KISSING THE NANNY

"I don't like surprises, Jocelyn, and you are full of them."

"Me?" She released his hand and straightened the collar of his polo shirt. Quinn hadn't bothered changing back into his uniform before responding to the trouble at The One Eyed Squid. The tips of her fingers skimmed up the strong, lean column of his neck. "What surprises you about me?"

"Everything." He played with a lock of her hair that had fallen across her shoulders. "You're not what I expected my kids' nanny to be like, yet you're wonderful at the job."

She grinned and teased, "Bet you won't say that about the housekeeping end of the deal."

"I'm not supposed to care about you, Jocelyn."

She wrapped both arms around his neck and pulled him closer. "I know." Then she reached up and playfully bit his lower lip, causing him to groan and finally kiss her the way she had been dreaming of night after night. . . .

Books by Marcia Evanick

CATCH OF THE DAY

CHRISTMAS ON CONRAD STREET

BLUEBERRY HILL

LET IT SNOW
(with Fern Michaels, Virginia Henley, and
Holly Chamberlin)

Published by Zebra Books

BLUEBERRY HILL

Marcia Evanick

ZEBRA BOOKS
KENSINGTON PUBLISHING CORP.
http://www.kensingtonbooks.com

ZEBRA BOOKS are published by

Kensington Publishing Corp.
850 Third Avenue
New York, NY 10022

All Kensington titles, imprints and distributed lines are available at special quantity discounts for bulk purchases for sales
promotion, premiums, fund-raising, educational or institutional
use.

Special book excerpts or customized printings can also be
created to fit specific needs. For details, write or phone the
office of the Kensington Special Sales Manager: Kensington
Publishing Corp., 850 Third Avenue, New York, NY 10022.
Attn. Special Sales Department. Phone: 1-800-221-2647.

First Printing: December 2003
10 9 8 7 6 5 4 3 2 1

Printed in the United States of America

This book is dedicated to the newest light within my heart. Welcome to the world Lilith Marie.

Love,
Grandmom

Prologue

"Are you sure you're all right, Joc?"

Jocelyn Fletcher heard the concern in her sister Sydney's voice carry over the telephone line and tried to lighten her tone. "I'm fine, Syd. Just tired, that's all."

"But to take a leave of absence from your job is serious, Jocelyn. What's wrong? What in the hell happened?"

For Sydney to use the word "hell," Jocelyn knew she was upset. She didn't want her sister upset. "Let's just say I had a few rough days."

"Days?"

"Okay, weeks. Maybe even months." She gave a weary sigh and slowly sank onto the couch. "Syd, I think I've made a mistake."

"About?"

"Following in Grandpop's footsteps." It was the first time she had said those words out loud, and it felt good to finally admit it to someone else. Sydney, who was a medical doctor and four years older than she, would understand and be supportive. There would be no crying and reprimands that she was throwing her whole life away. Gwen, her other sister, who was only a year older, would understand, too, but Sydney got the first call because she was the oldest. The Fletcher girls didn't do emotional scenes. They left the drama to the actresses of the world.

"Let me get this straight," Sydney said. "You don't want to be a lawyer any longer?"

"I didn't say that, Syd." Jocelyn picked up a jewel-tone throw pillow and hugged it to her chest. "I said I don't think I'm cut out to work in the district attorney's office. I love being a lawyer, but I don't think criminal law is my forte. I should be handling estates and adoptions. Maybe even a divorce or two."

"Oh, and watching dueling spouses scream at each other in court would brighten your day?"

"It would be a lot better than watching some two-bit drug dealer, with a spring in his step and a smirk on his face, waltz right out of the courthouse." Jocelyn shuddered at the memory from the other morning. Watching Joey G, as he liked to be called, stroll out of that courtroom had been the last straw on her career's back.

"Is that what happened?" asked Sydney. "A drug dealer got off?"

"Off? No, his case never even made it to the bench. He was released on a technicality. A young rookie didn't dot all the *i*'s or cross all *t*'s in the arrest report." Jocelyn hugged the pillow tighter. "No one seemed to care that he was walking back out onto the streets. I'm telling you, Syd, everyone there just acted so nonchalant about it. Like these things just happen."

"You've told me before about cases being thrown out for one reason or another, Joc. What made this one so different?"

"It wasn't different," sighed Jocelyn. "It was the one that made me realize I don't think I can do this for the next forty years."

"I think I'm beginning to understand now." Sydney's voice softened. "What did the DA say when you asked for a leave of absence? You hadn't been there that long."

"Well, let's put it this way, I probably won't have a job to go back to."

"So what are you going to do? What can I do to help?"

No condemnation from her sister, just a "What can I do to help." Jocelyn smiled for the first time in two days. "One of the other assistant DAs is having a house built. They just broke ground on it, and someone wants to buy his old house this month. He and his wife are going to sublet my apartment for the next six months."

"And where are you going to live?"

"That's where you and Gwen come in."

"Great, we'd love to have you. Erik says he wants to make some more *lutefisk* for you the next time you visit. He had never seen anyone turn that particular shade of green before." Sydney's chuckle was low and amused. "We'll get the guest room ready for you."

"I won't be staying with you and your sadist Viking husband." The Norwegian cod dish wasn't one she was willing to try again anytime this century.

"Ah, well, I'm sure Gwen and Daniel can put you up."

Jocelyn could hear the hurt in her sister's voice. "I wouldn't be staying with them either. It's embarrassing how those two can't keep their hands off of each other." She chuckled softly. "You and Erik aren't much better, either. I love you both dearly, sis. I even love both of my brothers-in-law, but this time I won't be staying with either one of you. I need you and Gwen to see what kind of apartments they have up there. A furnished one would be wonderful."

"I guess we can check around town for you."

"That would be great, and while you're at it, see what kind of jobs are available. I'm not fussy, as long as it hasn't got anything to do with the law. I want to put some distance between me and anything to do with being a lawyer as I try to work this out in my mind."

"Oh, I get it. You're coming up here to rethink the direction your life is heading in."

"Always said you were the smart one, Syd." Jocelyn felt good about herself for the first time in a long time. "I don't care what kind of job you can come up with. The more menial, the better. It'll give me more time to think about things." She added laughingly, "I'll even take a job on a tuna boat if that's all that's available."

Chapter One

Jocelyn Fletcher pushed the empty plate away from her and lightly patted her lips with the blue linen napkin. "There, you have fed me. Satisfied?" She studied her two sisters, Sydney and Gwen, who were sitting with her at the small table in the corner of Gwen's restaurant's kitchen. She didn't like the fact that neither of her sisters had wanted to discuss their plans for her when she arrived in Misty Harbor half an hour ago. All they had seemed interested in was making sure she was jamming food into her mouth. "Can we talk now?"

Gwen took the empty plate away and replaced it with another plate. This one contained a thick slice of blueberry pie. "Eat your dessert first. I made it especially for you this morning, after you called from the Connecticut rest stop."

"You never should have done that drive in one day," Sydney added. "Especially by yourself."

"Why? It's not like I could have gotten lost. You jump on Interstate 95 and head north." She reached for her fork and took a bite out of the pie. Delicious, warm, sweet blueberries melted against her tongue. She took a moment to savor the taste and then pinned both of her sisters with a knowing look. Being the youngest in the family had its drawbacks: the main one being everyone always treated her like the baby of the family. At twenty-six years old, she was hardly anyone's baby. "Both of you had made that same drive, so don't get all protective on me now." She smiled at Gwen as she forked up another mouthful. "This is delicious, Gwen, as usual. No wonder your restaurant is such a success."

"It's tourist season, and don't change the subject," Gwen said.

"Me change the subject?" Jocelyn shook her head at her sisters. "I'm trying to figure out what kind of job you've lined up for me, and you two are more concerned about my driving skills. What gives?"

"We didn't line you up with a job, Joc," Sydney said. "We lined you up with an interview, for tomorrow morning."

"Okay, that I can do. What about apartments? Small cottages? A place to rest my weary head after hauling in tuna all day?" Every time she had called her sisters during the past week, they had teased her about getting her a job with Bob Newman on his tuna boat. She wouldn't put it past them to actually think she was serious when she had made that comment to Sydney over the phone. Maybe she should have clarified that statement.

"The job you'll be interviewing for is a live-in position. You won't need an apartment." Gwen busied herself by pouring everyone more coffee. Sydney attacked her piece of pie as though she hadn't eaten all day.

"What kind of job am I interviewing for? I didn't think governesses were much in demand any longer, and I really don't think I'm merchant marine material." Her amused chuckle died in her throat when she saw the look Sydney gave Gwen. "What? What did you two do?" She was getting a horrible sinking feeling in the pit of her stomach. It was the same feeling she had when she had been four and had just eaten one of Gwen's mud pies that her sister had promised would taste exactly like a chocolate Easter bunny. It hadn't.

"Well, you're partially right," sighed Sydney.

"Partially a merchant marine? That would be what?" She stabbed at another piece of pie. "I know, a cruise ship director. I could be in charge of entertainment, right?"

"Not exactly," muttered Gwen as she glanced around the busy kitchen, keeping an eye on the staff and avoiding making eye contact with her baby sister.

"Oh, please don't tell me that you signed me up to be the aerobic instructor. I hate aerobics. All that moving, stretching, and sweating and you never go anywhere. Now, being the pool's lifeguard has possibilities."

Sydney rolled her eyes. "Jocelyn, it's not a cruise ship."

"Hell." She stared at her oldest sister. "Please tell me I'm not meeting with Bob Newman and the love of his life, his tuna boat named *Madison,* tomorrow morning."

"You're not," insisted Gwen. "The job interview we lined up has nothing to do with boats or even water."

"But Sydney said I was partially right." A horrifying thought entered her tired mind. "Tell me you didn't sign me up to be some nanny or something."

Gwen and Sydney didn't so much as breathe as they stared back at her.

"No! Absolutely not!" Her voice rose dramatically. Maybe the Fletcher girls did do drama after all. Right at this moment she felt as if she could try out for *Masterpiece Theater* as a homicidal maniac. She was about to strangle both of her sisters. "I would rather wrestle smelly tunas on the deck of Bob's boat all day long."

"It's only partially a nanny position." Gwen gave her a cheery smile.

"What's the other part?" She was a fool to ask, but she wanted all the facts before she killed her sisters. She was sure her brothers-in-law would want to know the reason behind their sudden status change to widowers.

Gwen looked helplessly at Sydney, who rolled her eyes and said, "Housekeeper."

"I'd rather wrestle *Bob* on the deck of his tuna boat! Are you two out of your minds? What do I know about being a nanny or a housekeeper?"

"You cleaned your own apartment, didn't you? Same thing, only more rooms." Gwen gave her a serene smile.

"You always said you wanted children one day, Joc. This would be the perfect opportunity for you to get some practice and see what it would be like." Sydney calmly finished her cup of coffee.

"I also said I wanted to get married, too. That doesn't mean I'm going to go around shacking up with different guys to get some experience and practice." She shook her head at her sisters. "What were you thinking?"

"We were thinking that our sister was looking for a temporary job and a place to stay. This particular job fits both of those requirements very nicely." Gwen got up, grabbed the coffeepot, and started to refill the cups. "Quinn Larson is a very nice man who just so happens to be in a very tight spot at the moment."

"Where's Mrs. Larson? Why can't she watch her own kids and clean her own house?"

"Diane Larson was killed six weeks ago in a car accident, down in Boston." Sydney added cream and sugar to her coffee and watched her sister carefully.

"Oh, the poor man." She felt horrible for voicing her objections when he had just lost his wife. "He must be devastated."

"They were divorced," Gwen said as if that would explain it all.

"Oh." What was she supposed to say to that?

"From what we know it was a friendly divorce. About two years ago, Diane took the three kids and moved to Boston. A year later the divorce was final. Quinn got the kids a lot during the summer months, holidays, and sometimes on long weekends. Quinn didn't seem bitter about the divorce, but he did seem to miss the kids when they weren't in Misty Harbor." Gwen glanced at Sydney. "Anything else you can think of to add?"

"The kids are in good health. Quinn brought them all in for a physical about four weeks ago."

"So, the wife picks up the kids, leaves the husband, and moves to Boston. The kids live with her full-time, except when they are visiting Daddy. The ex-wife dies in some tragic car accident, so Daddy rushes to Boston to pick up his kids and bring them back to Misty Harbor?"

"That's it." Gwen frowned at her coffee. "The kids have pretty much been through hell."

"But now Larson wants to add to that hell by having some stranger move in with them and take care of the kids and the house?" Didn't sound like a smart plan to her.

"What do you expect the man to do, Joc?" Sydney asked. "He has to work to support them all."

"True, but can't he put them in day care or hire a babysitter?" Millions of single parents did that all the time.

"Quinn is the sheriff, which means he's on call twenty-four hours a day for six days a week. He needs someone there at night, in case he is called out. He can't be waking the kids up and taking them to his mom's."

"What's he been doing for the past six weeks?"

"He took the first week off to handle Diane's funeral and get the kids' stuff packed up and moved. Then his younger sister, Phoebe, moved back to Misty Harbor and into his house to help out."

"So why can't this aunt keep the job?"

"Phoebe is going to be opening up a stained-glass business. She's using Quinn's garage now as a studio, but she can't be doing both. Quinn doesn't want her to either. He said they are his kids, his responsibility." Sydney shrugged. "The man is going nuts trying to handle it all. So is Phoebe. No one has applied for the job yet, so

Phoebe is very excited about this interview tomorrow morning with you."

"Even though I'll only be there temporarily?"

"So you are going to take the job?" Gwen asked excitedly.

"I didn't say that." Joc muttered something her sisters were better off not knowing into her cup.

"What was that?" By the sparkle in Sydney's eyes, Joc figured she had heard that word anyway.

"I asked how old were the kids? You said three, didn't you?" Three kids! What did she know about caring for one kid, let alone three? Baby-sitting never had been a favorite way to make extra money when she was a teenager. She had washed cars, mowed a few lawns, even pulled about a million weeds. But changing dirty diapers and wiping snotty noses wasn't easy money in her book. If this Diane Larson packed up the kids and moved away two years ago, the kids couldn't be that little, could they?

"Benjamin is five and will be starting kindergarten in September. I just did his physical needed for the enrollment." Sydney pushed away her empty pie plate. "Isabella and Victoria are twin girls who just turned three last month. I remember their birthday was the day after the physical I gave them. Tori wanted a pony, and Issy wanted a mermaid."

"Did they get them?" Jocelyn remembered wanting a pony when she had been about six or so. Her parents had allowed her to take horseback-riding lessons instead. She had kept up with those lessons until she discovered boys didn't appreciate a girl that smelled like a stable. A very ripe stable.

"I have no idea," Sydney said. "I think if Quinn had his way, he would have gotten the girls the moon if they had asked."

"He spoils them?"

"Wouldn't you?" asked Gwen. "Especially after what they have been through."

"Probably." She didn't like the pressure her sisters were placing on her. What did she know about raising kids? Especially those that had just lost their mother and had been forced to move from their home and into their father's house. The poor kids' lives must be in a total upheaval. Heck, she had come to Maine to get her own life straightened out. She wasn't in any position to help ease the fears and the minds of three small children.

She looked at her two sisters, who appeared to be waiting for her to say she'd take the job. "What other kind of jobs did you come up with?"

Disappointment flashed across Gwen's face, but Sydney just narrowed her eyes and said, "There's not much available, Joc."

"Most of the jobs are summer jobs, minimum wage, and filled by teenagers." Gwen glanced around her kitchen. "I could use an additional waitress, but it would only be part-time."

"The woman I hired to handle the phones, appointments, and filing is going to be taking some time off soon," added Sydney. "I could use you in the office. I would love to redo old Dr. Jeffreys' filing system and to get more stuff onto the computer. You could help me out there."

"I don't want sympathy jobs." She shook her head at her sisters. "I appreciate the offer, but since I don't even want to live with you two, what makes you think I would work for you?"

"Fine," sighed Gwen. "Misty Harbor Motor Inn is looking for a housekeeper. You get to clean rooms all afternoon and handle the laundry all morning. I didn't talk with Wendell Kirby yet, but maybe you can work something out with him for a room instead of a paycheck."

"Wendell Kirby? The same Wendell Kirby who proposed twice to me during my visit at Christmas?"

"The same." Sydney smiled.

"Didn't he get married yet?" Jocelyn had never seen a man so hell-bent on getting married. Someone would have thought they were giving away a free BMW with every marriage license.

"Not yet. He's still looking for wife number three. Maybe three is his lucky number," Gwen said. "Of course, he's going to be so happy once he learns you're in town for a while."

"Just think," Sydney added, "you can get to see him every day if you take the job at the Motor Inn."

Jocelyn shuddered at the thought. It had taken her a half an hour to shake Wendell from her side at Sydney and Erik's Christmas party. Then he had left only because Gwen's husband, Daniel, had seen the hunted look in her eye and had rescued her from the overzealous suitor. "What time did you say that interview is for tomorrow morning?"

The sick, queasy feeling returned to her gut when Gwen and Sydney shared a slow smile. She was four years old again, and she'd just been had.

Jocelyn followed the road around the bend and up the hill. Blueberry Hill Road twisted itself around a large hill, known by the locals as Blueberry Hill. Sadie Hopkins' blueberry farm was on the other side of the hill, and nestled at the bottom were the crystal waters of Blueberry Cove. A few houses were scattered around the hill. It was to one of those houses she was headed. Quinn Larson's house shouldn't be that difficult to find. After all, it was painted, what else, but blue.

Daniel had drawn her a map to follow. He had been born and raised in Misty Harbor and knew the area better than her sisters. He also knew where the Larson's house stood and filled her in on its history.

The house was built two years after the Civil War ended by one of Joshua Chamberlain's lieutenants, Thomas

Fuller. Thomas had purchased the entire hill, but over the generations parcels and pieces had been sold off for one reason or another. Seven years ago the last of Thomas's descendants, Ethan Fuller, passed on, leaving the house empty. Sadie Hopkins bought a good chunk of the land, but Quinn and his wife, Diane, bought the run-down house and the surrounding couple of acres for a bargain basement price. Quinn had been working on the house ever since, but he had concentrated mainly on the interior. The exterior looked about the same as when they had bought it, only more faded, chipped, and worn. Daniel had warned her not to be put off by the exterior of the house.

Jocelyn slowed her car as a relatively new white mailbox came into view. Someone had taken blue paint and neatly printed the name "Larson" on the side of the box. A number seven was below the name. Nothing was on either side of the road but trees, shrubs, and the occasional wildflower. She turned the car onto the gravel drive and headed through the trees. As she rounded a bend she slowly stopped the car.

Before her sat a huge, at one time blue house with wraparound porches. Most of the blue was now faded to a grayish color, but the roof looked brand-new. So did most of the windows, but only half the shutters were still in place. Spots of brilliant white, where Quinn had obviously primed and replaced rotten siding and deck flooring, stuck out like zits on a teenager's nose. The outline of flower gardens could be detected skirting the porches, but the weeds had overrun them. Choking most, if not all, of the flowers.

A big garage, which at one time had been painted the same shade of blue as the house, was off to one side. The garage didn't have the normal metal doors that rolled up in tracks. The two huge sets of wooden doors were on tracks that had to be manually slid to the side. One of the sets of doors was open, but she couldn't see into the dim interior. Someone, probably the original owner, had attempted to landscape around the garage.

Jocelyn drove another fifty feet and parked behind a dark green SUV that had a bar holding blue and red lights bolted across the top. *Hancock County Sheriff's Department* was neatly painted across the back and the driver's door. An old white Jeep, with a ratty-looking canvas top, was parked near the garage. A shiny red wagon and two pink tricycles were on the porch. A bent basketball net was attached above one of the garage doors. A soccer ball, a baseball bat, and a catcher's mitt were lying in the grass that had been due for a mowing job about two weeks ago. Now the grass was due for a herd of goats.

Jocelyn made her way up onto the porch and was happy to note, while the structure was in dire need of a paint job, it appeared structurally sound and safe. She knocked on the front door and stared at a miniature tea party that was going on in the wagon. Two Barbies were enjoying the imaginary meal. One Barbie was dressed in a whimsical gown of white satin and netting, a pearl necklace, and a shiny tiara. The other Barbie looked as if she had just competed in the WWF Smackdown. In a mud ring no less. Brown gooey stuff was caked in Barbie's blond hair and across every inch of her plastic, well-endowed body. Someone had dressed her in a leopard-print bikini and black leather, thigh-high boots. Jocelyn chuckled at the scene.

"Hi, you must be Jocelyn." A woman about the same age as her stood on the other side of the screen door. The door was pushed open. "Come on in, I'm Phoebe Larson."

"I'm Jocelyn." She stepped into the house and immediately had to step to the right to avoid walking into a tent made out of blankets and chairs. She heard a giggle or two coming from under the blanket and grinned.

Phoebe's smile grew. "I'm sorry that the kids aren't

here to meet you this morning. They went on a safari to Africa, but they promised to be back before lunch."

"Oh, that is a shame. I did want to at least meet them." She stepped around the end table that was holding down one end of the blanket. "I hope they are careful and watch out for lions and tigers. I hear that lions are particularly fond of little girls."

Phoebe led the way into the kitchen as more giggles erupted under the covers. "I heard just last week that some little boy was stepped on by an elephant. He was flatter than a pancake, and his father had to use a bicycle pump to blow him up again."

The giggles turned into full-blown laughter.

"It's good to hear their laughter." Phoebe walked over to the coffeepot. "Want a cup? It's fresh."

"Thank you." She took the cup Phoebe handed her.

"Sugar's on the counter." Phoebe opened the refrigerator and took out a carton of cream. "Quinn's upstairs on the phone. Business." Phoebe added cream to her cup and then handed her the carton. "So I hear you're from Baltimore."

"Yes." She glanced around the recently remodeled kitchen with approval. Big and bright, with plenty of room and light. The kitchen flowed into an eating area, which flowed into a family room. Two sets of patio doors opened onto a back patio. Someone had cleared a section of trees out back. From the doors and the patio there was an unobstructed view of the cove below. "Wonderful view."

"It's one of the first things Quinn did when he bought this place." Phoebe joined her by the patio doors. "Gwen tells me you're a lawyer."

"You know my sister?"

"Met her a couple of times. I know Daniel better. We were in some of the same classes at school. He was a year ahead of me."

"So you grew up in Misty Harbor?"

"Born and raised." Phoebe pulled out a kitchen chair and sat. "Take a load off." Phoebe's eyes narrowed. "Even though it's not much of a load."

"Is that a comment on my height?" Being five feet four inches in height sometimes was a disadvantage. Phoebe topped her by a good four or five inches.

"More about your weight." Phoebe chuckled. "Don't you eat three meals a day? If you are going to be staying up here for any length of time, we need to fatten you up some. A good nor'easter will blow you clear out to Dead Man's Island."

"I'm a lot stronger than I look."

"Good, because you will need it to keep up with these kids." Phoebe gave an extravagant sigh. "It's only nine o'clock, and so far I've made smiling-face waffles, unloaded the dishwasher, cleaned up the kitchen once, made the beds, and hung the first load of laundry." Phoebe nodded to the laundry basket filled with wet towels. "I was about to go hang the second load when you knocked."

"You obviously don't want me to take this job, do you?" She chuckled as she finished her coffee. Last night she had been bound and determined not to take this job. This morning she had pored over a stack of newspapers while sitting at Sydney's counter drinking coffee and working her way through a warm-from-the-oven Sara Lee coffee cake. None of the Help Wanted ads looked promising. The real estate rentals had been worse. At the height of tourist season, landlords were getting top dollar and seemed to be booked solid.

"Right now I'm desperate for you to take the job, but I wanted to be honest with you. You won't be doing anything that any other stay-at-home mom wouldn't do." Phoebe shook her head. "All these years I always envied those women who had kids and stayed at home. I thought how nice it would be to sleep late and never have to answer to a boss. The day would be yours to do with it as you please. As long as dinner was on the table for the hubby when he came home from work, your job was done."

"I take it Mr. Larson likes his dinner on the table when he walks through the door."

"With tourist season in full swing, my brother's hours are hectic and unpredictable. Usually he's reheating whatever I managed to cook for the kids earlier."

"He's not fussy?"

"Quinn fussy? Nope. Give that man the remote, clean uniforms, and socks and he's in heaven. The kids will drive you nuts, though. Benjamin doesn't like any of his food touching each other on his plate. Issy won't eat anything green, so good luck getting her to eat her vegetables. And Tori will live on macaroni and cheese if you let her. Can you cook like Gwen?"

"Afraid not." Jocelyn chuckled as a little blond head peeked around the corner and then disappeared. "Why are you so desperate to escape? You seem to have everything under control."

"In this house, control is an illusion." Phoebe finished her coffee. "I work with stained glass. Been apprenticing for years. A couple of months ago I decided it was time for me to come home to Misty Harbor and start my own business. I was working out the last week of my notice when Diane was in the accident and Quinn needed my help. Quinn had already agreed to let me use his garage as a studio until I find something I can afford. I was supposed to move back in with my parents."

"You moved in here instead."

"Right. But the kids need a full-time keeper, and that doesn't leave me any time for my business. I have my first major load of glass being delivered this morning. My hands are itching to go, but my feet are planted here. My mom helps out as much as possible, but at her age, she shouldn't be chasing three small kids around all day and night."

"Phoebe," a deep voice shouted from the top of the stairs. "I've got to run, something has come up." Heavy footsteps thundered down the stairs. "Jocelyn Fletcher obviously doesn't want the job, or she would have been here on time. I can't hire the woman anyway. How can I trust her with the kids if she can't even be on time?"

"Daddy, Daddy, Daddy," shouted two identical little girl voices.

"Um, Dad," came a boy's voice.

Quinn Larson was swinging both of his daughters up into his arms as he stepped into the kitchen. He was glancing over his shoulder at the boy. "What is it, Ben?"

One of the little girls was trying to whisper into his ear.

Phoebe rolled her eyes and gave Jocelyn a helpless smile and mouthed the word "men." "What your son and daughters were trying to tell you is that Jocelyn arrived right on time. You were the one not here to meet her."

Quinn's gaze shot to her, and for the first time Jocelyn understood the meaning of the word "magnetism."

Chapter Two

Quinn Larson took one look at Jocelyn Fletcher and knew he wasn't going to hire her. There was no way he would be able to live under the same roof with such a tempting woman. It would be asking for trouble. Big trouble. He had known Jocelyn was young, but he hadn't known she was gorgeous. He had played the odds, and lost. It wasn't the first time in his life, and it wouldn't be the last either.

He had met Jocelyn's sisters, Gwen and Sydney. Both of them were very attractive females. There were two ways it could have gone when he tried to conjure up in his mind what Jocelyn would look like. One, she could have been just as attractive as her older sisters. Two, the luck in the family gene pool wouldn't have held, and Jocelyn would have been the one with the sparkling personality. He had been praying for a sturdy, reliable home economics major who just happened to have the smarts enough to be a lawyer. Someone who could have captained the geek club. Instead, he ended up with the homecoming queen.

He had lived with a homecoming queen before. Hell, he had married her. Diane Bowman Larson had not only been the homecoming queen, but she had been the captain of the varsity cheerleading squad and the prom queen. His ex-wife had had the small, compact athletically fit body that had driven him to distraction back in high school. One look at Jocelyn and every one of his hormones thought they were eighteen years old again. Thirty-two was just too darn old to be experiencing that unsettling time all over again.

Discrimination be damned, he wasn't hiring her.

"Daddy," whispered Tori into his ear, "some lady is here."

Two pairs of small arms encircled his neck. Victoria's whisper had been loud enough to carry throughout the entire house. His ear was still ringing. "So I see, sweetie."

Isabella, Tori's identical twin in appearance only, didn't say a word. Her little fingers were playing with his badge as she glanced anxiously between Jocelyn and him. Ever since Diane had been killed in the car accident, Issy had grown more quiet. Issy had always been the quiet, refined little princess who hated getting her hands dirty. While Tori couldn't keep clean if someone sprayed her with Scotch Guard from head to toe. Tori also had a set of lungs a pearl diver would envy and tended to scream and shout her way through life. His three-year-old daughters were mirror twins, who just happened to be polar opposites. And he loved them both more than life.

He gave each of the girls a tight squeeze, causing Tori to giggle and Issy to frown, before lowering them back down. "You guys remember Dr. Sydney, right?" As both girls nodded, and Benjamin said yes, he explained. "Well, this is Dr. Sydney's sister, Jocelyn."

Benjamin stepped around him and into the kitchen. His five-year-old son stared at Jocelyn, who was hesitantly smiling back. "Are you a doctor, too?"

"Afraid not." Jocelyn's smile grew. "I'm a lawyer."

"What's that?" asked Tori.

"Well, you know how your daddy catches bad guys?"

"Yeah," said Tori and Benjamin in unison. Issy just nodded.

"Lawyers make sure that the bad guy goes to jail, pays a fine, or whatever punishment the law says he has to do." Jocelyn gave the kids a warm smile. "Your daddy does the hard physical stuff by catching the bad guys, and lawyers handle the paperwork."

"Our dad hates paperwork," Benjamin said. "He says it's a pain in his—"

"Benjamin Joseph Larson, don't you dare say what I think you are going to say." The other night when he had been complaining to his sister about the flood of paperwork overflowing his desk back at the office, he hadn't known Benjamin was right behind him. This morning he was paying for that slip.

"I was going to say, *butt*, Dad." Benjamin grinned, and his two little sisters giggled.

Phoebe laughed out loud, and Jocelyn looked as though she was going to join her any second. He could see the laughter dancing in Jocelyn's gray eyes and the enticing quiver at the corner of her lips. Their amusement was infectious.

He chuckled as he playfully ruffled the top of Benjamin's head. "You had me going there for a moment, son."

Benjamin's smile lit up the kitchen. "Fooled you, didn't I, Dad?"

"Sure did."

Phoebe stood up and carried her empty cup over to the sink. "How about I take the kids out back to play while you interview Jocelyn?"

Tori grabbed Issy's hand and practically dragged her to the patio doors. Benjamin beat his sisters to the door by a yard. He tugged open the sliding screen door, and a mass of blond ponytails, sun-kissed arms and legs, and bare feet tumbled their way outside. Phoebe picked up the laundry basket overflowing with wet towels and hurried after them. The slamming of the sliding screen door echoed through the kitchen.

Quinn cringed as he walked over to the coffeepot. "Want another cup?"

"No thank you," replied Jocelyn as she stood up and walked over to the patio doors. Her attention was centered on the backyard and the children. "Are they always so anxious to get outside?"

"Afraid so." He filled his cup and leaned against the counter. Since it was July, and all the windows were open, the sound of the children's shouts and laughter poured in through the screens. He could hear Benjamin and Tori, but not Issy. Nothing unusual in that. He never heard Issy. "They would spend all day and night out there if we'd let them."

"Can't blame them." Jocelyn's mouth tilted upward. "The view is fantastic." She turned away from the doors and faced him.

Quinn studied Jocelyn's small, compact body. His hormones were taking a slow, leisurely inventory of the lovely lawyer. Tan linen slacks skimmed her legs, and a sleeveless green silk blouse caressed her nicely rounded breasts. Long golden blond hair that fell halfway down her back was pulled neatly into a gold clip. He couldn't detect any sign of makeup on her beautiful face, but she was wearing gold earrings and a necklace. Her gray eyes were arresting, her nose delicate, and her lips were too wide. Jocelyn's mouth was sexy as hell, and made for sin. Jocelyn Fletcher didn't look like any courtroom lawyer he had ever seen, but she also didn't look like a nanny. She looked like a woman. A very desirable woman with an erotic mouth.

A good eight feet separated them, but he would swear in a court of law that he could feel her heat. He shifted his weight and took another sip of coffee. He needed time to gather his thoughts and get his body back under control. He was supposed to be interviewing Jocelyn for the housekeeper position, not a potential lover.

Curiously, he asked, "What made you give up being a lawyer?"

"I haven't given up being a lawyer." Jocelyn appeared offended by the question. "I just need some time to step back and reevaluate some things, that's all."

"So you're planning on going back to Maryland and picking up your career again?"

"Of course." Jocelyn carried her empty cup over to the sink and placed it next to Phoebe's. "I thought this was a temporary job."

There hadn't been a drop of hesitation in her voice. "Yes, and no." Quinn set his empty cup onto the counter. "I need a permanent housekeeper, but since no one is applying to fill that position, I will take a temporary one."

"So Phoebe can get on with her own life?"

He studied her for a long minute. "You did your homework."

"Lawyers always do their homework." Jocelyn gave him a fleeting smile that disappeared quickly. "The kids seem to be handling the situation nicely."

"They didn't have a lot of choice in the matter, did they?" Quinn turned away from her and stared out the screen door. His gaze swept the yard. Benjamin was hanging upside down on the crossbar of the swing set. Tori was sitting on a dirt pile playing with a big Tonka backhoe. Tori had more dirt on her than in the big yellow scoop. Issy was standing by the clothesline, watching her aunt pin up a load of towels. "Issy is taking it the hardest."

"I noticed that Tori seems the more vocal one of the two."

"Tori's always been the more outgoing one. Isabella is the quiet, reserved one."

"Are you trying to tell me that they're identical twins who aren't so identical in their personalities?"

"No one would have trouble telling them apart. Tori's the one covered in dirt." He stepped away from the door. "I guess I should give you a tour of the house and explain a little about the job." He walked into what should be the formal dining room. Diane had left her mother's dining room set when she moved to Boston. The fancy glass-front hutch stood empty. Diane had wanted the china, and he had never even thought about buying another set. He hadn't eaten in or used this room in two years.

"You named them after queens." Jocelyn walked into the room and looked around.

"Yes we did." He still remembered standing in the delivery room holding their tiny bodies minutes after their birth. He had thought they looked like princesses and had begged Diane to name them after royalty. Diane had amazingly agreed. He frowned at the piles of folded laundry on the table. "Please excuse the mess. Phoebe likes to use this table to fold the clothes."

"They've got to be folded somewhere." Jocelyn eyed the ironing board in the corner of the room and the three khaki uniform shirts neatly pressed and hanging from the rim of the hutch.

He stepped out of the room and into the living room. "As you can see, the kids kind of took over this room. We try to keep the family room only knee deep in toys, because that's where we spend most of the evenings. This room we've just given up hope of ever seeing the floor again until after they start college."

Jocelyn smiled at the blanket tents. When she was little, she and her sisters always made tents in their parents' formal dining room. Underneath the huge dining room table, which could sit twelve comfortably, made a wonderful playhouse, restaurant, or hospital. Depending on which sister got to be in charge that day. "I believe they were on a safari this morning."

"This month, Benjamin wants to be a vet when he grows up. He was probably rescuing elephants from poachers or something."

Jocelyn smiled at stuffed animals neatly lined up. Huge teddy bears, a giraffe, an elephant the size of a small child, two monkeys, and one dragon looked ready to march in some parade. "I did hear something about a tiger with a bellyache."

"Benjamin starts kindergarten the first week of September. He'll be catching a bus every morning, and someone will need to get him on it and then meet it about lunchtime." Quinn stepped around a scattering of toddler-size Legos. "I was thinking about starting the girls in a nursery school, but they seem too young to me. I think keeping them home for the next year will be good for them. They've had too many changes in their young lives as it is. Why add to the confusion?"

"True." The logic behind Quinn's reasoning sounded right, and they were his kids. What would she know about raising kids? She stepped over the same Legos and followed Quinn up the stairs. "I have to be right up front with you and tell you that I don't have a lot of experience with children."

"I know; but as Phoebe pointed out to me the other day, neither does she, and she's managing." Quinn gave her what she hoped was a reassuring smile over his shoulder. "The good news is they are all toilet trained; the bad news is, they are mobile. Infants kind of stay where you lay them. Three- and five-year-olds are never where you put them."

"Sounds challenging." She studied the enticing view of Quinn's backside as he climbed the stairs in front of her. Khaki never looked so good. Quinn's dark brown hair was the exact same shade of Benjamin's. His son also had brown eyes and the long lean look of his father. The girls blond hair and light blue eyes must have come from the mother's side.

"It's a challenge all right." Quinn turned left and headed down a short hallway. "Make no mistake about it. There is no rest from the time they wake up in the morning, 'til they fall exhausted into their beds at night. If I had half their energy, there would be no telling how much work I could accomplish in a day."

Quinn stepped into a room with twin beds and pink paint. One of the beds was done in a Snow White comforter and sheets, the other, Cinderella. There were mismatching curtains at the windows and framed posters on the walls. Either this was the girls' room, or she had just space warped into a Disney store. There was an adorable child-size white wicker table and two chairs beneath the window. A plastic tea set was on the table. A floppy-eared, brown-and-white stuffed dog sat in one chair. The other held a blow-up orange iguana. Someone had placed purple plastic sunglasses and a blue fright wig on the iguana. She chuckled at the sight.

"I take it this is where the princesses sleep." It was a bright, cheery room that was surprisingly neat and clutter free compared to the rest of the house. "I expected to see a lot more toys up here."

"We keep most of the toys downstairs. I've found it easier than going up and down the stairs all the time." Quinn left the room and stopped at the next doorway. He pushed the door wider and said, "Family bath."

She gave the room a quick glance and tried not to cringe at the amount of toys lining the tub's edge. A big green plastic clothes basket, overflowing with more water toys, was sitting on the floor. If she squeezed over the three rubber duckies, an assortment of baby shampoo and bubble bath, and avoided what appeared to be a complete fire station suction-cupped onto the tub wall, she just might be able to take a shower. An economy-size hamper that looked as if it belonged in the Kennedy clan bathroom sat in the far corner. When the hamper was full, it would take a forklift to move it.

Quinn quickly moved to the next door. This room was obviously Benjamin's. The boy definitely had a fixation with trains. Brightly colored trains were on the blanket and sheets. A matching wallpaper border printed with one continuous railroad track and an assortment of trains encircled the room. A bookshelf held an assortment of plastic, wooden, and metal trains. Along with books on trains and a conductor's hat.

"I take it that Benjamin loves trains?"

"Hard to miss, huh?" Quinn smiled at the room. "I have Lionel trains, from my boyhood years, up in the attic. When he gets a little older, I'll bring them down for him."

Quinn moved on to the other side of the stair landing. "This room I had been using as a den, but it's my room now. The position doesn't require you to clean up after me, only the children." He continued to the last doorway. "Phoebe's using this room now, but it goes to whomever I hire."

She followed him into the large room and knew immediately this was the master bedroom. A queen-size bed with a dark blue comforter and walnut posts at each corner dominated the room. A comfortable-looking tan chair and small table sat beneath the windows that had a vast view of the cove below. An armoire containing a television sat against one wall, and a five-drawer bureau sat along another.

"There's a private bath and plenty of closet space."

"You moved out of your bedroom?" Even with some of Phoebe's clothes tossed onto the unmade bed and a pair of pink slippers by the door, the room had a masculine air to it. A flower canvas suitcase was sitting on the chair. It was three-quarters of the way filled with clothes. She couldn't tell if Phoebe had been living out of the suitcase, or packing it. Was Phoebe so confident that Quinn was going to offer her the job, and that she would accept it?

Or was Phoebe really that desperate to get away?

Quinn frowned at the suitcase. "The job doesn't come with many perks. The hours are long, and it's six days a week. You will have every Tuesday off. The pay is room and board and only a small salary. When I'm home I usually can keep up with the kids, and we can fend for ourselves. I'm hoping that whoever takes the job will consider the larger room with a private bath as a perk."

She glanced into the bathroom and secretly studied the proud man gazing out of the window at the backyard and his children below. One of the girls was singing a song, but she had no idea what song. Benjamin was yelling, "Look at me, look at me," to someone. The corner of Quinn's mouth kicked up into a semismile, and she felt herself melt. There wasn't a doubt in her mind that Quinn loved his children.

Quinn obviously wasn't a wealthy man, but he wasn't destitute either. The weekly salary he had quoted was laughable, but she wasn't in Maine to enrich her stock portfolio. She was here to think about the direction in which she wanted her career to head, and this job was about as far away from the law as she could get. She wasn't sure this was the right job for her, but her options were limited. And Quinn really needed someone to help him out with the children and their home.

As job perks went, the bedroom suite wasn't much. Health insurance would have been her first choice. Dental her second. The salary Quinn had named would barely cover her insurance costs, let alone her car payments. Her savings would be dwindling for the next several months.

Jocelyn glanced around the room one last time and tried to offer Quinn some encouragement on the one and only perk. "It's a very nice room."

Quinn's shoulder shook for a moment with a silent chuckle. "Yeah, it is." He headed out of the door and for the stairs. "That's about it for the tour. You've seen it all."

She followed him down the stairs and through the living room. "What kind of activities are the children interested in? Does Benjamin do any sports, or have the girls mentioned ballet or dance?"

"They are a little too young for all that stuff. I'm sure in the next couple of years I will be running them from one place to another." Quinn entered the family room, bent over, and started to pick up pillows that were scattered in front of the television. With a casual aim that suggested he had plenty of practice, Quinn tossed them back onto the couch and chairs.

The coffee table was a jumbled mess of coloring books and a yellow box professing it held ninety-six nontoxic crayons. She counted only three crayons in the box. The rest were scattered across the table and on the floor. She knelt and started to gather up the crayons before someone stepped on them. "Gwen's the cook of the family, just in case you think I can whip up some gourmet meal from a box of crackers, frozen peas, and a can of tuna fish."

"Can you cook more than smiling waffles? I love my sister dearly, but I never want to see another round, grinning waffle as long as I live. Phoebe considers syrup a major food group."

She chuckled. "I know about six different ways to cook eggs, if that helps. Gwen still calls me useless in the kitchen because my gravy comes from a can and my cakes from a box."

"Phoebe's cakes come from the bakery."

"I heard that, Quinn," said Phoebe as she slid open the screen door and stepped into the room. "Is that any way to talk about your favorite sister?"

"You're my only sister." Quinn took the empty laundry basket from her and tossed it onto the chair.

"Remember that." Phoebe glanced out of the screen door to the children. "Jocelyn, why don't you go on out and talk to the kids for a few moments. My brother and I need to discuss a few things."

"No problem." Jocelyn stepped out onto the patio and closed the screen door behind her.

Quinn watched Jocelyn as she crossed the yard to where the children were. Benjamin was demanding all of her attention by trying to do a headstand in the middle of the overgrown yard. Tori was trying to imitate her older brother. Issy was sitting off to the side picking clover. Jocelyn sat next to Issy and laughed with Benjamin.

"You aren't going to hire her, are you?" Phoebe asked as she poured herself another cup of coffee.

"No." He continued to watch as his children vied for Jocelyn's attention.

"Why?" Phoebe leaned against the counter and studied her brother. "You know you can trust her with the children. You know and like her sisters. She's young and energetic enough to keep up with the kids. She's intelligent, and she is probably a better cook than me. So what's the problem?"

"Benjamin is a better cook than you." Quinn chuckled and grinned at his sister, before turning back to the scene out back. Issy was picking and then handing Jocelyn some flowers from the clover patch. He couldn't tell what Jocelyn was doing with the flowers, but Tori was now trying to do somersaults across the yard. Tori landed on her side every time.

"Don't change the subject, Quinn. Why won't you hire her?"

"Did you take a good look at her, Phoebe? If she moves in here, the entire town is going to be talking and speculating as to what is going on." Quinn watched as Benjamin helped his sister do a semistraight somersault.

"Let them talk, Quinn. Who cares?"

"I refuse to become the latest topic of gossip."

"Like you were when Diane left you?" Phoebe continued to look at him. "I wasn't here when all that happened, but Mom kept me up to date. She told me the whole town was speculating as to what caused the split and then the divorce."

"Why is it that everyone automatically assumes the worst when things like that happen? Why couldn't people just accept the fact that people change? That people fall out of love? And that it was nobody's business but Diane's and mine."

"Human nature, I guess." She set her cup down. "The same human nature that is going to speculate about Jocelyn and you if she takes the job. I'm sorry, Quinn, but put a good-looking, virile, single man living in the same house with an attractive, single female and rumors are going to fly."

"That's why I'm not hiring her. I don't need the hassle, and I'm sure she would appreciate not having her reputation dragged through the mud."

"Jocelyn seems like a big girl to me, Quinn. I think she can handle herself. Misty Harbor is a small town, but not too many people would want to piss off the only doctor in it by talking trash about her sister. I also don't know of too many people that would risk being blackballed from Gwen's restaurant. Then there are Daniel and Erik, Jocelyn's brothers-in-law, to contend with."

"That's true. Erik Olsen is as gentle as they come, but I will be the first to tell you, I never want to see that man mad."

"Erik's only got about two inches on you."

"Two inches in height, maybe. But, he's got about fifty pounds more of pure muscle." Quinn shuddered at the thought of what Erik, or his identical twin brother Gunnar, could do to the town if they ever went on a rampage. Phoebe was right; no one would dare say a word against Jocelyn.

Phoebe chuckled. "The only problem I see you having with Jocelyn living here is the parade of bachelors knocking on your door at all hours of the day or night. Your phone will be ringing constantly. It took me weeks to get them from bugging me all the time. The whole thing is going to start up again once Jocelyn moves in."

"Great! So what you are telling me is not only will I have a single, attractive woman living in my house, but I'm going to have another one working on her stained glass in my garage all day long. Hell, I'm never going to find a parking spot in front of my own house."

Phoebe grinned. "Just be thankful it's only temporary until you find someone else to fill the spot."

"True." He watched as Issy handed Jocelyn some more small flowers. Jocelyn was talking to Issy, who was talking back, but he couldn't hear what they were saying to each other. He could now see what Jocelyn was doing with the flowers. She was making a chain. Somehow, she was connecting the stems to one another to form a flower chain.

The one argument Phoebe could use, she didn't. His sister should be telling him to hire Jocelyn so she could get on with her own life. The children weren't Phoebe's responsibility. But she was the one taking care of them six days a week. Phoebe's dream of starting her own business had been put on hold long enough. Today her first large shipment of glass was due to arrive. How could he not hire Jocelyn and give Phoebe her freedom?

"I'll be working in the garage every day, so if Jocelyn has a problem or a question, she can ask me."

"What happens if she decides to go back to Maryland before someone suitable applies for the job? I will be stuck in a worse situation, because you will be busy with your business."

"We can work something out. Maybe put the kids in day care during the day while I work in the garage. Then I can help you at night with them."

"I don't want them back in day care, Phoebe. Right now they need the security of the house. Something solid. Being shuffled all over the place isn't solid."

"Then hire Jocelyn and place more ads in not only the local paper, but maybe Bangor's and Augusta's papers, too. Hopefully someone qualified will come along before Jocelyn gets bored with dirty laundry and small-town quaintness and heads back to the big city and the high court drama of being a lawyer."

"Let's not forget about the pay difference." Quinn heard the unmistakable sound of crunching gravel and the diesel engine of a big rig. It didn't take a genius to figure out a big truck had just pulled up in front of the house.

Phoebe's face lit up as the same sound reached her. "That's my shipment!" Phoebe tore out of the kitchen at a dead run. The banging of the screened front door echoed through the house.

He turned around to study the scene out back and think about what he should do. His smile slowly faded as he watched Issy interact with Jocelyn. Benjamin and Tori were rolling around in the grass like idiots. The grass stains were never going to come out of their clothes. Somehow, somewhere, he had to find an extra hour or two to mow the grass soon. Real soon. If the grass got any higher, he would lose the twins in it.

Jocelyn held up the chain for Issy's inspection. Issy's small fingers danced along the chain. Jocelyn laughed at something Issy said and then connected the two ends of the chain to form a circle. With a wide smile and a graceful sweep of her hand, Jocelyn placed the circle of flowers on top of Issy's head.

Issy's smile was radiant as she grinned up at Jocelyn. Joy was stamped all over his daughter's angelic face. In that one blinding instant, he knew he had lost the battle. He was hiring Jocelyn.

Chapter Three

Jocelyn looked at the three kids, sitting on what was now her bed, watching her every move as she unpacked. She felt as though she had just landed on Mars and the aliens were now trying to figure out if she was a hostile entity or had she "come in peace." For about the hundredth time in the past two hours, she questioned her sanity.

What in the world possessed her to accept the position of housekeeper to a hunk with a badge and playing nanny to his three kids? Maybe she was going through some type of midlife crisis at an early age. Twenty-six was just too young to have a complete nervous breakdown. Wasn't it?

"So, kids, what do we do now?" Maybe they would have a suggestion, because right now she hadn't a clue what to do with three-year-old twin girls and a five-year-old boy. Pony rides would work, but she hadn't seen a barn on the property, let alone a small horse. Obviously dear old Dad hadn't gotten Tori her birthday wish. Maybe she should speak to him about that. Ponies, she could handle.

"Play trucks," Tori shouted.

"Dance," whispered Issy shyly.

Benjamin shook his head in disgust at his sisters and hopped off the bed. "It's lunchtime," he declared in what was sure to become his I'm-the-man-of-the-house voice. His little blue sneakers and scabby knees carried him out of her bedroom, into the hall, and down the steps.

Tori and Issy quickly wiggled their way off the high bed. Tori left a butt-size dusty dirt print on the dark blue comforter and took off after her brother with pounding feet and a shout that seemed to echo throughout the entire house. Issy neatly and carefully replaced the pillow that had been knocked to the floor during their scramble off the bed and then slowly followed the other kids. Quinn had been right. There was no way you would confuse those identical twins.

She glanced at her three empty suitcases and the pile of neatly taped boxes still to be unpacked, gave a shrug, and headed after the kids. Phoebe's advice as she headed off to the garage and a truckload of stained glass earlier still rang in her ears. *Never let them out of your sight, and never let them see you sweat.*

What kind of advice was that to give an unarmed woman?

By the time she reached the kitchen, Benjamin had already gotten out the bread and two jars of jelly. Tori was standing on a chair and reaching into the pantry cabinet for something. Issy was in the middle of the family room with her hands stretched to the ceiling and twirling in circles.

Jocelyn hurried across the room and reached for Tori, just as the little girl was starting to teeter and lose her balance. With a quick grab, she set the girl safely on the floor and took the jar of peanut butter out of her little hand. "No more standing on chairs, guys. I'm way too young for gray hair." She closed her eyes as visions of broken arms, emergency rooms, and screaming little girls flashed before her. Hell, she didn't even know the direction of the nearest hospital. As soon as she had a free minute, she needed to call Sydney and find that out.

"Grandmom's got gray hair," announced Benjamin.

"So does Pop Pop," added Tori, not to be outdone by her brother. "He even has fuzzy gray hair coming out of his ears."

Jocelyn figured a change of subject was in order before the kids got really personal and slipped with some family secrets that were better left in the closet. She held up the jar and asked, "Who wants what for lunch?"

Ben and Tori shouted over each other, demanding that their sandwich get made first. Issy continued to twirl around the room and ignore them all. The child was making her dizzy just by looking at her. "Issy gets her sandwich made first, because she is the only one not shouting." Hopefully if she fed the kid, she would stop the spinning. The last thing she needed was for Issy to get sick all over the family room carpet. There were limits to any job, and that was definitely one for this job. "Hey, Sugar Plum Fairy, what kind of sandwich do you want?"

Isabella stopped in midspin and frowned. "I'm not a fairy; I'm a ballerina."

"I knew that, sweetie." Issy had trouble pronouncing her *r*s. Ballerina had come out sounding like bal-weena. "The Sugar Plum Fairy is from a famous ballet called *The Nutcracker.*" Jocelyn held up both the jar of grape jelly and the strawberry preserves. "What kind do you want?"

"Strawsbewwy." Issy approached the counter and watched as Jocelyn constructed the sandwich.

"Phoebe gives us chips with our sandwich," Tori said as she slid up onto a stool.

"Today you get grapes." She plucked a bunch of

green grapes out of the bowl that was sitting on the counter and placed them next to Issy's sandwich.

"I like chips better." Tori wrinkled her nose at the bowl of freshly washed fruit.

"So do I, but grapes are better for you." Jocelyn carried Issy's plate over to the table and set it down.

Issy quietly slid onto the chair in front of the plate and shyly said, "Thank you."

"You're welcome, sweetie." Jocelyn smiled at the little girl until Issy gave a flash of a quick smile and then bit into her sandwich. One contented kid down, two to go.

"What kind of jelly do you want, Tori?" She slapped two pieces of bread onto the next plate and looked at the child facing her across the counter. Some time between this morning when she had left the Larson household to go collect her belongings from her sister's house and half an hour ago when she had arrived back someone had attempted to cut the girl's bangs. At least that was what she was hoping happened. It was either some badly aimed scissors, or Tori had attempted to stick her head down the garbage disposal.

Over Tori's right eye, the blond bangs were straight and perfectly aligned with her delicate little brow. The same thing couldn't be said for the left half. Someone had taken a huge chunk out of the bangs. Tufts of baby-fine blond hair, about half an inch long, stood in every direction, giving Tori a shocked, fluffy duckling appearance. A bandage with Mickey Mouse riding a bicycle printed on it was plastered over Tori's tiny forehead. Everyone, including Phoebe, had pretended nothing had happened, and Quinn hadn't been around to question. She hoped the sheriff didn't think his daughter's fashion statement had happened on her watch.

"I want chips." Tori's adorable little chin took on a stubborn tilt.

Jocelyn grinned at Tori and wondered if the child got her stubbornness from her mother or father. Her money was on dear old Dad. "I want Brad Pitt, but neither one of us is going to be getting what we want." She spread the peanut butter over a slice of bread. "Besides, you will thank me for it later. Kindergarten is hard enough without having thighs that look like saddlebags. Your jeans will never fit right, and you'll be picked last for dodge ball." She slapped some grape jelly on the other half, pressed the two pieces together, and then with a flourish, sliced it down the middle. "You want to be able to reach the top of the monkey bars, don't you?"

Tori nodded, and Jocelyn placed a handful of grapes on the plate and started to carry it over to the table.

"Daddy," cried Ben.

Jocelyn nearly dropped the plate as she spun around and saw Quinn Larson leaning against the doorjamb frowning at her. "Jeez, Sheriff, do you always sneak into your own house like that?"

"I wasn't sneaking. You just didn't hear me come in, that's all." Quinn pushed away from the jamb and stepped into the room. "I had a few extra minutes, so I thought I would come home for lunch, considering it's your first day and all."

"I didn't make you anything." It was unnerving to have Quinn glaring over her shoulder. She knew it was his house, and his children, but still, he was paying her to handle both his home and his children. The least he could do was stay out of her way. By the storm of emotions brewing in his dark eyes, she knew she would be getting a lecture this evening. She wondered what upset him the most, claiming his daughter was going to get saddlebag thighs, or telling them she wanted Brad Pitt?

"I don't expect you to wait on me." Quinn opened the refrigerator and pulled out a pitcher of juice. "I told you, your job doesn't include taking care of me." Quinn poured the juice into three plastic cups and then carried them over to the table. He ruffled Ben's hair, kissed Issy's blond head, and then frowned at Tori as she scrambled up onto a chair. Quinn put his hands on his hips and stared at his scalped daughter.

Tori grinned back.

Jocelyn placed Tori's lunch in front of her and then cringed at the sight of her bangs. She had to give the little girl points for gumption. If her own hair had looked like that, she would have buried herself into the back of a closet and cried for a month. Tori seemed quite proud of herself. Quinn better not think she had been around when the Indian raiding party had attacked or she would be vacuuming rooms and changing bedding while trying to fend off Wendell Kirby marriage proposals. Taking care of three kids and Quinn's home was definitely the lesser of the two evils. "Tori's hair was like that when I got here."

"I know." Quinn's answer was a deep and resigned sigh.

"Oh . . . that's good."

Quinn turned to her and raised one of his eyebrows in a silent question.

"I didn't mean it looked good; I meant at least you knew I wasn't around when it happened." She gave Tori a comforting smile and a wink. "I'm sure a trip to the beauty shop could fix it up like new." Short of gluing her hair back on, she didn't think there was a thing anyone could do for the child. It would just have to grow back.

"Only if they are planning to give her a crew cut." Quinn shook his head at his daughter. "You're lucky you didn't poke an eye out with those scissors, young lady."

Tori raised her hand and felt her eye. Sticky little fingers left behind purple smears of grape jelly across her face and eyelid.

Jocelyn shuddered at the size of the bandage covering the girl's forehead and went to get a wet paper towel before the jelly got into her eye. "How bad was she hurt?"

"Tori only cut her hair, not her face."

"Why the bandage, then?"

"Because after I got done yelling at her and my heart finally stopped its frantic pounding, she wouldn't stop crying. The bandage made her feel better."

Jocelyn turned her laugh into a cough as she wet the towel. "I see." What she saw was that Quinn Larson was a big old softy when it came to his children. She also saw that Benjamin was attempting to make his own sandwich. He was doing a pretty good job of it, considering he was only five. "Here, Ben, let me help you." She handed Quinn the wet towel and walked back to the counter. She took the peanut-butter-smeared knife out of his hand. "What kind of jelly did you want on it?"

"I don't want jelly on it." Ben pressed the other piece of bread on top of the one smeared with peanut butter.

She cut the sandwich in half. "You don't like jelly?" She watched Ben carry his plate over to the table and join his sisters. She scooped up a handful of grapes and carried them over for Ben.

"I like jelly." Ben wrinkled his nose at what was left of his sisters' sandwiches. "I just don't like it touching my peanut butter. It makes it all smushy."

Jocelyn remembered what Phoebe had said about how Benjamin didn't like his food touching each other. Phoebe had also said something about Issy not eating anything green. She glanced at Issy's plate, and sure enough the only thing left of the sandwich was a couple pieces of crust. The green grapes hadn't been touched.

"Issy doesn't eat anything green," Quinn said as he popped one of Issy's grapes into his mouth.

"I just remembered." Jocelyn glanced around the kitchen, until her gaze landed on a bunch of bananas sitting by the toaster. "New rule, kids. You're allowed one swap per meal. Issy, do you want to trade your grapes in for a banana?"

Issy nodded.

Tori pushed her plate in Jocelyn's direction. "I want chips."

She hid her smile. Tori was definitely going to be the troublemaker of the three. "You can only trade in the same food group. Fruit for fruit, snack food for snack food."

"When's snack time," mumbled Ben around a mouthful of peanut butter and bread.

Jocelyn was amazed he hadn't choked.

"After nap time," Quinn answered as he finished wiping the jelly off of Tori's eyelid.

"I get nap time?" she asked in a half-joke, half-serious voice. A nap right about now sounded wonderful to her. She had been on the job only about an hour, and already she was exhausted. She started to peel a banana and then handed it to Issy.

"Not you," chuckled Quinn as he started to construct his own triple-decker peanut butter and jelly sandwich. "I was referring to Tori's and Issy's nap time. They usually sleep for about an hour or so after lunch."

"I don't take naps any longer," announced Ben proudly as he popped a grape into his mouth.

"What do you usually do while your sisters nap?" Whatever it was, she hoped it was restful and quiet. She could use some down time. Sydney and Erik had kept her up until the wee hours of the morning catching up on things. Then she had gotten up early to read the want ads and get ready for the interview. Add to that the countless things she had to do back in Baltimore to get ready for the move, and anything over four hours of sleep had become a luxury. A luxury she dearly wanted to experience soon. Real soon.

"Aunt Phoebe is teaching me to read," Ben said.

"Ummm, Mr. Larson?"

"It's Quinn. Mr. Larson is my father."

"Okay, Quinn, I've never taught anyone to read before." Wasn't reading some major building block in the foundation of life? She was willing to pick up after the kids and make sure they all had clean undies and didn't starve to death, but no one had mentioned the job required a teaching degree. Suddenly the prospects of hauling in tuna all day didn't look so tough after all.

"Do you know your ABCs?" Quinn sat down next to Ben and took a big bite out of his sandwich.

"Of course I do." She hadn't eaten a peanut butter and jelly sandwich in years. Since the Larsons all seemed to be enjoying theirs, she started to make herself one. "There's got to be more to it than that."

"Not much." Quinn swiped the rest of Issy's grapes. "When I registered Ben for kindergarten, they handed out this thick packet of papers. They are worksheets for kids to do at home to get ready for the upcoming school year. Every day Phoebe or I do a page with him. They're simple, and he enjoys doing them."

She carried her lunch over to the table and joined the family. "Okay, I'll give it a shot."

Ben grinned, and she noticed that he was missing one of his lower teeth.

"Nap and reading time I can handle. Anything else I should know about? Anything in particular I should be doing this afternoon?"

"Take the day as it comes. Your first priority is the children; after that it all kind of falls into place."

She chuckled and wondered who was living in some dream world? Quinn, for thinking everything just falls into place, or herself, for actually believing this would be easier than dodging Wendell Kirby every day. How fast could Wendell run anyway? He had a good fifteen years on her, and his belly hung over his belt by at least six inches.

"What's so funny?" Quinn had finished his sandwich and the last of the grapes.

"Nothing, I was just wondering if you eat peanut butter and jelly every day."

"Some days we have turkey sandwiches," Quinn said.

"Sometimes bologna and cheese if Phoebe remembers to buy it," Ben said.

"Mac and cheese is the best," added Tori.

"What about you, Issy?" She noticed the little girl didn't voice her opinion. "What's your favorite lunch?"

"Soup and cwackers," Issy whispered.

"What kind of soup? Vegetable, chicken noodle, or tomato?"

"Noodles."

She gave Issy a wide smile. "I'll write that down on the grocery list." She looked at Quinn. "You do keep a list, don't you?"

"We will now. Phoebe was a fly-by-the-seat-of-your-pants shopper. Whatever looked good that day, she threw in the cart, and that's what we worked with for the week." Quinn stood up and started to carry the dishes over to the counter. "Issy and Tori, go get ready for your nap, and I'll be up in a minute to tuck you both in."

Ben carried his empty cup over to the sink. "I'll go get my pages."

Issy and Tori headed for the stairs.

"What time will you be home, Quinn?" Sometime this afternoon she had to think about making dinner. All she needed to do was to start calling Quinn "dear," and she would sound like Hollywood's rendition of "the little woman." It was a sobering thought. One she would prefer never to have again.

"A little after six, if everything is okay at the office. If I'm not here, start without me." Quinn headed upstairs to tuck in his princesses.

Jocelyn stared at the empty doorway Quinn had just

passed through, and it hit her. Somehow, somewhere, she had crossed over into the Twilight Zone. A nineteen fifties sit-com starring Donna Reed or Danny Thomas. She always dreamed of getting married and having a couple of kids, but nowhere in her dreams had she become "the little woman." She would rather go without moisturizers, Snickers bars, and the Wonder Bra by Victoria's Secret than turn into June Cleaver.

She had seen *Nick-at-Nite* and all those black-and-white reruns they force-fed the children of America's chauvinistic attitudes. She had witnessed the horrors of vacuuming while wearing pearls and heels, dishpan hands, and the brain-dead zombie wives that said such things as "Wait until your father gets home," or "Daddy knows best."

Her vision of her future family life came complete with a loving husband who was her partner, two to four children, a fulfilling career, at least two vacations a year, and hired help. *The Brady Bunch* had Alice. *Family Affair* had Mr. French. Even her favorite show, *The Addams Family,* had the steady and ever-present Lurch.

Somewhere her life had been turned around. She was now someone else's hired help. Eight years of schooling and one law degree later, she had morphed into Hazel.

"Jocelyn," called Ben from the family room, "I'm ready."

She looked at the little boy sitting on the floor in front of the coffee table and had to smile. A thick stack of blue papers and two yellow pencils were laid out neatly in front of him. Ben looked ready to conquer *War and Peace,* or at least a Dr. Seuss book or two. How hard could it be to teach someone the ABCs? Resigned to expanding a child's mind, she walked into the family room and lowered herself to the floor.

Quinn stopped at the doorway and watched as Jocelyn showed his son how to make the letter *E.* Ben's tongue was peeking out the side of his mouth as he followed Jocelyn's instructions and tried his first lowercase *e*. Quinn's mother swore Ben got the tongue action from him. Per his mom, he had had the same habit when he had been Ben's age.

His gaze moved to the woman sitting next to his son. Long blond hair contrasted against Ben's dark head as they both bent over the paper on the table. Lord, Jocelyn was beautiful. The sunlight streaming in through the patio doors made her hair look lighter. Softer. More touchable. He had to have lost his mind to have hired her.

It was all Phoebe's fault. His sister had known exactly which buttons of his to push, and she had not only pressed them, but she had pounded on them without even mentioning them. Responsibility for the children was his, and his alone, now that Diane was gone. He couldn't allow Phoebe to continue to sacrifice her dream now that a resolution was at hand. Jocelyn was only a temporary solution, but an answer nonetheless. By not pointing out this fact, Phoebe had grounded his "hot" button into dust. There was no way he couldn't hire Jocelyn.

If he had told Phoebe the real reason he hadn't wanted to hire Jocelyn, his sister would have laughed herself silly or thrown him a party. The plain, simple truth was that Jocelyn Fletcher turned him on, and in a big way.

For the past year, since his and Diane's divorce had become final, everyone had been after him to get on with his life. To find a "nice" girl and settle back down. Phoebe had been the most vocal in her opinions, believing the best years of his life were slipping away. Twice in the past year his sister had fixed him up with one of her friends. Both times had been unexpected and if not disastrous, embarrassing for both parties. He had had to resort to threatening Phoebe with taking

the use of his garage away from her if she pulled another matchmaking attempt. He hadn't been looking
for love, or even getting laid, then.

That had been four months ago.

He still wasn't looking for love, because love was a
fleeting emotion, so why waste your time looking for
something that wouldn't last. As for getting laid, one
look at Jocelyn and he was seriously reconsidering his
priorities in life.

Which made this entire situation one big disaster waiting to happen. The sooner he found a permanent housekeeper, the better off he and the children would be.

He needed to get back to the office and the mountain
of paperwork awaiting him there. But before he tackled
his In basket, he was calling the Augusta newspaper and
placing a Help Wanted ad.

"The girls are down for their nap, and I need to get
back to the office." He gave Jocelyn a fleeting glance and
smiled at Ben. "I'll be home around six-fifteen. If I'm
not, don't hold dinner. The kids will need baths and
then in bed by nine."

"I guess I can handle that," Jocelyn said.

"My office number is by the phone in the kitchen if
you have any questions, and Phoebe will probably be
out in the garage all night."

"I'll help Jocelyn, Dad," Ben said.

"I know you will." He stepped into the room and ruffled the top of Ben's hair. "I like your lettering; it's getting better."

"Thanks, Dad." Ben beamed.

"See you both later." He turned and walked out of
the room.

He caught the front screen door before it slammed
behind him. He didn't want to give the girls any excuse
to get out of their beds and see what the noise was all
about. Without their naps, Issy tended to fall asleep
over dinner and Tori became grouchy. A crabby Tori he

wouldn't wish on anyone, especially if it was their first day on the job. If Tori got into her notoriously miserable mood, Jocelyn wouldn't last the week.

He stepped off the porch and frowned at the overgrown front yard. He really had to find the time to mow the grass. He had already given up totally on the flower beds. Maybe tonight, if he got home on time and Jocelyn wouldn't mind keeping an eye on the kids, he could at least get half of the yard cut before it got too dark.

Two months ago he had all the time in the world to mow the lawn, food shop, and fix up the house. Today, even with Phoebe's help, he couldn't even keep up with the clutter in the living room. That didn't say a lot about his parenting skills.

A flash of red in the tall grass caught his attention. He walked ten feet across the yard, bent, and picked up a battered and muddy Ken doll. Ken's red bathing suit had caught his eye, but his twisted and broken leg made him cringe. It looked as though Ken had gone ten rounds with the lawn mower, and lost. It was just his luck. He was now going to have to rake the yard of toys before he could even start to mow it.

He tossed the doll up onto the porch as a brightly painted Volkswagen Beetle chugged its way into the driveway. Edna McCain's car was an original, and not Volkswagen's updated version. Edna, who was at least seventy years old, kept the lime green car in a garage and only used it to make deliveries for her business. The huge yellow and white flowers that decorated the car looked as fresh and crisp as the day Edna's husband had painted them thirty some years ago. The name of Edna's business, Flower Power, was neatly written across the front hood in fluorescent orange paint.

Edna owned and operated the only florist in the Misty Harbor area. For the first three weeks Phoebe had lived with Quinn, the older woman and her flowery car had been an almost daily occurrence at the house. The men of Misty Harbor had smothered Phoebe with flowers and candy, and one creative soul had had champagne and a warm-from-the-oven blueberry pie delivered to the house. Phoebe's heart or interest hadn't been caught, but Quinn would be the first to agree that the pie had been delicious.

If the pie was any indication of the cooking ability of some of Misty Harbor's manly residents, maybe he should look into hiring a male housekeeper.

He watched Edna, with her ankle-length Indian print dress and sandals that appeared to have been made out of recycled tires, step out of her car carrying a bouquet of flowers. The elegant long-stemmed yellow roses clashed with the six seashell and metal disk necklaces Edna was wearing. The countless bracelets on both of Edna's wrists clanged and banged as she hurried toward him. Edna and her husband, Bill, had been hippies before "hippy" had been a word.

"Afternoon, Edna. Haven't seen you in a couple of weeks."

"Yeah, I got a breather there for a while, but now it's starting up again." Edna fussed with a lacy fern and then straightened the yellow satin bow wrapped around the dozen roses. "I'm getting too old for this. Bill says I need a cleansing period in my life."

"He should know." Quinn chuckled as he thought of Bill McCain. In the race between the tortoise and the hare, Bill was the tortoise. No one had ever seen Bill sweat, hurry, or get riled up about anything. He sometimes thought Edna had to walk around with a mirror in her pocket so she could occasionally place it under Bill's nose to see if the man was still breathing.

Edna snorted. "Yeah, that man's been in a cleansing period for the past twenty years." Edna tossed one of her long gray braids over her shoulder. "This time I'm seriously thinking about retiring. Being the only florist in this town is becoming a full-time job."

"What would we do without you, Edna? Town has to have flowers."

"Didn't say I would leave all you studs high and dry. My granddaughter's thinking about a change in careers. A person could do a lot worse than being a florist."

"True. How is your son, and all the grandkids?"

"Paul's still as stuffy and boring as all those old books he likes to read and analyze. How Bill and I produced an English Lit professor is beyond me. Fifty years ago there must have been more toxins in the water than I had thought." Edna's pounded silver and gemstone bracelets clanged as she shifted the roses from one hand to the other. "The grandkids seem to be following in his footprints. That's why I think it would be good for Mary to get away from Boston and move up here. Virginia's still in college, and Dylan's a lost soul being corrupt by materialism."

He chuckled. He didn't think Edna's and Bill's genes were twisted due to bad water. His money was on them smoking wacky weed way back when. Hell, Edna had probably baked brownies with the stuff in them. Being the sheriff, he wasn't going to get Edna to admit it now, and as far as he could tell, they hadn't so much as smoked a dandelion leaf in the past thirty years. "I don't think being a stockbroker corrupts a person."

Edna snorted. "The boy should be working for a living, not playing with other people's money. Just ain't right."

"I'm sure Dylan's working hard." He nodded toward the roses, then toward the garage. "Phoebe's in the garage working."

"Heard she is starting up her business. Nice of you to let her use your garage 'til she finds someplace else."

"She's helped me out a lot around here."

"Sad business that is." Edna glanced toward the house. "Little ones handling it okay?"

"As good as can be expected." He never knew what

to say to people when they offered up their sympathy and asked questions. Edna wasn't being nosey; she honestly was concerned for the children and him. The whole town had rallied behind one of their own when Diane had been killed. He just didn't know what to do with the rally.

"Good, good. Let me know if you need anything." Edna took a step toward the house.

"Phoebe's in the garage, Edna."

"I know, you already told me." Edna jiggled the bouquet of flowers. "These aren't for Phoebe. They're for Jocelyn Fletcher. Heard she's your new housekeeper."

He glared at the roses and felt like throttling someone. "Heck, Edna, the woman just moved in here less than three hours ago, and someone is already sending her flowers?"

Edna chuckled. "Those Fletcher girls are a bane to my existence. Last year my income jumped up into a higher tax bracket because of Gwen and then Sydney Fletcher. Lord knows what Jocelyn's presence in Misty Harbor will do to my bottom line. That coondog Wendell Kirby has already placed a special order for orchids. I won't be able to get them in 'til tomorrow or so, but let me tell you they are setting him back a bundle. Wendell's bound and determined to catch himself one of these Fletcher girls. How many more of them are at home in Baltimore do you suppose?"

"Jocelyn's the last of them." He couldn't believe this. Jocelyn hadn't even had a chance to unpack, and already the bachelors of Misty Harbor were sending gifts and trying to court her. The whole town was insane.

Edna was right. The water supply had to be polluted or something. Maybe it was a full moon or Mercury was aligned with Mars. It had to be something like that. How else could he explain the sudden twisting of his gut when Edna had said the roses were for Jocelyn?

If Jocelyn wanted the flowers, that was fine by him.

As long as it didn't affect her taking care of the kids, she could wear them in her hair and dance around the house as far as he was concerned. He had more important things to worry about than who was sending roses to his housekeeper.

"Just knock on the door, Edna. I've got to run." He hurried to his SUV and didn't look back.

Phoebe Larson had stood in the deep shadows of the garage and watched as Edna McCain and her Flower Power car pulled into the driveway. Her heartbeat had kicked it up a notch as the bouquet of yellow roses came into view. Was Gary Franklin finally going to acknowledge that she had moved back to town and that he was interested in picking up where they had left off eleven years ago? Gary had sent her a dozen yellow long-stemmed roses for her eighteenth birthday. She still had one of the blooms pressed in between two sheets of wax paper and tucked away in her memory box.

The small wooden box was cheap, crooked, and unevenly stained; but the hinges still held, and the tiny lock still worked. Gary had made her the box in shop class back in eighth grade. The box held every memory of him.

Movie stubs, pressed flowers, and Valentine's Day cards competed for space with mushy love notes, an empty bottle of perfume that had been his favorite fragrance, and the tie from the tux Gary had worn to their senior prom. A gold necklace with a tiny locket, complete with their pictures, was nestled in the bottom of the box. But the item that broke her heart every time she looked at it was the pre-engagement ring he had given her the night they had graduated from high school. The three tiny diamonds were no more than chips, but it had meant everything to her that night.

Gary Franklin and she had been engaged to become

engaged. It was one step up from going steady, and one step away from pictures in the local paper and setting a date. No one could have been happier than she had been that night.

Within two months, her world had crumbled, and the boy who professed to love her had walked away.

Or had she been the one to push him away? After all, she had been the one to choose to go away to college instead of staying in Misty Harbor. Gary had been the one to issue the ultimatum; him or college.

She couldn't say she regretted the choice she had made. Going to school and learning her craft had been very important to her back then. It still was. She just never could figure out why she couldn't have had her dream of working with stained glass and Gary.

In a perfect world, she would have had it all.

She held her breath as her brother gestured toward the garage. Her fingers crossed, and she said a silent prayer that the flowers were from Gary. It would be their first step to seeing if they still had any chance of a future together. Gary's first move. She had been waiting for his move for five long and lonely weeks.

A small sound escaped her throat as Edna shook her head and glanced toward the house. The flowers weren't for her after all. They were for Jocelyn, the new woman in town.

Quinn seemed disgusted with the flowers and the male population of Misty Harbor as he stormed his way toward his car. Edna's long skirt was teased by a summer breeze, and the distant sounds of jangling bracelets could be heard as she walked up the pathway to the porch.

Phoebe could feel her heart skip those extra beats and settle once again into its normal rhythm. Boring, normal, and just a tad broken rhythm.

Who ever said that the world was perfect anyway?

Chapter Four

Quinn was tired, disgusted, and hungry. He knew which side of the family Tori had inherited her miserable moods from; his. It was already after eight at night, and he was just now leaving the office. When he had tried calling Jocelyn around six, he hadn't gotten an answer. Concerned, he had tried back every fifteen minutes only to get a busy signal. By seven, Phoebe had been the one to answer the phone. His sister had sworn that the kids were fine and Jocelyn was handling everything. He wasn't to worry, and his dinner was in the microwave waiting for him whenever he got home.

Normally, he wouldn't have worried, but he had heard voices in the background. Male voices. It had almost sounded as if a party had been going on in his house, except he hadn't heard any music. When he had questioned Phoebe, she had laughed and once again told him not to worry.

He hated it when people told him not to worry. It meant something was going on that he wasn't going to like.

His stomach growled as he turned off Main Street and headed home. Hopefully Jocelyn had managed to

cook more than burnt hot dogs and a box of macaroni
and cheese, one of Phoebe's staples of life. The grapes
and peanut butter and jelly sandwich he had had for
lunch eight hours ago was long gone.

Who would have thought one simple fender bender
could turn into such a fiasco? Give a lawyer from New
York City too many beers with his lobster dinner, and
the man was ready to sue the founding fathers of the
town for daring to put streetlights up along the road.
The man should be thankful all he had hit was the pole
and not some innocent pedestrian. The front end of
the man's Cadillac had folded like an accordion, and
he had been demanding restitution from the town and
arguing with one of the deputies by the time Quinn had
arrived at the scene.

Mr. Fancy High Price Lawyer would be spending the
night behind bars, courtesy of Hancock County Sheriff's
Department. He'd deal with all the paperwork tomorrow morning. It had been his experience that lawyers
made the worst lawbreakers. For some reason, they all
thought they were above the laws they claimed to be
protecting.

He was beginning to dread the summer months and
all the tourists that the season brought to his town. Misty
Harbor needed the tourists, and the majority were really nice people. But every summer there were a select
few who should be banned from the state of Maine for
the rest of their lives. This week alone, he had already
run into two such individuals, and the weekend wasn't
even here yet.

As he turned onto Blueberry Hill Road, the tension
in his shoulders started to increase. What in the world
had been going on at his house, and why hadn't Jocelyn
answered the phone earlier? He believed his sister when
she had assured him the children were fine. Phoebe
wouldn't have lied about that. So what had been going
on?

The gravel crunched under his tires as he turned onto his driveway and rounded the curve. His foot pressed the brake gently as he slowed his SUV and pulled in behind Jocelyn's sporty red car. In the fading evening light, he studied his house. Jocelyn's was the only car parked out front. Phoebe, and whoever else had been there, was gone. A few lights were already lit in the house. Everything looked peaceful.

The confusing thing was, someone had mowed his yard. From what he could see they had done a fine job, too. No shredded toys littered the neatly cut grass. Even the front walk appeared to have been swept. By the amount of grass still littering it, he would have to guess Benjamin or one of the girls had done the broom work. So who had climbed on his temperamental John Deere and ridden it around the yard?

His sister wouldn't have done it. Not that Phoebe couldn't. Phoebe was capable of doing anything she darn well pleased. He just knew her well enough to know that she wouldn't have stepped foot outside of the garage now that the glass shipment had been delivered. He was surprised she still wasn't here inspecting each piece of colored glass and planning her first piece.

Jocelyn should have been watching the kids all afternoon and worrying about what to make for dinner. She wouldn't have had the time, and the yard work was definitely not on her to-do list. So who had saved him a couple of hours' worth of work, and how much was he going to owe them?

Quinn shook his head as he moved up the walk and spotted a small mountain of toys piled on the front porch. The yard had yielded a treasure trove of goodies. It looked like Santa wouldn't need to stop here this Christmas. Thankfully, all the toys appeared to have been picked up before the mower blades mutilated them into recyclables. The simple task of picking up the toys had to set someone back at least an hour or two.

He walked into the house and silently groaned at the sight of the living room. How was it possible that it appeared worse than when he had left at lunchtime? He detoured into the dining room and saw that someone had taken the time to fold one load of laundry. The unfolded dry towels were sitting on the table still piled in a plastic laundry basket.

The kitchen was a disaster. Take-out containers were everywhere. So were empty cups, sticky plates, crinkled paper napkins, and used silverware. He counted at least three paper airplanes littering the floor and countertop. For some odd reason a Barbie doll, wearing a hot pink string bikini, a black feathered boa, and green high heels, was floating in the sink. A few stray bubbles clung to her firm plastic chest and the sides of the stainless steel sink. He stepped closer and shook his head. A colander, assorted cookie cutters, and one rubber ducky with a hole in its side lay at the bottom of the water.

The bouquet of yellow roses Edna had delivered earlier was in an old mayonnaise jar proudly sitting in the middle of the kitchen table. A six-foot weeping fig tree, which he had never seen before, was near the family room's fireplace. What appeared to be a five-pound box of very expensive chocolates was open on the coffee table. Someone had obviously picked through the candy already. At least a dozen or so brown wrappers were scattered across the table. The toys from the living room had overflowed into the family room.

The last time he had seen the house look this bad, Phoebe had been suffering from a twenty-four-hour flu bug, and the Harbor Jazz Weekend had been in full swing, taking all of his time. What in the world had his newly hired housekeeper been doing all afternoon? Obviously not cooking or cleaning.

The noise and racket coming from upstairs told him bath time was at hand. Tori's squeals of delight echoed through the hallway and down the stairs. He better go up and see how Jocelyn was managing hair-washing time. He found washing the twins' long hair the hardest part of having little girls instead of little boys. That and trying to get a comb through the tangles. He had mastered a ponytail, but any other style was beyond his abilities. Much to his daughters' disappointment, his DNA was missing the braiding and pigtail gene.

Benjamin's door was near the top of the stairs, so he checked on his son first. Ben was sitting in the middle of his bedroom floor, playing with trains. A line of books ran across the carpet, and his son was using them as tracks. "Hi, Ben. Waiting your turn for the bathtub?"

Ben spun around. Beneath a dirty face, his son's smile lit the room. "Hi, Dad. You're late."

"You're dirty." He stepped into the room and squatted down. "What were you doing, cleaning the chimney?" It looked as if Ben had been rolling around in a pigpen all day. The grass stains on his beige shorts were from this morning. But how did his dinosaur T-shirt and every inch of exposed flesh get covered in dirt? Hell, his shirt even appeared to have damp spots.

Ben laughed. "Nope, we helped Jocelyn clean up all afternoon."

"Clean up what?" From what he had seen of the house, there was no way anyone put a single toy back where it belonged, let alone spent a whole afternoon doing it.

"Outside. Jocelyn said it was too nice to spend the day indoors. We had to pick up all the toys that were in the yard."

"Who cut the grass?"

"Jocelyn did." Ben grinned. "We had to stay on the porch where she could see us; but she gave us buckets of soapy water, and we got to clean all the toys. Tori made a mess, but we gave Issy all the Barbie dolls to clean. She liked that."

"I can imagine." What kid didn't like a bucket of water and bubbles. He had to give Jocelyn credit, for not only cutting the grass, but keeping the kids entertained while she did it. "So, your afternoon with Jocelyn went okay? You like her?"

"She's cool, Dad." Ben leaned in closer and whispered, "She must not have any kids at her house."

"Why do you say that?"

"She let Tori and Issy play in the kitchen sink, and she let us all have a piece of candy before dinner. She didn't even yell when Tori helped her take down the clothes and dropped all the socks into the mud."

He hid his smile. If that was all of Jocelyn's faults Ben could list, he'd consider his new temporary housekeeper a gift from heaven. For now. "You're right, Ben. Jocelyn doesn't have any kids. All of this is kind of new to her, so I need you to help her out, okay?"

"Sure." Ben started to pick up all the books and replace them back on the bookshelf. "All those guys came over again."

"What guys?"

"The ones that kept pestering Aunt Phoebe until she told them all to go away." Ben carefully set the two engines back on the shelf. "This time when Phoebe saw them here she didn't get mad; she laughed real hard and offered everyone a soda."

"What did Jocelyn do then?" He now knew what had been happening at the house while he had been giving some drunk lawyer a Breathalyzer test.

"She gave Phoebe a real funny look, and then she filled the sink with bubbles and water for the girls to play in."

"What were you doing?"

"Mr. Newman was showing me pictures of his tuna boat, and Mr. Martin was teaching me how to make a paper airplane."

"Bob Newman and Abraham Martin were here?"

"So was some other guy, but I forgot his name. He brought Jocelyn a tree, and Mr. Martin bought her the candy."

That explained the weeping fig tree and the box of candy. He wondered what Bob Newman had come a-courting with? The men of Misty Harbor never dropped in on a lady without something in hand. It was a town tradition, one that was forcing Edna McCain into a higher tax bracket.

"Don't eat all of Jocelyn's candy." He ruffled the top of his son's head and stood back up. "I better go help Jocelyn with the girls. You know how Tori gets when you try to comb her hair."

Ben shuddered. "Tori's a whimp."

"It's not nice to talk about your sister like that."

Ben rolled his eyes. "It's not nice the way she screams bloody murder every time you try to comb her hair."

He chuckled. He couldn't argue with Ben on that one. "What do you know about 'bloody murder'?"

Ben's face scrunched up as he thought for a moment. Quinn knew the exact moment an answer came to his son by the relaxing of his small, adorable face and the flash in his dark eyes. "It's red."

Quinn was still chuckling when he stepped into the bathroom's doorway. His laughter slowly died as he took in the noisy scene before him. Both of his daughters were still in the tub, and the bubbles were so thick they were tickling their chins. Their faces were scrubbed clean, and mounds of wet hair was piled on top of their heads. Every bath toy they owned was in the overflowing tub with them.

Wet, dirty clothes were scattered across the floor. The rug in front of the tub looked saturated, and Jocelyn was on her hands and knees using a bath towel to soak up the rest of the water that had been splashed onto the floor. Bubbles were everywhere. A few even floated in the air. His bathroom had turned into a Lawrence Welk nightmare.

His gaze landed on Jocelyn's khaki-covered butt as it moved side to side with every swipe of her arm. Sometime after lunch she had changed from her stylish linen slacks and silk blouse to a pair of shorts and a light blue top with the tiniest straps. No way was his housekeeper wearing a bra under that skimpy top, and her long, lightly tanned legs should be illegal. Somehow she had twisted her long hair up into some type of messy bun that got it off her neck but looked as though it would all come tumbling down at any moment.

No wonder his house had become the strutting grounds for the single male population of Misty Harbor. Jocelyn Fletcher was one sexy babe.

"Daddy, Daddy, Daddy," shouted Tori as she tried to stand up in the slippery tub.

Jocelyn reached for his daughter before she could fall and hurt herself. "Easy, kid, I don't need you to crack your noggin."

Tori giggled as she started to step out of the tub. Hundreds, if not thousands, of bubbles clung to her skin. "Hi, Daddy. Jocelyn gave us a bath and washed our hair. She didn't even get shampoo in my eyes like you do." Tori shook her arm, trying to dislodge some of the bubbles. It didn't help. "She let me pour in the bubble juice."

"So I see." By the look Jocelyn was casting him, he knew she regretted that decision. "I think we need to hose you down some before you can get out of the tub." Somewhere in the sea of floating toys was a large blue cup he used to rinse the girls' hair. He smiled at Issy, who had on a sparkling tiara holding her wet hair in place. "You look like a bubble princess, sweetheart."

Issy slowly smiled. "My Barbies had a bubble bath, too, Daddy."

"So I heard, princess." He gave Jocelyn a quick glance. His housekeeper looked to be on the frazzled side of life. A few stray bubbles were in her hair, and somehow she had managed to get the front of her top soaked. Either the water had been very cold, or Jocelyn was very happy to see him. Twin hard nipples were pressing against the softness of her top. He forced his gaze back onto his daughters. "How about I finish up in here?"

"No, I've got this handled. All these two need is a quick rinse job and they're done." Jocelyn started to dig into the tub of bubbles looking for the cup. "You go eat your dinner. It's in the microwave; all you have to do is heat it up."

Quinn watched as Jocelyn stretched farther and lower. Her breasts brushed the froth overflowing the tub. Jocelyn pulled back in triumph. One hand was clutching the blue cup; the other was busy swiping bubbles off her chest. For a moment, he forgot how to breathe as desire flared hot and heavy. All in one very obvious place. With a hasty good-bye he left the room.

Ten minutes later Quinn had gotten himself under control, changed into jeans and a T-shirt, and was taking his dinner out of the microwave. Paradise was on his plate. Heaven consisted of Cajun swordfish, a bed of spicy rice, and a vegetable medley complete with a dinner roll and a thick slice of key lime pie for dessert. Jocelyn hadn't cooked it. He would recognize her sister Gwen's cooking anywhere. Jocelyn had raided the kitchen at Catch of the Day, the best restaurant for miles around. His housekeeper deserved a raise for ingenuity. It was a real shame he couldn't afford to give her one.

He closed his eyes as he took his first bite of the swordfish. Spicy hot seasonings scorched his mouth and almost made his eyes water. Almost. He washed it down with a cold beer. There was no way he was ruining this meal with milk, orange juice, or red Kool-Aid. A fine wine would have been his first choice, but since he hadn't bought a bottle of wine in over two years, beer would do. One beer wouldn't hurt him, and he was off duty, even though he was still on call twenty-four hours a day.

He took another bite of the swordfish and closed his eyes to the mess surrounding him. The roses were fragrant, and the cool evening breeze brought the scent of the sea into the house. Wonderful smells. Maine's smell. The smell of home. He couldn't imagine living anywhere else besides Misty Harbor. What did the people in Nebraska smell? Corn? Cattle? What about Minnesota? Did the evening breeze there carry the scent of forests, lakes, and wolves?

Quinn could hear the girls in their room. Ben was in the bathroom now, and Jocelyn was going from one room to the other. He should have stayed and helped her, but was glad he hadn't. Trust was a double-edged sword and was a very important part of their working relationship. He had to be able to trust Jocelyn with the children, in all things. She in return had to trust him to be a gentleman, or their living arrangements would never work. There had been no way to hide his reaction after seeing her breasts covered in strawberry-scented bubbles. It hadn't mattered one bit that she had been the one wearing a skimpy top while bathing his daughters. Jocelyn would have taken one look at the heat in his eyes and the bulge in his pants and either walked right out the front door, or she would have been barricading her bedroom door and sleeping with an ax. It didn't take a genius to figure out where she would be swinging that sucker either.

There was something about the combination of bubbles and breasts that had turned him on. He stabbed at a piece of broccoli and then a carrot. Amazingly, at thirty-two, he was still discovering stuff about himself. Who would have thought bubbles could be an aphrodisiac?

He closed his mouth and savored the lightly seasoned vegetables. Even having been warmed up in a microwave, Gwen's cooking was delicious. If he didn't count the clutter surrounding him, and the fact that his housekeeper had been entertaining potential suitors, with his own sister's encouragement, he could live like this every evening. The yard was mowed, kids were on their way to becoming presentable, and the meal was the best he had had in weeks. Who cared that it had come out of Styrofoam containers?

All in all, it was a very good beginning.

"Daddy, we're squeaky clean," announced Tori as she and Issy scrambled into the kitchen on bare feet and smelling like strawberries and baby shampoo.

"So I see." Both of his daughters were dressed in pink pajamas. Issy wore a knee-length, lace-trimmed night-gown with Belle printed on the front. Tori's pajamas had shorts and a sleeveless top with a roaring Beast printed on the front. Their choice in pajama wear said it all. "I also see that Jocelyn combed your hair."

Issy's hair was straight and damp. Her bangs were perfectly straight across her brow. Tori's hair was combed, too, but the left half of her bangs was already dry and sticking straight up. In the ten hours since Tori had cut her bangs, he would have thought they would have grown somewhat. Thankfully the bandage had been re-moved from her forehead. He hadn't been looking for-ward to pulling it off. Tori might act like the tough one in the family, but give that child an inkling of pain and she would scream the house down.

"You two climb on up here and tell me what you did all afternoon." He pushed a pile of dirty dishes and empty Styrofoam to the other end of the table as the girls scrambled up onto the chairs. "What did you guys have for dinner?"

"Fish and pie," said Tori.

He looked at Issy. Ever since Issy became infatuated with The Little Mermaid, she refused to eat any fish, ex-cept tuna from a can. "Ham and cake."

"Did Aunt Phoebe watch you while Jocelyn picked up dinner?"

"Nope, Jocelyn took us with her." Tori snatched a piece

of carrot off his plate and popped it into her mouth. "Phoebe put our seats in Jocelyn's car."

"I see." He finished the last bite of his swordfish and made a threatening face at Tori as she swiped the last carrot. His daughter giggled. "So what did you do this afternoon besides pick up toys from the yard and wash them?"

"I helped Jocelyn take down the clothes," Tori said. "And she didn't even yell at me."

"Well, that's good, right?"

"Right." Tori eyed the remaining rice on his plate. He shook his head and pushed his plate and fork in front of her. Tori dug in.

Around a mouthful of rice, Tori mumbled, "Jocelyn says we get a snack before bed."

"Are you sure you ate your whole dinner, young lady?" Maybe Jocelyn had been right about his daughter acquiring saddlebag thighs. If Tori continued to eat like this, she wasn't going to fit on the school bus seats.

"Yep. Jocelyn's a great cook."

He wouldn't know about that. So far she hadn't made anything fancier than a peanut butter and jelly sandwich. The thundering sound of feet pounding down the stairs announced Ben's arrival.

"Hey, guys, Jocelyn says we have to pick up some of the toys before we get a snack." Ben frowned at the messy family room. "Come on, you two, I'm not doing all the work."

Quinn nodded toward the mess. "Both of you go help your brother."

Issy quietly slid off her chair and went to pick up crayons. Tori rolled her eyes and muttered something under her breath before joining her siblings.

He tried not to chuckle.

Jocelyn stepped into the kitchen, took one look around, and groaned. "It's worse than I remembered." She started to carry the dirty dishes over to the dishwasher, tossing empty Styrofoam containers as she went.

"Things aren't that bad. It will calm down around here after a few days." He noticed that she had taken the time to change into a clean, dry T-shirt. This time she was wearing a bra underneath. He stood up and carried over his plate and tossed the empty beer bottle into the recyclable container in the corner of the room.

Jocelyn unplugged the kitchen sink and started to wring out Barbie's long blond hair and boa. She gave him an amused look over her shoulder. "If you say so, boss."

"Dinner was excellent."

"I didn't make it."

"I know." He picked up some plates and stacked them into the dishwasher. "How much do I owe you for the meals."

"Nothing." Jocelyn tossed the paper airplanes into the trash.

"On your salary you can't afford meals from Catch of the Day. I insist on paying for them."

"The only thing they cost me was my pride." Jocelyn started to wipe down the kitchen table.

"Your pride?"

"Yeah, my pride. When I called Gwen at five minutes to six and told her I forgot all about dinner, she thought the whole thing was hysterical. She offered up the meals because she feels somewhat responsible for me taking this job in the first place." Jocelyn bent closer to the roses and took a deep whiff. "I figure I can play on that guilt for about a week or so."

"You took advantage of your sister?"

Jocelyn's grin was positively wicked. "Darn straight I did. Wouldn't you?"

He chuckled and then glanced at the small mountain of Styrofoam containers in the trash can. "Any chance you could guilt her out of her poached salmon with her famous sour cream dill sauce?"

"You didn't like the swordfish?"

"Loved it, but if you've only got a week's worth of guilt to work with, I want to put my order in now." He glanced into the family room and smiled as Issy straightened all the pillows and Tori picked up the candy wrappers. "Did Gwen and Sydney force you to take this job?" He was pretty sure Jocelyn could have landed some other job, one that definitely paid more, even if she was only going to be in Maine temporarily. One that didn't include bath time, getting out grass stains, or handling yard work.

"Forced me? No." Jocelyn wiped down the countertops. "There weren't a lot of job opportunities available, and I'd be the first one to admit this wasn't exactly what I had in mind; but it's not too bad." Jocelyn dumped the cookie cutters into the dishwasher and then squeezed the colander onto the lower rack. "It beats hauling in tuna or computerizing Sydney's office files."

"That's the kind of competition I was up against?" He couldn't picture Jocelyn wrestling tuna with the likes of Bob Newman. The desk job should have been right up her alley, though. Lawyers did a lot of computer work, whereas he couldn't stand the blasted machines. He was only a hunt-and-peck typist, and it didn't matter what type of printer the department bought; it was usually toast within a year. He was tired of being looked down upon by repairmen who still wore braces and had acne. If he got one more "Invalid Command" on his desktop, he was chucking it out the window.

The rubber ducky, with the hole in the side went into the garbage. "There wasn't any competition really."

"So you're planning on staying?" He held out his hand, and Tori dumped all the crinkled and crushed candy papers into his palm. "These little monsters didn't scare you off yet?"

Ben growled, Issy gave a shy smile, and Tori wiggled her eyebrows, which made her new partial-spiked haircut flutter.

Jocelyn's laugh was light and honest. "Scared, no, but they sure did tire me out today."

He studied her face and for the first time noticed the faint shadows beneath her beautiful gray eyes. Jocelyn did look beat. "Why don't you call it a night, and I'll give the kids their snack and tuck them in. I had forgotten you drove all the way up here from Baltimore yesterday." Jocelyn looked as if she might be about to argue. "I have to be in the office early tomorrow morning, and Ben's been known to rise with the chickens."

"Well, I do have some more unpacking to do." She knelt down and put out her arms. "Any hugs before I head off to dreamland?"

Tori was the first one in her arms. Ben was next, followed by Issy. All of his children were friendly and openly affectionate with their hugs and kisses. Jocelyn seemed to enjoy herself being the object of all that affection. He was glad to see the children appeared to like their new temporary housekeeper and nanny. Jocelyn seemed to return their feelings.

Two minutes later Jocelyn was gone, and the arguments started. Ben opened the pantry door. "I want cookies."

Tori's voice tried to drown out Ben's. "I want chips. Lots of chips."

Issy twirled her way around the counter as Ben pulled down a bag of sprinkle-covered chocolate chip cookies. Tori tried to reach the bag of potato chips, but couldn't. "Hold it, you two, I thought you guys had cake or pie after you ate your dinner."

"So?" Ben frowned, and Tori looked mutinous. Issy was still spinning in circles.

He knew Diane had never loaded the kids down with junk food. Their current feeding habits came from Phoebe's food shopping and her willingness to buy anything they wanted, and his own tendency to spoil them. Jocelyn's example of grapes over chips at lunch was excellent. They already had their junk snack for the night. "If you guys are hungry, I'll cut up some bananas for you, but that's it. No cookies, chips, or even ice cream."

After a few minutes of arguing, Issy and Ben ate their bowls of banana slices without further comment. Tori glared at the offending fruit, but ate every bite.

Twenty minutes later, the kids were all tucked in, and he could hear that slice of key lime pie calling his name.

Quinn raised his hand for the third time and knocked a little harder on what at one time had been his bedroom door. This time he softly called Jocelyn's name. He didn't want to wake the kids, but he needed to tell Jocelyn that he was leaving. There was a major accident out on Route 1, and they needed him. It didn't matter that it was two in the morning and he hadn't even managed three hours of sleep.

After finishing the pie earlier, he had had to clean the entire bathroom before he could even take a shower. The mountain of bubbles had dried up and left a gray film all over everything, and no one had thought to empty all the toys back out of the tub. Damp towels had littered the floor, and globs of toothpaste spotted the sink. The bathroom was clean, but now he wished he had gone to bed instead. He also wished Jocelyn would wake up and answer the door.

He listened for a moment, shook his head, and then opened the door. "Jocelyn, it's me." He hesitated for a moment and then added, "Quinn." No response. He stepped into the moonlit room and saw her lying under the covers. At least he had to assume it was her. The body seemed to be the right size, but her head was buried under the pillow. Strands of long blond hair were in every direction. The slight rise and fall of the blankets proved she was breathing.

He felt like a Peeping Tom in his own house. He really didn't want to know what Jocelyn wore to bed at night, but he was praying for flannel. Lot's of flannel. It didn't matter that it was about seventy degrees in the room with the windows wide open. Jocelyn should be covered from neck to toe.

The scent of flowers filled the room. A vase of flowers sitting on the table in front of the window was silhouetted in the moonlight. He couldn't tell what kind of flowers they were, but he now knew what Bob Newman had given Jocelyn when he came a-courting earlier. If his current housekeeper stayed any length of time in Misty Harbor, Edna McCain would definitely be hitting a higher tax bracket.

He stepped closer to the bed and raised his voice above a whisper, "Jocelyn?"

A low moan was muffled by the pillows.

A chuckle was threatening to emerge, but he held it back. Jocelyn obviously wasn't a light sleeper. He took the final step to the edge of the bed and picked up the pillow. "Jocelyn, I've got to go."

"Go away," muttered Jocelyn as she tried to bury herself deeper into the bed.

His laughter filled the room, yet his housekeeper didn't even budge. He had to wonder if she was always this sound of a sleeper, or did keeping up with the kids for one afternoon put her in a coma. Hell, would it even be safe to leave the kids in the house with her? This time when he called her name, he shook her shoulder. "Come on, Jocelyn, wake up, sleepyhead."

Jocelyn's eyes finally cracked open, and in the light spilling in from the hallway he saw a frown pull at her lower lip. "What time is it?" Her gaze shot to the darkened window. "Is something wrong?"

"I've got to go out. Didn't you hear the phone ring?"

"Phoebe had it unplugged." Jocelyn pushed her hair out of her face. "Where are you going all dressed up?"

She made it sound as if he was in a suit with a tie instead of his usual khaki summer uniform. "Four-car pileup on Route 1." He had to wonder what she would say if he told her he had a hot and heavy date?

"Ouch." Jocelyn snatched her pillow back out of his hands. With that wondrously expressive sentiment, Jocelyn buried her head back under the pillow.

He chuckled. "You will take care of the kids if they wake up, right?"

The pillow nodded.

"Will you hear them?" Considering what it had taken for him to wake her up, he wasn't too sure. Then again, Tori had a habit of jumping on beds to wake the occupant. No one slept through Tori's bouncing. In her past life, Tori must have been related to Tigger.

"Leave the bedroom door open," mumbled Jocelyn.

"Will you—"

"Go away, Quinn." Jocelyn picked the pillow up, turned her head, and glared at him. "I need my beauty sleep."

He could argue that point with her. If she got any prettier, he would be tripping over his own tongue. Drooly, the eighth sex-starved dwarf. "I'll try to be home before breakfast so I can help you out." Thankfully, Jocelyn didn't sleep in the buff. She slept in a short-sleeve T-shirt. It wasn't flannel, but it was a nice safe second.

Jocelyn waved him off as she buried her head once again.

He turned and was almost out of the room when her sleep-rumbled voice stopped him. "Quinn?"

"What?"

"Drive carefully."

A slow smile broke across his face. Jocelyn sounded concerned for his welfare. It had been a long time since someone, besides a family member, cared enough to voice a worry. "I always do."

Chapter Five

"No, Mom, I haven't fallen in love. I'm not getting married, and I'm not staying in Maine permanently." Jocelyn moved the telephone receiver away from her ear, looked at Phoebe, and rolled her eyes before continuing the conversation. "I know I've only been here five days, but honestly, Mom, I think I would know if Mr. Perfect had walked into my life and swept me off my feet."

Phoebe chuckled and took a long, slow drink of pink lemonade. Soldering all afternoon in the garage had left Phoebe's face flushed and hair damp around the edges. But there was a glow about her face that said she would keep on soldering, no matter how hot it got inside that garage.

"Okay, Mom, I'll call this weekend when Dad's home so I can talk to him and convince him to stop worrying about how he is going to pay for another wedding so soon." Jocelyn laughed, told her mother that she loved her, and then hung up the phone.

Having a conversation with her mother while being surrounded by the Larson family was a bit disconcerting. Phoebe and the children she didn't mind too much.

It was a six-foot male, lying on the floor between Issy and Tori and coloring in a Scooby Doo coloring book, that had made the whole conversation feel awkward. Quinn hadn't said a word. In fact, he hadn't even looked at her once during the phone call, but she knew he had heard every word she had said.

"I take it that your mom is worried that she is going to be losing another daughter to the wild bachelors of Misty Harbor?" Phoebe pressed the cold, empty glass against her cheek.

"My parents were already contemplating getting a summer place up here, so they could visit anytime they had a few extra days. Now my dad says he should just buy a boat and sail up and down the eastern seaboard; it would be cheaper than paying airfare all the time." Jocelyn picked up her glass of lemonade and sat back down on the stool. During the past five days, Phoebe and she had become fast friends. "As for 'Wild Bachelors,' I haven't seen any of those yet. What time did you say their boat was scheduled to dock at the harbor? I definitely wouldn't want to miss it."

Phoebe laughed. "What about your date tonight? Don't you consider Gregory Patterson a wild bachelor?"

"Do you?" countered Jocelyn right back. Greg seemed like a very nice guy, but there hadn't been any instant attraction on her part. She had only agreed to go out with him because tonight was her first official night off and Gwen was working and Sydney had already made plans with her husband. She had spent the morning and a good part of the afternoon shopping with Sydney at the nearest mall, and she needed something to do with the evening hours. Quinn needed to spend some time alone with his kids, without her playing the part of the fifth wheel. Besides, she was bored.

"I couldn't help but notice the other day that Greg wasn't averse to your company, Phoebe. You both seemed to have a lot in common."

"We were in most of the same classes in high school."
Phoebe grinned. "And no, I never went out with him."

"So Greg's not one of the wild bachelors?"

"Hardly, the man brought you a six-foot weeping fig
tree, for goodness sakes." Phoebe glanced at the tree
standing in the corner of the family room and shook
her head. "Not what I would class as wild and crazy.
Besides, Greg's into computers."

Jocelyn chuckled. "Computers are a bad thing?"

"Bad, no. Boring, yes," Phoebe said.

"What do wild bachelors come calling with, just so I
know one when I see one." She still wasn't used to gift-
bearing men just showing up at the door, all hours of
the day, unannounced. In Baltimore, they would probably be arrested for stalking. Here in Misty Harbor she
was assured by both of her sisters and Phoebe it was the
norm. In the five days she had been there, she had accumulated four bouquets of flowers, two boxes of candy,
a fig tree, an exotic hothouse orchid that was currently
dying in her bathroom upstairs, a bottle of wine, and a
three-foot-tall wooden lighthouse that actually lit up
when plugged in.

She was going to need a moving van when she went
back home to Baltimore.

"Erik tried courting Gwen with redfish, and then
ended up not only cooking them, but swapping recipes
all afternoon with her sister in the restaurant's kitchen.
Gunnar had tried the allure of lobsters, but with the
same results."

"Erik and Gunnar are now both happily married, and
it would take more than dead fish to turn my head and
make me want to spend my winters here. From what my
sisters say, it's darn cold up here."

"I'm sure neither of your sisters have trouble keeping warm."

"True." Both of her sisters had moved to Maine and
found the love of their lives. She wasn't looking for the

love of her life, but a couple of those wild bachelors would definitely liven up her summer. "So what you are telling me is that I should be on the lookout for Vikings bearing slimy sea creatures?"

Erik and Gunnar Olsen were six-foot two-inch, long blond-haired identical twins from Norway, who just happened to look as though they just stepped off a Viking ship. Erik had taken one look at her sister Sydney, and that was all it took. Gunnar had fallen in love and eventually married a local girl. The most she had gotten from the Viking twins was a slow dance or two at Gwen's wedding. As fantasies went, it didn't even register as a naughty thought.

Sometimes life wasn't fair.

"There aren't any more Vikings around. I looked." Phoebe put her empty glass into the dishwasher. "I've got to run. You and Greg have a great time at the movies. I'll talk to you tomorrow, and I will be wanting details." Phoebe gave her a big smile and wiggled her eyebrows. "All the details."

She laughed back. "I'll try to remember all the plot twists in the movie, okay?" Whatever Phoebe might be thinking was going to happen tonight with Greg, wasn't. Greg seemed like a nice guy, and she was bored. End of story.

Quinn was mentally wading through a bloodbath of a crime scene, looking for clues, when he heard a car pull up out front. He glanced at the clock sitting on the mantel. Eleven thirty-five. It wasn't even midnight and Jocelyn was home from her date. The early hour didn't brood well for Greg. Of course, the fictional town of Silver, Colorado, wasn't doing much better with a knife-wielding serial killer carving up the residents and an incompetent sheriff in charge of the case. *Slicing Up Silver* was topping the *New York Times* best-seller list, but he had no idea how the bumbling sheriff was going to solve the crime. His money was on the new female deputy, the one with long legs, a smart mouth, and a bad attitude, becoming the hero and saving the day.

He thought about closing the book, but decided if Jocelyn saw him just sitting in his favorite chair twiddling his thumbs, she would think he had been waiting up for her. It wasn't the impression he wanted to give her. Jocelyn was free to go out with whomever she wanted to, and if she found geeks like Greg Patterson attractive, who was he to argue?

There were more important things to do with his one and only evening off. Spying on his kids' nanny wasn't one of them. He had taken the kids into Sullivan for happy meals and then to the corner store to rent a video. They had spent a pleasant evening watching some movie about a cat and two lost dogs trying to find their way home and eating bowls of popcorn. After bath time he had read them a book about raining meatballs and tucked them into bed. Then he had mopped the kitchen floor.

Jocelyn wasn't big on the housekeeping end of things. He wasn't going to complain, though. She was great with the kids, and they did keep her busy. Last night she had actually made meatloaf for dinner. The potatoes had come from a box and the gravy from a can, but all in all it was one of the best meals he had had in a long time. Besides, his lawn was looking good, and there were even flowers in the garden. He had come home for lunch on Sunday only to find Jocelyn and the kids planting flowers in the beds that at one time had surrounded the house. A lot of the flowers had been crushed or broken off by little helping hands, but most had survived the experience. The kids had been so proud of themselves that he hadn't had the heart to tell Jocelyn he was running out of clean socks.

He had done two loads of laundry this morning before Jocelyn had made it out of bed.

The sound of a car driving away accompanied Jocelyn into the family room. "Oh, you're still up?"

The book was lying forgotten in his lap. "I was reading." He shoved a piece of paper into the book to mark his spot, closed it, and then placed it on the end table. "Did you have a nice time?"

Jocelyn chuckled as she kicked off her sandals and curled up onto the couch. "You sound like my father."

Quinn watched those long, tanned legs fold up beneath her and felt anything but fatherly. Jocelyn's skirt was a couple of inches above her knee when she was standing. When she sat like that it rose to midthigh. A sleeveless silk blouse and a couple of pieces of understated gold jewelry and she looked like a fashion model displaying the latest summer style. At five feet four inches she was short for a fashion model, but she was as gorgeous as the women that covered the pages of glossy magazines.

Gregory Patterson must have thought he had died and gone to heaven when Jocelyn had agreed to go out with him.

"Sorry, I didn't mean to pry. Must be the father in me." He had already resigned himself to both of his daughters hating him when they turned into teenagers and wanted to date. They would be allowed to date, once they had their college degrees in hand.

"No problem, you're going to need the practice. Tori and Issy are going to have the boys lined up by twos and a mile long."

"Don't think so." He grinned.

"You don't?" Jocelyn frowned. "Your daughters are beautiful now; I would hate to see what they are going to look like when they turn sixteen. Resign yourself to a lot of gray hair and antacids."

"I know they are beautiful; they look like their mother." Quinn's smile grew. "But you forgot one thing."

"What's that?"

"I'm armed."

Jocelyn's laughter joined his. "I'm taking it that you aren't above using your position as sheriff to make that point."

"Not where my children are concerned." Quinn settled back and enjoyed the conversation. "So, did you have a nice time with Greg?"

Jocelyn's white teeth worried her lower lip. "Dinner was good and the movie was great. Had a surprise ending that I didn't see coming."

He wished she wouldn't do that to her lip. It was driving him nuts. "I take it Greg didn't fair so well?"

"Greg's a very nice guy. He's just a little too . . ." Jocelyn's hands waved in the air, searching for the right word.

"A little too what? A little too birdie? Flapping? Waving?"

Jocelyn sighed and dropped her hands. "A little too desperate."

"What do you mean by desperate?" A sick feeling twisted his gut. Jocelyn wasn't big enough to fend off some six-foot desperate man. He sat on the edge of the recliner and demanded, "Did that nerd try anything funny with you?"

"Of course not. Greg was a true gentleman." Jocelyn glared at him. "Even if he did try something *funny,* as you so eloquently put it, I can take care of myself."

He snorted. "Not with those arms you couldn't."

Jocelyn looked at her biceps and frowned. "What's wrong with my arms?"

"Nothing is wrong with them. They are very nice and shapely arms, for a woman. But, I honestly don't think you would be doing a lot of damage with them."

"It's not my arms he would have to worry about." Jocelyn's smile turned wicked. "It would be my knees."

"Ouch." Quinn cringed as her meaning became clear. "Since I know you don't have any brothers, I would have to assume your father gave you some well-aimed pointers."

Jocelyn chuckled. "My father's a pacifist. He believes every confrontation can be solved with logic, compassion, and words. Our mother taught us girls how to protect ourselves against unwelcomed advances. Our grandfather bought us each the biggest baseball bat he could find and told us to aim for the knees."

"Remind me to never get your family mad." He vaguely remembered seeing Jocelyn's mother around Christmastime. She had been bundled up against the cold and doing some last minute shopping down on Main Street. The woman had been no bigger than Jocelyn, and from what he had heard, she was also a very gifted heart surgeon. She definitely hadn't looked the type to drop a man with a well-aimed knee. Neither did Jocelyn, but there was something in her eyes that told him she could and would if the situation ever arose.

He was still curious as to why Jocelyn only now referred to Greg as desperate. The man had paid an uninvited visit and brought her a six-foot weeping fig tree as a token of his desire, for God's sakes. If that wasn't asinine, he didn't know what was. He couldn't imagine what the computer geek had done during dinner and a movie that had been worse than that act of stupidity. "So what did Greg do to scare you off? Boring you to death with computer jargon isn't what I would consider an act of desperation."

"He took the hint to stop talking about his job once my eyes glazed over." Jocelyn tugged at the hem of her skirt. "Religion is a heavy topic for a first date, but I could have handled it if he hadn't asked which faith I would be raising my children under during the main course."

Quinn groaned and shook his head. There was no doubt about it; Greg was an idiot. "You're kidding, right?"

"By dessert he wanted to pick out baby names."

"Ummm . . . You do know there isn't an abundant amount of single females around here, right?"

"Yeah, I heard we're scarcer than palm trees lining the streets of Misty Harbor. I just hadn't been expecting a near marriage proposal on the first date."

He chuckled. "Bet that scared the socks right off you." By the sound of her voice, Jocelyn hadn't taken Greg's enthusiasm as a compliment.

"Socks? No, but I did hear my fallopian tubes start to slam shut while eating my cheesecake." Jocelyn shuddered. "You don't think Greg's a little off balance, do you? I'm talking Norman Bates *Psycho* kind of sick. He's not going to pull a Glenn Close *Fatal Attraction* number and start cooking up bunnies, is he?"

"I don't think so." He chuckled at her imagination. "Greg's harmless. Desperate maybe, but harmless." He nodded to the coffee table. "Which reminds me, a package came for you while you were out."

Jocelyn looked at the plain brown wrapped package and frowned. "At least it's not flowers."

"True. The house is beginning to smell like a funeral home." He really didn't mind the fragrance of the flowers that was beginning to fill his home. What he did mind was the fact that all the single men, from twenty to sixty, were pressuring his housekeeper and kids' nanny to either go out with them, run away and get married, or bear their children. And not particularly in that order. "My guess is that it's a book."

"By the size?" Nothing was written on the wrapping. No return address. Not even her name. Just an ordinary piece of string tied into a bow.

"That, and the fact that Gordon Hanley delivered it."

"Who's Gordon Hanley? I don't believe I met him." Jocelyn picked up the package and untied the bow.

"Gordon owns the little bookstore down on Main

Street. The Pen and Ink sells books, magazines, postcards, and a bunch of tourist stuff. The book isn't from him; he was only the delivery person."

"My grandfather and I were in his shop when we were up for Sydney and Erik's wedding." Jocelyn smiled at the memory. "Granddad bought a box of expensive cigars, and I found an old book of Keats' poems." The brown wrap opened, and Jocelyn smiled at the book in her hands. *The Poetry of Edgar Allan Poe.*

He shuddered. "Isn't he the one who wrote *The Murders in the Rue Morgue* and *The Pit and the Pendulum?* Not the kind of stuff that I would class as romantic."

"They were stories, not poems." A folded note card was tucked into the front of the book. Jocelyn opened it up and started to read.

"That's right. Poe wrote such romantic sonnets as 'The Raven.' " He nodded toward the slim volume. "So who's trying to court you with demented birds of prey? This one just might be capable of boiling those bunnies." He couldn't believe the stupidity of the men in town. What were they trying to do? Send Jocelyn screaming in terror all the way back to Baltimore?

"Paul Burton, and I love Poe." Jocelyn placed the note card back into the book. "He's just confirming our date for Saturday night. Phoebe did tell you that she'll be hanging around here Saturday night, so I can go out with Paul, didn't she?"

"She mentioned it." Of course, there had been a flash of glee in his sister's eyes when she informed him that she would be helping out on Saturday night. Like he needed his sister to tell him his housekeeper/nanny was one popular lady.

"You have a problem with that? I could cancel."

"I don't have a problem with Paul. He's a nice enough guy, if you discount his taste in poetry."

"I meant with me going out." Jocelyn uncurled her

legs and stood. "It was Phoebe's idea. I just went along with it because Paul was standing right there holding a dozen long-stemmed red roses."

"Where's he taking you?"

"Jazz festival down in Boothbay Harbor." Jocelyn crumbled up the wrapping and tossed it into the kitchen trash can.

"That's over an hour away."

"I know. That's why we need an early start. Phoebe said she'll be here by four in the afternoon." Jocelyn bent and picked up her sandals. "Well, I'm beat and the kids want to get an early start tomorrow morning. We're going on a hike, and then a picnic."

"Hiking?" He didn't know if he liked the sound of that one. Three-year-olds shouldn't be hiking.

"It's not really a hike, Quinn. They just think it is. There's a path that goes all around Sunset Cove. We are going to catch it behind Sydney's father-in-law's house. Sydney tells me there's a nice spot for a picnic about half an hour away, and the kids are looking forward to the adventure."

"Just be careful around all that water. Kids and water are a bad combination."

"You should have warned me two days ago when I took them down to Blueberry Cove. I told them they could only wade in the water, but Tori and Ben ended up sitting in it and getting soaked. It took them an hour to dry off. Issy went in up to her knees and not an inch higher."

He chuckled. "Tori told me she slipped and that you didn't yell at her once."

Jocelyn's laughter joined his. "If you believe she slipped, I have a desert oasis right down the street that I want to sell you." Her arms tightened around the book as she hugged it closer to her chest. "Good night, Quinn. Enjoy your book."

He glanced at her tempting mouth and wondered

again at the foolishness of men. If he had had Jocelyn all to himself in some nice romantic restaurant, he sure as hell wouldn't have been discussing religion or future names of babies. He'd be telling her how beautiful she was and that he was the luckiest man in the world. He nodded toward her book of strange and bizarre poems. "You, too."

Phoebe watched her brother as he dumped the box of noodles into the boiling water. Great, Jocelyn was probably just sitting down at some outdoor restaurant ordering lobster and a fine wine with Paul Burton, while she was going to get Quinn's famous spaghetti. Boiled-to-mush noodles and a heated-up jar of sauce. *Yum.* Jocelyn was going to be toe tapping to some of the best jazz in the state and getting serenaded by smoldering saxophones all night long. By the video clutched in Tori's little hands, she was going to be entertained by the multimillion-dollar corporation known as Disney.

Sometimes life wasn't fair.

By the look on her brother's face, he was feeling the same way. Interesting. Quinn wasn't one to mope around the house, especially in front of the children.

Ever since Diane had died, Quinn had tried and succeeded to make a happy, safe, and loving home for the kids. She thought the children were handling the change and grief in their life extremely well. Issy was a little too quiet, but she was coming out of her shell more and more with every day. All the credit had to go to Quinn, but having Jocelyn around was definitely helping.

"Know what I noticed?" She nibbled on a piece of carrot she was supposed to be slicing up for their salad and was thoroughly satisfied that she no longer had to worry about feeding Quinn and the kids. She much preferred to swelter her days away in Quinn's garage working on her art.

"What?" Quinn frowned as he stirred the noodles with a wooden spoon.

"Issy's talking more." She watched as her brother observed his children playing in the family room. Ben was practicing his letters, Tori was now coloring, and Issy was playing with a Little Mermaid doll. Issy was making Princess Ariel twirl in circles.

"She's only humming." Quinn reached for a pot and the jar of sauce sitting on the counter.

"When was the last time you heard her hum?" She polished off the carrot and picked up a slice of cucumber. There was nothing better than fresh-picked garden vegetables sold at roadside stands throughout the summer months. Okay, chocolate fudge brownies and butter pecan ice cream, just to name a few of her weaknesses, came to mind. There was nothing healthier and better for her jean size than fresh-picked vegetables.

Comparing her body to Jocelyn's compact and athletic build would lead to depression. At five feet eight inches, her bones were definitely bigger than Jocelyn's, and she had the meat on them to prove it. A nor'easter would never blow her over, but she didn't class herself as fat. She was solid. Solidly into double-digit jean sizes. And if she didn't start watching what she ate, she soon would be buying the next double-digit size.

Quinn opened the jar and studied Issy. "I don't ever remember hearing her hum before."

"I think she's trying to sing that sound from the movie, something about under the sea, but she can't remember the words."

"I can. Issy must have watched the video a hundred times since her birthday. They're drummed into my head so deep I will be remembering those lyrics when I'm collecting Social Security." Quinn dumped the sauce into the pan and grinned. "You might be right about Issy. The other day she went on and on about the hike Jocelyn took them on and the things they collected."

"Jocelyn is good with the kids."

"She's only been here nine days and the kids already love her. What's going to happen in a couple of months when she heads on back to Baltimore? She's going to break their hearts."

"She might be breaking a whole lot of hearts in town, but I don't think she'd break the kids'. They might miss her, but they'll be fine."

"How do you know that?"

"I heard her talking to them. She told them all about her home in Baltimore, and how she has to go back there." Phoebe selected another cucumber slice. "How she's only here until you hire a new housekeeper and nanny. But she promised the kids she'd visit every time she came up to see her sisters and their families."

"The kids understood this?" The sauce started to splatter all over the stovetop. Quinn cursed under his breath and turned down the burner.

"Yes and no. Only time will tell." Phoebe selected a piece of carrot. "How's the search going on finding a new housekeeper?"

"Nowhere." Quinn gently scooped up a single noodle from the boiling pot of water. "Only received one response in the post office box I set up. Every other word was misspelled, the paper smelled like cigarette smoke, and there were ashes smeared across the bottom of the page."

"Well, Jocelyn seems content to stick around until you do find someone."

"When she's not too busy going on dates, taking phone calls, and entertaining uninvited guests. Do you know that yesterday, when I got home, Abraham Martin was on the front porch teaching Ben how to tie a half hitch and a square knot? Dinner hadn't even been started and old Abraham was entertaining everyone with the story about the time he hauled in a shark instead of a tuna and almost lost his leg during the ensuing battle.

Ben thought he was a damn war hero and ended up inviting him for dinner. The man talked my ear off, ate two burgers, and drank three of my beers."

"Remember he brought one of his mother's famous carrot cakes for dessert. Mamie Martin might be eighty-two, but she sure can cook."

"Mamie just wants to see Abraham finally get married and out of her house. She would probably shred carrots until her fingers bled just to get rid of him. Putting up with Abraham for the past sixty years would make a saint drink."

"Mamie's wasting her time and energy. Jocelyn's not interested in Abraham." From what she had been seeing, her new friend wasn't interested in any one man in particular. The only man Jocelyn had been eyeing with something akin to desire in her eyes had been Quinn. Of course, Quinn had been out back, without his shirt on, splitting firewood for the upcoming winter. Quinn might be her brother, but even she had to admit he was one fine-looking guy.

"I should hope not. The man's pushing sixty, and his pickup truck has been around since World War II. Abraham even tried to get Jocelyn to go for a ride with him after dinner." Quinn shook his head in disgust. "The old coot probably wanted to take her up to Look Out Point and show her his slip knot collection."

"I take it she didn't go?" Everyone knew Abraham's truck was a death trap waiting to happen. The old lobster fisherman swore he wouldn't buy a new one 'til this one died and was beyond resurrecting. Last she heard, the old tugboat of a pickup had over two hundred thousand miles on it. And she had still been in high school at the time.

"No, she claimed she wasn't allowed to leave, just in case I got called out on a double homicide or something."

Phoebe chuckled. Hancock County had only had

one murder in its history, and it had happened back in the early nineteen hundreds. And there hadn't been any mystery to it at all. Estelle Baker had been caught standing over the body of her abusive husband with the bloody pitchfork still clutched in her hands and a smile upon her face. "Bet you that impressed old Abraham."

"Nope, he offered to take the 'little tykes' with them. Claimed they could ride in the back of the truck with his lobster pots."

Phoebe's laughter drew the kids' attention. She could just see Quinn's expression as his precious children climbed in the back of Abraham's rusty truck to snuggle in between the seaweed-encrusted lobster pots. The stench alone would have killed them. "What did you say to that?"

"I threatened to have him arrested." Quinn tested another noodle. "What I want to know is, why you volunteered to give up your Saturday night and practically forced Jocelyn to accept Paul Burton's invitation?"

"Jocelyn needs more than one night a week off. Besides, what can she do on a Tuesday night?"

"Maybe she didn't want to go out with Paul."

"Did she say that?" She rested her hip against the counter and studied her brother. Quinn was acting awfully interested in what his housekeeper was doing with her time off.

"No." Quinn frowned at the pot of boiling noodles.

"Then, maybe she did." She snatched up a wedge of a tomato and popped it into her mouth. "Paul's good looking, nicely set financially, and sweet. Jocelyn could do a lot worse."

"If Paul is such a catch, why did you turn him down, at least twice that I know of?" Quinn pinned her with a knowing look.

"He's not my type." The vegetables in her stomach turned to a rolling pitch of acid. The last thing she wanted to talk about with her brother was her type of men. Quinn tended to be a tad overprotective with his baby sister. "Jocelyn didn't seem that opposed to a date with Paul."

"Did it ever occur to you that she might not appreciate your meddling in her love life?"

"Jocelyn's more open-minded than you are, dear brother. She needed a break from the house and kids, Quinn. All work and no play will have Jocelyn running back to Baltimore. Paul's a great date. Besides, she loves jazz."

"She does?"

"Don't you ever talk to her about anything besides dirty socks, how much starch you like in your uniform, and the fact that your old riding mower needs a tune-up?" Phoebe stared at her brother in amazement. Quinn at one time had been the catch of the local high school. Star quarterback, honor-roll student, king of the homecoming court. It had been rumored that her brother had more moves off the field than on it. At least he had, until he fell in love with Diane Bowman in the twelfth grade. Quinn had come out of their marriage a changed man. He seemed to have lost his ability to have fun.

"I think you need to get out more, big brother. Go on a date and converse with the opposite sex. Let your hair down and have some fun."

"Maybe you should get your own dating life in order before you start handing out advice."

"What do you mean by that? Plenty of men have asked me out."

"And you have turned every one of them down, haven't you?" Quinn turned off the burner beneath the pot of noodles. "One has to wonder why that is."

She wanted to scream at Quinn that it wasn't any of his business who she dated, but she didn't. They were family, and family always cared about each other. "Maybe I'm just highly selective." Or maybe it was because the right man hadn't been the one doing the asking. Gary Franklin was sure taking his own sweet time to work up the nerve to pick up a phone and punch in seven little digits. *Maybe it's about time I helped him along in that direction.*

"Maybe you're living in the past."

"Pot calling the kettle black, Quinn." As far as she knew Quinn hadn't had a serious relationship since his divorce had become final. Diane had been the last woman she had ever seen Quinn with. The Larsons were batting zero when it came to the opposite sex.

"Have you spoken to Gary Franklin since you moved back here?"

Quinn's question stole her breath and pierced her heart. It was one thing for her to think of Gary and to play all those little mind games with herself. It was another thing to have her brother throw Gary's name up at her like that. Quinn knew how much Gary had hurt her all those years ago.

Quinn had been one of the few people who had understood her decision to go to college in Massachusetts to study the art of stained glass. Quinn had understood her dream. Most of the town residents thought she should have stayed in Misty Harbor and married her high school sweetheart, Gary Franklin.

Gary hadn't understood. Two weeks before she was to leave for college he had given her an ultimatum; college or him. She had wanted both and seen no reason why she couldn't have both her dreams of working with some of the finest stained-glass artists in the country and the love of her life. Gary had forced the issue, and she had chosen college.

Phoebe turned and walked out of the kitchen without saying a word. Tears were clogging her throat, and she needed some privacy to compose herself before she faced her nephew and nieces. Behind her she heard Quinn curse and then softly call her name. She didn't bother to stop.

It wasn't Quinn's fault that Gary still held the power to hurt her. She had only herself to blame.

Chapter Six

Quinn pulled into his driveway and studied his home. A wagon and tricycle were abandoned in the neatly cut yard, and a colorful display of flowers and weeds were haphazardly circling the porch. A flowerpot overflowing with pink geraniums and a yellow plastic sand shovel were sitting on the lowest step. Two plastic pots, dripping flowers and some type of vine, were neatly spaced and hanging from the porch roof. Four white wooden rockers, with fat flowery cushions, sat patiently on the porch waiting for someone to sit and relax away a few hours. Even needing a fresh coat of paint, his home looked comfortable and inviting. It was how he always envisioned his home to be.

In the two weeks Jocelyn had been in charge of his home and children, changes had been made. Jocelyn loved flowers and working outdoors, and his home benefitted from that love. His children had experienced a wide variety of activities that he just didn't have time to explore with them. Maybe he should start making the time. Before he knew it, the kids would be grown and making lives for themselves. The years would pass, and he would be sitting alone in one of those rocking chairs, wondering where the time had gone.

It wasn't a very pleasant vision of the future.

He wasn't due home from work for a couple of hours yet. Since he had been called out in the middle of the night to break up a barroom fight and toss a couple of drunken lobster fishermen into jail to sleep it off, he deserved to knock off a couple hours early. He missed his kids and was determined to be more active in their lives. He was also curious to see what Jocelyn was up to today.

Jocelyn was always up to something, and his kids followed her every step. She was the pied piper of Misty Harbor. Not only did she charm his children to go where she led, but she had entranced every male above the age of eighteen to follow right along with them.

Just yesterday Jocelyn had taken the children down to the docks to visit her sister Gwen. They had ended up not only getting lunch, but "Crazy" Simon had taken them all out to Sunset Cove to fish away the afternoon. Ben had sworn Simon had talked the fish right onto their hooks. None of the fish had been big enough to keep, but that hadn't stopped the fun. Tori now wanted to be a fisherman, and Ben wanted to go out fishing for the day with Simon and Jocelyn's brother-in-law Erik Olsen. The invitation was still open. He wasn't sure how he felt about taking the kids out for the day.

He was one of the few residents in town who preferred the solid feel of land beneath his feet. In his youth he had been teased unmercifully. Thankfully, with Dramamine, he had stopped turning puke green and tossing up his cookies every time he felt the roll of the ocean beneath his feet.

When he had walked in the front door last night at six, he had discovered Simon in the kitchen giving cooking lessons to Jocelyn and a very amused Phoebe. A blushing Simon had stayed for dinner, seated like a king between Jocelyn and Phoebe. The baked mackerel and boiled red potatoes had been delicious, and Simon really wasn't a bad guy. A little strange in the head, but he had told the most wondrous tales to entertain the kids. He just wished Simon had been paying more attention to Phoebe instead of to his kids' nanny.

Quinn locked his service revolver in the glove compartment and got out of the SUV.

Heaven only knew what kind of following Jocelyn had accumulated today. It was barely three o'clock in the afternoon. She had probably filled in the rest of her calendar for August and fended off two marriage proposals already today. His housekeeper was one popular lady, and Jocelyn seemed to be enjoying the status of being Misty Harbor's "hottest" date.

He didn't know what was aggravating the hell out of him more—the parade of men vying for Jocelyn's attention, or her delight in having that caravan of available men.

The sound of children's laughter reached his ears before he made it to the porch. He veered to the right and headed for the backyard. Ben's shouts joined Tori's. If he wasn't mistaken, Issy's laughter joined her siblings'. Whatever was happening in the backyard sounded noisy and fun.

"Look out!" shouted Tori.

Ben and Jocelyn yelled, "Max!" in unison.

Quinn stopped walking and frowned. *Who in the hell is Max?* He didn't know any Max. There hadn't been any strange cars parked in the driveway, so this Max hadn't driven here. The way Jocelyn was attracting males, Max had probably parachuted into the backyard with a bouquet of roses in one hand and a diamond bracelet clutched between his teeth. Here he had been planning on spending the rest of the afternoon and evening alone with his family. He shouldn't have locked up his weapon yet. A loaded .45 just might scare off some of Jocelyn's less determined admirers.

Jocelyn must have been standing right around the side

of the house from him, because he heard her clearly say, "Quinn might not like this."

The knot in his gut twisted tighter. There were a lot of things he wouldn't like. Things that were too numerous to count. What was Jocelyn up to now, and why were his kids sounding as though it was Christmas in July?

He took a step closer and faltered as Jocelyn said, "I can't let him into the house, he might have parasites or something equally disgusting."

That did it. He was going back to the SUV and getting his weapon. Just as soon as he snuck a peak to see who, or what, was causing the distress in Jocelyn's voice and the giggles from Issy. What was the name of the man who sold bait over in Sullivan? The one who smelled worse than the squid, and had only two teeth left in his mouth? He couldn't remember if it was Max or not.

He took another step forward and slowly peeked around the side of the house. The first thing he saw was Jocelyn's bare back and a pair of cut-off jean shorts that just covered her sweetly curved tush. Two tiny ties held on what was surely a bikini top. A golden lopsided bun was piled on top of Jocelyn's head, and a cell phone was pressed to the delicate shape of her ear.

"Yes, Phoebe bought flea shampoo, but you should see all the hair, Sydney. He's covered in it." Jocelyn listened for a moment and then raised her voice to be heard over the children's shrieks and the barking. "You're the doctor, sis; you tell me what to look for and I'll look."

Quinn pulled his gaze away from Jocelyn's delectable rear and with a sense of dread looked to where all the laughter and barking was coming from. A huge soapy dog was sitting in the middle of the twins' plastic wading pool. Bubbles and water were everywhere. Three soaking-wet kids surrounded the dog. Ben held the hose and was trying to rinse some of the bubbles off the mutt, but was managing to get water everywhere but on the dog. Issy held one of the good bath towels open, ready to dry the hundred-pound dog. The dog was bigger than Tori and Issy combined, but none of the kids seemed to have noticed that fact. Tori was laughing and tugging on a red Frisbee the dog had clamped between its teeth.

Jocelyn was on the phone arguing with her sister about medical degrees and fleas.

The opening in the Twilight Zone had finally appeared in Misty Harbor.

He stepped into the zone and was rewarded with a thunderous bark and a hundred-pound sudsy animal dashing from the pool, and across the yard. He braced himself for the impact as two soaking-wet paws landed in the middle of his chest. Medicinal-smelling soap bubbles coated his uniform as foul doggie breath bathed his face. He stared into the gentlest and biggest brown eyes he ever saw and said, "I take it this is Max?"

"I've got to go, Syd. Quinn's home early." Jocelyn closed the cell phone, placed it on the patio's table, and faced him. "Hi, we didn't expect you home so early." Jocelyn's hands pushed at the large, wet, and hairy dog.

Max didn't budge.

Quinn wasn't positive, but he would have sworn the dog smiled. He purposely kept his gaze on the fur face in front of him. It was either that or stare at Jocelyn's chest. His darn housekeeper was wearing a bikini top. Two tiny lime green triangles covered everything that had to be covered, and not an inch more. "Who's your friend here?" He gently pushed at the dog, and Max obediently lowered himself to all fours and sat.

Ben, Tori, and Issy came running over. All three hugged the dog, bubbles, soap scum, and all. "We found him," Ben said.

"He found us, Daddy," Tori added.

Issy's little arms encircled the beast's neck. "He's my Max."

"Max? Does he have a collar?" There had to be a collar. How else would the children know his name. The dog tag would tell him where to deliver the beast. He saw the love and possessiveness in his children's eyes and wanted to get the mutt away from them as soon as possible. There was no way he wanted the dog to get the idea he would be staying.

"No collar." Jocelyn cringed and then carefully took the squirting hose out of Ben's hands. "Issy named him Max, after the dog from *The Little Mermaid.*"

Quinn stared from his soaking-wet shoes to the water squirting from the hose his son had been holding. A sick feeling twisted his gut. "Issy named him?" The look of possessiveness in his daughter's eyes was now understood. You didn't name a dog you weren't planning to keep.

"About thirty seconds after he wandered into the backyard." Jocelyn aimed the hose at Max. "The kids started begging, and Phoebe was suckered into running to the store to pick up food, bowls, and flea shampoo."

Max ran around in circles barking and trying to bite the squirting spray. Water splattered in every direction while the kids ran around the dog laughing, shouting, and slipping all over the place. For his size, Max appeared about as vicious as a goldfish. This wasn't good. If he wasn't careful, he would be stuck feeding the horse-size dog for the rest of his life. Along with vacuuming up shedding dog hair and probably having every left shoe he would ever own chewed beyond recognition.

In a firm voice he said, "We can't keep him." What he needed to do was to be decisive yet compassionate. "I'm sure some little boy or girl is missing Max horribly right about now. We need to find out where Max lives, and then see that he gets home."

All three kids stopped in their tracks and stared at him in horror. Jocelyn bent her head and seemed to study her bare toes wiggling in the grass. He noticed that she had changed the color of her toenail polish.

Yesterday her toenails had been the color of apricots; today they were a ripe raspberry color. He had to wonder if she had a thing for fruit, or was it the fact that Jocelyn always made him hungry that had him comparing her toenail color to produce.

Ben patted Max's head. "But, Dad, he needs us. He was hungry and real thirsty. He emptied both of his bowls."

"Max came here, Daddy." Tori ran her hands up and down the dog's back, causing Max to lather more. "He likes us."

Issy's small arms encircled Max's hairy and soapy neck. She said only one word, and by the look of determination in her bluish gray eyes, she meant it. "Mine!"

He stared at Issy and wondered if he had somehow gotten her mixed up with Tori. Tori was the determined one of the two. Tori was the one to pitch fits and make demands, not Issy. Isabella was the quiet, shy twin who had to be coaxed into saying what she wanted. He glanced at Tori still rubbing the dog's back. Sure enough, it was Tori. The butchered bangs were soaking wet and plastered to her little forehead. About two whole inches above her eyebrow. There was no mistaking those two for the next several months.

Great, Tori had taught Issy how to be stubborn and demanding.

He knelt down in the mud so that he was now on eye level with his kids. "Listen, guys, I know you like the dog, and the dog seems very nice; but he's not yours. Some little boy or girl is probably sitting at home right this minute crying because they lost their doggy. If you had a dog, and he got lost, wouldn't you like for whoever found him to return him to you?"

All three kids nodded, but then Issy went and ruined it by silently crying. Two fat tears slowly rolled down her cheeks as she whispered, "My Max."

"How are we going to find out where he lives, Dad?" Ben asked as he took the hose back from Jocelyn and started to rinse one of Max's back legs.

"I'll take him to the Humane League out by Franklin." It was the only plan he could come up with on such short notice. He needed to get the dog out of there before the kids became more attached.

Jocelyn gasped, "The pound?" She looked at him as if he had just sprouted another head.

Ben's eyes grew wider. "The pound? He can't go there, Dad. Without dog tags they will lock him in a smelly cage and make him do that long lonely walk. You know"—Ben rolled his eyes toward his sisters—"the one he would never come back from."

Damn Disney and its black, money-grabbing heart. Don't they realize the trouble they cause with their movies like Lady and the Tramp? Next thing he'd know, Issy would be accusing him of trying to skin Max to make a furry coat and a set of matching earmuffs.

He didn't know how it was possible, but Issy's tears became fatter and slower as they trailed down her cheeks. Tori's expression was stubborn, with a hint of murderous intent thrown in for good measure.

Jocelyn glared at him and silently mouthed the words, "Not the pound."

With a resigned sigh he looked at the object of his problem, Max. Walt Disney, himself, couldn't have drawn a more pathetic-looking face. He was in deep do-do. Deep doggie do-do.

He glared at Jocelyn. "Since you object to the pound, what do you suggest we do with him?" He reached out and shifted the running hose so that the water actually hit the dog. "And remember, I heard that comment about fleas and parasites."

Jocelyn had the grace to cringe and then face the children. "Your father's right, kids. Max here might belong to some family already. I think we should hang posters to see if we can find his family for him."

"Where would he stay in the meanwhile?" Locking Max in the garage would have been his first choice, but Phoebe had stuff all over the place in there. Breakable stuff. But then again, Phoebe had been the one to rush out and buy food and shampoo for the mutt. It would serve her right if he did reclaim his garage as a giant doghouse.

"I think we can make Max comfortable out back here until his family shows up." Jocelyn gave a decisive nod at her own suggestion. "He'll have plenty of room to run and to do his business."

"Speaking of 'his business,' who will get cleanup duty in that department?" By the size of the dog, he would need to unbury the snow shovel from the back of the garage.

"I'll do it, Dad," Ben said.

"Me, too!" shouted Tori.

"Me, too!" cried Issy as she scrubbed at her tears.

By the smiles on the girls' faces, he knew they hadn't a clue as to what they were agreeing to. He knew exactly who would be cleaning up after Max. "Dogs come with a lot of responsibilities, and you three have to remember Max won't be staying here forever. For now he will be our guest."

Issy hugged Max tighter and started to sing, "Be our guest, be our guest," but it came out all wrong and muffled. The cast of *Beauty and the Beast* would never have recognized it.

Tori shouted with glee, and Ben's grin widened as he squirted Max with the hose.

He glanced at Jocelyn to see what her reaction was to this latest development. Jocelyn was looking at him as if he had just single-handedly saved Christmas. For one insane minute he was actually happy the dog would be staying with them.

Reality crashed through his utopia when Max bit the hose and knocked Tori down into the wading pool. His daughter landed on her bottom and screamed at the top of her lungs. Tori splashed Ben when he started to laugh at her. Ben then turned the hose on Tori, causing her high-pitched screaming fit to shatter all records.

He looked at Jocelyn and said, "You do realize how much extra work Max is going to be, don't you?"

"I'm beginning to." Jocelyn smiled as though she didn't mind at all and then went to help Tori and the rest of the kids finish bathing the mutt.

He stood there for a moment and watched as his family crowded around the dog, giving advice, demanding attention, and just having a great time. This was what family was all about. Togetherness. So why was he standing on the sidelines in soaking shoes and a muddy, paw-printed uniform.

Throwing caution to the wind, he kicked off his shoes and socks and rolled up the cuffs of his pants. He placed his muddy button-down shirt and his wallet on a chair and waded into the pool to help. If Max was staying, then it was up to him to make sure the animal didn't have an entire ecosystem living in all that hair.

Jocelyn leaned back on her elbows and studied the ocean before her. As far as the eye could see there was nothing but blue skies, gray seas, and the occasional swooping and diving bird. Her stomach was full of lobster, the blanket beneath her was soft and comfortable, and the man sitting beside her was handsome in a rough and muscular way.

Life was indeed good.

Her date, Ned Porter, worked for her brother-in-law Daniel, constructing log homes. Ned looked as if he could lift the logs without the use of heavy machinery. The amazing part was, Ned was more than just a piece of eye candy; he actually had a working brain and ambition. Ned was a freelance writer for nature magazines when he wasn't working for Daniel. He was a cross between Henry Thoreau and Paul Bunyan.

So why wasn't she exploring some of those rippling muscles or at least enjoying herself more? Wasn't that one of the main reasons she had hightailed it to Misty Harbor when things got confusing back in Baltimore? Sure her sisters were here, but so were a couple dozen single men. Males who didn't care if her career was suddenly put on hold due to her indecisions and doubts. Men who knew how to show a woman a good time and not expect her to fall in bed with them on the first date. The men of Misty Harbor weren't looking for one-night stands; they were looking for wedding vows, matching monogrammed bath towels, and the honeymoon suite at the local Motor Inn.

She was more adept at handling lecherous male octopuses than men with forever gleaming in their eyes.

Thankfully, Ned Porter didn't have their silver pattern picked out yet. So far during her stay in Misty Harbor, she had avoided going out with men who wanted her to see their homes, their boats, or to meet their mothers. Ned was sweet, gallant, and if the meal they had just consumed was any indication, an incredible cook. So why was she staring at the churning sea and wondering what Quinn and the kids were doing today and if Max was behaving himself?

She looked at her sexy date and decided to break the silence. Ned wasn't one for talking. "It's a beautiful day for ocean watching." *Great, the kiss of death to all conversations, the weather.* Her sisters would laugh themselves silly if they could see her now. She quickly added, "Do you bring all your dates to Dead Man's Island for a lobster bake?"

"Local women aren't impressed with lobster, baked or otherwise." Ned stretched out his long legs and finished off the last of the water from his bottle. "Besides, not too many of them would step foot on this island."

"Why not?" She glanced around at the rugged shoreline, pine trees that were weathered and beaten by the wind, and shrubs. Lots of shrubs. Wild and uninhabited beauty surrounded them. Their blanket practically covered the only tiny patch of sand on the entire island. As far as she could tell, they were the only people on the small island. Ned's boat was anchored a good twenty feet offshore, and they had waded in carrying their lunch. The fact that they were alone on a deserted island would have made her a bit uneasy, except Daniel had vouched for Ned, and Quinn knew where they had been going. There was nothing like living with the sheriff to keep your dates in line.

"Truth?"

"Of course." She studied Ned as he frowned at the empty water bottle.

"It's supposed to be haunted."

"Really?" She glanced around her with renewed interest. "By who?"

"The dead man." Ned seemed to relax now that she hadn't freaked out or anything.

"What dead man?"

"The one they named the island after." Ned chuckled and handed her a fresh, cold bottle of water. "In the mid-seventeen hundreds someone came out to the island to do some exploring. They found the bones of a man staked out in the center of the island with a cutlass still through his rib cage. Legend has it that pirates had hid their treasure somewhere on the island and that the poor soul had helped the captain bury it. The captain in turn permanently silenced him for his efforts."

"Ah, the old dead-men-tell-no-tales theory." She cracked open the bottle and took a long, cool sip. "So is the legend true?"

"Don't know. Plenty of people have looked for the treasure, but no one ever found anything."

"It's a pretty small island. I guess someone would have found something by now if there was some treasure chest filled with gold and jewels."

"True. It's only a mile long by about half a mile wide. Plenty of places, but not that unmanageable if you were really into treasure hunting." Ned took another bottle of water from the cooler he had carried ashore. "My brothers and I used to spend many a summer vacation looking for that buried treasure."

"How many brothers do you have?"

"Three older brothers, no sisters."

"Are all your brothers as big as you?" If they were, she couldn't imagine how his parents afforded to feed them all. Ned had packed enough food to feed an entire NFL defensive line. Most of which was now gone. Considering Ned had commented on her eating like a bird, she didn't think she was the one to have consumed it all.

"Bigger." Ned grinned. "I'm considered the runt of the family."

She nearly choked on her water. "Good Lord. Your poor mother must have been chained to the stove just to feed you all."

"Afraid not. As soon as we were old enough, she taught us all to cook, do our own laundry, and which end of the vacuum sucks up the dirt. She prefers hauling in tuna with Dad, than baking pies and crocheting afghans."

She frowned and studied the clear liquid in her plastic bottle. Ah, a woman who had known her own mind. "Your mom sounds wonderful."

"And you sound like you miss yours." Ned studied her face for a long moment. "Can I ask you a personal question?"

"You can ask, but I won't promise to answer." She ac-

tually had a date once ask her if she was into black
leather and pain. When she had found her voice and
answered no, her date had taken her home immediately and thanked her for a wonderful time. He never
called her again. Being the son of a very wealthy and
highly visible politician, he had a very busy schedule,
she was sure. If Ned mentioned leather, whips, or pain,
she was going to personally strangle her brother-in-law.

"You've gone out with half a dozen or so men from
the area, but you never dated anyone twice. From the
comments Gwen has made to me, you have been bom-
barded with gifts, telephone calls, and the occasional
mackerel from another couple of dozen guys."

"What's your question?"

"Why haven't you dated anyone twice?"

"I don't think it would be right in letting someone
think that we were starting a relationship. I'm not looking for a relationship, Ned. I'll be going home to Baltimore before Christmas."

"Fair answer." Ned rubbed at the dark stubble shad-
owing his jaw. "So why did you agree to go out with me
when I called?"

"You seemed sweet and nice, and Daniel said you
were the best. Besides, you didn't send me weeping fig
trees, cod, or enough candy to make a diabetic comatose."

"Daniel talked to you about me?" Ned seemed to
find something very amusing in the idea of her brother-
in-law talking to her about other men.

"Only about five times a week. Why?" She knew Daniel
had been trying to fix her up with one of his friends.
There had been nothing subtle about it. It had taken
her two weeks, but she had finally relented and agreed
to go out with Ned if he called.

"While Daniel had been working on you, Gwen had
been listing all your great qualities to me."

"Such as?" Last time her sister had listed her qualities

they had been anything but great. Annoying, nosey, and being a spoiled-rotten tomboy had been at the top of her list. Of course, that had been over ten years ago, and she had just been caught spying on Gwen and one of her boyfriends while they had been making out on the family room couch.

"Gwen said you were almost as good as she is at cooking." Ned's expression looked hopeful.

Jocelyn couldn't contain her laughter.

Ned's face fell. "What about you being the 'outdoors' type? Hiking, camping, canoeing?"

"I watch some National Geographic specials on TV. Does that count?"

This time it was Ned's turn to laugh. "I think we have been had. I saw it coming, but I just didn't pay any attention to all the signs. In my mind there was no way I could reconcile the Jocelyn Fletcher I met at Daniel's wedding with the woman Gwen was describing."

"Daniel and Gwen meant well, I think." She would have to give her sister and her husband the benefit of the doubt in regard to their matchmaking. "Gwen wants me to find love, happiness, and to settle down up here in Misty Harbor. Daniel probably did it just to shut my sister up and to keep harmony in their marriage. What was your first clue I wasn't Ms. Treehugger?"

"I told you where we were going and what we would be doing today, and that is how you dressed."

"What's wrong with how I'm dressed?" She glanced down at her neatly pressed khaki shorts and white spagetti-strapped top. Her hair was pulled up into a ponytail, and she had worn a khaki baseball cap advertising the Misty Harbor Lighthouse and a pair of wildly expensive sunglasses she just couldn't pass up in the town's only boutique. A pair of strappy Italian leather sandals, which matched her handbag, completed her outfit. The cap had been a gift from Phoebe.

"If you walk more than fifty feet into the surrounding forest, you will break an ankle wearing those shoes. They are utterly useless."

"I like my sandals." She held up her foot and examined her toes. Somehow she had managed to chip her nail polish while wading through thigh-high water to get to the island.

"The second clue was when you screamed as you entered the water. It was only up to your knees."

"I wasn't expecting it to be so cold, and it was way past my knees." Nor had she been expecting this date to go downhill so fast. Daniel and Gwen were going to be extremely disappointed in her. "Sorry for the scream, okay. I'm usually not that vocal."

"That's not what Wendell Kirby is saying around town." Ned chuckled and settled back down onto the blanket. "He's telling everyone you practically shattered his eardrums last week."

"Wendell ought to be darn happy I didn't tell either of my brothers-in-law what he had done to deserve that scream. His eardrums wouldn't have been the only thing shattered."

Ned's eyes narrowed, and the bottle he had been raising to his mouth stopped in midmotion. "What did he do?"

"I was in the frozen food aisle of Barley's Grocery Store. Tori was begging for chocolate ice cream, but Ben wanted peanut butter fudge. Ben won the coin toss, and Tori wasn't a very good, or quiet, loser. I was bending into the freezer chest sorting through the quart containers searching for Ben's favorite kind and getting freezer burn on my fingers when Kirby's hand landed on my ass. Years of living in a big city must have taken their toll. I came up screaming and swinging a quart of Rocky Road like it was a boulder. I almost clobbered him with it before I realized what I was doing.

"Wendell claimed it was an accident, that he lost his

balance, but I hadn't been in the mood to believe him. I dragged him down the aisle, where I could still keep an eye on the kids without being overheard. I read him such a riot act that I'm sure his ears are still blistered and ringing."

"You didn't tell anyone else what happened?"

"No, and neither are you." She didn't like that predatory gleam in Ned's eyes. The last thing she needed was another protector in town. Daniel and Erik were enough. "Promise me you won't say a word about Wendell to Daniel or Erik."

"Why would I promise you that?"

"Because even though we are totally wrong for each other, I thought we could be friends at least. Friends don't tell other friends' secrets."

"Wendell's a secret?"

"No, Wendell's a nightmare. One that won't be bothering me again." She gave Ned a charming smile, one she reserved for the male population when she wanted to get her way. "Promise?"

"I promise not to tell Erik or Daniel."

She raised her water bottle and lightly knocked his with hers. "To friendship, as long as hiking up mountains isn't involved."

"To friendship," Ned said.

Chapter Seven

Jocelyn slowly replaced the telephone receiver. Sydney's highly amused laugh was still ringing in her ear.

Ned Porter was going to die. Slowly and very painfully. Friend or not, he was toast. The fink had kept his promise, though. He hadn't told either of her brothers-in-law about Wendell Kirby's straying hand. Ned had told Quinn.

Sydney had called to tell her that Quinn had just written out his third ticket to Wendell, in two days. Hell, the ink on the citation probably wasn't even dry yet. Sadie Hopkins had just shown up in Sydney's office for her three o'clock appointment and had related all the details to her sister. Sadie also told the story to the receptionist and two other patients. By five o'clock there wouldn't be a person left in Misty Harbor who hadn't heard about Wendell's beat red face and Quinn's flashing lights and revengeful grin.

There was also a story going around town that the county's fire marshall had paid a visit to the Misty Harbor Motor Inn this morning and had written Wendell's inn up on three seemingly simple, yet very expensive, violations. It was all her fault. She never should have told Ned. Then again, Wendell shouldn't have tried to play "grab ass" in the frozen food aisle. She should have clobbered him with a quart of Rocky Road ice cream and been done with the whole matter when she had the chance.

Now it seemed everyone in town was placing bets. The odds were four-to-one that Wendell would be behind bars within the week. There were also ten-to-one odds that Quinn and she would be married before the first frost. Her life was being run by bookies, and her sister had wanted to know where to place her money.

Tonight, after the kids were tucked into their beds, Quinn and Jocelyn were going to have a nice long talk, and it wasn't going to be pretty. How was she ever going to get another date if a man walking around with a weapon strapped to his hip was ticketing every guy who got fresh with her? If she stayed in Misty Harbor, she would surely die a lonely old maid who never had any fun.

Hours later Quinn sat on Issy's bed, with a daughter on each side and Ben at his feet, reading about some little mouse who was afraid of the dark. Tori and Issy were enjoying the story, but Ben kept rolling his eyes. The kids should have been in their beds with the lights out fifteen minutes ago. He was stalling for time. Jocelyn was downstairs waiting for him. She wanted to talk with him. His housekeeper hadn't said about what, but he knew. The rumors were already circulating around town about his and Wendell's private little battle.

Hell, Gordon Hanley was running a betting operation out of his back room at the bookstore. The odds were four-to-one that Wendell would be occupying one of the three cells down at the office within the week. If it wasn't illegal, he would take those odds. He was just looking for any excuse to toss the president of Misty Harbor's Chamber of Commerce into the cage and let him rot. Wendell Kirby should be ashamed of himself for molesting his kids' nanny in Barley's frozen food section.

Maybe he could talk Jocelyn into pressing charges. It was a long shot, but one that would give him immense joy. He didn't know what upset him more—the fact that Wendell grabbed her ass, or that Jocelyn hadn't punched his lights out right in the middle of the ice cream aisle of Barley's store. Maybe that would have taught the jerk some manners.

He had seen Jocelyn roughhousing with the kids and wrestling Max, who had to weigh at least a hundred pounds. When their guest pet played, he played hard and for keeps. Jocelyn could have taken pudgy belly Wendell with one hand tied behind her back if she had wanted to.

Jocelyn had single-handedly whipped the gardens and lawn into shape. Granted she had the aid of three pairs of little hands, but he knew his children were probably more hindrance than help. She had done everything outside but split the firewood for the upcoming winter. She probably would have attempted that, too, but he had taken the precaution and hid the ax in the back of his SUV.

If she used some of those supremely toned and tanned muscles to scrub the kids' tub once in a while, he might appreciate it more. But if he had to choose between scouring a bathtub ring or planting petunias, he'd take the soap-scum ring every time. Besides, she was the only person he knew who could wash and comb the girls' hair without making them cry, and he really didn't mind ironing his own uniforms. In an odd way they made a great pair.

If he was a betting man, his money would be on Jocelyn cleaning Wendell's clock in the first round. Since his housekeeper had elected not to make Wendell part of the frozen orange juice display, it was his responsibility to make sure the jerk realized the error of his ways so he wouldn't be tempted to ever pull a number like that again on Jocelyn or any other female.

Jocelyn was a woman, and as such she needed to be protected. And that was the gist of his whole problem. If he expressed that chauvinistic and outdated view to Jocelyn, he would be the one getting decked. Hell, after he picked himself up off the floor, he would probably be short a few teeth. He was in a no-win situation, and he hated the feeling.

"Daddy, where's mousey?" Issy was pulling the book toward her to get a better look at the picture. Tori was trying to yank it in her direction. Ben looked as though he had fallen asleep.

"The mousey's right here." He turned the page and showed both of his daughters the little mouse tucked into her bed with a night-light glowing softly beside her. He read the last two pages and closed the book. "The end."

Issy smiled as she snuggled down under her blanket with one of her stuffed animals. Tonight a cute brown-and-white floppy-eared dog got the honors. Tori bounced off Issy's bed and onto her own. "Nighty night."

Ben mumbled something as he headed for his own bed.

Quinn bent down and kissed Issy's soft cheek. "Good night, princess." The good-night routine with his kids had become very special to him. He loved knowing they were tucked all safe and warm into their beds and that they would be there in the morning. Every morning.

Issy wrapped her arms around his neck and squeezed him tight. "Night, Daddy."

"Night." He gently tucked the lightweight blanket up to Issy's chin. "I'll see you in the morning."

He turned to Tori and wiggled his eyebrows. Issy liked her good-night kiss soft and gentle. Tori preferred the more active approach. He reached for Tori and pretended he was going to rub his stubbled jaw against her cheek. Tori screamed and giggled as he made buzzing sounds while trying to tickle her. "Daddy, no, stop," shouted Tori in between fits of laughter. "You'll scratch me."

He teasingly buzzed his daughter's neck and laughed as two small hands cupped his jaw. "I'll stop if you give me a kiss."

Tori quickly complied. "There."

His kiss was soft and gentle as he brushed her forehead with his lips. Half of Tori's bangs were still soft spikes, and he tried not to let it bother him anymore. For some strange reason the reckless haircut suited his daughter. He frowned at the huge and ugly stuffed warthog that took up half her bed. Only Disney would make a movie with a warthog as one of its main characters. No cute little puppies for Tori. "Good night, princess. Sleep tight and don't let the bedbugs bite."

Giggles erupted from both beds as he tucked Tori's blanket around her. He knew the blanket would be kicked off within half an hour of her falling asleep. Issy cuddled under her blankets no matter what the season. Tori was a cold weather sprawler who would probably sleep in a snowbank and never ask for a blanket.

He turned off the light, but left their door open. Ben was already tucked into his bed. A gentle evening breeze was lightly blowing the curtains. It was a great night for sleeping. He bent over and kissed the top of Ben's head. "Night, son."

"Night, Dad." Ben rolled onto his back and looked up at him. "Can Jocelyn go berry picking with us tomorrow? She said she never picked blueberries before."

"Sure, if she wants to come, she can come." Tomorrow afternoon he didn't have to go into the office, but he was still on call. He had talked Phoebe into leaving her glass workshop for the afternoon to go berry picking with him and the kids. His sister would have handled the kids if he had to leave in a hurry, and he was going to offer Jocelyn the time off. Jocelyn might consider it a nice gesture, but in reality it was a peace offering so she wouldn't be too mad at him for butting in where Wendell Kirby was concerned. "Maybe Jocelyn knows how to make those blueberry muffins like her sister, Gwen."

"Wow," whispered Ben, "Mrs. Creighton makes the best muffins in the world, Dad."

"I know." Gwen had come out to the house yesterday morning to visit Jocelyn. She came bearing a dozen of the most mouthwatering muffins he had ever tasted. He and his son obviously had the same taste. "Get some sleep, and we'll ask Jocelyn in the morning."

After turning off his son's light, he headed downstairs for a conversation he wasn't interested in having. There was no way to explain to Jocelyn his deep-seated need to realign Wendell Kirby's nose. With his position as sheriff, he couldn't very well deck the guy, so he settled for the next best thing. He got Wendell where it really hurt. Right in his pockets. Wendell was notoriously cheap.

He entered the kitchen and glanced around. For once it was clean. After dinner, he had been the one to put everything away and clear off the counters while Jocelyn and the kids played a game of catch with Max. When he had taken the kids upstairs for their bedtime story, the counters and table had held the messy remains of their snack. Jocelyn and the girls had made a sponge cake this morning. Or at least he assumed it was supposed to be a sponge cake. It had been about that color, and it did have the tendency to bounce back with every bite. The girls had been extremely proud of their cake, and everyone had a great time piling on strawberries and Cool Whip before gobbling it down. Max had especially liked the Cool Whip Tori had fed him under the table.

Jocelyn must have cleaned up the mess while he tucked in the kids. There wasn't a trace of squished strawberries or whipped cream anywhere. The table was scrubbed clean, and all six chairs were neatly pushed into place. The yellow roses that had graced the table were now wilted, dead, and gone. A mayonnaise jar filled with assorted wildflowers the kids had picked this afternoon sat in the center of the table. The constant barrage of flowers Jocelyn had been receiving had slowed to a trickle.

The bouquet of snapdragons and irises Edna McCain had delivered this morning had been surprisingly for Phoebe, not Jocelyn. His sister had joked about getting flowers on the rebound from men Jocelyn was turning down, but she had taken the flowers home with her anyway. Amazingly, since he had arrived home at six o'clock, the phone hadn't rung once.

The men of Misty Harbor were finally taking the hint and leaving his housekeeper alone.

He looked into the empty, and halfway neat, family room. No Jocelyn. The dining room yielded four clean, but unpressed, uniforms lying across the ironing board waiting for the ironing fairy to appear. There was a stack of folded bath towels, one chewed-on bone that appeared to have come from a brontosaurus's thigh, and a trio of inflated ducky-printed inner tubes. Someone had taken it into their head to use the empty antique glass front hutch as a Beanie Baby display cabinet. For a formal dining room it lacked ambience and dishes.

He didn't even bother looking into the living room. Jocelyn called it no man's land, and refused to clean it or even go in it without combat pay. He didn't blame her since he had given up on that room weeks ago.

Since Jocelyn was the one who wanted to talk, he didn't think she'd be in her bedroom, so that left either the front porch or the back patio. Knowing how well his housekeeper liked to sit out back and relax in the evening, he headed out the patio doors and found her reclining on a cushioned chaise enjoying the view.

Max came bounding up to him with a slobbered tennis ball in his mouth. If the dog had had a tail, it would have been wagging. What kind of dog didn't have a tail? The "Found" posters Jocelyn and the kids had plastered all over town and the surrounding area, a week ago, had turned up nothing. No one knew who owned Max or how the dog had ended up in his backyard. The frightening thing was, it appeared he had just acquired a dog. A big, hairy, one-hundred-pound mutt that was eating him out of house and home.

It would break the kids' hearts if someone came to claim the big gloop now.

He reached down and pulled the wet ball out of Max's mouth and smiled as the dog danced around in circles waiting for him to throw it. He tossed the ball in the direction of the swing set. Max took off like a crazed mop.

"Doesn't he ever get tired of chasing things?" He pulled out a chair from the patio set and sat. The night was cooling down and filled with the sounds of nature and the fragrance of the sea. Moths battered against the screened patio door, trying to get to the light burning in the kitchen. Jocelyn hadn't bothered to turn on any of the outside lights and was reclining in partial shadows.

"No, but I get tired of throwing them," Jocelyn said in a lazy voice.

He wondered if he had just awakened her. "Tired?" He stretched out his legs and slouched farther into the chair. It felt good to sit and relax finally. Between work and three small children he didn't get the chance very often.

"Being a mother should be an Olympic endurance event." Jocelyn gave a small laugh and stretched. "The kids wore me out by lunchtime. I was actually envious of the girls when they had nap time and I didn't."

Max came bounding back onto the patio and nearly knocked him off the chair. He patted Max on the head,

"Good dog." He pried the ball out from between his canine teeth again and gave it another toss. Max's toenails slipped, clicked, and scored the slate patio in his hurry to retrieve the ball. Quinn had no idea which direction the ball had gone because he was too busy eyeing Jocelyn's long, luscious legs.

"I've got to tell you the kids really love having you here." He shifted his gaze away from her legs and watched a moth beat itself against the screen. Both he and the moth were getting a lesson in futility. "I also have to be honest with you and say that I really didn't think you were the right person for the job, but you proved me wrong."

"I know you only hired me because of Phoebe and the fact that her first glass shipment was due that day, Quinn." Jocelyn surprised him by laughing softly.

"True, I will admit that I was a desperate man." He liked the sound of her laugh and that she did it often. "I'm glad you proved me wrong."

"This would be a great time to hit you up for a raise," Jocelyn gave a slight pause, "if I was asking."

"Are you asking?" She deserved a lot more money than he was paying her. If you added up all the hours she put in during a week and divided it by what he was paying her, it didn't even add up to minimum wage. Of course, she got free room and board, but somehow it still didn't seem fair. Jocelyn was used to making a lot of money. For cripes sake she was a lawyer. Maybe he could come up with a few more bucks a week if he put off painting the house for another year or two.

Max trotted back up onto the patio, but this time he went to Jocelyn. He noticed that she held out a hand and Max dropped the ball right into her palm without even being asked. Jocelyn tossed the ball in the opposite direction of the swing set, and Max scrambled away.

Jocelyn wiped her palm on the edge of her shorts. "The money's fine, Quinn. I'm not looking for a raise."

He gave a deep sigh of relief and prayed she didn't

hear it. "So that's not what you wanted to talk with me about?"

"No, the terms of my employment are fine." Jocelyn swung her legs over the side of the chaise and sat up straight. There was now only three feet separating them, and with him slouching, they were eye to eye. "I have another issue I wish to discuss with you."

Now that Jocelyn was sitting in the soft light pouring through the patio doors, he could see the frown on her mouth matched her voice. "What's that?" He already knew what this was about, but he was curious as to what she was going to say about Wendell.

"I'm a big girl, Quinn. I can fend for myself and fight my own battles. I don't need a big brother."

"Good, because I don't want to be your brother. One sister is plenty, thank you." He wasn't going to comment on her being a big girl. She was a good eight inches shorter than him, and he outweighed her by at least eighty pounds. Unless she was a black belt or knew some fancy martial arts stuff, there would be no way to win any battle against him, or any other male his size. Wendell Kirby was a slug, so he didn't qualify.

It didn't matter what her mother had taught her. Jocelyn might have the heart of a warrior, but she still had the physical strength of a woman. Every instinct he possessed told him that she was a woman under his care, so he must protect her. His sister had always claimed he had been born into the wrong century. His sister was right.

"What's wrong with Phoebe? She's a wonderful sister and aunt." Jocelyn sounded incensed for her new friend.

He smiled. "There's nothing wrong with my sister, and a person couldn't ask for a nicer one." The last thing he wanted to be was Jocelyn's brother. The first thing he had to be was her employer, and hopefully her friend. "Let's just say Phoebe used up all my brotherly patience by the time she turned eighteen."

"You were one of those overly protective brothers that grilled every one of her dates, weren't you?"

"That's what brothers do, Jocelyn." Phoebe had hated his overprotective ways, but it had been his shoulder she had cried her eyes out on when her heart had been broken. He had dried her tears, given her back her confidence, and then helped her move into her dorm room at college so she could reach her dream. Then he had gone looking for Gary Franklin, the boy who had broken his sister's heart. He hadn't been sheriff then.

"Poor Phoebe." Jocelyn shuddered. "And here I thought having two older sisters was bad."

"Phoebe lived through it, and so did you."

"Maybe I'm emotionally scarred."

"Maybe I'm Spiderman." He shook his head and was thankful he only had one baby sister.

Jocelyn laughed. "Red and blue spandex isn't you, Quinn. I see you in black and with a cape."

"Dracula?" His male pride took a beating at the thought of Jocelyn comparing him to some blood-sucking monster. Was he that bad of an employer? His deputies didn't seem to complain that much.

"I was thinking more along the lines of Batman."

He grinned as he straightened up in his seat and puffed out his chest. "Didn't George Clooney and Val Kilmer play Batman in the movies?"

"Yes, and they got the likes of Nicole Kidman." Jocelyn shook her head at him. "Superheros don't write out a ridiculous number of tickets to the bad guys, Quinn."

"If they were the sheriff, they would." He felt his chest deflate, and he sank lower into the chair. "Why didn't you tell me what Kirby did?"

Jocelyn thought about lying, or at least stretching the truth, to Quinn, but decided against it. Quinn obviously knew the whole story. "I'm going to kill Ned."

"Ned did the right thing by coming to me." Quinn's

eyes narrowed as he studied her face. "I understand that you got him to promise not to tell either of your brothers-in-law."

"That's right, and he shouldn't have told you either. The whole incident was an accident and is totally blown out of proportion."

"Says Wendell."

"Says me." She had had enough of Quinn's interference, and she wanted to put the whole thing behind her. After the blistering she had given to Wendell's ears, she doubted very much that he would be grabbing any woman's butt in the future, and surely not hers ever again. "The whole incident was forgotten, until you started this moronic ticket campaign. Now everyone in town knows about it, including my brothers-in-law."

"The town is also taking bets that I will throw his butt into a cell and maybe forget about him for a few days or weeks."

"I know. Four-to-one odds, as of this afternoon." She had to wonder if he had heard about the odds on them being married by fall. She felt a tide of heat sweep up her face. If Quinn had heard of one bet, he had heard of the other. "Are you going to lock up Gordon Hanley, too, for running a bookie operation out of his bookshop?"

"I warned Gordon that I better not be hearing about any more bets, if that is what you mean."

"So you aren't going to arrest him?" That was a small relief. She didn't want to be blamed for causing a one-woman crime spree through the town.

"I'm not going to arrest anyone, unless you want to press charges against Wendell."

"I'm not pressing charges. Don't be ridiculous." She couldn't believe this. Next time Wendell so much as looked crooked at her, she was hauling off and clobbering the guy. Hell, maybe she should just drive down to the docks, wait for Wendell to stroll by, and then toss his sorry ass into the harbor just so everyone would be satisfied.

"Didn't think you would press charges."

"Listen, Quinn, I want you to stop harassing Wendell."

"Why?"

The man was as thick as a brick sometimes. Exasperated by the whole subject, she snapped, "Because people are getting the wrong idea about us. They think this overprotective attitude of yours is on a more personal level."

Quinn's gaze was on the buzzing and fluttering of a few insects trying to get in through the screen door. "I'm sorry about that, Jocelyn. That wasn't my intention."

"What was your intention?" He didn't have to look that upset about having his name linked to hers, did he?

"To teach Wendell Kirby a lesson."

"I think you succeeded in that, Quinn. Can you please let it go now?"

"I will on one condition."

"What's that?" She hated conditions. They had always bothered her. Being a lawyer only compounded the hatred because it seemed every case she worked on had conditions. Conditions set by someone else.

"Next time something like that happens you either tell me or one of your brothers-in-law."

The hair on the back of her neck bristled. "No."

Quinn's mouth dropped open in shock as he stared at her. "No?" His shoulders stiffened, and his chin took on that stubborn tilt that she had thought was so sexy only yesterday. "What do you mean, no?"

"No means no, Quinn. I'm not going to run to Daniel, Erik, or you the next time someone wants to play 'grab ass.' I'm going to break the guy's nose and cram his privates up to his tonsils, and then I will call one of my sisters to come bail me out of your jail."

"I'd pay to see that." Quinn's laughter was low, sexy, and sent a delicious shiver running down her spine. Was it any wonder the man had been driving her crazy for the past couple of weeks.

"You would pay to see someone grab my tush? Sounds kinky to me, but to each his own." She tried to keep the laughter out of her voice and wondered just how far she could push him. "Must be a Maine thing."

Quinn actually sputtered. It was a real shame they were sitting in the dark. She would have loved to know if she could make the straitlaced sheriff blush. Ten-to-one she could, and had.

"I was referring to you decking some guy." Quinn shifted in his chair. "But it better not come to that. I believe the rest of the male population of Misty Harbor has better manners than Wendell."

"A slug has better manners than Wendell." She stretched out her legs until her toes were nearly touching Quinn's. Her size six and a half foot looked so tiny against Quinn's size eleven. *Big feet, big hands, big. . . .* She quickly cleared her throat and mind and said, "Ben's still bugging me about going out on Erik's boat with Simon. Erik said it doesn't have to be a whole day out if you don't want to. He'll gladly take us for a morning or an afternoon, so the kids can try their hand at fishing at sea." Erik was excited about taking the kids out and was just waiting for her to confirm a date. Erik was going to make a wonderful father whenever Sydney and he were ready to start their own family. By the contentment on both Erik's and Sydney's faces lately, she wouldn't be surprised if that family would be coming sooner rather than later. "Sydney even offered to come along to help with the kids."

"It would have to be a Tuesday."

"No problem. Erik said he's flexible."

"Tuesdays are your days off. I wouldn't want to interfere with your social life."

"My social life is just fine, Quinn." Was that a hint of jealousy she heard in his voice, or was it wishful thinking? "You pick the Tuesday, and if the weather's good, those fish are history. Neptune, himself, will be shaking in fear of our arrival."

Quinn chuckled. "Don't tell Issy that, or she won't go. I don't think she will fish anyway. Disney has ruined that child."

"Simon has that already taken care of. He told her they were going to be looking for mermaids and shipwrecked princes all day." She could still picture the excitement on Issy's face when Simon had said that.

"Great, that's all I need is a prince to feed and house. We already have the dog." Max came bounding up onto the patio and flopped down. Quinn moved his feet at the last second. "Maybe next Tuesday, okay?"

"Sure, I'll run it by Erik and Sydney." She watched as Quinn slowly got to his feet and stretched. Muscles rippled beneath his T-shirt, and his faded jeans rode low on his hips. They didn't make sheriffs like him back in Baltimore. She knew, she worked with a lot of law enforcement guys, and no one came close to Quinn in looks, manners, or even sexy laughs.

"Tomorrow afternoon I talked Phoebe into taking a couple of hours off and going blueberry picking with me and the kids. Sadie Hopkins allows us to pick as many berries as we want from her fields. You can have the afternoon off or if you like, you can come with us."

It was the first time Quinn had invited her along on a family outing. She didn't want to read anything into the polite invitation that wasn't there, but her crazy heart wasn't listening to reason. Joy brightened her voice. "I've never been blueberry picking before, so sure, I'd love to come."

"Great." Quinn's smile flashed in the dim light as he reached for the screen door handle. "Ben wants to know if you can get Gwen's recipe for her blueberry muffins. They were delicious."

She kept her smile on her face by pure force and spoke around her clenched teeth. "No problem. If we pick enough of them, I'll whip up a batch of those muffins for Wednesday's breakfast, okay?" *Fat chance!* Quinn was the one who usually had breakfast cooked, or at least started before she even made it downstairs in the morning. Part of that problem was she refused to pull a robe over her pajamas and stumble downstairs to face Quinn with her hair and teeth unbrushed. Besides, Quinn's coffee tasted better than hers.

"There's no rush on the muffins." Quinn's gaze traveled the length of her legs before turning back up to her face. His voice held a slight edge as he said, "I've got some paperwork that needs to be done before I hit the sack. I'll see you in the morning, and we'll head out into Sadie's fields once the girls wake up from their nap."

That lingering hungry look had just saved Quinn from being told where he could shove those muffins. "Good night, Quinn." She watched as he entered the house and then quickly disappeared from sight.

Max stayed by her feet for company, and she scratched him behind his big floppy ears and grinned at his doggie sighs. In the week since he had joined the family, he had become an intricate part of it. The children and Phoebe loved Max. Quinn was growing more fond of him every day. Max, now that he was declared insect free, was allowed to spend the nights in the house. He could be found at the foot of Issy's bed every morning. The only problem she had with the massive dog was that he required more hair care than both girls combined, and he tended to splash water all over the kitchen every time he drank from his bowl. If Max's owner showed up now, more than one heart in the Larson household would be broken.

Jocelyn stared at the screen door and the room beyond as she continued to give Max a good scratching.

Why was Quinn so hell-bent on protecting her? He had to have known the town would start putting two and two together and come up with eight. Yet, he didn't seem to mind too much. Could there be a more personal level, one she wasn't aware of yet? Oh, there was an attraction between them, one that Quinn obviously wasn't interested in pursuing. Or was he?

No one would ever claim she was slow on the uptake. She noticed the way Quinn looked at her sometimes when he didn't realize she was watching him. Quinn had a fascination for her legs, and her lime green bikini top. Her legs were one of her best features, but much to her disappointment, her breasts were on the small side. The Wonder Bra had to work double time to give her cleavage. She had always heard that blondes had more fun. Since she had naturally golden hair, she believed that big-breasted women were the ones having all the fun. The last time she had any serious fun was back in law school with her then steady boyfriend, Jared, who now worked for NBC in New York City.

The sad truth was, Quinn had been the perfect gentleman and had treated her with nothing but kindness and respect since she accepted his job offer. He went out of his way to make sure they were never in any situations that could be misunderstood. When two people were living in the same house, there were many opportunities for miscommunication, which meant Quinn tended to avoid her a lot. He also used the kids as a natural buffer between them.

Now that she thought about it, she had to wonder why Quinn avoided her so much. Wasn't that strange? Quinn trusted her with his house, his kids, but he didn't trust being alone with her. Interesting.

Very interesting.

Chapter Eight

Quinn enjoyed the cool water lapping at his toes. Blueberry Cove was one of his favorite places during the hot summer months. The air was always fresh and clean, and the water cold. Fishing was only so-so, but the swimming was great. More importantly, fewer than a handful of tourists ever found the place, and it was only a short hike downhill from his house.

"Daddy, look what I can do!" shouted Tori as she crab walked around the stretch of sandy shoreline and pretended she was a crab, or maybe she was supposed to be a lobster. With Tori, it was hard to tell which crustacean she was imitating.

"That's great, sweetie." He watched Tori scuttle to and fro, all arms and legs and belly toward the sky. When she tilted her head back, to try and see where she was heading, her long blond hair dragged across the sand. Jocelyn was going to have fun getting all the sand out of Tori's hair tonight. Maybe he and Max would go for a long walk tonight, say around bath time.

His sister and Issy were standing farther down the shoreline tossing a stick into the water and watching Max swim out to get it. Max loved the water. Hell, the dog even loved to get baths in the kids' wading pool. His daughter was chatting with Phoebe about something. Issy's small arms were waving with every word she said. Whatever she was saying must have been funny because Phoebe was laughing right along with his daughter. It was good to see Issy laugh and smile.

Ben was sitting on the blanket in the shade grousing to Jocelyn about the amount of sunblock she was rubbing onto his back. Ben had wanted to take off his shirt, and Jocelyn had insisted on more lotion. Lucky kid.

He was tempted to take off his own shirt just to feel Jocelyn's small, delicate hands run across his back. His housekeeper was driving him crazy. Strange part was, it was a good crazy. For the first time in years, he felt alive. He got out of bed in the morning with a sense of anticipation as to what the day would bring. He came home from work looking forward to seeing his children and hearing what they had done all day. In truth, he not only rushed home to see the kids, but their nanny as well. Jocelyn had a way about her that just made everything seem okay. Nothing appeared to frazzle her. Not even when Max chewed apart one of her good shoes or when Tori got into her makeup and perfume and stank up the entire house.

He loved the way she interacted with the kids. She didn't talk down to them or treat them like babies. She also didn't let them walk all over her and become spoiled brats. Issy was starting to talk more. He wasn't sure if that was Jocelyn's doing or the dog's. Tori had stopped screaming to get her way and now only occasionally raised her voice, usually to be heard over whatever commotion was going on in the house.

Ben was starting to take an interest in sports. While he made time to toss a ball around with Ben, it was Jocelyn who had rushed down to Krup's General Store and bought his son a soccer ball and a T-ball stand for batting practice. Jocelyn was attempting to teach Ben how to throw a curve ball. Ben couldn't even catch a regularly thrown ball, and his aim was all over the place; but Jocelyn didn't seem to mind.

Jocelyn had all the makings of a perfect mom.

For days now he had been trying to find the big city lawyer in her. He couldn't. It wasn't just the power suits, business lunches, and arrogance that were missing. It was the attitude. With ten years in the business, he had dealt with enough lawyers to know which ones were the sharks. Jocelyn was no more of a shark than Issy. So what in the hell had she been doing in the DA's office in Baltimore? Places like that would chew someone like Jocelyn up for breakfast.

It would explain her recent temporary move north to Misty Harbor and her current employment situation.

The key word here was "temporary." He had to keep reminding himself that Jocelyn would be heading back to Baltimore within a couple of months, or sooner if he found someone to fill the position permanently.

"I'm going to head back and pick some more berries." Jocelyn stood beside him holding an empty pail. "We are going to need more if you want a pie or two."

Oh, he wanted something, and it wasn't a pie or two. They had been picking berries for only about an hour when the kids decided they needed a break. Most of his time had been spent supervising the kids and keeping Max from running all over the place. As berry picking went it was a wasted hour; but the kids were having a blast, and that was all that really mattered. He could always stop at one of Sadie's stands and buy the berries.

"You don't have to do that. We'll pick more on the way back home." He didn't want her to go off on her own. This outing was more about fun and relaxing with the kids than picking berries.

"But I want to. You, Phoebe, and the kids stay here

and enjoy yourselves." Jocelyn plopped her big, floppy straw hat back on top of her head and started up the hill.

He watched the delicious sway of her hips and the enticing view of her long, tanned legs as she climbed up the incline. Her navy-colored shorts were guaranteed to stop traffic down on Main Street and raise more than a few men's blood pressures.

"Why don't you go help her, Quinn," Phoebe said as she handed him another empty pail. "I would rather watch the kids than go pick berries anyway. Working like I am now, I don't get to spend as much time with them as I would like. I've been missing the little monsters."

He tried to hear any ulterior motives in Phoebe's voice, but couldn't. His sister, at one time, had been dead set on seeing him remarried and settled back down. Phoebe's matchmaking had been embarrassing both to him and the poor women she tried pushing his way. He had been expecting Phoebe to push him and Jocelyn together since she took the job. But amazingly, Phoebe hadn't been playing matchmaker, and that was beginning to worry him.

"I did have this dream about blueberry pie last night." He didn't add that it also involved Jocelyn and one very large bed. He took the empty pail and glanced at the kids playing with Max. The dog seemed to enjoy shaking himself right next to the kids just to hear them scream when they became soaked. Who was he to deny Aunt Phoebe some quality time with her nieces and nephew? "I'll be right up the hill. Give a yell if you need any help with the little monsters."

"I can handle them." Phoebe headed back over to the kids and tossed a stick back out onto the water. Max dashed after it with the kids all yelling encouragements from the shoreline.

Quinn sat down on a large rock and put his socks

and sneakers back on. He could see Jocelyn's big hat bobbing up on the hill. The hat not only kept the sun off her face and out of her eyes, but it was a homing device. As long as she kept the hat on, there wasn't a chance in hell he wouldn't be able to find her.

Feeling younger than he had for quite some time, he picked up the pail and headed up the hill after Jocelyn. Today he was just going to go with the flow. The flow was pushing him directly up the hill so he could enjoy the company of his housekeeper on this beautiful summer's day.

Fifteen minutes later he was working his way down the same row of bushes as Jocelyn. She was picking berries off the ones facing the cove, while he worked the ones behind her. He wasn't getting too many berries into his bucket. He was too busy eyeing the delicious curve of Jocelyn's tush. In the blinding glare of the afternoon sun he could see the dusting of freckles across Jocelyn's lightly tanned shoulders. Enchanting freckles that he knew scattered their way across the top slopes of her breasts. Freckles that seemed to whisper to him with her every movement.

He was in sad shape, and he knew it. Jocelyn seemed to like all the attention she had been getting from what he considered the horny male population of Misty Harbor. Yet, she actually went out with very few of them, and then she never dated anyone twice. She was playing the field and having a blast. By the amount of men who had called her, it wasn't a field. It was a damn prairie.

A very crowded prairie.

He wasn't looking to become one of the masses. He also knew that he would be jeopardizing their working relationship if he tried throwing his hat into her arena. As a housekeeper, Jocelyn wasn't the world's best, but she kept the house from falling in on them all. Plus, her cooking was improving. But where she really shone was with the kids. He couldn't have asked for a better nanny. Having his kids happy and well taken care of was her first priority, and Jocelyn handled it well.

The kids were happy and healthy. He had never wished for any harm to befall Diane, but he was delighted to have the children now living with him full-time. His days were filled and his career challenging enough to keep him on his toes. He had his health, and while not rolling in dough, he had enough to meet his bills. Even his baby sister had finally returned to Misty Harbor. He should be a contented man, but he wasn't.

For some obscure reason, he wanted more from life.

Quinn popped a ripe berry into his mouth and studied Jocelyn as she worked. Her fingers were quick, agile, and covered in blueberry juice. His weren't in any better condition. It was one of the drawbacks of berry picking. Of course, one of the benefits was that you got to eat as you worked. *One for me, one for the pail.* He popped another sweet berry into his mouth and savored the taste.

"You never will get your pail filled that way." Jocelyn reached over, swiped a couple of berries from his nearly empty pail, popped them into her mouth, and grinned.

"Hey, no fair." He tried to reach for her pail, but she hid it behind her back. He knew it was about halfway filled already. He had two choices. One, he could play the gentleman and leave her berries alone and let her win this round. Two, he could take her pail and taste her berries.

Since he had missed lunch today to handle a problem at work so he could be home on time, he reached for her pail. Jocelyn's surprised screech echoed in his ear as she bolted away clutching the pail to her chest and laughing. He rubbed his ear and tried to think past the ringing. The sound of her laughter was contagious. The little minx wanted to play games, and he was just in the mood to oblige.

He took off after her and rounded the end of the row at a dead run. Jocelyn was faster. Her long, tanned legs churned and pumped their way up to the next row. His own breathing was harsh, and his heart pounded as he put more effort into the chase. He couldn't hear Jocelyn breathing heavy, but she at least stopped laughing. He didn't think he could live with the humiliation of his dainty, five-foot four-inch housekeeper beating him in a footrace.

He had to lay off the muffins.

A bush scratched his forearm as he tore around it and gained on Jocelyn. The sound of her rapid breathing finally became noticeable as he reached out and wrapped his arm around her waist and swung her in a circle.

Jocelyn tried to cover the top of her pail with her hand, but many of the berries flew out of the wildly swinging bucket. "I give! I give," she half-laughed and half-shouted as her feet left the ground.

"Say uncle." He slowed the rotation, but kept her back pressed to his heaving chest. He didn't know what caused his heart to pound more, the run or having Jocelyn held against him so close he could feel her every breath. His arm tightened. The bucket clamped in his other hand was now totally empty. So much for blueberry picking.

"Never." Jocelyn kicked her feet and tried to elbow him in the stomach. He could tell she was only half-heartedly trying to get away from him.

The floppy hat Jocelyn had been wearing had been blown off and was now lying on top of a nearby bush. Her golden ponytail whipped back and forth, and the enticing silky skin on the back of her neck was mere inches away from his mouth. All he had to do was tilt his head downward and he would be able to taste the bewitching texture of her skin. "Say uncle." He silently added the word "fast."

Jocelyn went limp in his arms. She glanced over her shoulder and softly smiled. "Uncle."

How could he have thought her eyes were plain, ordinary gray? The color seemed to shift with her mood. Today, they were more blue than gray. A smokey blue that deepened and swirled with emotions the longer he looked into them. His gaze dropped to her mouth, and a hunger, unlike anything he had ever experienced, clawed at his gut. He slowly lowered Jocelyn. "Were you on the track team in college?"

Jocelyn took a hesitant step back, but she seemed to be studying his mouth as intently as he was still regarding hers. "No, my legs weren't long enough."

"There's nothing wrong with your legs, Joc." He glanced down to the shapely limbs, just to refresh his memory, and frowned. "You're bleeding." A thin, six-inch scratch ran down the side of her calf.

Jocelyn glanced down and shrugged. "Oh, that's nothing but a scrape. I must have grazed it on one of the bushes."

He grabbed her hand and pulled her over to where a medium-size boulder was nestled between two bushes. "Sit down and let me see it."

Jocelyn laughed. "I'm not one of the children, Quinn. I don't need a Band-Aid and a . . ." Jocelyn's voice trailed off as a tide of red swept up her face.

Either Jocelyn was embarrassed, or four minutes in the sun without her hat had caused one heck of a sunburn. He knew exactly what she had been about to say. *A Band-Aid and a kiss.* It was the same remedy the girls asked for whenever they got an ouchy. At home they went through almost a box of cartoon Band-Aids in a week and one truckload of kisses. He was more than willing to supply Jocelyn with the same remedy, or at least half the remedy. He didn't have a Band-Aid with him.

Seeing Jocelyn's blush and her loss for words, he couldn't help but tease her more. "A Band-Aid and a what?" He took her pail from her hand and placed it on the ground. She had lost about half the berries during their game of tag. He moved in closer, backing her legs up against the large stone.

"Nothing." Jocelyn sat down, but she wouldn't meet his gaze. "My leg's fine, Quinn."

He knelt in front of her and gently lifted her leg so that he could get a closer look. "Let me be the judge of that. I'm the one with medical training." The scratch wasn't very deep. A dozen drops of blood were beaded along the shallow slice.

The medical training he and his deputies received was mainly for emergencies. They learned how to give CPR and how to make a tourniquet so someone hopefully wouldn't bleed to death before an ambulance arrived. He also had learned how to deliver a baby, and he had prayed more than once that he would never have need of that particular knowledge. Jocelyn's scrape didn't rate in the emergency category, but the sight of her legs sure got his blood pumping faster.

He balanced his weight on the balls of his feet and gently placed her ankle across his one knee. She wore scuffy white sneakers and low white socks that had a band of baby blue running around the edge. The same blue as her low-cut tank top and the ribbon that had been used as a band on her straw hat. Her calf was warm and smooth beneath his fingertips. With a quick tug, he pulled the hem of his T-shirt out of his shorts and used it to gently wipe away the few drops of blood.

He heard Jocelyn suck in a quick breath, but he knew he hadn't hurt her. Concentrating on the scratch to see if it was still bleeding, he said, "When we get back to the house I want you to use soap and water to clean it out better, and then some antibiotic cream to make sure it doesn't get infected."

Jocelyn's voice sounded weak and shaky. "Your arm is bleeding, Quinn."

He glanced at his forearm and for the first time noticed the long, thin scratch of his own. A dozen or so drops of blood were smeared across his arm. "We have matching boo-boos."

He was using the hem of his shirt to wipe his arm when Jocelyn said, "If we put them together, we can be blood brothers." Jocelyn still had her leg up on his knee, even though he wasn't holding her ankle any longer.

His gaze shot to hers. "As I told you before, the last thing in the world I want to be to you is your brother, Joc." Out of habit, or possibly impulse, he leaned down and placed a soft kiss on her shin. He saw the heat flare in her gaze. Now her eyes were smokey gray and sparked with the same desire he had been feeling for weeks. He wondered if she would admit to those feelings. "What do you have to say to that?"

Jocelyn slowly smiled as she lowered her foot back to the ground and leaned forward. "I'm extremely thankful that I shaved my legs this morning in the shower."

He met her halfway and captured her smile in a heated kiss directly out of one of his nightly fantasies. Jocelyn tasted like an erotic combination of sunshine and blueberries. There was nothing tentative about the way she kissed. Jocelyn kissed the same way she met life; bold, forward, and totally thorough.

Jocelyn's arms wrapped around his neck as she playfully nipped at his lower lip and then deepened the kiss.

Either Jocelyn moaned or he did; he couldn't tell who, nor did it matter. His tongue swept into her mouth as he hauled her off the boulder and into his lap. His butt landed in the dirt as Jocelyn's bottom settled on a very sensitive, yet hard part of his anatomy.

He was as hard as the boulder she had just been sitting on, and they hadn't done anything more than kiss. And what a kiss it was. On the scale of one to ten, it ranked at least a twelve. His fingers gently cupped Jocelyn's cheek as his tongue tangled with hers, and he tried to push the kiss to fourteen.

He could feel Jocelyn's fingers tremble against the back of his neck as Max's barking finally pierced the haze of desire surrounding them. He took his time to break the kiss and silently cursed when he realized the barking was growing closer. The tips of his fingers trailed down the satiny smoothness of her cheek as Jocelyn slowly opened her eyes. There wasn't a hint of blue in her gorgeous eyes now. They were a deep, turbulent gray. A desperate man could read a lot of things in their depths if he wasn't careful.

Ben's voice could be heard above the barking. "Where are they, Max? Find Dad and Jocelyn."

His son was about three rows over, and from the sound of it, his daughters and Phoebe weren't far behind.

The pad of his thumb skimmed the moisture on Jocelyn's lower lip. "We are about to have company." For the first time since Benjamin's birth, Quinn actually wished he and the twins were somewhere else. He didn't resent his children; he just wished their timing could have been better.

Jocelyn scrambled off his lap just as Max came barreling around the corner, all humongous paws and flying fur. Quinn tried to get to his feet before the dog reached them. Both pails, and the remaining blueberries, went flying as Max slid into them and the back of Quinn's knees.

Ben rounded the corner just in time to see his father get knocked on his butt by a slipping and sliding hundred-pound, soaking-wet dog.

Four days later, Jocelyn was confused and hurt. After the kiss she had shared with Quinn up on Blueberry Hill, she had expected something more. What, she wasn't sure, but she knew there had to be something. She hadn't really thought Quinn would ask her out on a date or anything; hell, they were eating dinner together nearly every night and sleeping in the same house. Maybe after the kids were tucked in for the night they could have tried for a repeat of that kiss.

There was no way that kiss could have been as great as she remembered. She was more than willing to test that theory.

Problem was, since that afternoon of berry picking, Quinn had been avoiding her more than ever. If she was in the kitchen, he was out back with the kids. If she was in the family room watching television, he was upstairs in his room catching up on paperwork. If she was out back tossing a ball to Ben, Quinn was out front with the girls washing his SUV or taking Max for a walk. It was to the point where Quinn preferred the company of a hundred-pound furball to hers.

Even the children were beginning to notice something wasn't quite right between her and their father. Phoebe had given her some encouraging smiles during the past couple of days, while glaring at her brother. Phoebe wasn't stupid. She had known what had been going on between them the minute she and the girls had joined them in the middle of the blueberry farm.

If Quinn wasn't attracted to her, she could understand his behavior. But after the kiss they had shared, and his reaction to it, she knew he wasn't immune to her. Hell, she had been sitting on his reaction. She had been pressed so close to him that she had felt the rapid pounding of his heart. Hell, she would have had to climb under his T-shirt and shave his chest hair to get any closer.

The attraction was mutual. So what in the world was Quinn's problem?

The sound of wood being chopped reached the kitchen where she was enjoying a tall glass of iced tea and the peace and quiet of the house. The girls were taking their nap, and Ben, who had already finished his lesson for the day, was busy building a tower with Legos in the living room. He was hoping to have the thing completely done before his sisters had a chance to knock it down.

Jocelyn headed for the screen door but didn't go outside onto the patio. Quinn was at the very back of the yard chopping wood. He had taken off his T-shirt and tossed it onto the grass. His well-worn jeans rode low on his hips. The muscles in his back and arms flexed with each blow of the ax. Under the heat of the afternoon sun, he had worked up a fine sheen of sweat.

With every swing of the ax, wood went flying. Quinn was male perfection in motion. By the amount of wood littering the yard and already piled by the garage, she would have to guess Quinn was planning on supplying firewood to the entire town this coming winter.

She pressed the cold glass of tea against her cheek and felt the condensation coat her heated skin. If Quinn was that good at chopping wood and working up a sweat, one had to wonder what else he would be good at.

"Even for being my stubborn and pigheaded brother, I would have to concede, he's easy on the eyes." Phoebe stood beside her and had followed her gaze to where Quinn was chopping wood.

"Oh." Her one hand flew up to her suddenly pounding heart while the other one clutched at the slippery glass. "I didn't hear you come in, Phoebe."

"You were distracted." Phoebe chuckled as she headed for the refrigerator and helped herself to a glass of iced tea. "I needed something cold to drink. It's got to be ninety out there. Even with the two fans going in the garage, it still feels like an oven."

"It's ninety-two." She frowned at the scene in the backyard. Quinn's short hair was plastered to his head with sweat. "I don't understand why your brother would want to chop wood on one of the hottest days of the year."

"He's frustrated." Phoebe downed half the glass in one long gulp.

"Something wrong at work?" Quinn didn't talk much about his job, besides bitching about all the paperwork, which he blamed on the lawyers. Quinn hadn't believed her when she told him most lawyers hated paperwork as much as he did.

"Nope." Phoebe downed the rest of her glass and then poured herself another one. "Ever since Diane left him and asked for a divorce, no one has ever seen Quinn with another woman."

She was dying to know what had happened between Quinn and his ex-wife, but she wanted to hear it from him, not Phoebe or the town's gossip mill. "He must have loved her very much."

Phoebe shrugged. "The girls were only nine months old and Ben was barely three when they left. Having them move to Boston tore him up inside."

She noticed how Phoebe avoided the subject of Diane. "Anyone could see how much he loves them."

"Yes he does." Phoebe wet a paper towel and bathed her face and the back of her neck. "Once in a while on his days off he used to go up to Bangor for the night."

"I don't think you should be telling me this, Phoebe." She didn't want to hear about Quinn's trip to see another woman. The entire time she had been there the only women who ever called Quinn were his mother, the receptionist down at the office, and some teenage clerk from the video rental place to tell him the movies he had rented were late.

"Since the kids moved in with him, he hasn't made one trip into Bangor."

"And the reason you're telling me this is?" She didn't want to hear about Quinn being sexually frustrated because the kids were cramping his style.

"I gave Quinn plenty of opportunity to go visit and even spend a night away from home. He never took me up on it." Phoebe took another long sip out of her glass and smiled. "Which leads me to believe whoever's in Bangor isn't important to him."

Jocelyn moved away from the screen door and started to hunt through the freezer, looking for something she could make into dinner. She refused to dwell on the happiness Phoebe's words had caused. "What makes you think I'm interested in Quinn's past?"

Phoebe snorted. "Get real, Joc. The way you two spark off of each other, I'm afraid the whole house is going to burn down one of these nights." Phoebe jiggled her drink and seemed to enjoy the sound of ice cubes rattling in an empty glass. "Quinn puts on a great show, Joc. He never bad talks about Diane, and not just because she's dead now. He never did it, not even when she ripped out his heart and packed up his children and moved them to Boston."

"So, he's a saint of an ex-husband." What would make a man so complacent when it came to the children that he so obviously loved? If someone had tried to take her children and move them hundreds of miles away, there would have been hell to pay. Yet, per Phoebe, Quinn had probably helped them pack.

"I'm going to let you in on a secret where my brother is concerned." Phoebe's gaze wandered to the backyard where her brother still was chopping wood. "Quinn has a flaw. A major flaw. He puts everyone else's happiness above his own. When Diane informed him she and the children were moving to Boston, Quinn was willing to give up his position here to go with them."

"But he loves it here." She had been here only a few weeks and she knew that Misty Harbor was in his blood. It was where Quinn belonged.

"I know, and thankfully, so did Diane. She could have roped him along until they were settled comfort-

ably in Boston, and then divorced him. He would have
been alone in a city he never wanted to be in, and then
the decision would have been his to move back here,
away from the children."

"Quinn never would have left the children."

"I know." Phoebe dumped her ice into the sink.
"Diane made the break clean and filed for the divorce
the same week she moved there. Diane assured him she
was happy there, and so Quinn gave her everything she
wanted."

"Did Quinn want the divorce?"

"Hard to say. I was living down in Philadelphia at the
time. I do know that he wanted the children."

"But not his wife?"

"You have to ask him that." Phoebe filled a plastic
bottle with ice cubes and water to take back with her to
the garage.

Fat chance that would ever happen. Quinn couldn't
even stand to be in the same room with her, let alone
have a personal conversation. "Why are you telling me
all of this?" She considered Phoebe a friend. There was
friendship, but then there was family. Phoebe and Quinn
were family.

"I think you're very good for my brother, Joc. During
the past several weeks I've seen signs of life coming
back to him. Even the hint of the old green-eyed monster, jealousy, once in a while. Quinn's not as cool and
unaffected by your presence as he wants everyone to believe. Just because he isn't saying anything to you, doesn't
mean he's not thinking about you. Quinn's known to
be too stubborn for his own good."

"Such as putting everyone's happiness above his
own?"

Phoebe saluted her with the water bottle and smiled
as she opened the side door. "Use the knowledge wisely."

Chapter Nine

"Abraham, I can't practice law in Maine." Jocelyn gave Abraham Martin a gentle smile. "I'm sure there has to be a lawyer in the area who could give you and your mom some legal advice." No one could have been more surprised than she when Abraham showed up on the doorstep five minutes ago seeking advice. Knowing she was about to disappoint him, she had invited him in for something cool to drink. From her seat at the kitchen table she could keep an eye on the kids playing out back.

"There's Francis Haskel over in Sullivan." Abraham turned a letter over in his rough, work-reddened hands. This afternoon he had cleaned himself up for the visit. His jeans and T-shirt were clean, his jaw was clean shaven, and his wide orange suspenders boasted cute little puffins.

Jocelyn had to wonder if his mother had been the one to comb his thin, graying hair over his growing bald spot. "Why don't you call him and make an appointment?"

"Frank's been practicing law since before he landed on the beaches of Normandy. Half the time he only goes into his office to take a nap and to puff on his cigars, because his wife won't let him smoke them in their house."

She tried to hide her smile. "I'm sure there has to be another attorney nearby."

"Not close enough for Mom. She doesn't like to ride in my truck, and she refuses to talk to Frank."

She could sympathize with Abraham's mom. There wasn't enough money in the world to make her climb into the cab of his pickup truck. The stench of rotting bait alone could make a person lose consciousness, along with their lunch. "Why won't she talk to Mr. Haskel?"

"Mom had been engaged to him when he went into the army during World War II, to do his duty for God and his country. She promised to wait for him, and wait for him she did."

"What happened?"

"Frank came home to Maine a war hero and with a French wife named Fifi in tow." Abraham chuckled. "No one can hold a grudge like my mom."

She studied the ice cubes in her glass and bit the inside of her cheek to keep from laughing. "I still can't give you any legal advice, Abraham. As I told you before, I'm not licensed to practice law in Maine, only in Maryland." Here she had thought Abraham was pushing sixty, when it now appeared he was probably only fifty-five or so.

Abraham slid the envelope he had been clutching across the table to her. "Could you at least look at the letter and tell me if it's worth driving all the way to Bangor? The starter in my truck is going, and I was hoping to get another couple hundred miles out of it. A trip to Bangor means I've got to replace it before I go."

Curiosity was burning a hole in her gut. In the past several weeks she hadn't really been giving her career a lot of consideration. She still had no idea what she was going to do once she returned to Baltimore. Lately she had been acting as though this trip to Maine was one very long vacation. Maybe it was time to start considering her future. The only thing she knew for sure was that the law would definitely have a big part in it. "Who's the letter from?"

"My cousin, John. He's the son of my mom's brother, Harris, who passed away about three months ago."

Jocelyn turned the white envelope over. The return address was John Eldred's. "It's addressed to your mom."

"Yeah. Years ago my mom gave her brother some money so he could buy this hunting lodge up near White Cap Mountain. She became a thirty-percent owner in the lodge, and once a year her brother sent her a check for her share of the profits. It wasn't much, but Mom sure did get a kick out of receiving it."

"Now your Uncle Harris is gone, and his son is running the lodge?"

"John wants to sell the lodge and retire to someplace warmer."

"Doesn't your mom want to sell?" As a thirty-percent owner, Abraham's mom didn't have a chance to stop the sale, unless she was willing to buy out whoever now owned the other seventy percent.

"Mom doesn't care one way or the other what John does with his father's hunting camp."

"So what's the problem?" She still hadn't opened the envelope.

"John says his dad left him the whole lodge free and clear and that my mom gets nothing. He says my mom has to sign the enclosed release and everything would be settled and done. Doesn't seem right to me or my mom."

"If Harris Eldred owned the lodge free and clear, as John says, your mom wouldn't have to sign a release, Abraham."

"That's what I thought." Abraham pulled the papers from the envelope and handed them to her. "Could you at least read it and tell me if my mom should sign."

"I can't do that, Abraham."

"Can you at least tell me if it stinks like week-old squid under a July sun?"

Jocelyn fingered the papers and frowned. If there was a legal release, then an attorney had to be involved somewhere. If the story Abraham had just told her was true, a corrupt attorney. One who was trying to cheat Abraham's mom out of her share of the business.

Curiosity won. What harm could it do to read a page or two. She already knew she was going to tell Abraham to find his mom a good attorney. She skimmed the letter from John Eldred first. Nothing surprising there. It was just as Abraham had told her. No money would be coming, but could you please sign the release?

The release was more interesting to read. It consisted of a bunch of legal jargon that would baffle any second-year law student. Underneath all the legal gobbledy-gook it basically said that Mrs. Martin would be signing her share of the hunting camp over to Harris Eldred's heir, his son John. If Abraham's mom signed the paper, she would be signing away all her rights and thirty percent of the lodge.

She handed Abraham back the papers. "I have only two words for you, rotting bait."

"Then they are trying to cheat my mom?"

"Your mom needs a lawyer, Abraham. Tell her not to sign this until she sees a good lawyer."

"How do I find a 'good' lawyer?" Abraham's voice held anger and confusion. "Don't say the yellow pages, because I don't trust them. Anyone could put their names in there and call themselves a lawyer. Went to a dentist once who had the biggest and flashiest ad. The guy pulled one of my back molars and charged me a fortune to do it. Mom's not going to want to sign over her Social Security checks to some fancy lawyer."

She hadn't thought about the financial burden this would place on Abraham's mom. She didn't want Mrs. Martin to spend her Social Security check on lawyer's fees. "Do you have any idea how big this hunting lodge is? Are we talking a lot of acres?" The building might be falling into itself, but the land surely would be worth something.

"It's about five hundred acres, including the small lake. Plus it backs up against state game land. The lodge has about ten rooms, and Uncle Harris built about a dozen small cabins for those who wanted more privacy."

Five hundred acres! "Tell your mom to get a lawyer, a good lawyer." She had a feeling Abraham's mom wouldn't have to worry about stretching her Social Security checks any longer. "Does your mom have any paperwork supporting her claim to be a thirty-percent owner in the hunting camp?"

"She said she has it somewhere. Should I tell her to look for it?"

"Yes. The lawyer will want to see everything she can find."

"Can you help us find a lawyer?" Abraham's cloudy gray eyes seemed to plead with her. "Please."

It was the *please* that did it. How could she possibly tell Abraham no? She didn't know Maine's laws, but she knew how to find a reputable lawyer. She could even do some checking on the Internet and find out what Abraham's mom could expect to go through. "All right, but you have to give me a couple of days to see what I can find out."

Abraham's smile was wide and genuine. "Thanks, Jocelyn. I knew we could count on you. Mom wasn't too sure until I told her you were Doc Sydney and Gwen's sister. Mom loves Doc Sydney so much that I don't have to fight with her to go see the doctor anymore. Last month I took her to Gwen's restaurant for her eighty-second birthday. Mom said that Gwen's clam chowder was almost as good as hers."

"High praise, indeed." She grabbed a pen and a piece of junk mail she had carried in earlier and jotted down both John's address and the name of the lawyer who had typed up the release. "I should have something by Friday afternoon."

"I'll stop by then." Abraham stood up and glanced out back to where the kids and Max were playing. "I see Quinn finally broke down and got the kids a dog."

"The dog found the kids. Quinn still hasn't accepted Max as a permanent part of the family, but I think he's fighting a losing battle on that one." Issy was holding a tea party and serving imaginary cookies. Tori was pouring water from the teapot into the plastic cups. Max was slurping water out of his cup and making a mess all over the table. Both girls were laughing and scolding Max.

Ben had taken all the pink plastic silverware that matched the tea set and stuck them straight up into the dirt pile. He was currently using the big metal Tonka truck to run over every piece.

"Ben," she yelled through the screen door. "Don't break your sisters' silverware."

"I'm not," yelled Ben right back.

"Benjamin!" She could see the fork he had just run over was still bent.

"Oh, all right." Ben started to yank the tableware out of the dirt and pile it into the back of the dump truck. There was some distant mumbling, but she couldn't hear Ben's words.

Abraham chuckled. "If you ever decide you don't want to be a lawyer anymore, you would make a great mom."

"Why can't I be both?" She had never considered it an either-or occupation.

"Guess you could if you really wanted to." Abraham picked up his baseball cap and tugged it on over his bald spot. "Would be a shame to let all that education go to waste."

She walked Abraham to the front door. "You're right, no sense wasting it." Even though she hadn't been using it for the past several weeks. "I'll see you Friday afternoon."

"I'll be here." Abraham stepped off the porch and started to walk toward his truck.

She hurried back to the kitchen and the children. She had never thought of not being a lawyer or wasting the education she had worked so long and hard at obtaining. As for becoming a mother, that had always been in her future plans down the road. Two, maybe three kids. A loving husband, and at least two vacations a year. A big, comfortable house with some hired help to take care of the kids and house while she was at work. This temp job was like a trial run for her future in regard to the family end of her dreams. Except she was playing the part of the hired help.

As far as she could see, there wasn't a reason why she couldn't have the career and the family. Of course, she had to get her career back on the right track first. Then find that loving and incredibly sexy husband, before the kids arrived on the scene. Her parents might be hinting at a grandchild lately, but she didn't think they would take the joke if their only unmarried daughter was the one to supply them with that bundle of joy.

Phoebe pulled away from her brother's house and smiled at her passenger. "Thanks for coming with me."

"Hey, thanks for asking." Jocelyn fiddled with the old seat belt and finally got it to latch. "It's been a long while since I participated in a 'girls' night out.' "

"Since there's only the two of us, we make a pretty pathetic group, but I'm sure there will be other women where we are going." Phoebe didn't bother to add that the women who hung out where they were heading weren't the professional type. At least she didn't think so.

"Are you finally going to tell me where we're going?" Jocelyn laughed as she rolled down the window and allowed the evening breeze to fill the Jeep. "Quinn didn't seem too happy when you refused to tell him."

"Quinn's a natural-born worrier." She shifted into third gear and headed out of town. "It's Friday night, and both of us could use the break. Who needs big brother looking over our shoulders?"

"It was real nice of your mom to come up and stay at the house just in case Quinn got called out." Jocelyn rummaged into her purse and pulled out a tube of lip gloss.

Phoebe shook her head. Whoever heard of applying lip gloss when wearing jeans? Leave it to Jocelyn to look classy while slumming. "Mom wanted to spend some time with the kids, but she didn't want to be stepping on your toes. This way, everyone is happy, except Quinn."

"Why? Don't Quinn and his mom get along?"

"My brother gets his worrying from our mom. She's always after him to find a nice girl and settle back down. She's worried that he's lonely and that he needs a wife to make his life complete."

Since moving back in with her parents she had been getting the same lecture nearly every night. Her mom was insisting that all her daughter needed to make her life complete was the love of a good man. Phoebe didn't put much stock into a man making her life complete, but she wouldn't turn down some good loving. As long as it was coming from the right man.

The Jeep took a curve a little too fast as she drove along the road heading north. She slowed down 'til she was only about five miles per hour above the speed limit. Anticipation was making her foot heavy. The last thing she needed was for one of Quinn's deputies to pull her over for speeding. She would never hear the end of it from Quinn. "Mom's got it into her head now that the kids need a mom, and that it's Quinn's duty to supply them with one."

"The kids had a mom. It doesn't seem right just to replace Diane like that." Jocelyn looked out of the window. "If something had happened to my mom when I was little, I wouldn't want anyone to try to replace her."

"Mom doesn't want to replace Diane in the kids' hearts. She believes the kids need a 'female' touch in their lives."

"But they have her, you, and whoever the housekeeper will be." Jocelyn frowned. "Unless Quinn hires a male nanny and housekeeper."

"True." She chuckled as she thought about her brother hiring a male housekeeper. "But Mom doesn't consider me as having a very feminine touch. I own exactly two dresses, and one of those is an old bridesmaid dress I got suckered into wearing at a friend's wedding. It's periwinkle blue and comes equipped with its own hoop skirt and parasol. I can't cook or sew, and have no desire to learn either. Makeup makes me break out, I clip my fingernails to the quick, and I consider conditioner for my hair a total luxury."

Phoebe wiggled her hands, and a gentle clanging filled the Jeep. "My one claim to femininity is my love of jewelry." Three hammered copper bracelets adorned her right wrist, and she counted six different rings. "Then again men are beginning to wear more jewelry than some women I know. Have you ever seen the size of some of those diamonds athletes have on their lobes? I'm telling you, Jocelyn, it's enough to make a grown woman cry."

Jocelyn chuckled. "I think football players are the worst."

"Nah, my vote is for professional basketball players."

"I have three bridesmaid dresses in the back of one of my mother's closets, none of which I have worn twice," said Jocelyn. "I'm getting better at cooking, but I still would rather be doing anything else but cleaning. I chew my nails when I'm nervous, and I can throw a mean curve ball."

"I knew there was a reason we became fast friends. I was the pitcher for the girls' softball team all four years in high school." Phoebe relaxed into the worn and sagging seat. During the twelve years she had been driving the old and battered Jeep, the seat had permanently curved to fit her body. Of course, her body at twenty-nine was a lot different from when she had been seventeen.

The Jeep was now on its last leg, but she didn't have the heart to get rid of it. Gary Franklin had been the one to spot the ad for the Jeep in the local paper. He had been the one to drive her out to see it for the first time. He had been the one to help her give it its first tune-up and oil change. Gary also had reached third base with her in the front seat one summer's night. Memories like that you didn't trade in.

"So, friend, where are we heading?" Jocelyn asked. "Into Sullivan?"

"You up for a little adventure?" Her palms were damp against the wheel, and her stomach felt as if she had just eaten a bucket of worms. Maybe this wasn't such a great idea after all.

"Sure." Jocelyn's voice sounded interested.

"There's a bar up the road. It's not the type of place that attracts tourists or the affluent. The words 'class' and 'upscale' have never once been attached to it."

"A local hangout?"

"You could say that. I believe most of the patrons are hardworking fishermen who need a place to kick back and relax." She owed it to Jocelyn to be up front about the place. "It's called The One Eyed Squid."

Jocelyn chuckled. "Sounds perverted."

She joined in the laughter. "It was probably meant

that way, too." She shifted gears as the Jeep followed the winding coast road next to the crashing dark surf. The sound of waves pounding the rocks never failed to calm her or to bring her peace. She was finally home. Eleven years of running, only to return to the place she had been running from. She hadn't been running from Misty Harbor; she had been running from a boy. Gary Franklin had been eighteen when he had broken her heart. Tonight she was finally going to put that demon to rest and get on with her life.

She glanced over at Jocelyn and added, "The food is barely edible, the music loud, and the crowd rowdy. But, I've been told that the beers are always cold."

"What you are telling me is, the place has atmosphere."

"Wouldn't know about atmosphere. I've never stepped foot in the place."

"So why tonight?"

"Promise not to laugh, and if you think I'm pathetic, could you keep it to yourself?"

"Now I'm intrigued. Spill the dirt, girlfriend."

Jocelyn was easy to talk to, and something told her her new friend wouldn't laugh. Those were the main two reasons she had invited Jocelyn along for the night. That, and courage. Walking into The One Eyed Squid with Jocelyn would be a lot easier than strolling in alone. "When I left for college eleven years ago, my boyfriend and I broke up. Now that I'm back, I'm curious to see if there's any spark left between us." She hoped it didn't sound too pathetic or desperate.

"This old boyfriend hangs out at The One Eyed Squid?"

"Gary's a lobster fisherman. I asked around town and found out he bartends there on Thursday and Friday nights. Quinn's usually busy on Thursday nights, so I figured Friday night would be a good time just to stop in and show you one of the county's more colorful attractions." She slowed the Jeep and nodded toward an old weather-stained building up ahead.

Phoebe drove her Jeep into a pothole-infested parking lot. Both lights that should have been lighting the lot were broken. The beam of her headlights glistened off a couple shards of glass beneath one of the poles. Rusty pickup trucks, a few cars, and half a dozen heavily chromed motorcycles halfway filled the lot.

The One Eyed Squid boasted flashing neon beer advertisements in every window that cast the parking lot into a rainbow of colors. A lousy hand-painted sign was nailed above the scarred wooden door. The squid looked like a demented octopus wearing an eye patch and a red bandanna. Hyperactive second graders could have done a better job drawing him.

Phoebe frowned at the salt-stained building, which was listing toward the right, as she turned off the Jeep. In the dozen or so times she had driven by the place, it had never seemed this bad. Daylight had actually improved its appearance.

"Maybe this isn't such a great idea."

Jocelyn chuckled. "I can definitely see why you didn't want Quinn to know where we were going." Jocelyn opened her door and got out of the Jeep. "Come on, Phoebe, it can't be that bad. I hear music, and if I'm not mistaken, it's an old Doors' song."

Phoebe got out of the Jeep and took a reassuring breath. Gary's relatively new pickup truck was parked at the far end of the lot. Jocelyn and she would be safe as long as Gary was there. She didn't know the man Gary had become, but she had known the boy. He couldn't have changed that much. Besides, if the patrons of The One Eyed Squid made a habit out of accosting unescorted females, her brother would have shut the place down in a heartbeat. Quinn would never tolerate such a threat in his county. Apart from the rare barroom fight, she hadn't heard anything really bad about the tavern.

The music got louder as they approached the door. She could hear the voices and laughter of people over the hum of distant air conditioners. It wasn't the rowdy patrons that caused her feet to freeze; it was the thought of seeing the man behind the bar. Gary was her ghost and her demon, all rolled up into one delicious package. "We could go back to town now, and no one would know we were here."

"And do what?" asked Jocelyn. "Get double-scoop ice-cream cones down at Bailey's, walk the docks, and play tourist?" Jocelyn reached for the knob. "Come on, Phoebe, this was your idea, and there's no way I'm leaving without seeing your old high school boyfriend. He must be something for you to remember him after all this time."

She took a deep breath and followed Jocelyn into the boisterous and smoke-filled bar. Half the conversations stopped before the door was shut behind them. Smoke hung a good two feet beneath the ceiling rafters. Small candles flickered on every tabletop. Low lighting was behind the bar, but she couldn't bring herself to look in that direction. She followed Jocelyn to an empty booth along the side wall. She refused to dwell on the fact that nearly every man in the place stared at them as they made their way through the shadowy room.

Jocelyn walked between the tables and around a few gawking males as if she owned the place. Hell, she wouldn't have been surprised if her new friend frequented biker bars and honky-tonks. She chuckled at what Quinn's reaction would be if he could see his dainty little housekeeper now.

Jocelyn slid into the booth and grinned. "It isn't as bad as I first thought." She nodded to the three pool tables taking up the back room. "You play?"

"Our dorm had one, but most of the time the balls or the sticks were missing." She slid onto the empty seat and faced Jocelyn. Most of the conversations had started back up, and she was afraid she knew what the hot topic was. She had an unobstructed view of the bar, but she still hadn't looked to see Gary's reaction. Hell, maybe in all this haze he wouldn't recognize her.

"Cues, not sticks," Jocelyn corrected automatically.

Phoebe glanced over her shoulder at the poolroom and counted five men and two women. She recognized three of the men and the hard-looking woman. Karen Kelly had been the toughest girl in her graduating class at Hancock High. K.K., as she liked to be called, had been wild, outspoken, and rumored to have slept with half the male student body and all of the male teachers. Now K.K. looked at least ten years older than what she was. Her once proud thirty-eight Ds were down around her waist, or at least where her waist should have been. Perched on a bar stool watching the men play, she looked like a fat, bleached-blond troll with a mammoth red rosebud tattooed on one of her biceps and a cigarette dangling from her painted lip.

There was no way she was going into the back room. K.K. had had it out for her back then, because Gary had turned down every overture the hussy had made toward him. K.K. hadn't handled the rejection very well, and she had blamed Gary's refusal on his girlfriend, Phoebe. "I'm not moving from this booth until we leave."

"Why? I think this place is cool." Jocelyn grabbed the laminated menu that had been perched between the salt and pepper shakers and gave it a quick glance. "Think the chili is edible?"

"Only if you drink Kentucky bourbon with it to kill the germs." She snatched the one-page menu from Jocelyn's hand and started to read.

A waitress, wearing skin-tight black shorts and a sleeveless khaki blouse with the bar's logo printed across her

one breast, approached their booth. "What can I get
you two?" The girl didn't look old enough to vote, but
she had both her eyebrow and tongue pierced. In the
dim light it was hard to tell, but her hair might have
been blue.

"I'll take a bowl of chili with cheese on top, and a
glass of whatever you have on tap." Jocelyn turned to
face the waitress, but her gaze was on the far side of the
room, where the long bar was located.

"I'll have the same." What the heck, it had been a
long time since lunch.

She watched as the waitress threaded her way back
through the tables. Most were empty, but a few held
mainly men and the occasional woman enjoying a meal.

Jocelyn turned around and raised one brow. "So
that's Gary?"

Her gaze shot to the bar and was immediately snagged
by a pair of angry green eyes. She couldn't see their
color, but she knew they were green with tiny flecks of
amber. By the scowl on his face, Gary obviously wasn't
happy to see her. Her stupid heart refused to listen to
reason. It soared as if the past eleven years never happened. How was it possible to still be in love with the
thickheaded jerk? She forced herself to give him a
friendly smile and a small wave, before turning back to
Jocelyn. "That's him."

"He's hot, Phoe. Why don't we go sit at the bar and
you can flirt a little with him. See if he bites?"

"Oh, he'll bite all right." She toyed with one of her
bracelets clanging on her wrist. "He'll bite my head
completely off. In case you haven't noticed, he doesn't
seem real pleased to see us here."

Jocelyn did a quick glance over her shoulder. "Nah, I
think you shocked him." Jocelyn smiled. "Is he really
that cute up close?"

"Gary's not Brad Pitt cute; he's more the Harrison
Ford type. Rugged, and all man. He spends just about

all his time on his boat, or working here." She should know. She had been trying to run into him again in town for weeks.

"What's he been doing the last eleven years? You said you broke up when you went to college, right? Is he married? Was he married?"

"He's been working. He's got his own boat now, and a small house back in Misty Harbor. Never got married, and as far as I know never been in a serious relationship." She would know, too. Her mother had been keeping her filled in on all the gossip going on in town for the past eleven years. It got so that her mother just mailed her the weekly local newspaper along with her weekly letters of news and updates that would never be printed in the paper. Her mother would have told her if Gary had been seeing anyone.

"Seems strange, doesn't it?"

"What?" She twisted the silver thumb ring, with an ancient Celtic design, around her thumb a couple of times before she forced herself to stop it. If Gary saw her playing with her jewelry, he would know how nervous she was. It was an old habit, one she still hadn't managed to break.

"A man as good-looking and reasonably financially stable as Gary seems hasn't got a wife and a couple of little ones by now. Hell, Phoe, I can even picture him helping to coach his son's Little League team."

"He doesn't like baseball." Her gaze darted back toward the bar as Gary handed the waitress a tray holding two beers and two bowls of chili. "Gary prefers football or soccer."

"Hmmmm." Jocelyn smiled as the waitress set their steaming bowls in front of them. "Thanks." A bottle of Tabasco sauce, napkins, and two spoons joined the beers on the scarred wooden table.

"If you need anything else, just give a holler." The waitress's attention wasn't on them or their meal. The young woman was eyeing a muscle-bound man sitting at the far end of the bar. The man looked as if he could bench press tuna boats just for the fun of it.

Jocelyn tasted the chili first. She said, "Not bad," as she dipped her spoon back into the bowl.

Phoebe blew on her spoonful and then tasted it. "You're right." She added a splash of Tabasco sauce and wondered who had made the chili. Surely not Gary, and the waitress didn't appear to be the domestic type. "It could use some more fire, though."

"Tell me more about some of the local people in here." Jocelyn took a long sip of beer, but didn't add any Tabasco sauce to her chili.

"You know your sister Sydney's husband, Erik, and his twin brother, Gunnar?"

"The Norse gods of Misty Harbor."

"Gunnar married Maggie Franklin Pierce earlier this year. Gary is Maggie's older brother."

"Maggie has an adorable little girl named Katie," added Jocelyn. "I'm trying to get a convenient time for everyone to come over to Quinn's house for a cookout. Katie and Benjamin will be in the same kindergarten class, and I want them to get to know each other before school starts."

She sighed, "Sounds wonderful." It also sounded like something she should have thought of first. Benjamin needed to make some friends before the first day of school. Quinn's house was too isolated and away from the center of town where the majority of the kids lived.

"You'll be invited of course."

"I wasn't hinting for an invitation, Jocelyn. I'm just upset that I hadn't thought of that first. Ben and the twins had lots of friends back in Boston. There were neighborhood kids and kids in the same day care. Now they only have each other. They need to get out more and socialize."

"I agree. Issy wants to take ballet lessons, but when I

mentioned this to Quinn, he said she's too young." Jocelyn frowned at her beer. "What do you think? Is three years old too young for dance lessons?"

"I think we definitely need to look into dance lessons for Issy. As long as we aren't the ones pushing her into it, I think it would be great." The sad truth was, she hadn't been paying attention or putting in the time needed to be a good aunt. Even with Jocelyn living there, Quinn and the kids still needed her help, and she had been too busy and self-centered working all the time. More than likely Quinn didn't know the first thing about ballet lessons, and he was too stubborn to ask. "All it would take is Quinn seeing Issy in one of those cute little tutu things spinning in circles and smiling, and he'd pay any price. Heck, he'd probably head up the car pooling."

"Tori wants to ride a horse, but I'm not too sure about that one. Tori's awfully little, and horses are awfully big."

Phoebe thought about Tori, her three-year-old daredevil niece. She could definitely see Tori sitting fearlessly on the back of one of those beasts. Of course, she could also picture Quinn having heart failure when she took her first tumble. "Maybe she can start off with pony lessons. A very small pony."

Jocelyn grinned. "I hadn't thought of that one. You know anyone who has a pony around here?"

"No, but I'll do some checking on ponies if you look for a dance studio. We'll gang up on Quinn and get the kids involved with activities outside of the home."

Jocelyn scraped the last of her chili from the bottom of the bowl and glanced around the room. Quinn's nanny seemed to get enormous pleasure out of telling her, "Gary's still staring at you."

She shot a quick glance at Gary and then went back to scraping the bottom of her own bowl. Jocelyn was right, but she refused to read anything into it. There could be a hundred reasons why Gary was staring daggers at her. Her gaze quickly scanned the room. "He's not the only one staring at us." With a heavy sigh, she added, "If I'm not mistaken, we are about to get company."

Chapter Ten

Two local fishermen approached their table. The one wearing a T-shirt with a beer advertisement tipped his cap and slurred, "Evening, ladies."

Manners dictated that Phoebe give them both a polite smile. Clem, a forty-something fisherman, whom she had recognized from her youth, appeared to have drunk his dinner. Last she heard, Clem was married with a boatload of kids. Someone should definitely take the keys away from the other guy, Mr. Miller Time. He was swaying on his feet.

Clem was trying to hold in his gut, but he wasn't succeeding. It would take more than a few clenched stomach muscles to hold in that amount of blubber. "Would you ladies care to dance?"

Phoebe looked around for a dance floor, but couldn't spot one. There was maybe a ten-foot area between the tables and the first pool table. Lynyrd Skynyrd's "Free Bird" was playing on the jukebox. "Thank you for asking, Clem, but we're just getting ready to leave." She gave Jocelyn a soft kick to the shin under the table. There was no way she wanted to dance with Clem or his friend. "We only stopped in for something to eat before heading to the mall to do some shopping." She couldn't think of a better excuse, and most men would run in the other direction as soon as a woman mentioned the word "shopping."

Clem blinked his red-rimmed eyes in surprise. "You know me?"

"Just about all my life." Her smile grew in proportion with Clem's discomfort. Served the bozo right for trying to pick up women in a bar. Someone should tell his wife. "Phoebe Larson. I live down the street from your in-laws." Either Clem got a whopper of a sunburn today out in his boat, or he was blushing. "Speaking of in-laws, how's Dolores and all the kids. Last I heard you have what, four or five of those little tykes?"

"Six, all girls, and Dolores is as big as a house with number seven." Clem's eyes narrowed as recognition finally dawned on him. "You're Quinn's baby sister."

Jocelyn chuckled, and then tried to cover it up by coughing.

"That's me." She gave Jocelyn another kick under the table. "Baby sister to the sheriff."

Mr. Miller Time gave a wide smile that showed off the fact he was missing a bottom tooth. "Clem, you can have that one." His smile widened as he stared at Jocelyn. The light from the flickering candle on the table gleamed off a silver cap in his mouth. "I'm taking this one."

She saw Jocelyn flinch and watched as her polite smile grew harder. The best thing they could do was to make a hasty retreat and avoid any unpleasant scenes. "Sorry, boys, but as I already told you, we're on our way out." She quickly figured out what their meal should have cost and mentally added a tip. She pulled a few bills from her purse that would more than cover it and tossed them onto the table. "Ready, Jocelyn?"

Jocelyn reached for her purse and casually slipped the strap over her head. "Ready as I'll ever be."

Clem took a quick step back as Phoebe slid out of the

booth and stood. She didn't know what he respected more, the fact that she knew him, and about his wife and kids, or that she was the sheriff's baby sister.

The other guy wasn't so smart. Mr. Miller Time blocked Jocelyn's escape. "Now, that ain't very friendly of you, sweetheart." He pressed himself in closer. "All I want is one little dance."

Jocelyn held her ground at the edge of the seat. "We're leaving now, sorry." Jocelyn swung her jean-clad legs out and nearly got her feet tangled with the stranger's. "If you would be so kind as to back up, I would like to leave now."

Clem cleared his throat. "Um . . . Dave, maybe we should go get another cold one." Clem obviously was the brains of the dynamic duo.

"You go." Dave's voice grew louder. "I want to dance with this sweet thing."

A guy flaunting a long gray ponytail, a full beard, and a loud parrot-print silk shirt joined them. "Dave, the lady said she wants to leave, so back off."

Phoebe had noticed the man eating his solitary meal at a nearby table a while ago. The man could be a ringer for the now-deceased Jerry Garcia on a Hawaiian vacation. He looked vaguely familiar, but she couldn't place him. She gave him a small smile, "Thank you."

He nodded, but his attention was on Dave, who was turning more belligerent by the moment. "Butt out of this, Karl, it ain't your business."

"Dave," sighed Karl as he sadly shook his head. "The lady wants to do some shopping. Let's step over to the bar, and I'll buy you another cold one."

"You got a filthy habit of always butting your nose in where it doesn't belong, James." A huge, towering man, half the age, but twice the size of Karl, joined their group.

Phoebe's heart sank. She had a feeling this was going to get ugly fast. At least she finally placed Karl. Karl James was a fellow artist whose medium was wood. He was relatively new to the area and the art scene, and was considered by many a man of mystery. Articles she had read about him labeled him a recluse. Obviously they weren't accurate, because everyone in the bar seemed to know who he was.

"Go back to your pool game, John," said Karl. "This doesn't concern you." Karl didn't seem rattled by the sheer size of John or the fact that Dave looked ready to take a swing at him.

John took a threatening step closer. "Where in the hell is my wife, James?"

One of Karl's gray and bushy brows rose in astonishment. "How would I know? Did you lose Marla?"

"You know damn ass well where she is!" shouted John. "I want her and the boy home, now!"

She glanced at Jocelyn, who was definitely feeling the same apprehension. In about two seconds, all hell was going to break loose, and they were going to be stuck right smack in the middle of it. Dave was still crowding Jocelyn into the booth.

A few of the patrons picked up their meals and drinks and headed for the far end of the room. Most of the men hurried forward, either to see the action up close, or to join in the melee. By the look of anticipation on their faces, Phoebe wasn't sure which.

Karl drew John away from the booth, by backing up a step or two. He relaxed on the balls of his feet and smiled. "What? Is it awfully lonely living by yourself with no one to punch around anytime you feel like it?"

The next moment, utter chaos erupted in the bar. John flew over the few feet that separated him from Karl. Dave decided it was the perfect opportunity to reach for Jocelyn. Clem, finally coming to his senses, grabbed Dave. Dave swung at Clem as Jocelyn's foot connected with his thigh.

Dave and Clem were both knocked into the gathering crowd. A few patrons took exception to having the drunks land on them and came out swinging. The sound of flesh connecting with flesh, groans, and grunts could be heard over Steppenwolf's "Born to Be Wild" now blaring from the jukebox. Somewhere a table was knocked over, and the sound of breaking glass and cursing echoed off the walls.

Phoebe looked at Jocelyn, jerked her head toward the poolroom, and shouted, "Back door!" Jocelyn nodded in agreement, and they started to make their way around flying fists and staggering bodies.

They had gotten about four feet when someone grabbed Phoebe's left arm and tried to pull her to the right. She reacted on pure instinct and her brother's many lessons. Her right fist connected with someone's face before she even looked to see who it was. Pain radiated from every finger as her rings dug in.

"Damn it, Phoebe!" shouted Gary Franklin as he hauled her and Jocelyn to a far corner of the room. The back door was blocked by sweating and heaving bodies pulverizing each other. Gary's right eye was turning red and watering.

She fought an extreme urge to giggle. In all likelihood she had just given Gary a black-and-blue eye. Quinn would be so proud of her. Of course, her brother was going to have a cow once he learned she had been in the middle of a barroom brawl. Gary shoved her and Jocelyn behind his back and into the corner as a bar stool landed on a nearby pool table.

In all the commotion she could hear K.K. laughing and cheering someone on. She tried to peer around Gary's shoulder, but he quickly shifted his position and blocked her in more. She glanced at Jocelyn, who had her back pressed against the paneling. Her nieces' and nephew's nanny was standing on her toes, looking over Gary's other shoulder, and grinning ear-to-ear. Quinn wasn't going to have a cow; he was going to kill his one and only sister for putting his housekeeper in danger.

Quinn hadn't even admitted it to himself yet, but there was more than a spark or two between him and Jocelyn. She just hoped her brother wasn't stupid enough not to act on it before Jocelyn headed back to Baltimore.

With her breasts pressed against Gary's back, she was close enough to smell his aftershave and feel the heat of his body. Gary smelled of sunshine and the sea. She wiggled in closer and smiled as she felt Gary stiffen in response. Her fingers clutched at his waist, and her breath bathed his neck and the back of his ear. "Sorry about the eye."

Gary grunted something, but didn't turn around. His concentration was on the fighting and the rare piece of flying furniture.

She felt incredibly safe and protected behind Gary. She still couldn't believe how fast he had gotten her and Jocelyn out of the thick of things. It was extremely sweet of Gary to come to their rescue, even though they didn't need the rescuing. Jocelyn and she might not have made it out the back door, with the two oafs on steroids pounding each other and blocking the way. But they could have made it to the ladies' room and either barricaded the door or snuck out the window if there was one.

The fighting was finally quieting down. She glanced over Gary's shoulder to see if people were just tired from beating on each other, or if there were bodies littering the floor. John, the big brute who had started the whole thing, was lying on the floor either dead or unconscious. Karl was standing idly by the body drinking a beer. Karl wasn't even breathing hard.

Gary followed her gaze and shouted, "Did you kill him this time, Karl?"

"Nah." Karl nudged John's rib cage with the toe of his boot. "He's just taking a little nap." Karl's gaze searched for her and Jocelyn. "You took care of the ladies, Gary?"

"Yeah, I grabbed them."

As the music died down, the sound of distant sirens could be heard. She looked at Jocelyn and silently mouthed the word, "Quinn."

Jocelyn rolled her eyes and stepped around Gary. The fighting was done. Most of the grunts and groans were coming from men picking themselves up off the wooden floor. The patrons at the far end of the bar were leisurely finishing their meals and surveying the damage.

Gary finally turned around and demanded, "Are you all right?"

She frowned at his eye. It was not only swelling shut, but she had managed to cut him on the cheek with one of her rings. Tiny drops of blood marred his wind-burned cheek. She tenderly traced his cheekbone, being careful not to touch the small scrape. "Ouch, that must hurt."

Gary's gaze was busy skimming her from head to toe. "Only when you touch it." He pulled away from her finger. "Are you sure you aren't hurt?"

"Positive. The only one who laid a hand on me was you." The sirens came to a screeching halt out front of the bar, causing her to frown. "Tell me you didn't call Quinn."

"I didn't call Quinn." Gary shook his head at such a ridiculous question. "I called the cops as soon as John confronted Karl."

"I take it they have a history." She was half-relieved to know she and Jocelyn hadn't been the cause of the free-for-all. Somehow she didn't think Quinn would be as thrilled.

"You could say that." Gary instinctively stepped in front of her again as the front door burst open. Quinn was the first one through the door, followed quickly by a deputy. "Now the shit is going to hit the fan."

The deputy trying to make it through the back door was having a harder time of it. Over five hundred pounds of pressure was holding it closed. Both men, who moments before were trying to arrange each other's faces, were sitting against the door, trying to catch their breath and grinning at each other. K.K. handed each of them a beer.

One look at Quinn's face and she knew she and Jocelyn were never going to hear the end of this. Big brothers were a pain in the ass sometimes. She waved at Quinn, but he didn't seem to notice. Her brother was too busy taking in the sight of Jocelyn, who was removing the bar stool from the center of the pool table.

Quinn marched across the room, stepping over John, who was now groaning. Her brother reached out and yanked the bar stool out of Jocelyn's hand. "What in the hell do you think you are doing?"

Jocelyn's chin rose an inch. "I don't *think* I'm doing anything. I *am* putting the stool back where it belongs."

Phoebe held in her laughter and whispered to Gary, "This is about to get interesting."

"I take it this is Doc Sydney and Gwen's sister, Jocelyn?" Gary leaned against the wall and watched. "She looks like them. Still can't picture her playing nanny to Quinn's kids, though."

"The kids adore her."

"Seems to me, more than the kids adore her." Gary chuckled at Quinn's frustration.

Quinn turned and faced Phoebe. His voice shook the rafters. "What in the hell were you thinking, coming in here?"

Gary pushed off the wall, but she stepped in front of him and confronted her brother. The last thing she wanted was for Gary and Quinn to get into it. "I was thinking about a nice bowl of chili and a cold beer."

Quinn waved his arm in Jocelyn's direction. "I can't believe you were stupid enough to bring her in here."

Gary moved her aside. "Now, wait a minute, Quinn. That wasn't very fair."

"Keep out of this, Franklin." Quinn looked ready to

take someone apart with his bare hands. She had never seen her brother react like this before.

"Excuse me, Quinn, but I walked in here on my own free will." Jocelyn turned to Quinn and jammed her finger into his chest. "Phoebe didn't drag me in here." Her finger jabbed again. "I'm twenty-six years old, and I surely don't need you or anyone else telling me where I can and can't go."

Phoebe watched as her brother, for the first time in his life that she knew about, was at a loss for words. Quinn stared at Jocelyn with his jaw clenched and his eyes burning. In frustration, Quinn turned on Gary. "What in the hell happened to your eye?"

K.K. ambled over, stared at Gary's rapidly swelling eye, and snorted. "Hey, Phoebe, you have one hell of a right hook." K.K. took a long swallow of beer and grinned. "Always figured you for one of those artsy types. Too busy trying to save the dolphins and making flowers out of tissue paper to get down and dirty with the rest of humanity."

Before she could form a response to such high praise, Quinn rounded on her and demanded, "You did that to Gary?"

She held up her right hand and gently blew on her throbbing fingers. "Yeah, and it hurt like hell."

Gary grabbed her hand. "Here, let me see." His fingers were gentle as they skimmed the back of her hand and over her rings. "Guess I should consider myself lucky that you didn't take out an eye with all these rings."

She glanced at his eye. "I think it needs ice."

"Come on." Gary started to drag her over to the bar.

"Franklin, I'm closing you down for the rest of the night." Quinn nodded to his deputies, who started to usher patrons out the door.

"Fine with me," said Gary as he headed for a small room behind the bar. A moment later lights went on throughout the bar.

Quinn looked around the place in disgust and then asked Karl, "Which one of these hotheads started it?"

"John and Dave Brown." Karl finished picking up a table that had been knocked over and then joined Quinn.

"Dave gave you a hard time?" Quinn kept frowning at Jocelyn as she went around the bar straightening up the occasional chair and bar stool.

"Naw, Dave was giving"—Karl nodded in Jocelyn's direction—"that one a hard time. Seems he wanted to dance and she didn't. When John came after me, Dave made a grab for her, but Clem halfway stopped him."

"Who stopped him the other half?"

Phoebe tried to gauge Quinn's reaction. On the temper scale, it was one step below explosive. Over the last four minutes, her calm, cool, and always in control brother had developed a tick in his jaw. Amazing.

Karl chuckled and grinned at Jocelyn, who was pretending to ignore the entire conversation. "The little lady. She gave him such a kick that he went stumbling backward into the crowd of onlookers, who didn't take kindly to his bumbling ways." Karl helped a deputy get John to his feet. "If Clem hadn't knocked Dave off balance at that precise moment, let me tell you, Dave would be singing soprano for the rest of his life."

Quinn stood in the middle of the bar with his eyes closed. Phoebe wasn't sure, but he might have been counting. She chuckled until Gary emerged from the back room with a plastic bag of ice and carefully placed it on her hand. "Ouch, what are you doing?"

"You said it needed ice." Gary held on to her hand and the ice bag as he glanced around the bar. "Jocelyn, stop straightening up. There's a cleaning lady who will handle all that in the morning, and she gets paid by the hour."

"Hey, it's in the blood." Jocelyn grinned at Phoebe and Gary. "I'm a housekeeper you know."

Quinn growled something, but she couldn't catch the words.

K.K. helped usher the two behemoths from the back room. "Come on, you two. We've got some cold ones back at our place."

"Who's driving, K.K.?" asked Gary.

"I am. We'll pick Stan's bike up in the morning." K.K. gave a wide smile that didn't actually make her beautiful, but it did soften her face. "Nice to see you two finally back together."

She could feel Gary's stare, but refused to meet his eye. K.K. made an honest mistake. Anyone seeing them standing so close together, with Gary holding her hand, would have jumped to the same conclusion.

The waitress, who actually had teal-colored hair, finally left the arms of the towering hulk at the end of the bar. She had taken refuge there when the fight had broken out. "Does this mean I can go home now?"

Gary smiled. "Sure, Jen."

Jen hurried back to the hulk. "Quinn, someone needs to drive Clem home." Gary nodded to Clem, who was sitting in a booth with a cold bottle of beer pressed to his jaw. Gary released Phoebe's hand and the ice bag to pull a set of keys out of his pocket and tossed them to Quinn. "These are his. I took them about an hour ago."

Quinn caught the keys with one hand and then tossed them to the nearest deputy. "Can you drop him off on your way in with Dave?"

"Sure." The deputy shook his head at Clem. "Anything else?"

"See if you can get a hold of Doc Sydney and see if she can stop by and examine John. He was out of it for a while."

"Will do." The deputy escorted Clem from the bar.

"Well, shoot, there goes my Friday night." Karl placed a couple of bills onto the bar and headed for the door.

Quinn gave his sister and Gary a long, hard look before turning to Jocelyn and saying, "Come on, I'm taking you home."

Half an hour later, Phoebe followed Gary into his house. She had been dying to see what his home looked like, but she refrained from gawking at every room. She got right down to the business of treating his eye. "I'll go get some ice. Got anything to put it in?"

"I told you, I can take care of my own eye." Gary winced as his fingertips caressed the swollen skin. "It doesn't even hurt."

She rolled her eyes and headed for the kitchen. "If that's the case, I'm running you into the emergency room. Nothing that swollen can't hurt, unless there is some nerve damage." The whole time back at The One Eyed Squid, Gary had refused to allow her to take the ice pack off her hand or to look at his eye. Her fingers were now beet red and frozen, but at least the pain was gone.

"Fine, it hurts like an S.O.B.," snapped Gary as he rummaged through a drawer and came up holding a plastic Ziploc bag. "Are you happy now?"

"I'd be happier if it had been Dave's or John's face I connected with instead of yours." She snatched the bag from his hand and opened the freezer door. *Stubborn, pigheaded men!* Gary probably couldn't even see out of his eye, yet he had insisted on driving home. She had followed closely behind with her Jeep, worrying the whole time that he would go blind and wrap his pickup around some tree. Gary had then expected her to wave him good-bye, at his driveway, and be on her way. Fat chance that was going to happen. She had been the one to give him the shiner; she would be the one to treat it.

Besides, tonight was going a lot better than she thought it would. She was now alone with Gary in his house. His cute little white cottage with its red door and shutters.

The main floor of his home consisted of a living room, kitchen, and an eating area. Above them were the bedrooms and a bath. From what she had seen already, Gary's home was clean but slightly cluttered. Gary obviously liked the color green.

She reached for the last handful of ice and smiled at the carton next to the plastic ice bin. "Nice ice pops." Winnie the Pooh and Tigger stared back at her from the box. "You actually eat those?"

"They're my nieces' favorite." Gary grabbed the bag from her hand and placed it over his eye. "There, it's all better. You can leave now."

She chuckled and shook her head. She would have been insulted if she hadn't seen the way Gary had cringed when the bag touched his eye. "Go make yourself comfortable on the couch and tell me where you keep the aspirins?"

"I can get my own aspirins, thank you very much." Gary sounded like a bear rudely awakened from his nap.

"Go sit down," her voice held a hard edge, and her finger pointed to the living room.

Gary glared at her with one green eye. "When did you become so bossy?"

She glared back and refused to allow him to intimidate her. "When did you become so stubborn?"

"Fine, have it your way." Gary turned and walked out of the room. "The aspirins are in the cabinet above the toaster. I definitely feel a headache coming on now."

She suppressed a rude comeback and glanced around the kitchen. Damn if Gary wasn't domesticated. Toaster, coffeemaker, microwave, and even curtains fluttering in the evening breeze. A couple of dishes were draining in the rack, but not a single dirty dish was in the sink. The wooden cabinets were old, but boasted a new coat of dark green paint. The walls were the same color as the living room and small dining area, beige. Pine floors were throughout the house, but each room had a soft area rug.

By the contents of his freezer, Gary knew how to cook more than frozen dinners in the microwave. The dining room held a wooden table with four mismatched chairs and two overflowing bookshelves. A month's worth of newspapers were piled on one of the chairs. Another held magazines, and an open book lay facedown on a green plaid place mat.

There was only one place mat at the table.

Was Gary's life as lonely as hers?

She turned from surveying the rest of the room and opened the cabinet directly above the toaster. The lower shelf was filled with a mishmash of over-the-counter medicines. She reached for the aspirin bottle and shook two into her palm. After filling a glass with water, she headed for the living room.

Gary was stretched out on an old leather recliner that should have been driven to the dump a decade ago. The green couch looked relatively new, so did the television. The rest of the room looked worn, comfortable, and very much like she had pictured Gary's house.

"Here, sit up and swallow these."

Gary lowered the ice pack, popped the two tablets into his mouth, and washed them down with the entire glass of water. "Thank you, Florence Nightingale."

She took the empty glass. "If I didn't know better, I would swear you're upset that a mere girl gave you that shiner instead of some hulking biker brute."

"You know better than that." Gary replaced the ice bag.

At one time she had known everything about Gary. His one and only fear had been of sharks, and his secret fantasy had included her, naked, a bottle of coconut oil, and a private sandy beach. Gary had whispered that fantasy to her in the front seat of his truck when they had been eighteen and a hairbreadth away from hitting a home run.

As fantasies went, it was a pretty tame one. She had to wonder what the man Gary had become would fantasize about.

She returned the glass to the kitchen before Gary could see the blush her secret fantasy had wrought.

Hope had leaped into her heart the moment Gary had stepped in front of her to protect her during the brawl. When it had been over, Gary had turned to her first and demanded to know if she was all right. Not Jocelyn. Not any other patron. Her.

A smile curved her lips as she found a tube of antibacterial cream. She yelled, "Where do you keep your towels?"

"In the bathroom."

"No, your kitchen towels?"

"Second drawer, to the right of the sink. Why?"

"You'll see." She found a clean towel and wetted one end of it. A moment later she was standing by the recliner and gently removing the ice pack. "I want to see that cut."

"It's fine, Phoebe." Gary tried to grab the ice out of her hand.

She tossed it onto the rug and leaned against the arm of the chair. "Don't move, this will only take a second." She tenderly wiped at the dry blood and was thankful the cut was small and shallow. She shuddered to think of the damage her ring could have caused.

"Phoebe, I don't think—"

"Shhh . . . Don't think and be still." She wiggled farther onto the arm of the chair to get a better look at the damage. The eye was nearly swollen shut, but if she wasn't mistaken, the ice was helping some of the swelling to go down. "It's going to be a beaut by morning." She softly patted his cheek dry. With the tip of a finger, she applied the medicated cream. "This should kill the germs."

"Why, you have a lot of them?" Gary was staring at her mouth.

Phoebe capped the tube and frowned at her hands. Rough hands, that bore the scars of working with stained glass all day long for years. Nicks, small cuts, and the occasional burn mark lined her fingers. Hand creams could only do so much. "Probably millions." She quickly lowered her hands, slid off the arm of the chair, and retrieved the ice bag. "Put this back on." She handed him the bag. "Could I get you something before I go? Maybe a cold drink or a cup of coffee?" The night was still young. It was barely ten o'clock.

"Coffee sounds great"—Gary rose from the chair—"but I'm making it. You're a guest." Gary headed for the kitchen.

She followed him. "I'm not your guest. In case you forgot, I kind of barged in here."

Gary put a filter into the machine and added the grounds. "So, you're a pushy guest."

"I'm not pushy." She walked into the dining room and started to scan the titles of his books.

Gary snorted as water dripped through the filter. "Since when?"

She felt it would be better for both of them if she ignored that remark. "I see you still like history." The shelves were crammed with fat tomes of boring history. Mostly American, with an occasional European or Irish one crowded in between. Gary had struggled with algebra, but had aced every history exam he had ever taken. Curiously, she asked, "Ever make it to Gettysburg?"

"Five years ago." Gary lifted the lid off a bright red lobster cookie jar. "You still like Oreo cookies?"

"Regular or double stuffed?" She felt her heart jerk at the thought of Gary at Gettysburg. One summer afternoon, long ago, they had been playing the basketball game of twenty-one at his house. Winner was going to choose where they would be spending their honeymoon.

Gary had wanted Gettysburg, while she had been holding out for Disney World. Gary had won.

"Double stuffed." Gary pulled out a plate and started to load the cookies on.

"My favorite." Gary had once claimed there was nothing more erotic than watching her pull apart an Oreo cookie and lick the creamy white filling.

Gary slid the plate onto a tray and added two cups. "They're Katie's favorite, too."

So much for twisting those cookies apart and turning him on tonight. She nodded to a basket sitting in the corner of the room. The woven basket held coloring books, crayons, books, and a couple Beanie Babies. "You get Katie a lot?"

"At least once a week. Maggie and Gunnar are still newlyweds, and they could use some privacy. Five-year-old little girls aren't conducive to romance, or so I've been told. Besides, she's a great kid, and we have a ball together." He filled the cups and carried the tray out into the living room.

She slowly followed and sat on the far end of the sofa. "You have a lovely home, Gary." She glanced around the room and realized for the first time Gary had indeed made a home out of the cottage.

His books lined the shelves. A breathtaking oil painting of a deep pine forest, after a winter's storm, graced the wall above the mantel. The far wall held a portrait of Joshua Chamberlain, a Civil War hero, and at one time the governor of Maine.

There were ice pops in the freezer and a cookie jar filled with double stuffed Oreos for his niece.

Gary had achieved his dream of owning his own lobster boat and becoming his own boss. His truck was new enough that he was probably still paying on it. Gary had reached every goal that he had set for himself.

And he had done it all, without her.

Chapter Eleven

Jocelyn was ticked at Quinn. An uncomfortable silence had reigned during their drive home from The One Eyed Squid. She guessed she should be thankful that Quinn had allowed her to sit up front in the SUV instead of being locked behind the thick metal mesh screen that protected Quinn, the sheriff, from unsavory and crazed criminals. Quinn should be thankful that she had gotten in the car without an argument in the first place.

If Karl James hadn't already left, she might have been tempted to hitch a ride home with him. At least Karl had seemed like a gentleman. Quinn had acted like a dictator. Orders to his deputies she understood. Orders to her, especially when they had nothing to do with the children or the house, were inexcusable.

For the first time since arriving in Misty Harbor, something exciting had been happening in her life. She had never been in a barroom brawl before, and it had been electrifying watching furniture flying, glasses shattering, and grown men duking it out for no other reason than it was Friday night and the beer had flowed a little too freely. She knew the main reason she had enjoyed the show, and not been scared out of her wits, was because of Gary Franklin's wide shoulders and protective stance.

Anyone with a lick of sense could have seen the way Gary had protected Phoebe. Jocelyn had just been lucky enough to get included in that protection. There obviously had been plenty of history between Gary and Phoebe, and if tonight was any indication, there just might be a future. When Quinn and she had left the bar, Gary had still been fussing over Phoebe's hand. There had been no way she would have intruded on their reunion and asked Phoebe for a ride home.

Hence she had been stuck with sourpuss Quinn.

Tomorrow morning she was going to be grilling Phoebe for all the juicy details of her and Gary's reunion.

As for tonight, she was heading for bed. The last thing she wanted to do was to get into a fight with Quinn, and if the man opened his mouth one more time tonight, it wasn't going to be an argument. It was going to be a battle. And she was probably going to lose her job, along with her temper.

Spending the rest of her time in Maine updating Sydney's patient files and living with Gwen and Daniel didn't sound like fun in her book. Besides, she wasn't ready to go back to Baltimore quite yet. She hadn't figured out her life.

When she first came to Maine, she figured her life was such a jumbled mess that it could only get better. She had been wrong. Now she was more confused than ever as to which direction she wanted her life and her career to go.

She walked through the kitchen and locked the patio doors and turned off the lights. Quinn was out front, seeing his mother to her car, and the children were all asleep in their beds. So far she hadn't seen Max, but her money was on the mutt sleeping with Issy. Max had de-

veloped a fondness for hundred-percent cotton sheets
and fluffy pillows.

Through the dining room window she could see
Quinn talking to his mother and shaking his head. She
also saw the row of neatly pressed uniforms hanging from
the top of the hutch cabinet. Starched collars, just the
way Quinn liked them, and creases in his pants sharp
enough to cut cheese hung exactly one inch apart across
half the hutch. Quinn's mother obviously had been busy
pressing the five uniforms. Not even Quinn could have
been that meticulous of an ironer. The rest of the laundry that had been folded and piled on the table when
she had left with Phoebe was now gone. The mahogany
table gleamed from a recent polishing, and the blanket
fort that had taken up half the room had been disas-
sembled. Mrs. Larson had been one very busy woman.

Nothing like being shown up in the cleaning category by a woman old enough to be your mother. So she
wasn't the best housekeeper on the East Coast. Sue her.

With a weary sigh, she headed upstairs. Ben's door
was wide open, and the little boy was asleep on his back
and with the covers kicked off. She stepped into his
room and gently pulled the lightweight blanket up to
his shoulders. Her fingers tenderly brushed a lock of
his dark hair off his forehead, before placing a soft kiss
on the spot.

Over the past several weeks Ben and his sisters had
become very special to her. Maybe too special. She knew
Quinn was worried the children would be upset when it
was time for her to head back to Baltimore and out of
their lives. Quinn had talked to his kids about the meaning of temporary. She had talked to the kids about her
apartment and life back in Baltimore. Even Aunt Phoebe
was helping them to understand. No one, including
herself, had figured her feelings into the equation.

Who would have thought a trio of munchkins with

bad eating habits and worse personal hygiene would steal their way into her heart. It wasn't fair. They were supposed to be showing her what having children of her own one day would be like, not confusing her life more.

So far this job had confirmed her belief that one day she would want children, two, possibly three. It also pointed out one very important fact that she, and her future husband and father of those two-point-five kids, better be raking in the bucks. Life was not cheap. Life with children was going to get downright expensive. First there was the cost of a nanny. Since she and her future husband would be working, someone needed to be home with the babies. Then there was the housekeeper's salary. She didn't mind riding around Quinn's lawn on the mower, or even tending the flower gardens. So doing the yard work at her upscale, suburban fantasy house somewhere outside of Baltimore would be okay.

The one thing she would not do for the rest of her life was scrub toilets, wash floors, and try to get stubborn grass stains out of clothes. The housekeeping gene was definitely missing from her DNA. Cooking dinner seven nights a week was out of the question. Where in the world was she supposed to find the time for all of that while putting in seventy- to eighty-hour workweeks, like she had been doing back in Baltimore?

Then again, if she started to put that many hours in again, she wouldn't have the time to find that future husband, let alone squeeze in an hour or two to make those babies she had always dreamed about.

Maybe there was more to the fact she had walked away from the DA's office besides watching a drug dealer go free.

She heard Quinn's mom drive away and a moment later the front door close. She quietly left Ben's room and headed for the girls' room. She was sure their grandmother had done a wonderful job tucking them in, but checking up on them had become a nightly habit. One that she would eventually have to break, but not tonight. Now she needed to make sure Issy and Tori were tucked safely into their beds.

Max, who was indeed lying across the foot of Issy's bed and using one of her Cinderella shams as a pillow, turned his head and looked at her as she entered the girls' room. At least she thought the dog opened his eyes. With all that hair covering his face, it was hard to tell if he even had eyes, let alone if they were open or not. She patted Max's head. "Good boy."

A warm pink tongue licked her hand.

Jocelyn wiped the back of her hand on her jeans and refused to think about what else Max might have licked recently. She removed two large stuffed animals and three plastic dolls that were crowding Issy against the wall. Between Max and the Disney Corporation the poor girl barely had enough room in her own bed. As gently as possible she moved the sleeping girl back into the center of the bed, tucked in one cute and cuddly stuffed animal, and kissed the top of her head. A soft, contented sigh whispered through perfectly formed rosebud lips. The light from the hallway made Issy's hair look like fine golden silk, and there was a touch of summer's color on her baby-soft cheeks. Issy looked like a fairy-tale princess when she slept.

She glanced over to the other bed and grinned. Tori looked like a combination of the mythical Medusa and Roy Rogers. The only thing missing was Trigger. Tori's nightshirt was covered in horses, and even in the dim light she could tell Quinn's mother had not gotten a brush through the girl's hair. Waves of golden tangles were everywhere, giving Tori's hair that writhing snake appearance. Quinn hadn't been too thrilled with her when she had trimmed Tori's remaining bangs halfway up her brow. But he had to agree, her hair was looking a lot better now that the scalped bangs were growing back. In another month or so, Tori just might have bangs that were all the same length. Short.

With three steps, she was at the edge of Tori's bed. Tori had kicked off all the covers, which wasn't unusual. What was strange was that Quinn's mom had allowed Tori to wear her red cowboy boots and fringed faux leather vest to bed. Tori and her sister were identical twins, but in the place of soft, gentle sighs, Tori snored. Instead of being some helpless princess who would need rescuing, Tori was some kick-ass heroine who would probably rescue the prince. Together, the twins would make the perfect Disney movie.

As gently as possible she removed the vest and tugged the first boot off the little girl's foot. Tori hadn't bothered with socks. Then again, Tori didn't bother with a lot of things unless one stood behind her and gave explicit instructions. Like, brush your teeth, wash your hands, get the tricycle off the hood of your daddy's car, and stop feeding the dog garlic. Tori's latest heart-attack-provoking trick had been trying to ride Max down the stairs. She had thought Quinn had recovered nicely from that episode until she caught him downing a shot glass full of brandy about an hour later. Heck, she hadn't even known the brandy had been hiding in the back of the kitchen cabinet. A shot or two would have helped her nerves the morning Tori had taken it into her head to use the porch railings as a balance beam. Luckily Tori's head was hard and the azalea bush, where she had landed, had been soft.

"We need to talk." Quinn stood in the doorway watching her.

"Sh . . ." She didn't want the girls to wake up. The second boot came off, and she placed both on the floor near the foot of the bed. It took her a moment to untangle the sheet from the comforter and assorted stuffed animals. When she had Tori tucked back in, she bent and placed a kiss on those uneven bangs.

By the time she straightened back up, Quinn was kissing Issy good night. It was a touching scene. One that brought home the fact that if someone looked in on them right this moment, they would think they were all one big, happy family. The atmosphere was a little too *intimate* for her, so she slipped quietly out of the room.

She took refuge behind her closed bedroom door. Quinn rarely came into her bedroom. On the occasions when he was called out in the middle of the night, she usually heard the phone ring, or he pressed sticky notes to her door to let her know he was gone, in case she awoke. Her laptop and a small mound of papers were on the table in front of the window. Quinn had given her permission weeks ago to use his Internet account to check on her own e-mail.

Since it was still early, tonight would be the perfect time to check further into Abraham Martin's mom's problem. This afternoon when Abraham had stopped by, she had some of the answers for him, but not all. Abraham's mom was still leery about going to some unknown attorney. Jocelyn was bending over and plugging into the phone line when there was a knock on the door. *Damn, he is persistent.* "Come in," she called.

Quinn stepped into the room and watched as she booted up the computer. "Checking for messages?"

"Nope, doing some research for Abraham Martin." She clicked on the dial-up icon, and the grating sound she so despised filled the room. "You should look into getting DSL for the Internet. It's faster."

Quinn chuckled. "Yeah, like that would happen this decade. We didn't even have a local AOL number until two years ago." Quinn stepped farther into the room, but left the door wide open behind him. He leaned against one of the bedposts. "What kind of favor is Abraham asking?"

Quinn hadn't been around during Abraham's two visits, and she hadn't brought it up in any of their conversations. "His mom needs to find a good estate attorney, and I promised him I would look into some legal stuff for them."

"Are you allowed to do that?" Quinn nodded toward the computer.

She sat down in the big comfortable chair and kicked off her shoes. "I'm not hacking into anyone's computer system, Quinn. I'm just verifying what I already know." Quinn looked more concerned than relieved. "Don't worry, I'm not doing anything illegal. You won't have to arrest me or anything."

"That's good to know." Quinn relaxed and sat on the end of the unmade bed. "Be hard to explain to the kids why I'm handcuffing their nanny."

She laughed at the image. "I don't know, Quinn, sounds kind of kinky to me."

Quinn looked ready to say something, but he only shook his head and stared down at the floor. "You like being a lawyer, don't you?"

"You don't pass the bar exam unless you live, eat, and sleep the law. Liking it has nothing to do with it; you have to love it." She pulled both her feet up onto the chair and rested her chin upon her knees. Quinn had never talked about her "real" career before.

"If you love it so much, why did you leave the DA's office in Baltimore? Why come all the way to Misty Harbor to play nanny to a bunch of preschoolers?"

"That's a difficult question to answer." She closed her eyes and thought back to the smirk on Johnny G's face when he had waltzed right out of the courtroom. "Sometimes when a person is standing in the middle of the forest, she gets overwhelmed by all the trees. Dreams of never being able to find her way out become nightmares. Nightmares become fears, and soon you're questioning why you're standing in the forest in the first place."

"Sounds like a typical case of work overload. Why didn't you just book a two-week vacation to the Bahamas and lie around soaking up the sun and frozen daiquiris?"

"I didn't need a vacation, Quinn. I needed a change in my life and my career." She watched Quinn as he struggled to try and understand what she was saying.

"I thought you loved being a lawyer?" His hand waved in the direction of the laptop and pile of paperwork. "You're still doing it."

"I do love being a lawyer. I'm even getting a kick out of helping Abraham and his mom. There are many shades and directions in the law, Quinn. My grandfather, on my dad's side, was the most beloved, hard-ass DA Baltimore ever saw. His name is legendary down there."

"He sounds like my kind of guy."

She wasn't surprised by his comment. Most law enforcement personnel liked a hard-nosed DA who went after criminals with a vengeance. There also was a lot of friction between the two departments. For the DA to get convictions, the police had to do their job, and do it well. Even then, it was never a sure thing. A lot of deals were made in the name of justice. How many little fish did you let go free, so that one day you could nail that bigger fish?

"He died one night at his desk. Massive heart attack at the age of sixty-two. I was only eight years old at the time, and I worshipped the ground he walked on. I made a vow then and there that I would follow in his footsteps."

"You were doing a pretty good job of it. What happened?"

"The footsteps became too big. My grandfather wore a size eleven shoe." She raised one foot and wiggled her toes. "I wear a six and a half."

Quinn seemed to study her foot for a long time. "I'm betting your grandfather never wore peach-colored toenail polish."

She chuckled at the thought of big, burly Grandpop Fletcher painting his toenails. "Peach wasn't his color."

"Always heard that the money was in defense, not the prosecution." Quinn leaned back on his elbows and studied her. "A lot of DAs or assistant DAs leave the office for a lot of different reasons. Political or big money offers from private practices mostly, but a lot of mystery books are being written by former DAs and cops. Ever have the desire to write a murder mystery?"

"No." She shuddered at the thought. "I grow faint at the sight of too much blood, and per my sisters I always miss the best parts of movies because my eyes were either closed or I was screaming my head off."

Quinn's smile was downright sexy. There was something deliriously sensual about the way he was lying across her rumpled bed. It was as if he was waiting for her to come join him. She had to wonder what he would do if she made the first move. The kiss they had shared out on Blueberry Hill had been too mind-numbingly wonderful never to experience it again.

"I thought you liked Poe?" asked Quinn.

"Only his poems."

"Then," said Quinn, "don't go reading any of my books downstairs."

"I already skimmed the titles and know none of them have earned the *Good Housekeeping* seal of approval. You and Sydney should do a book swap. She loves that kind of book. Heck, when I unpacked her books last Thanksgiving, she had many of the same ones you have. You both shop at Serial Killers-R-Us.com or what?"

"Really? A fellow mystery fan?"

"I wouldn't call her a fan. Sick, twisted, and plain old weird, yes, fan no."

"Hey, that's my kids' pediatrician you are talking about."

"She was my sister before your kids' doctor. I get to call her anything I want because I had to live with her and her twisted horror movies for all those years. You know what kind of damage those movies can do to an innocent kid's psyche? I can't even watch a hockey game now without hearing chain saws in my mind."

"I'll concede the point. Sydney is weird and twisted." Quinn's smile grew. "So what type of books do you like to read?"

"Romance."

"Ah, Prince Charming or the lonely billionaire ready to sweep you off your feet?"

At least he didn't tease me about the sex. "Neither, I'm more the Scottish Highlander type."

"Mel Gibson in a kilt?"

"Never underestimate the power of a kilt." She leaned her head back and grinned. "Or Sean Connery's voice."

"So you read them for the same reason I read mysteries, the escapism?"

"I wouldn't call it escapism." She frowned up at the ceiling.

"What would you call it, then?"

"Happily-ever-after." She never even admitted it to her sisters, but for some reason with Quinn she didn't mind telling him the reason behind her love of the genre. "I love knowing that with every book I pick up there will be a happily-ever-after. It's guaranteed. With a mystery, the puzzle is solved by the end of the book, but you aren't guaranteed that happy ending. Heck, there are some mysteries out there where the bad guy is never caught, and he's guaranteed to keep showing up in future books.

"With fantasy it's all about good triumphing over evil. That doesn't mean that the people you came to care about for four hundred pages live." She was really getting into the subject now. "Working in the DA's office, the last thing I wanted to read for pleasure were books about child abuse, politics, or mob bosses with a heart of gold." She sat on the edge of the chair and looked at

Quinn. "You like to study the workings of a criminal mind. I prefer the emotions of the human heart."

Quinn's dark brown gaze seemed to bore into hers. "Do you honestly believe there is a happily-ever-after for everyone?"

"Are we talking in general, or in a relationship? To a great majority of people, simply adding a couple of zeros to their bank accounts would be happiness. If you're talking about a relationship between a man and a woman, that's a whole different ball game."

"How so?"

"If growing prize-winning roses makes a person happy, they can grow the roses. If having a lot of money makes someone happy, that person can get a better job, or do something to bring in the money. If nursing the sick, or volunteering for the needy, or teaching a child to read makes you happy, it's all possible. They are all individual ideas and dreams, all possible of obtaining individually."

Quinn rubbed his jaw. "Makes sense."

"If we're talking the princess kisses the frog, the frog turns into a prince, they get married and live happily-ever-after, it's not the same thing. The difference is love takes two people to obtain one result. If the princess loves the prince, but he doesn't love her in return, there will be no happily-ever-after. One-sided love will only lead to heartbreak."

"So what you are saying is that one person's happiness depends on another person."

"No, what I'm saying is each of them will depend on each other and themselves. Alone they fail. Together they could win."

Quinn snorted. "You've been watching too many Disney movies. Issy's a bad influence on you."

"There's nothing wrong with Disney movies. *Beauty and the Beast* is my all-time favorite." She understood Quinn's skepticism when it came to the happily-ever-afters. He not only had his wife pack up and leave him, but she had also taken his children with her. Quinn now had his children back with him, but the cost had been high. Too high.

She wanted nothing more than to show Quinn there were happily-ever-afters, but life wasn't produced or directed by Disney. One enchanting kiss wasn't a prelude to walking down an aisle wearing white lace and her grandmother's pearls. Life was never that simple.

"You said something about needing to talk to me." The best thing she could do was to change the subject. "What about?"

Quinn stood up and paced to the door and back. "I wanted to apologize to you for being such an ass at The One Eyed Squid. I had no right to jump down your throat like that."

She could see the twitching of the muscle in his jaw and wondered how much this apology was costing him. Was Quinn afraid she would pack her bags and leave him, too? There was a world of difference between having your wife walk out the door and your housekeeper leave. "Apology accepted."

"Just like that?" Quinn looked at her with astonishment.

"Yeah, just like that." She stood up and smiled. She was awfully glad they weren't going to get into an argument. There were a lot of things she wouldn't mind doing with Quinn; fighting wasn't one of them. "I'm not the type to hold a grudge."

"That's good to know." Quinn paced back to the door and seemed to look everywhere but at her. "You do realize how much trouble you could have gotten into there, right?"

She shook her head and sighed. They had been so close to ending this night on a good note. "Drop it, Quinn. You're not my father."

"No, I'm not your father, or your brother, or even your mother." Quinn's voice rose with every word.

"You're my employer, Quinn." The tic in his jaw grew more pronounced. "It's none of your concern how or where I spend my free time."

Quinn's eyes blazed as he turned to her and demanded, "Do you have any idea what went through my head when I pulled into the parking lot of a bar where a brawl was going on and saw Phoebe's Jeep there?"

She took a step back and took a wild guess. "You thought Phoebe could be hurt inside."

"Phoebe can take care of herself; besides, no one would harm a hair on her head knowing she was my sister." Quinn took another step closer. "Phoebe didn't even enter my mind in that moment it took me to get from my car into the bar."

Her back pressed against the wall, blocking a further retreat. She didn't know if she liked or feared the gleam burning in Quinn's eyes. It took her a moment to swallow the lump in her throat. "She didn't?"

"No, she didn't." The sides of Quinn's sneakers brushed against her toes as he took one final step. "The only thing that kept running through my mind was that you were in there, and no one in there knew what I would do to them if they so much as touched you the wrong way." Quinn's hand came up and tenderly stroked her cheek. "No one inside knew how much I cared. Hell," muttered Quinn, as his fingertip outlined her mouth, "I hadn't even known until that moment."

He cared! The heat of his fingers and his gaze melted away her anger. Quinn hadn't been upset that his kids' nanny had been in a bar. He had been worried about her safety. "What would you have done?" She reached up and covered his hand. The intensity in his gaze seared her heart.

Quinn shuddered. "I don't know, Jocelyn, and that's

the part that frightens me." His lips brushed her knuckles. "I'm not a violent man. Or at least I never thought I was, until tonight." He gave her a small smile. "I don't like surprises, Jocelyn, and you are full of them."

"Me?" She released his hand and straightened the collar of his polo shirt. Quinn hadn't bothered changing back into his uniform before responding to the trouble at The One Eyed Squid. The tips of her fingers skimmed up the strong, lean column of his neck and then lightly stroked where the tic had pulsed in his jaw. "What surprises you about me?"

"Everything." The blunt end of his fingers played with a lock of her hair that had fallen across her shoulder. "You're not what I expected my kids' nanny to be like, yet you're wonderful at the job."

She grinned and teased, "Bet you won't say that about the housekeeping end of the deal."

Quinn didn't jump at the bait. "My lawn and gardens never looked so good."

"And this surprises you?" She didn't know if she should be insulted that he didn't mention her improved cooking skills or not. Her fingers traveled upward and wove their way into his dark hair. Quinn's hair might have been cut short, but it was thick and soft to the touch.

"Not really. You're a smart, loving, and caring woman, Jocelyn, and it shows in everything you do." Quinn leaned closer. "What shocked the living tar out of me was the paralyzing fear I felt not knowing if you were safe or not." His mouth toyed with her lower lip. "I'm not supposed to care about you, Joc."

She wrapped both arms around his neck and pulled him closer. "I know." She reached up and playfully bit his lower lip, causing him to groan and to finally kiss her the way she had been dreaming of night after night.

A moment later, when the kiss was just turning interesting, Quinn broke it and took an unsteady step back.

She could hear his rapid breathing and see the heat flare in his eyes. It matched her own. So why did he stop?

"I need to get out of here"—Quinn ran a trembling hand through his hair—"while I still can."

The man had just declared he cared about her, then kissed her into mush and announced he was leaving. She didn't know if she should laugh or cry. She took a step toward him. "No one asked you to leave, Quinn."

Quinn's gaze shot to the open doorway and the hallway beyond. "This is going to complicate things, Joc."

She grinned as she shut and locked the door. "I should hope so." Her fingers shook as they undid the two buttons on his polo shirt. "Whatever happens we'll handle it, Quinn." A jagged fingernail, which she had broken earlier in the evening while righting a chair at the bar, skimmed the embroidered emblem on the shirt. "Do you know why I never dated anyone twice since moving here?"

Quinn shook his head, she tugged his shirt up and over his head. A "Why?" was muffled under the shirt.

A fine sprinkling of dark, curly hair covered the upper portion of Quinn's muscular chest. His stomach was flat and tanned. An enticing trail of dark curls arrowed their way into the waistband of his jeans. A weaker woman would have drooled. She prided herself on the fact that her mouth had gone completely dry, yet she managed to say, "Because none of them were you."

The next thing she knew the room spun around, and she found herself flat on her back in the middle of her unmade bed. Quinn's hard and heated body covered hers as his mouth stole her breath and her reason.

Quinn's fingers fumbled with the buttons on her blouse and the front clasp of her bra, while hers tugged at his belt and tried to undo his straining zipper. Denim rubbed against denim as they both tried to get closer to each other. The feel of his skin against her palms caused her to curse the clothes they still had on. She wanted to feel all of him, now.

Friction built, and she nearly screamed when his hot mouth closed over one of her nipples and he bathed the nub with his tongue. Nothing had ever felt so wonderful, or so inadequate. "More, Quinn. I need more." She arched her back and pressed the junction of her thighs against the strength of his desire. She was already teetering at the edge of her desire. All she required was one small nudge from Quinn and she'd shatter into a million pieces.

Quinn swore as he rolled off the bed and stripped the rest of the clothes from his body.

She watched as every hard inch of Quinn was revealed. Her breath hitched in her throat as she breathed one word, "Beautiful."

A smile flashed on Quinn's face before he leaned down and traced her mouth with the pad of his thumb. "Yes, you are." He tenderly helped her remove her opened blouse and bra. Warm kisses caressed each of her shoulders before trailing down and torturing her breasts. Heat exploded as his lips and tongue brought her closer to the edge. She shifted her body and silently demanded more.

Quinn's fingers danced and teased their way over her skin as he reached for the snap of her jeans. One slow slide of denim and lace and she was naked to his gaze. Instinct told her to reach for the blanket, but the heat in Quinn's gaze stilled her hand.

Quinn's smile slowly faded as he stared down at her. "You aren't beautiful; you're a dream."

She reached for him with one arm. "I'm not a dream, Quinn." She didn't want Quinn mistaking tonight for some fantasy or one-night stand. What he had said earlier about this complicating things was going to hold true. She had a feeling this was going to change her life. "I'm real, very real, and I want you, now."

Quinn's gaze burned into hers, and in the depths of his eyes she saw a vulnerability she never thought possible. "Give me one reason why you want me, Jocelyn. Just one."

She could give him a hundred. Most had to do with the way he was with the children, his family, the community, or even his job. She didn't want them all in their bed. Tonight was about Quinn and her. There wasn't any room for anyone else. She wrapped her hand around the back of his neck and pulled his mouth down to hers. "Because you kiss like sin and taste like heaven."

Quinn was still growling when he closed the distance between their mouths and kissed her. A work-roughened palm slid up her thigh, and fingers teased the golden curls. His tongue plundered her mouth as a finger slowly slid inside her. Her hips arched in demand. Now was not the time for teasing or playing. She was too close to climaxing—dangerously close—and she wanted Quinn with her when she came. There would be plenty of time for playing later.

She reached between them and wrapped her fingers around his heated shaft and gently squeezed.

Quinn thrust himself deeper into her hand, threw back his head, and groaned in pleasure.

"You know what would feel better than this?" She gave him a few strokes.

Quinn's gaze was unfocused and dazed as he stared down at her. A groan that sounded suspiciously like "What?" emerged from his throat.

She shifted her weight and wrapped her legs around his waist. "You being in me." She positioned the head of his penis against her opening and released him.

With a wild, not quite tamed sound, Quinn plunged. She felt the length and thickness of him fill her. His second stroke drove her over the edge, and she climaxed.

The quaking of her release was still stealing her breath when Quinn shouted his own climax into the pillow next to her ear. A smile spread across her face as she felt his weight press her farther into the mattress.

Chapter Twelve

Quinn woke to the sound of Max barking and Tori yelling. Without fully coming awake or opening his eyes, he pulled a pillow over his head and wondered why he was so tired. Memories of last night flashed in his mind as he jerked up in bed. His bed, not Jocelyn's. Sometime around dawn he remembered regrettably stumbling back to his own bed, in case the kids woke up.

Jocelyn! Erotic, breathtakingly beautiful, loving, and sensual Jocelyn. What had they done? A slow smile spread across his face as he remembered exactly what they had done. Not once. Not twice. But an amazing three times. He should be thankful his heart hadn't given out.

The sound of more laughter drew his attention to the open window. After a huge stretch and jaw-popping yawn he walked to the window and looked out onto the scene below. His children were running around the backyard with the canine mop, Max. How one dog could have so much hair was beyond him. The kids were still wearing their pajamas. On top of his head Max was sporting a puffy ponytail tied with a satiny blue ribbon.

Issy was wearing her Winnie-the-Pooh slippers and a

sparkling tiara that glistened under the morning sun. Tori was prancing around the yard on her stick pony and wearing the same red cowgirl boots she had tried sleeping in last night. A white cowgirl hat and a long piece of rope completed the ensemble. Tori was trying, without much success, to lasso Max. Ben was barefooted and kicking around a soccer ball, but he did have on his favorite conductor's hat.

In the middle of all the chaos was Jocelyn. Thankfully she wasn't wearing what she had slept in last night. Which had been nothing but a smile of complete satisfaction. He had been the one to put that smile on her beautiful face. He was going to do it again, just as soon as they didn't have an audience. Lord, she was gorgeous in the morning light. Her denim shorts showed off her long, tanned legs, and the pale pink T-shirt clung to every nicely rounded curve.

Her hair was damp and pulled back into a ponytail, and she was pouring cereal into bowls for the kids. Plastic cups and a pitcher of orange juice sat on a tray, along with a bunch of bananas and Pop-Tarts. Breakfast was being served on the patio this morning.

Below him was every dream he had ever had about a family. The kids were already his; it was Jocelyn who could shatter that dream, along with his heart. Somewhere during the past several weeks Jocelyn had captured not only his children's affections, but his own as well. It wasn't just about the sex, even though last night had been an experience he had never had before. There was something between them that went beyond the instant attraction and lust. His feelings for Jocelyn went deeper than the bulge in his pants.

He was afraid to examine his emotions any closer for fear of what his own heart would reveal. Loving Jocelyn was a no-win situation. How could it be, when she was still planning on returning to Baltimore and her high-power career? Of course, knowing the outcome of their relationship didn't stop the leap of his heart when her laughter reached his ears.

He glanced at the clock and knew he was going to be late for work. It wouldn't be the first time, but it was the first time he wasn't going to rush. He needed a shower, and then he was joining his kids and Jocelyn for breakfast on the back patio.

Three minutes later he stood under the spray of the hot shower and wondered what he had to offer a woman like Jocelyn. Three kids, that weren't her own. While they owned his heart, he couldn't see any woman putting them on the plus side of the equation. His steady job, and willingness to do it, was a plus, but the salary had to be put on the minus side. In Misty Harbor his salary was adequate, but to a career woman like Jocelyn his salary probably landed in the pathetic category. He loved his home, but again he couldn't see it as an asset in Jocelyn's eyes. The last time his house had a real coat of paint, man hadn't even walked on the moon.

He dried off, slipped on a clean pair of boxers, and started to shave. What did it matter what he thought anyway? Jocelyn was old enough to make up her own mind on what she wanted, and last night she had wanted him. He was reading far too much into their one night together. What he needed to do was to step back and take it one day at a time. Starting with this morning's breakfast.

After buttoning up his shirt and tucking it into his pants he headed downstairs. He could imagine the "morning after" being a bit awkward to most men. Having three pairs of young eyes watching and listening to his every word or move was going to be uncomfortable to say the least.

Issy was the first one to greet him as he stepped out of the house. His daughter threw herself into his arms and pronounced she was a fairy princess.

He swung her up into the air and laughed. "So I see,

Princess Isabella, guardian of the forest creatures." He gave her a loud kiss and gently placed her in her seat at the round glass-topped table.

His gaze met Jocelyn's. He wasn't sure how she would react this morning. Her slow, easy smile stole his heart and his breath. He felt himself grinning like a fool, and quickly tried to squash the gesture. "Morning."

No regrets or embarrassment shone in Jocelyn's smokey gray eyes. If he didn't have an audience, he would have swept her up in his arms and carried her back upstairs. The residents of Hancock County would survive without him for a couple more hours. Maybe even days.

"Morning, yourself." Jocelyn motioned to an empty chair. A steaming cup of coffee and a bowl of Cheerios was already there. "I heard the shower running, so I got your breakfast ready." Jocelyn handed him a banana and a knife. "We are doing cereal with banana slices this morning."

"And Pop-Tarts," added Tori, who was munching on a frosted square filled with sweet red stuff. "You have to finish all your cereal first."

"And your bananas," added Ben. His son's bowl was empty except for a small lake of milk and one lone Cheerio bobbing in the current. "How come you slept so late, Dad? Jocelyn said we were to be quiet and not to wake you up."

"She said you were too tired to come down and play," said Tori before taking another large bite of her breakfast. Somehow she had managed to spill orange juice down the front of her pajamas, and a Cheerio was caught in the tangled mess she called hair. He didn't relish Jocelyn's job of brushing out those tangles later on.

He glanced at Jocelyn, who if he wasn't mistaken, was actually blushing. "Did she now?" He didn't know if he should be insulted by Jocelyn's lack of faith in his stamina or pleased that she cared enough to let him sleep.

Jocelyn seemed very interested in stirring her coffee. "You were snoring when I walked by your room this morning. I figured an hour extra sleep wouldn't hurt."

"I snore?" The only woman he had ever spent the entire night with had been Diane. His ex-wife had never once mentioned that he had snored.

Ben made horrible grunting and snoring sounds, which caused the girls to break out in high-pitched giggles and then try to imitate him. Max ran around the table making his own growling sounds, which caused the kids to laugh more. When Jocelyn started to laugh, he gave up the battle and joined them, too. So he snored. Jocelyn didn't seem too upset by the development.

He watched, enthralled, as Jocelyn's entire face lit up. Her eyes sparkled and filled with tears of merriment. Her rich, husky laughter tugged at his heart and called to his soul.

His future was sitting directly across from him. All he had to do was figure out a way to make Jocelyn see that they had more going for them than incredible sex.

Somehow the morning seemed to get a little brighter. The air a little fresher. The impossible didn't quite seem so insurmountable when it came to his relationship with Jocelyn. Stranger things had been known to happen.

Gary Franklin studied Phoebe Larson as she hauled another lobster out of one of his wire mesh pots and then held it out toward him. He took in the nice-size catch and knew it was a keeper by the government standards. Using the bander he quickly snapped an elastic band around each claw, to keep them from opening. Lobsters could not only do some damage to your fingers with their claws, but they also could attack and eat each other. The last thing he needed was for his catch to kill and devour one another. He placed the lobster into the container holding the rest of their catch. The container held more lobsters than he had seen in quite a while.

Phoebe's presence had brought him good luck today. When she had been waiting on the wharf, as dawn broke the sky, he had been at first surprised. Then leery. He didn't need a helping hand for the day. His eye hadn't been swollen that much that he couldn't manage his own traps. But he didn't have the strength to turn down her offer of help, especially since she obviously went through a lot of trouble. A full picnic basket and small cooler stocked with bottled water and soft drinks had been the deal breaker.

Of course, with Phoebe standing there all sleepy-eyed and fresh out of her bed, he had been surprised his mind hadn't suffered a meltdown. She also had been wearing the most incredible pair of shorts and smelling like lavender. How could he have refused her anything?

He should have remembered Phoebe had nearly failed home economics back in high school. Phoebe had been the only girl in the history of Hancock High to cheat on her final in cooking class. Eleven years ago he had thought it was hysterical. Two hours ago when he had hungrily unpacked that basket only to discover three peanut butter and jelly sandwiches, a half-eaten bag of chocolate chip cookies, and a crushed box of Animal Crackers, he hadn't been laughing.

Phoebe and he had ended up splitting the roast beef on rye and the container of potato salad he had packed for himself at four-thirty this morning. He had helped himself to one of her sandwiches and more cookies than he should have. Lunch had been a quiet affair filled with awkward silences and polite inane conversation.

They had too much history between them to become such strangers. At one time he not only loved Phoebe, he had considered her his best friend. There hadn't been a subject they couldn't discuss. No topic had been off limits. From sports, to school, to sex, they had covered it all. Phoebe had been the easiest person in the world to talk to. Surely they could overcome their past and become friends once again. He had missed her terribly over the years.

He watched as Phoebe tied a freshly baited pocket into the mesh pot, the last on this string of traps, and then dropped it back into the water. "I see you haven't lost your touch." Phoebe had tagged along with him and his father for years, hauling up traps and wrestling with snapping lobsters. His extra pair of thick gloves were way too big and clumsy on Phoebe's smaller hands, but she managed quite well.

Phoebe grinned and tossed the thick gloves onto the deck. "It's been a few years, but I guess it's like riding a bicycle. Once you learn to do it, you always remember." Phoebe tilted her face up toward the sun.

She looked adorable in an extra pair of his foul-weather bib overalls. The light brown color went well with her green T-shirt and the thick braid hanging down her back to her waist. The red baseball cap advertising Savannah, Georgia, and shielding her face from the relentless sun added a nice touch. Today she wore only three bracelets and four silver rings. If she fell overboard, he just might be able to save her before she sank to the bottom of the sea.

He never saw a woman wear so much jewelry, and all at the same time. No gold, no fancy diamonds or other precious gemstones adorned Phoebe's hands. She preferred silver and woven intricate patterns that appeared to be Celtic. The ring that had cut his cheek last night had had a hunk of amber the size of a quarter mounted on it. No wonder her hand had hurt after landing that punch. Phoebe was lucky she hadn't broken a finger or two.

"You'll make a fine sternman if you ever decide to give up stained glass." He reached up and unhooked the buoy from the hydraulic winch he used to haul the traps up from the bottom of the sea and onto his boat. He tossed the buoy into the sea. The brightly colored green, white, and red-striped buoy bounced playfully on the water. His buoy and his colors marked where his traps were. The Maine coast was a rainbow of buoys.

Phoebe snorted as she reached into the cooler for a cold bottle of water. "A day or two a week, in beautiful weather, is about all of this I can take. It will keep me from looking like the living dead, but I'm never giving up stained glass." Phoebe took a long swallow of water and recapped the plastic bottle. Her light brown gaze bore into his. "I gave up too much to get where I am today."

Her verbal attack was as deadly as ever. Phoebe had a knack for hitting what she aimed at.

He knew exactly what she had given up. *Him!* Eleven years ago, when he had been both young and stupid, he had given her a choice, a full scholarship at one of the best colleges on the East Coast or him. He had been naive and foolish enough to believe Phoebe would choose becoming his wife and the mother of his future children over leaving Misty Harbor and everything and everyone she had ever known. She had chosen furthering her education over love. His reckless pride hadn't listened to her tearful promises of returning to him, and everyone knew long-distance relationships never worked. He had hardened his heart and stood silently by as she packed up her old Jeep and drove out of town and out of his life.

He couldn't believe she still drove that old Jeep. They had made a lot of memories in the front seat of that vehicle. If it hadn't been for the gear shifter, on more than one occasion he would have batted a home run instead of rounding third base.

"So how's your new venture going?" He wasn't going to bring up the past. Why bother? It wouldn't change a damn thing.

"It's not a venture; it's my business." Phoebe moved out of his way as he piloted the boat to the next bobbing buoy that marked his traps. "And there's nothing new about it. I've been working exclusively with stained glass for seven years now."

"Yeah, I remember your mom saying you were living in Atlanta once. Something about an apprenticeship."

Phoebe handed him a cold bottle of water, leaned against the starboard side of the boat, and watched the wake churning up behind them. "I've been in a lot of places over the years. Mainly on the East Coast doing repair work. Churches mostly." Phoebe's gaze drifted toward the horizon, where the sea merged with the sky. "Sometimes I helped with a commissioned piece or two."

"Ever get to Florida?" He remembered how she wanted to see Disney World, pink flamingos, and palm trees. They had had an ongoing argument as to where they would be taking their honeymoon. He had won the disagreement by beating her at basketball during their senior year. To this day he never knew if she had allowed him to win that game of twenty-one or not.

"No, the farthest south I got was Atlanta." Phoebe picked up a pair of his sunglasses that had been lying on a bench seat and slipped them on. "How come you don't have a sternman? Wouldn't it make it easier for you?"

"Sure, but I prefer my own company most days." A lot of the lobster fishermen went out in pairs. It was easier and faster if there were two pairs of hands to do the work. He had been his father's sternman for many years while he saved every dime he could. When he finally had enough money saved to buy his own boat, his father hired on another sternman. His father had nearly twelve hundred traps, too many for one man to handle. Especially since his father was getting up in age. "I make my own schedule and stay out as long as I want or need. The profit's all mine this way. Besides, it's just easier this way."

"Don't you ever get lonely?" Phoebe turned and looked at him.

He couldn't see her eyes behind the dark lenses of his sunglasses, but her voice had sounded sad. The last thing he wanted from Phoebe was pity. He was alone because he preferred it that way. "No." Up ahead was another one of his buoys. He eased up on the throttle. "Get the gaff ready, we're almost there."

Phoebe replaced her bottle of water, pulled on her gloves, and picked up the long pole with the hook on the end. With one try she had hooked the sink rope and the buoy and pulled them in.

He came up beside her, took the buoy and the line, and hooked it up to the hydraulic winch. The whirl of the motor prevented any further conversation as the wire mesh pots came up from the bottom of the sea. In perfect harmony they went to work. Out of the four traps, only one had a lobster that didn't meet the government standards. Phoebe tossed the little fellow back in before he got off a good pinch. The three other lobsters joined the rest of their catch.

"You're bringing me good luck today," he said. Only five of the traps so far were either empty or had other sea creatures sleeping in them. With the little fellow Phoebe had just tossed back in, it brought the total up to six undersize lobsters so far. A record for him.

"Maybe I should come out with you more." Phoebe glanced at him and quickly added, "Of course, I would want my share of the catch then. Today was a one-shot deal."

He brought his hand up to his eye, but didn't touch it. The area around his entire eye throbbed and hurt like a bitch, no matter how many aspirins he had swallowed. He had seen the damage this morning in the mirror but couldn't imagine what it looked like now, nearly eight hours later. "I'd say more like a one-punch deal."

Phoebe cringed. "I already apologized for that, Gary." With fumbling fingers she tied the baited pockets into the pots. "Does it hurt as bad as it looks?" Phoebe glanced over her shoulder at him as she pushed the first trap over the side of the boat. "There's a little ice left in the cooler. I could wrap it in something for you."

"Why did you really invite yourself along today, Phoebe?" He unhooked the buoy and line from the pot hauler and watched as the rest of the traps fell into the sea. A moment later a lone buoy bounced on the waves. "You know me well enough to know I could handle this," he waved his hand around him to encompass the boat, "all on my own. I was practically raised on a lobster boat."

Phoebe smiled. "Your mother would have heart failure if she heard you say that."

He frowned. "You're avoiding the question." He never thought to see the day when straight-shooting Phoebe Larson hedged an answer.

"Don't you have more lobsters to haul up?" Phoebe went back to the bait tub and started to fill more bait pockets to be used in the traps.

He stood there and watched her do one of the less thrilling jobs of the day. He hadn't asked her to fill the small mesh bags with remains of discarded fish. He was used to the ripe odor they had, especially under a hot summer sun. "Why?"

"Why what?" Phoebe concentrated on the messy job as if she were building a nuclear device.

"Why did you come to The One Eyed Squid last night? Why did you follow me home and play Florence Nightingale? And why in the hell were you standing on the wharf this morning?" Three different times Phoebe had placed herself directly in front of him. No way was it a coincidence. Phoebe was purposely seeking him out, and he wanted to know why.

Fish parts and guts, better known as racks, slipped from her gloved hand as she turned and faced him. Her head tilted to one side as if she was confounded by a puzzle. "I don't know you at all, do I?"

Seagulls screeched overhead. A few of the braver ones made a dive for the open bait tub. "What do you mean you don't know me? You know me better than anyone." She wasn't making any sense. He had poured out his heart and soul to this woman. Told her every dream he ever had, and yet she claimed not to know him at all. Hat or no hat, the relentless sun had obviously fried her brains.

Phoebe shook her head. "No, I don't, Gary. At one time I thought I knew the boy you had been, but I was wrong." Phoebe waved away a brazen seagull and closed the lid on the bait tub. "I was curious to see and to get to know the man you had become."

"Why?" He couldn't imagine why she would be interested. For eleven years they hadn't spoken one word to each other. On her rare visits home she had gone out of her way to make sure their paths never crossed. But then again, so had he.

"As I said, curiosity." Phoebe shooed another seagull away. "Aren't we going to the next buoy?" Phoebe glanced at a half dozen seagulls sitting on the roof of the wheelhouse. More were circling above. "It's beginning to look like a sequel of the movie *The Birds.*"

He nodded toward the bait tub. "You couldn't think of a better way to satisfy your curiosity than playing with fish guts in ninety-degree weather?"

"Yeah"—Phoebe flashed him a teasing grin—"but somehow I didn't think you would be interested in playing a game of strip poker."

His gaze automatically dropped to her chest. His baggy foul-weather pants did nothing for her, but for some obscure reason he found her sexy as hell in them. The light green T-shirt that advertised some seafood restaurant in Maryland clung to her well-rounded breasts. Phoebe had filled out very nicely over the years. Beneath his oil-gear overalls were a set of hips wide enough for a man to hold on to without fear of doing any damage. Phoebe wasn't some hothouse orchid that a man would be afraid to touch and to take on the occasional trip over to the wild side of love. Phoebe was as sturdy and as beautiful as the wild lilies of the valley that grew along Maine's coast.

He raised his gaze and grinned right back. "You should have asked last night. I have a deck of cards sitting in one of my kitchen drawers."

"I have to warn you, I cheat at cards."

"I remember." He remembered the good laugh he had had when he caught her cheating at solitaire. Phoebe hated to lose at anything. That fact was the reason he suspected she threw that basketball game years ago. That and the fact that Phoebe usually won every game they played. Phoebe was a physical dynamo who had always given it a hundred percent, while he tended to pay more attention to her bouncing breasts than to the ball. If they were to meet on a basketball court now, she would win every game hands down. "Over the years I learned a few moves of my own."

One of her dark brows rose above the rim of his glasses. "I should hope so."

He didn't know if she was commenting on his game playing or on the fact that when she had driven her Jeep out of Misty Harbor eleven years ago, he had still been a virgin. So had she. They weren't kids any longer. Life had gone on, and now they were right back where they had started. Older, hopefully wiser, and more skeptical than ever. He flashed her a wicked grin as he headed for the helm. "You just let me know when you want me to break out that deck of playing cards."

Phoebe's smile sent his heart racing and his blood pumping. "I'll do that." With those cryptic words, she opened the bait tub and went back to filling the pockets with racks.

Three hours later he finally called a halt to the day's work. All the traps that had to be checked were done. The rest would have to wait until Monday morning. He headed the *Winter's Rest* back toward the wharf and home. A smile tugged at his mouth as he watched the antics of the seagulls swooping and diving for the remainder of the bait Phoebe was dumping overboard.

His sternman didn't smell like lavender anymore. She smelled of the sea and looked a little wilted around the edges. It had been a long day.

Phoebe was beautiful, and his life had never looked so empty. Saturday night and the most he had to look forward to was selecting his dinner before the derrick lifted the container holding his catch of the day into a lobster car, where they would stay until a market was found. The History Channel was also having a special on at nine tonight about Civil War surgeons. He didn't think he could stand the excitement.

Wondering if he should press his luck and open the door he had closed years ago, he selected two of the biggest lobsters and placed them and some water into a bucket. The worst that could happen was Phoebe would decline his invitation to dinner, and then he would eat lobster two nights in a row.

He watched as Phoebe straightened everything up on the boat while he pulled up to the wharf. Within minutes the derrick was unloading his catch, and Phoebe was using the water hose to wash down the deck and everything else in sight. The derrick operator gave a long, loud whistle as Phoebe stepped out of the foul-weather pants and proceeded to rinse them down. He would have joined Hank, but one look at Phoebe's long legs and short shorts and his mouth had gone dry.

Phoebe rewarded Hank with a big smile and then hung the pants up to dry.

Phoebe flashed him a bigger smile and held out her hand. "Toss me your pants, Gary."

Hank started to choke, and the container holding his catch swung a little wild before settling back down. "Pay attention to what you are doing, Hank. That's next month's truck payment in there." He stepped out of his oil gear and tossed the pants onto the deck of the boat. Unlike Phoebe, he had worn jeans beneath the protective pants.

He boarded the boat and helped get everything cleaned and put away. Phoebe set her basket and cooler up onto the wharf and then turned to him and said, "Well, that was fun."

"Thanks for all your help." He could hear the two lobsters' claws scraping the sides of the metal bucket as they tried to escape their destiny. He said, "I was wondering . . ." the same instant she said, "I was wondering . . ."

They both laughed. "You first," he said.

Color was riding high on Phoebe's cheeks when she asked, "I was wondering if you would like to get something to eat later."

He couldn't tell if she was blushing, or if the flush was from too much sun. He had never had the experience of having a woman ask him out before. Leave it to Phoebe to be the first. He swung the bucket holding the lobsters onto the wharf. "I was hoping you would join me later to celebrate our catch."

"You're cooking?" Phoebe eyed the bucket hungrily.

"Of course." He shuddered to think of Phoebe trying to steam those two prime specimens. "I'm thinking about an hour and a half at my place?"

"What can I bring?" Phoebe stepped up onto the wharf.

"Not a thing. You already did more than your share." His gaze was level with the top of her thighs, and he was finding it extremely difficult to breathe. Where had all the heat come from all of a sudden? "I do have one question, though." Something had been bugging him for most of the afternoon.

"What's that?" Phoebe picked up the cooler and the empty basket.

"Earlier you said you didn't know the boy I had been." She had been right about one thing. At eighteen he had been only a boy, not a man. "What makes you think you didn't know me?"

Phoebe's gaze locked with his. He could read the indecision swirling in the depths of her light brown eyes. Finally with a heavy sigh she said, "The boy I thought I knew never would have issued that ultimatum. The Gary Franklin I knew would have been fairer to us both."

"Are you sure about that?"

Phoebe tugged her baseball cap lower, so the setting sun was no longer in her eyes. "I would like to think so."

"So would I." He nodded toward their dinner. "See you in about an hour and a half?"

"Just try to keep me away." Phoebe gave him a playful smile, turned, and walked away.

He stood there and watched Phoebe as she made her way down the dock. She stopped two or three times to talk to a couple of the locals, but she didn't linger long. Nor was she flirtatious with anyone in particular. She seemed to save all that playfulness for him. Or maybe he was just imagining the whole thing.

Wishful thinking on his part.

He knew for certain that Phoebe hadn't gone out with any guy from town since she had been home. Over two months and not one date. So why had she suddenly changed tactics and asked him out? After eleven years he couldn't believe she still had any feelings for him or what they had once shared. Maybe she was telling the truth after all. Maybe she was just plain curious.

If that was the case, he would do well to guard whatever was left of his heart.

Chapter Thirteen

Jocelyn glanced up from the mound of paperwork scattered across the kitchen table. "Are you sure I can't help you with something, Millicent?"

"You are." Millicent Wyndham, the monarch of Misty Harbor and probably the richest woman in the county, nodded her stylish gray head. "You have already saved me from eating a boring evening meal with only myself for company by inviting me to join you for dinner." Millicent smiled at the twins. "The company will be so much more entertaining here. You just keep reading, Jocelyn, and tell me what you think."

"I think I should be the one cooking that haddock, not you." Jocelyn smiled at Issy and Tori, who were seated at the counter watching every move the older woman made. "I am the housekeeper after all."

"Nonsense." Millicent started to expertly gut and clean the first of the two fish. "You're a lawyer, not a cook. When your brother-in-law handed you these two fish, I thought you were going to pass out."

Issy and Tori wrinkled their noses and said, "Yuck." Ben, who had joined his sisters, smiled and said, "Cool," as Millicent started to fillet the eighteen-inch fish.

"Gwen's the cook of the family, but I'm improving. I can even manage a couple of the fish dishes as long as the fish comes from the market fillet and ready to cook." She shuddered as Millicent wacked off the second fish's head. "I draw the line at gutting and cleaning." Erik, her brother-in-law, had known that; that was why he had been laughing so hard when he left ten minutes ago. Knowing her sister, she wouldn't have been surprised if Sydney had put him up to delivering the fish. Thankfully Millicent had been present to take the slimy, glassy-eyed creatures.

Millicent carefully waved the knife she was using in the direction of the kitchen table. "And I draw the line at reading forty pages of incomprehensible legal jargon that would cause the attorney general to start drinking. All that for one simple project."

"Setting up a scholarship fund in your late husband's name isn't a simple project." She frowned at all the scattered papers and wondered how she had gotten herself into this one. "In fact, it's quite complicated."

"Believe me, I realized that by the time I was reading the third page." Millicent rinsed the fillets and placed them into a shallow baking pan. "I had a raging headache by page four, and that idiot lawyer in Bangor just wanted me to sign where he told me to sign."

"If you think he's an idiot, why did you go to him?"

"Because Jefferson's family had been using that law firm for as long as anyone could remember. Jefferson trusted them completely, and I've just been following suit. The lawyers Jefferson used have all retired, and these younger ones all seem to be in such a hurry nowadays." Millicent's voice deepened to do a perfect imitation of an impatient male. "Sign this. Initial here. Print your name here." A heavy sigh of disgust filled the room. "He couldn't even bother to offer me a cup of coffee or ask how my day was. All he wanted was for me to sign those documents and be on my way. You should have seen his face when I told him I sign nothing that I haven't read and understood."

"What did he say to that?" She glanced down at the pile of papers before her and wondered why the lawyer hadn't jumped with glee. The billable hours alone would have been a nice tidy sum.

"He started to huff about being late for his next appointment, so I picked up all the papers, told him I'd call if I had any questions, and left." Millicent placed the sharp knife into the dishwasher and away from little hands. "By the time I read page five, I knew I was out of my depths and that I needed legal help. That's when I thought of you."

Millicent wrapped the uneatable parts of the fish in a thick wad of newspaper and handed it to Ben. "Could you please be a gentleman and put this outside in one of the trash cans with a lid?"

"Yes, ma'am." Ben puffed out his chest with pride because he was given such an important job and headed for the side door.

"You two ladies"—Millicent smiled at Issy and Tori—"can help me with the seasonings."

Both girls nodded so fast they nearly fell off the stools. Jocelyn chuckled and wondered what Quinn was going to think of the "hired" help in the kitchen when he got home in a couple of minutes. That was if he managed to get home on time tonight. After all, he had been late getting to work this morning.

A warm blush threatened to sweep up her cheeks when she thought about their heated good-bye, far from prying eyes. No one had ever kissed her like Quinn did. Who needed coffee in the morning when she had Quinn to rev her engines?

"Why don't you just change lawyers if you're not happy with them."

"To which law firm?" Millicent, making herself right at home in the bright sunny kitchen, went to the refrigerator and got out the lemon juice. "It's bad enough I have to drive into Bangor every time I need something or someone needs a signature. I'm just not comfortable driving that kind of distance any longer."

"Yeah, Abraham Martin was telling me that this area is pretty dry when it comes to lawyers. Abraham mentioned one over in Sullivan."

"Francis Haskel got his law degree before I was even allowed to date." Millicent chuckled as she helped Issy sprinkle the salt onto the fish. "If I can't remember the first boy I dated, how am I supposed to believe he remembers all that legal stuff they teach you in school."

She couldn't argue that point. She watched the older woman as she helped Tori sprinkle on the paprika and remembered that Millicent and her late husband, Jefferson, never had any children of their own. It was a shame, because the town's monarch would have made a wonderful grandmother. "You do understand that this kind of stuff"—she waved an arm over a pile of paperwork—"wasn't my specialty back in Baltimore."

"You do understand it, though, right?" Millicent didn't seem too concerned if she understood it or not. The seventy-three-year-old woman was too busy playing Julia Child with the munchkins.

"Most of it makes sense, but I need to check out some state laws before I feel comfortable enough to tell you to sign it." Twice now she had been made to feel uncomfortable in regard to her chosen career. Back in Baltimore she never would have told anyone she needed to check the laws that were on the books. It was a humbling experience for the youngest assistant district attorney in Baltimore's history. Of course, she had checked and rechecked the law numerous times back in Baltimore; she just never went around advertising that fact.

"You can do that, right?" Millicent allowed Issy to hold the pepper shaker.

"The Internet is a wonderful tool."

"Of course it is. That's how I got your sister, Gwen, to move to Misty Harbor." Millicent chuckled over the memory. "Gwen and I met in a cooking chat room. I believe we were discussing lobster Newburg, or was it baked scallops? Doesn't matter, I guess. Anyway, she told me her dream was to open up her own restaurant." Millicent smiled at the two little girls listening wide-eyed to her every word. "Wouldn't you know it, but Misty Harbor had an empty restaurant just waiting to be bought. Three months later, The Catch of the Day was open for business."

Jocelyn chuckled at her own memories. At first she had thought Gwen had been throwing good money down a bad drain, but she had stood by her sister's decision and offered nothing but encouragement. After flying up for the grand opening, she realized just how wrong she had been. Gwen had not only fitted into Misty Harbor, but Misty Harbor fitted Gwen. Her sister had not only found and realized her dream of owning her own restaurant, but she had found the love of her lifetime, Daniel.

"Eight months later your other sister, Sydney, opened up her own medical practice, to the delight and sincere gratitude of nearly every citizen in town."

She now felt like a slug compared to both of her sisters. She had been the one to run away from a lucrative career and become a temporary nanny. "Classic overachievers, both of them."

"Now you're here." Millicent gave her a soft smile and overlooked the overachiever comment. "One has to wonder if you soon will be opening up your own law practice in our beautiful little town."

There was no denying the need for a good honest lawyer in the area, but it wouldn't be her. "I already told you, Millicent, I can't practice law in Maine." She had a life back in Baltimore just waiting for her to step right back into it.

"Poppycock, all you have to do is take Maine's bar

exam and you'll be staring at paperwork"—Millicent waved her hand at the kitchen table—"just like that for more hours than you would like. I'll even be your first client."

"Just like that?"

"Of course, just like that. I eat at your sister's restaurant more often than is good for my waist, and your other sister has seen me in my unmentionables while poking and prodding in places better left unsaid." Millicent glanced at the two girls, who were now giggling. "Why wouldn't I allow you to handle my legal affairs? I'm sure you would have the decency to offer me a cup of coffee and explain everything to me in English I could understand."

"I'm flattered that you would trust me with such a responsibility, Millicent, but that wasn't what I was referring to when I asked if you thought it would be easy."

"What were you referring to?"

"Taking the Maine bar exam." She never wanted to take another bar exam in her life.

"Oh, did you have trouble passing the Maryland one?"

"Of course not. I passed it on the first try." She was extremely proud of that fact, but it didn't mean she wanted to take it again. She would rather get a root canal done on every tooth in her mouth than to suffer through such a grueling test again.

"Then I don't see what the problem is." Millicent turned to one of the cabinets and started to hunt around. "Do you have any potatoes? Rice? Something that would go with this fish? Girls, what would you like?"

Tori jumped off the stool and ran to a different cabinet. "Mac and cheese. Mac and cheese."

Issy hurried to the freezer side of the side-by-side refrigerator and opened the door. A big plastic red-and-white bag was clutched in her tiny fist as she slammed the door. "Fries!"

Millicent looked bewildered for a moment, but then shrugged and smiled. "Wonderful choices girls. I think we'll do both. It's been ages since I had chips with my fish." She took the blue-and-yellow box out of Tori's hands and tried not to grimace at the picture on the front. "I can't ever remember eating macaroni and cheese shaped like a Sponge Bob Square Pants."

"He lives in a pineapple," sang Tori at the top of her lungs.

"Under the sea," added Issy in a much softer voice.

Ben came in through the side door singing, "Drop on the deck and flop like a fish."

All three children dropped to the kitchen floor and started to flop around like psych patients receiving shock therapy. Millicent looked alarmed for a moment. "Oh, my."

Jocelyn laughed. "Relax, Millicent, they're singing about some cartoon they all like to watch."

"Did all that make sense to you?" Millicent carefully stepped around Tori, so as not to mash a toe or finger.

"Nope, and I've watched that show at least half a dozen times with the kids. Believe me, nothing makes sense in it, but they love it."

"Okay, Millicent, did you let in all these jellyfish?" Quinn stepped into the kitchen and pretended to frown at his wiggling children.

With a loud chorus of "Daddy! Daddy! Daddy!" the kids all got up off the floor and rushed Quinn.

Quinn was nearly pushed off balance, but he kept his feet under him. He bent over and swept up both girls into his arms as Ben scrambled up onto his back and held on for dear life. "What were you guys doing down on the floor like that?"

The children all looked at one another and giggled.

"It was my idea, Quinn." She loved the way his one brow shot up when he was waiting for an answer. "I didn't feel like cleaning the kitchen floor today, so they were all pretending to be mops." She nodded to the wooden floor. "See how shiny it is now?"

The twins giggled more. Ben said, "We were fishes, Dad, not mops."

"Something about a sponge named Bob," added Millicent as she stirred a pot of sauce that was starting to bubble on the back burner. "We're having him for dinner along with some nice haddock Erik dropped by."

Quinn eyed the nice fillets lying in the pan. "Erik cleaned and fillet them for you?"

"No, I told him to go on home. I can do that." Millicent straightened the strand of pearls around her neck. "Jocelyn invited me for dinner, so the least I could do was cook it while she's checking out a legal headache for me."

Quinn lowered all the kids back to the floor and raised another eyebrow at the amount of paperwork scattered across his kitchen table. He gave a low whistle. "Problem, Millicent?"

"No, at least I don't think so." Millicent poured the sauce over the fish and then slid the whole pan into the oven. "Jocelyn's going to attempt to explain all that to me, before I sign it. I'm starting a scholarship fund in Jefferson's name."

"That's a great idea." Quinn shuddered at the amount of paperwork. "Of course, I'm not the one who has to read all that."

"That's why I'm cooking." Millicent picked up the bag of frozen fries. "Jocelyn won't hear of taking my money, so I have to do something." Millicent glanced at Ben. "Since your sisters each picked out a side dish, you get to pick out the vegetable."

"I do?" Ben ran across the room, opened the refrigerator, and stared at its contents. "Are eggs vegetables?"

"No." Quinn came over to help his son. "We could make a salad, and that would count as lots of vegetables." Quinn closed the refrigerator and opened the freezer. "There's also corn, squash, peas, and spinach."

"Can I help make the salad?" Ben wrinkled his nose at everything in the freezer.

"Sure. You and I will do the salad, since Millicent is busy cooking up fries and Bob." Quinn glanced at Jocelyn and smiled. "You can keep reading."

"We do, Daddy, we do?" asked Tori.

"Millicent, since you're the guest, do you want to eat in the kitchen, the formal dining room, or out back?"

"Definitely out back. I love eating outside when the weather is nice."

"Out back it is," said Quinn. He handed Tori a wet dishcloth. "You can wipe down the table." He handed Issy a few paper towels and a bottle of glass cleaner. "You polish it up real nice after your sister is done."

Both little girls ran outside, forgetting to close the screen door. Quinn closed the door and then proceeded to get the ingredients for a salad together. "Ben, you will wash and tear the lettuce into pieces while I do the chopping."

She sat there watching father and son work side by side. Max had joined the girls outside, and Millicent was spreading the fries on a baking sheet. Before her sat a legal challenge, one she would normally be sinking her teeth into and forgetting about all else happening in the universe. So why wasn't she reading Millicent's papers? Why did she have this incredible urge to get up and start slicing cucumbers with Quinn?

When in the hell had her life become so domesticated?

With a disgusted sigh she went back to reading and trying to ignore cucumbers, tomatoes, and even those crunchy little croutons Quinn loved so much.

Half an hour later, she was the one developing a headache. On the legal pad next to her were more questions than answers. Millicent had been right not to

sign the documents. Their sole purpose seemed to confuse an already complicating issue more. Surely there
had to be an easier way than this mess?

"Dinner's ready," said Millicent as she carried a bowl
of macaroni and cheese out to the patio table. Ben carried two bottles of salad dressing. Issy brought the salt
and pepper, Tori the basket filled with napkins. Quinn
brought up the rear by carrying the baking pan filled
with fish and giving her a sexy wink as he walked by.

With a lighthearted feeling, she got up and managed
the bowl of salad in one hand and the fries in the other.

Aluminum tube chairs with fat flowery cushions scraped and banged their way across the slate patio. Kids yelled
and jostled for their spots. Millicent got the seat of honor,
right between the twins. Ben sat next to his father, and
she ended up on Quinn's other side.

She helped Tori load up her plate, but her attention
was on Quinn. "How come you didn't change out of
your uniform?" Quinn always came home from work
and immediately changed into shorts or jeans.

"I've got to go back after dinner." Quinn gave her a
very intimate smile. "Sorry about that, but Rick's wife's
water broke about an hour ago. He's not going to make
his shift, and I get to fill in for most of it."

"Your deputy is about to become a father?" She vaguely
remembered Quinn mentioning a Rick before.

"Melissa is finally going to have that baby?" asked Millicent as she cut Issy's fish into bite-size pieces. "I saw her
in church last Sunday, and I've got to say, I've never seen
a woman so pregnant, and so uncomfortable, in all my
days. I wouldn't be surprised if it's triplets."

Quinn chuckled. "Rick's a nervous wreck thinking
it's one. I would hate to see him if Melissa gives him a
surprise or two."

"What's triplets?" asked Ben, who was making sure his
fish didn't touch the macaroni and cheese on his plate.

She couldn't imagine delivering twins, let alone triplets. "Three babies at once."

"We're two babies at once," stated Issy.

"Yeah," added Tori with a wide smile, "we're twins."

All the adults chuckled as they glanced back and forth between the two girls. She saw the confused and hurt look on the girls' faces and quickly reassured them. "We aren't laughing at you girls. We just think it's funny that for being identical twins, right now you don't look anything alike."

"We don't?" Tori stared at her sister.

Issy stared right back.

Jocelyn chuckled some more. Both girls were wearing an identical expression. Maybe they were more alike than she was giving them credit for. Issy was dressed in one of her favorite outfits, pink plaid shorts, a sleeveless pink top with Tinkerbell printed on the front, lace-trimmed pink socks, and perfectly white sneakers. Two fat pink bows held her neatly combed pigtails in place.

Tori looked as if she had wrestled a grizzly all afternoon. Her little denim shorts were covered in grass stains, and one of the back pockets was dangling by a thread or two. Her dirty red T-shirt proclaimed she was 99 percent mischief, 1 percent angel. There was truth in the advertising. Somewhere within a quarter-mile radius of the house were her sneakers and socks. Chances were both were wet and covered in mud. The red bow that had been in her hair this morning was long gone and probably lost forever. Tori had washed her hands and face before Millicent had arrived, but she was now sporting a streak of mud across one cheek. As of ten o'clock this morning, there were three different Band-Aids gracing minor cuts and bruises on her little legs.

Issy thrust out her chin and lower lip and announced, "I don't look like her."

Tori mirrored the expression. "I don't like pink."

Quinn, obviously seeing the same fight brewing she had, said, "Issy, why don't you tell Mrs. Wyndham what you want to be when you grow up."

"A ballerina, Mrs. Wyndham," Issy said.

"Call me Millicent, and you will make a lovely ballerina, Isabella." Millicent turned to Tori. "What about you Victoria?"

"I want to be a cowboy." Tori stuck her tongue out at Issy.

Quinn gave Jocelyn a look that clearly said *Where did we go wrong?* Beneath the table, away from the curious eyes of the children and their guest, Quinn's fingers trailed up her bare thigh. A shiver slid down her spine as she remembered last night and where those same fingers had trailed up to. Her hand lowered to Quinn's and stopped their upward movement. Quinn turned his hand up and threaded his fingers with hers.

Millicent smiled at the girls. "I must admit, Quinn, you have a delightful family." Millicent's gaze went around the table and seemed to linger on the spot where both of their hands were joined out of sight. Millicent gave Quinn a knowingly warm smile. "You must be doing something right."

Quinn's fingers squeezed hers. "I sure hope so, Millicent. I sure hope so."

Ten minutes after the stroke of midnight Quinn pulled in front of his house and stared at the darkened windows. Jocelyn had left on the porch light, but every other light in the house was off. So much for his daydream of Jocelyn waiting up for him. It was his own fault. He had told her not to wait up for him, because he had no idea what time he would be home.

The good news was Melissa Roberts had delivered a healthy baby boy three hours ago. Mother and son were doing fine. Rick, his trustworthy, calm, and always in control deputy, had barely made it through the experience. The bad news was he had worked Rick's entire shift and had missed spending some time alone with Jocelyn.

He locked his weapon in the glove compartment and then locked the SUV. He had never once brought the loaded gun into his house; he made it a habit to leave it locked in the glove compartment. Even when the children were living in Boston with their mother, he never once broke that habit. Curious children and guns were a bad combination.

The safest spot to secure his weapon was in the car. Anyone could break into his house, especially if they weren't from around this area and knew he was the sheriff. Not too many criminals were foolish enough to break into a well-marked sheriff's car.

The house was dark and silent. The only light was coming from the low-wattage bulb in the hood of the stove. He locked the front door and headed for the kitchen. Jocelyn had promised to save him a piece of the cake she and the girls had baked that morning. Sure enough, the plastic cake holder sitting on the counter held more than half a chocolate cake. He got a plate, knife, and fork and sliced himself a big piece of the lopsided cake. The icing seemed a little runny, and it looked as though someone had smeared it on with a garden trowel; but it tasted great. He was halfway done with the cake and a tall glass of milk when he heard Max's paws clamoring down the stairs. *Ah, the guard dog approaches.*

Max padded into the kitchen, didn't even bother to look at him, and headed for his bowl of water. "Either you are the smartest security dog and knew who it was before I entered the house, or you're a discredit to your kind." He reached down and patted the mutt on top of his hairy head. He'd be the last to admit it, but the darn dog was growing on him. "I'll give you the benefit of the doubt for now, but next time could you at least bark once or twice when the front door opens?"

Max tilted his head and drooled.

"I'm taking that as a yes." He opened the back patio door and stepped outside with the dog. "Go do your business." Max trotted away, leaving him alone in the yard. The moon was nearly full, casting ripples of light across Blueberry Cove below. From his yard he couldn't see the sea or the harbor, just thick woods on the other side of the cove, and the occasional light peaking through that let him know he wasn't alone in the world.

He glanced up at the master bedroom window. Jocelyn's window. He could tell both windows were open, but no light shone within the room. Jocelyn was asleep. He couldn't blame her after the night they had shared. He figured she couldn't have gotten more than three hours' sleep total. During dinner he had noticed how tired she looked and really regretted not being home earlier to help her with the kids.

Max rejoined him, and they both silently reentered the house. He made sure everything was locked up for the night and then headed upstairs. When he checked on the girls, Max was already asleep at the foot of Issy's bed. The princess and the beast. He chuckled at the scene and then gently kissed both of his daughters good night after retucking Tori back in under the covers.

Ben didn't make a sound as he pulled up his son's blanket and kissed his tousled head.

He stood at the doorway to Jocelyn's room for a full three minutes debating if he should just crawl in bed with her and hold her throughout the night. She had left her door open, but he wasn't sure if it was an invitation to him, or if she just wanted to hear the kids in case they woke up. A cool evening breeze was blowing in through the windows, but Jocelyn was buried under the covers. He couldn't very well tuck her in and give her a kiss on top of her head like he had just done with the children. Jocelyn was not a child. She was a very desirable woman. One who was maneuvering her way into his heart faster than he could build the barriers to keep her out.

What in the hell was he going to do when she headed back to Baltimore and the life she had built for herself there?

With a weary sigh, he turned away from her doorway and headed for his lonely cold bed.

Chapter Fourteen

Jocelyn could hear the girls giggling and laughing upstairs. Max barked once or twice, and the sound of running feet could be heard from the girls' room to Ben's room, and then back again. She lit another candle and tried not to think about how long Quinn was taking to tuck in the kids. The nightly ritual usually ran about half an hour. Tonight was no exception.

She turned off all the family room's lights and only left the dim light in the stove's hood burning. Six candles flickered as the evening breeze blew in through the patio doors. She would have lit a fire in the fireplace, but it wasn't cool enough. Setting a scene for seduction was nearly impossible when three little kids would be asleep one floor above you. There was no telling when one of them would wake up wanting to use the bathroom or begging for a glass of water.

What did married couples do for a few romantic moments? Or weren't you supposed to seduce each other after the kids arrived on the scene. Now that was a depressing thought.

The candles were pushing it, but she wanted to do something romantic with Quinn. She had bought a bottle of white wine earlier in the day, and it was cooling in the refrigerator. Quinn had spotted it earlier, looked directly at her, and raised that one brow in question. Her only response had been to grin like some brain-dead cheerleader who was about to reel in the quarterback. Problem was, Quinn didn't seem to be a "white wine" kind of guy. His taste ran toward the couple bottles of beer he kept chilling in the refrigerator.

She was still surveying the family room when Quinn came downstairs. Strong arms wrapped around her waist from behind, and warm lips trailed a wide path of kisses from the edge of her blouse to the very sensitive spot behind her ear. Quinn's teeth playfully tugged at her ear before he asked, "Are you trying to seduce me?"

"Would it work?" She tilted her head and gave him more access. Last night she had missed him in her bed. One night of Quinn, and she was already addicted.

"You don't need candles or the wine." Quinn's mouth closed over the rapidly throbbing vein in her neck.

"I don't?" She tried to turn around, but he held her fast.

"Nope." His tongue traced the thundering pulse. "All you have to do is walk into the room, and I'm seduced."

She melted farther back against him and could feel his erection through his jeans. "You're easy."

"Only for you." Quinn glanced around the room and smiled. "I love the thought, but I have a better idea." A kiss landed on the curve of her jaw. "One that would offer us more privacy."

"Now I'm intrigued." Short of locking themselves into her bedroom, she would love to know how to get some privacy with him.

"I take it the wine was for tonight?" Quinn went to the refrigerator and pulled out the bottle.

"I'm in the mood for a beer if you don't mind."

Quinn gave her a funny look, but replaced the wine and pulled out two bottles of beer. He took down two glasses and picked up the afghan from the back of the couch.

"Where are we going?" She took the two glasses from him.

"Right out back." Quinn walked around the room and blew out the candles. "Don't worry, we'll hear the kids if one of them needs us." Quinn led the way out back, handed her the two beers, and pulled the chaise farther into the shadows.

With the two sets of patio doors open, they would be able to hear the kids, the phone, or anything else set on interrupting them. Quinn sat on the chaise and then pulled her down so that her butt was snuggled in between his thighs and her back was against his chest.

She nuzzled against him as he tried to pour the beers. "Stop that," growled Quinn, "or we are going to end up smelling like a brewery."

She took the glass he handed her and enjoyed the view of the night sky and the cove below. "This is better than what I came up with."

Quinn's lips played with her ear. "I loved your idea, Joc. I just wanted us to have a bit more privacy."

"Privacy, or more time to pull ourselves together just in case one of the kids comes downstairs?" She liked the warmth of his hand as it lay across her stomach. So far Quinn hadn't done one thing that could be considered out-of-line.

"Both." Quinn kissed the top of her head and then settled deeper into the chair. "This is my favorite spot to just sit and think."

She watched the way the moonlight flickered across the cove. Trees rustled in the wind, and the occasional seagull was still crying into the night. Peaceful sounds. The scent of sea and pine were thick on the breeze. "What do you think about?"

"Life, the kids, the job. The same type of things I'm sure everyone else thinks about when they are alone."

They sat in contented silence for a while just enjoying the evening. Curiosity finally got the better of her. There was so much concerning Quinn she didn't know. So many questions. She wanted some of those answers. "Quinn, tell me about Diane."

"My ex-wife?"

She had felt him stiffen for a moment at the mention of Diane's name, but he quickly relaxed. "You know another Diane?"

"Can't say that I do." Quinn took a drink and then set his glass down next to the chair. "What do you want to know?"

"Anything you're willing to tell me, I guess." She didn't want to know the really personal stuff, but she was curious about the woman who had bore Quinn's children.

"I guess I knew Diane my entire life, or close enough to it. She and I were both born the same year, in Misty Harbor. We were in just about every class together from kindergarten on up. We started dating when we were in the eleventh grade. By the twelfth grade we knew we were in love. We even went to the same college in Bangor."

"Sounds like you were inseparable." Jocelyn tried to think about the boys she had dated in the eleventh grade. A few of them stuck in her memory, but she couldn't imagine being married to any of them.

"We were. We were married the month after we both graduated from college. I joined Bangor's police force, and Diane got a job in retail management."

"When did you move back to Misty Harbor?"

"Three months after Diane found out she was pregnant with Ben. We had both agreed to raise our family here, instead of Bangor. We scraped together every penny we could and bought this place. I was lucky enough to get a deputy's job for the county. Diane worked part-time down at Claire's Boutique in town. She was overqualified for the job, but Misty Harbor didn't offer a whole lot of choices for someone with a degree in retail management. Ben was born, and we were managing nicely. Between both of our moms Diane still kept her part-time job, and we started to slowly fix up the house.

"I guess Ben was around two when the old sheriff retired and I ran, and was voted in, for the job. My pay went up, and Diane found out she was pregnant again. She was in her third month when the doctor ordered an ultrasound, and we discovered it was twins."

"That must have been an exciting time." She couldn't imagine what went through a woman's mind when the doctor told her she was carrying twins. Probably fear, anxiety, and incredible exhaustion all mixed with spectacular joy.

Quinn was quiet for a long moment. "Truth, Diane wasn't real thrilled with the news. Don't get me wrong, she loved both the girls, but she wasn't looking forward to handling newborn twins and a very active three-year-old. Ben turned three two months before the girls were born, and I was putting in some long hours. The job was still relatively new, plus we needed the overtime money. Diane had to give up the part-time job because it wasn't fair to ask either one of our mothers to watch three kids. She started to regret not using her education and talked about moving back to Bangor."

"I thought she moved to Boston?"

"She did, but that was after I said no to Bangor. We had agreed to raise the kids here, and I wasn't open to changing my mind. I told her if she wanted to go back to work part-time, she could. All her salary would be going to baby-sitters, but if it made her happy, that was okay. I told her if we stopped working on the house, and saved whatever we could, that by the time the girls were ready to start kindergarten, she would be able to open her own shop in Misty Harbor or in one of the other surrounding towns."

"She wasn't willing to wait, was she?"

"No, and in a way I couldn't blame her. Back in Bangor

when we were first married she was making more than I was. She was employed by an upscale store and was loving the responsibilities that went along with it. Back here in Misty Harbor she felt her parents went into debt to send her to college for nothing. She didn't need the college degree to be a glorified cashier down at Claire's.

"The twins were nine months old when Diane announced one night after dinner that she and the children were moving to Boston. Her old college roommate had not only found her a job, but a nice little house in a good section of the city to rent."

"What did you say to that?" She could hear the sadness in Quinn's voice, but no anger.

Quinn picked up his glass and finished the beer. "I told her if it was that important to her, we would sell the house, and I would move to Boston with her."

She closed her eyes against the beauty of the night. "Diane didn't want you to come, did she?"

"She thought it would be better if we made a clean break of things. The divorce was civil and friendly. I got to see the kids whenever I wanted. We had drifted apart, and the kids were stuck in the middle. Neither one of us wanted to hurt the children, so everything was handled with the children's happiness and stability in mind."

"Sounds like it was all very"—she almost choked on the word—"civil." If she had a husband and children, and one day he announced he was taking the kids and moving to another city, hours away, civil would be the last word to describe the ensuing scene. Heads would have rolled.

"It was civil, Joc." Quinn's arms tightened around her, and his chin rested on the top of her head. "Diane was a wonderful mother to the kids. She loved them more than life. She just wanted something more than what I could give her. Than what Misty Harbor could give her. I had no right to deny her that dream."

"She was your wife. They were your children." She

knew there was anger in her voice, but she couldn't help it. How could Quinn have done nothing?

"You can't force a person to love you, Joc." Quinn's voice sounded old and tired. "Forcing or preventing Diane from leaving wouldn't have solved anything. What we once had together would have crumbled into hatred. As it was, we parted as friends, and our children benefitted from that friendship. Weren't you the one who said a person alone in love would fail, but two people in love would win?"

"Yeah, they sound like my words." She still couldn't imagine not fighting for your own children, but on the other hand, Quinn and Diane's way of handling the whole thing sounded very mature and open-minded.

She felt Quinn's mouth form a smile against the back of her head. "Okay, enough about me," said Quinn. "I happened to run into your sister Gwen tonight when she was closing up the restaurant, and she told me this amusing little story."

A sense of dread slid down her spine. "About?"

"About how you used to trick your dates into thinking you had cooked their meals, when in fact it had been Gwen all along doing the cooking." Quinn's chest shook with his merriment. "What kind of guys did you go out with that dumped you because you couldn't cook?"

"Guys that obviously thought more about their stomachs than of me." Quinn already knew she wasn't the world's greatest cook, and he didn't seem to be running in the other direction. "And I can cook, just not like Gwen. Heck, I can even cook better than Sydney if I put my mind to it."

"Didn't realize that there were that many stupid men living in Maryland."

She turned her head and looked over her shoulder at him. "Thank you."

Quinn leaned forward and quickly kissed her. "You're welcome."

She settled back into his arms and shivered as the evening turned cooler. Quinn was wearing jeans and a polo shirt, while she was still dressed in a sleeveless top and shorts.

"Cold?" Quinn's palms lightly rubbed her bare arms. "Get under the blanket; that's why I brought it out here with us. Even in the middle of the summer, the nights tend to turn chilly around here."

She leaned forward and pulled the afghan up over her legs and arms. "I like how the nights cool down. Back in Baltimore you sweat all summer long, and the nights are just as bad as the days. We live in air-conditioning for months on end. We all hurry from our air-conditioned homes to our air-conditioned cars, to our air-conditioned offices, and then back again at the end of the day. Heat waves last for weeks on end."

"We get the occasional heat wave up here; but it only lasts for a few days, and the nights are usually bearable."

"Speaking of nights?" She wasn't sure if she should be concerned that Quinn hadn't slipped into her bed last night once he got home from work, or relieved that he hadn't taken their one night together as an open invitation.

"What about them?"

Quinn's chin rested on top of her head, and the heat from his body warmed her beneath the blanket. Dating, she understood. Dinner, movies, occasional picnics in the parks, and maybe even dancing. A relationship was built over time, and if everything was going great, you took it to the next step. Then the next step. The next thing you knew your toothbrush ended up at his apartment and you were discussing guest lists for the wedding. With Quinn it was different. They were already living together. They shared the same dinners and watched the same movies, but they had never been on a date.

"I'm not quite sure how to handle the other night, Quinn."

Quinn's body stiffened, and his hands froze upon her arms. "Regrets?"

She quickly turned in his arms and looked at him. Because of the deep shadows, she couldn't read his face. "Never." She brushed her lips across his mouth. Quinn returned the gesture with a heated kiss that had her melting in seconds. Why was she so concerned about the other night when they had this together? Why did she insist on analyzing everything to death? Maybe it was the lawyer in her.

Quinn slowly broke the kiss and brushed at a lock of her hair the wind had tossed across her cheek. "You want to lodge a complaint?"

She snorted at the absurdity. "Yeah, the night was too short."

Quinn's teeth flashed white in the darkness. "As long as that was the only *short* thing."

Her elbow playfully jabbed him in the gut, and then she wiggled closer into his arms. She could spend the next month or so right where she was and love every moment of it. Quinn's arms made her feel warm and wanted.

"What about the other night is making you uncomfortable?" asked Quinn softly.

"I'm not uncomfortable, just a little taken aback that everything happened pretty fast between us." *Fast, hell, I practically attacked the man in my bedroom.*

"So what you are telling me is that you want to slow it down?" Quinn's arms stayed around her and held her tight. His voice held a resigned sadness.

She shook her head. "No, I like your speed just fine, Quinn." She couldn't very well blurt out that she was falling in love with him. The last thing she wanted was for Quinn to go running for the hills and barricading his bedroom door at night. From what she heard about the male-female relationship only one word scared a guy more than love, it was "pregnant." It was a good thing she was already on birth control pills, because they hadn't used anything the other night.

"Spill it, Joc. Something is upsetting you, and I want to know what."

She took a deep breath and blurted out, "I don't do one-night stands, and I have never even thought about sleeping with my boss before."

"I've never had a one-night stand, and my boss is sixty-two years old, fifty pounds overweight, and bald." Quinn gently cupped her chin and forced her to look at him. "I know this whole situation is not what either of us is used to, with us living in the same house and with three pairs of curious, yet innocent eyes following our every move. Then there's the fact that you're only here temporarily, and that both of your brothers-in-law would use me for fish bait if I hurt you. But I can't stop wanting you." Quinn leaned forward and kissed her tenderly. "I've got the feeling that I'm going to be the one with the trampled heart."

Her fingers shook as they pressed against his chest. She could feel the steady beat of his heart beneath her hand. She didn't want to hurt Quinn, and she didn't want her own heart to get trampled. If they were going to have any type of relationship, Quinn needed to know the truth. "I think something very special is happening between us, Quinn. I'm not sure what to call it, or where it will lead, but I want to find out."

"So do I." Quinn's mouth brushed hers. "I'm glad you are feeling the same things I am, Joc."

She wrapped her arms around his neck. "Why is that?"

"Because where we are going, it takes two to get there." Quinn's mouth descended and captured her smile.

Jocelyn allowed Quinn to be the aggressor for all of two minutes. Then she not only returned his heated kisses, but she turned them up a notch. Quinn's groan gave her all the encouragement she needed. With a gentle kick she knocked the afghan onto the grass and straddled Quinn's lap. His thick, heavy arousal was nestled right where she wanted it, but they were both wearing way too many clothes.

Quinn's hands stroked their way up her bare thighs as his tongue slow danced its way into her mouth.

Her breasts grew heavy, and her nipples hardened against his chest. Desire thundered fast and furious throughout her body. She wanted Quinn, and she wanted him now. She broke the kiss and arched her back.

Quinn's mouth found her nipple through her blouse and gently tugged. She nearly climaxed.

"Quinn"—she cupped his jaw and moved his head away from her breasts—"do you think the kids are asleep yet?"

"Probably." Quinn was having a hard time trying to catch his breath. "We've got to slow down, Jocelyn, or I'm never going to make it upstairs."

She wiggled her bottom and chuckled at the inventive curse Quinn uttered. "This chaise is looking better by the minute."

Quinn groaned as his hands grasped her hips and tried to keep them still. "We're too old to be making love on a lounge chair."

She slid off Quinn and spread the blanket on a patch of grass that was deep in the darkness and on the other side of the chaise. With a quick snap and a zip, her shorts and the small triangle of silk called underwear hit the ground. "Speak for yourself, old man." Her fingers worked the buttons on her blouse. "Will the ground be better for your decrepit old bones?"

Quinn shot out of the chaise and pulled his shirt over his head. "I'll show you what these decrepit old bones can do."

She laughed softly as she lay down and her blouse and bra joined her shorts. "I love it when you talk dirty."

Quinn growled as he slid his naked body over top of hers. "Tell me how much you want me." The tip of his penis nudged her opening.

She wrapped her thighs around his hips, and she felt him slowly sink into her moistness. "I won't tell you." Her breath hitched in the back of her throat when he was fully inside and filling her beautifully. "I'm going to show you."

A low rumbling could be heard from Quinn as he slowly pulled back out, only to thrust more deeply.

With a low cry, she arched her back and met him thrust for thrust. Her body turned liquid soft and accepting as his hardened and drove toward completion. Harsh breathing mixed with moans of pleasure. Flesh met flesh as they climbed higher.

She felt her climax start the same instant Quinn muffled his shout of release against her neck.

Four minutes later she was still trying to catch her breath as Quinn slowly rolled off her and onto the grass. He missed the blanket by a good foot or two. By his sudden grunt of surprise he had either rolled onto a stone or one of the kids' toys. She just prayed he hadn't rolled onto one of Max's pooh piles, as the girls liked to call them. "You okay, Quinn?"

Quinn reached under him and yanked out Ben's baseball bat. "Nothing a little tender loving care won't fix."

She opened her arms. "Come here, and I'll rub it."

White teeth flashed in the darkness. "You don't know where it hurts." Quinn rolled toward her and pulled her into his arms.

"It doesn't matter." Her palms slowly stroked his muscular buttocks. "I'll just keep rubbing until it starts to feel good again."

Quinn flexed his hips, growled, and then slowly released her. "We need a soft bed before I start showing you how good it can feel." He tossed her her clothes. "Lord sakes, woman, put something on, or we are never going to make it back into the house."

Phoebe pulled her Jeep into Gary's driveway, but didn't turn it off. Away from the crowded movie theater, she felt nervous and unsure of what she was doing. She hadn't felt like this since she was sixteen and Gary had just gotten his license and they were alone for the first time. Well, she wasn't sixteen anymore. "Thanks for coming, Gary. The movie was as good as everyone said. The critics were right for once."

Gary turned in his seat and looked at her. Strong, capable hands lay silently in his lap. "Thanks for asking. I've been meaning to see it, but the opportunity had never arose until you called earlier and suggested it."

She had finally broken down and called Gary, because he hadn't called her. Four days and nights since they had gone lobster fishing together and then had a very nice dinner at Gary's. Four days and nights she had stood staring at the silent phone and praying he would call. No one had ever accused her of being patient.

She might have been the one to ask Gary out, but he had paid for the movie, while she sprang for the popcorn and drinks. The movie she chose hadn't been some chick flick or the latest romantic comedy. She didn't want to see beautiful movie stars kissing and sweating up the sheets while sitting next to Gary. She had picked some tough-ass war movie that she knew Gary would appreciate. "I'm glad you liked it." She would have enjoyed it more if Gary had been the one to suggest it.

Gary glanced away from her and toward his house. "I guess I better get going. Four in the morning comes awfully early."

"I imagine it does." The other morning when she had gotten up at four to be on the docks before Gary, it had nearly killed her. There had to be something wrong with anyone willing to get up at that ungodly hour, day after day. It was almost ten o'clock now. That meant by the time Gary got to bed, he would have less than six hours of sleep before he had to get back up. She shuddered at the thought. She needed at least eight hours straight before she could begin to function properly. Nine hours straight and a pot of coffee might actually put her in a decent mood.

Gary opened the door and stepped out of the Jeep. "Thanks again, Phoebe." He closed the door and looked in through the window opening. "I guess I'll be seeing you around."

"Sure." She willed herself not to cry, scream, or to say something incredibly stupid. She forced herself to smile nicely at the man who was breaking her heart all over again as tears burnt the back of her throat.

She watched as Gary slowly walked to his house and unlocked his front door. He turned once, gave her a small wave, and then disappeared inside. For all of Gary's enthusiasm, she could have been dating her brother.

Tonight was the fourth time she had made the first move in their awkward relationship, if one could call it that. She wouldn't even label it a friendship. They were more like acquaintances. Dinner the other night had consisted of nothing but conversations concerning the local residents and mutual friends. Gary hadn't even attempted to kiss her good night when she had left.

She was scared to death Gary was going to break her heart all over again, but so far she was still brave enough to keep trying. She needed to see if there was anything left between them. Sometimes she thought she saw something in Gary's eyes when he looked at her. Some magical little spark that said there was plenty left and he was feeling it, too.

Other times, like tonight, Gary hid behind a cool, polite mask.

The Gary she had known and loved back in high school never would have worn that mask. Gary had been passionate about everything he had done, be it hauling in lobsters or discussing some obscure little-known Civil War battle. Gary had also been passionate about her, about them, about their future together. He always had been holding her hand or touching her in sweet, gentle gestures that he probably hadn't even realized he had been doing while they had been out in public. In private, Gary had known exactly how to touch her and make her ache. They had grown up together. They had experimented with their growing sexual feelings and had enjoyed every minute of it. She had always regretted never hitting that home run of completion with Gary, but she never regretted his touch.

Tonight any touching had been purely accidental. Each casual touch had sent a jolt of electricity through her and made her edgy.

Gary had changed over the years. She wasn't foolish enough to think he wouldn't have, but it still was a shock to compare the boy against the man he had become. She liked the boy better.

The boy had made her want.

Yet that illusive gleam in Gary's green eyes told her the boy was still there, somewhere. The question was, did she have the patience or the desire to unbury the boy?

She stared at Gary's house for a long while before putting the Jeep in reverse and driving away. She would give Gary a couple of days to see if he would contact her. If not, she'd be back.

She had to come back because he still held something very precious of hers. Gary still held her heart.

Chapter Fifteen

Jocelyn finished putting away the stack of towels in the family bath and straightening up the room. Thankfully the kids were learning to pick up after themselves more, and their dirty clothes actually made it into the hamper. Issy and Tori were in their room having an imaginary tea party, while Ben was downstairs busy building with his Legos. She was unloading the hamper when she heard the phone ring, but she didn't rush to get it. Quinn was downstairs ironing his uniforms.

Domestic bliss was alive and well at the Larson household.

After checking on the girls, she carried the full laundry basket downstairs and put it on top of the washing machine. She wasn't going to do a load this morning because it was pouring outside. Quinn's and her plans to take the kids out on Erik's fishing boat this afternoon were a wash. They had already made arrangements to try it again on Quinn's next day off.

She closed the laundry closet doors and noticed Quinn standing at the back patio door staring out into the rain. Her heart gave that familiar little catch. The one she had been growing accustomed to over the past several weeks.

Her lover looked incredibly sexy, yet lonely.

She slipped up behind him, wrapped her arms around his trim waist, and pressed her cheek against his back. She just held him for a moment, breathing in his scent. Quinn didn't wear aftershave, but he smelled of fresh soap, clean shampoo, and just a hint of fabric softener. She closed her eyes and thought that she would know his scent anywhere. She had been sleeping and dreaming in that scent every night now for over a week.

Quinn's hands pressed her arms against his stomach, but he didn't break the silence.

It wasn't very often they got to hold each other in the daylight. Any minute now, one of the children would come thumping down the steps demanding something.

She rubbed her cheek against his shoulder blade. Something was upsetting Quinn, yet he had been fine when she had gone upstairs to put away the towels. "Who was that on the phone?"

Quinn gave a weary sigh and turned around. "A Mrs. Krugle."

She lowered her arms and took a step back. She didn't like the dismal expression on Quinn's face. It was giving her a bad feeling. "Who's Mrs. Krugle?" She had never heard the name before. Today was Quinn's day off, so she didn't think the phone call had anything to do with his job.

"A woman applying for the position of nanny and housekeeper." Quinn's gaze never left her face. "She'll be here in two hours for an interview."

"I see." The only thing she could see at the moment were the questions burning in Quinn's eyes. Questions she didn't have answers to. They had both known this could happen. She just hadn't expected it to be so soon. "I guess I'll go clean up a little bit more, and then get out of your way."

She turned to go, but Quinn's hand latched on to her arm. "You're not in my way, Joc. Besides, today is supposed to be your day off."

She didn't turn to face Quinn. There were tears blurring her vision, and she didn't want him to see them. Quinn's first duty was to his family, and she not only understood that, but she accepted it. They both knew she wouldn't be staying. Quinn needed that housekeeper. "The interview will go a lot smoother if I'm not around, Quinn. I think I'll go visit my sister this afternoon, okay?"

Quinn's hand slowly released her. "If that is what you want to do."

It wasn't what she wanted to do. It was what she had to do. She would have liked nothing better than to lock the front door and pretend they weren't home when this Mrs. Krugle showed up. That wasn't going to happen. She couldn't spend the rest of her life hiding out in Misty Harbor trying to figure out her life, while playing nanny. "I'll be home in time to help with dinner." She hurried from the room and headed upstairs.

For the next hour and a half she ran around the house making beds, vacuuming rugs, and dusting. The kids pitched in on the cleanup, and the living room even had a nice-size path through the maze of toys. Quinn had explained the upcoming interview to the children, but they seemed awfully quiet as they picked up their toys. Quinn had finished the ironing and had straightened up the dining room.

The house never looked so clean and tidy as she pulled on her raincoat and headed out the door, with fifteen minutes to spare. Even Max got a pretty blue bow on top of his head.

By the time she drove to Sydney's, tears were rolling down her cheeks. She parked the car by the curb in front of her sister's cottage and frowned at the driveway. Not only was Sydney home, but Erik was there as well. She didn't mind her sister seeing how upset she was, but there was no way she was crying in front of Erik. A quick search through the glove compartment unearthed three clean, but wrinkled, McDonald's napkins. It also revealed two happy toys, a pair of pink, sparkly plastic sunglasses, and a chewed-on tennis ball.

She allowed herself another two minutes of crying, and then she pulled herself together, blew her nose, and wiped away the last of the tears. As she slowly walked around the white picket fence and up the walk, she got soaked, but it didn't bother her. The weather and rain were warm enough, and hopefully walking through the downpour would wash away the evidence of her crying spell.

Sydney opened the front door, took one look at her, and ordered her upstairs to the only bathroom in the house.

Five minutes later she made her way back down, feeling and looking a whole lot better. She found her sister in the kitchen putting on a pot of coffee. "Was that Erik I just saw leaving?" Erik's pickup truck had been pulling out of the driveway when she had walked through the living room.

"He wanted to go visit his grandfather," Sydney said as she took three coffee cups out of the cabinet. "Gwen's on her way over."

"I thought she was working." She had a sinking feeling Sydney had kicked Erik out of his own home and called their sister to come over. She was about to be grilled.

Gwen came hurrying through the side door bearing a box and a worried look. "I brought food." Gwen looked straight at her and asked, "Are you all right?"

"Of course I'm all right. What did Sydney tell you?" She frowned at Sydney, who was looking just as concerned as Gwen.

"That you've been crying." Gwen hung up her slicker and opened the box. "Cherry cheesecake, your favorite."

She looked at the mouthwatering cake and had to bite her lower lip to keep from bawling like a baby. Gwen had always known exactly what to do to cheer either her or Sydney up when they were down. Sydney preferred anything chocolate, while she wanted cheesecake. She gave Gwen a quick hug, and then Sydney. What would she ever do without her sisters? "Thank you both."

Sydney carried the cups over to the table and started pouring the coffee. Gwen got down the plates and napkins. She snatched up a knife and three forks and joined her sisters at the table.

She was on her third forkful of cake when she noticed that Gwen was pushing hers around the plate instead of eating it. She narrowed her eyes and studied her sister's face. Gwen looked horrible. "Are you sick, Gwen?"

Gwen glanced at her, then at Sydney. "No, I'm not sick. I'm just a bit off this morning." Gwen managed a wide smile, and some color did seem to be returning to her cheeks. "It must be this weather getting me down, that's all."

"Who's your doctor?" asked Sydney as she picked up her sister's wrist and started to feel for the pulse. "When was your last checkup?"

Gwen yanked her arm away from Sydney and chuckled. "You're my doctor, Syd. Why would I go to anyone else when we live in the same town?"

"I've never seen you as a patient." Sydney tried to feel Gwen's forehead. "Any fever? What about nausea?"

Gwen swatted at Sydney's hand. "The reason you have never seen me is because I haven't been sick since you opened up your practice in Misty Harbor. I'm fine now. Nothing that a good night's sleep won't cure."

Sydney snorted. "Then tell Daniel to let you sleep for God's sake."

Gwen's chuckle had Sydney and Jocelyn joining right in. It was a well-known fact that even after a year of marriage Daniel and Gwen couldn't keep their hands off of each other.

As their laughter died down, Jocelyn's sisters shared a glance and then looked directly at her. The inquisition was about to begin. Sydney fired off the first volley. "So, how's Quinn and the kids?"

"Fine." She stabbed a cherry and popped it into her mouth. They were more than fine; they were wonderful, loving, and becoming her whole world. She didn't think her sisters wanted to hear that she was losing her mind and becoming Alice from *The Brady Bunch.*

"What are they doing on this rainy afternoon?" asked Gwen as she took a sip of coffee. Gwen still hadn't eaten one bite of cake.

"Quinn's interviewing a prospective nanny/house-keeper." She stared hard at her cheesecake and refused to meet either of her sisters' looks. The damn tears were back. "I figured it would go easier if I wasn't standing around looking over his shoulder."

Her sisters were quiet for a long moment. Finally, Sydney broke the silence by softly asking. "You're in love with him, aren't you?"

"What does it matter?" She looked at both of her sisters, and in one blinding instant she was jealous of the happiness they both had found. "Contrary to your two perfect lives, not every story has a happy ending." She regretted the words and her sarcastic tone as soon as they left her mouth. "I'm sorry, neither one of you deserved that." She reached out and grabbed their hands. "I'm really happy that both of you found the love of your lives and will be living happily-ever-after. I'm jealous, and it's the green-eyed monster talking."

Both Gwen and Sydney squeezed her hands back. "We understand completely, Joc. Love is never easy. In fact, it can be downright painful at times," said Sydney.

"Got anything in your medicine bag for it, Doc?" She

chuckled at a childhood memory. "Remember that little black leather medicine bag you got for Christmas one year? You used to carry around jelly beans and Hershey Kisses in it so that you could prescribe them to me whenever I had an ache or a pain."

Sydney chuckled at the memory. "Mom swore that keeping me in medicine for my patients was more expensive than paying for medical school."

"Maybe, but you cured me every time." She gave her sister a small smile. "It won't be that easy this time."

"How does Quinn feel about you?"

She shrugged. "I don't know."

"You don't know?" asked Gwen. "Haven't you discussed your feelings for each other?"

"Yeah"—she played with the handle on her fork—"we both agreed that something special was happening between us, and that we both wanted to see where it would lead."

"And where exactly is it leading?" asked Sydney.

"To him interviewing someone for the position of housekeeper, and me without a job or a place to stay. I probably will be heading back to Baltimore sooner rather than later."

"You can stay here," offered Sydney.

"We have plenty of room for you, Jocelyn," added Gwen. "Where do the children fit in this?"

"What do you mean?"

"You can't fall in love with just Quinn, Joc. He comes as a package deal. It's not like Daniel and me, where it is only the two of us. Or like Sydney and Erik. You have to love the children, too."

She stared at her sister as if she were nuts. "Who do you think has been living in that house for over a month now? Who do you think has been taking care of those children? Cooking their meals? Teaching Ben to throw a curve ball and Issy how to do the five positions in ballet? Who do you think is calling every horse farm in the phone book looking for pony-riding lessons for Tori?"

Sydney and Gwen looked at each other and smiled. "Well, that explains a lot."

"It also explains why my heart is going to break four times over when I pack up my bags and move back to Baltimore." Why couldn't her sisters see that she and Quinn hadn't had enough time together. Everything was too new. Love needed time to grow, and Quinn probably needed more time than most men. After what he had been through with Diane, could he chance falling in love again? Would he chance it? He had known Diane his entire life, been in love for years with her, and one day, poof, she was taking his children and moving away. She didn't see how he would ever risk falling in love again.

Sydney seemed to be mulling the problem over in her mind, while Gwen slowly stirred her coffee. "Remember when Grandmom Augusta passed away and we found out we were in her will?" asked Gwen.

"Yeah, she left us each a nice-size chunk of cash and requested that we invest it in our dreams. She called it our dream inheritance."

"That's right. Want to know what I invested in?" Gwen gave both of her sisters a wide smile. "My restaurant."

Both Sydney and Jocelyn shook their heads. "Like we wouldn't have guessed that." Jocelyn looked at Sydney. "What have you invested in?"

"Erik and I are renting this cottage, and I rent my medical office. I didn't need it to start up my practice here. I'm using it as my share of an emergency medical center a bunch of doctors from the surrounding area and I are trying to get built nearby. The nearest hospital is just too far away for all of our peace of mind."

"Wow," muttered Gwen. "Now I feel stupid for investing in my restaurant while you're out there trying to save human lives."

Sydney chuckled. "Nonsense. Grandmom Augusta wanted us to use it for our own dreams, not someone else's. My dreams are different from your dreams, Gwen. That's all." Sydney leaned over and hugged Gwen. "By the size of the crowds you get in the restaurant, I would have to say your dream is making quite a few people very happy."

Both of her sisters turned and looked at her. "So, baby sister," asked Gwen, "what's your dream?"

Quinn glanced at Mrs. Krugle and tried to hazard a guess at her age. He failed miserably. The woman had to be a good ten years older than his own mother. How was she ever going to keep up with three very active children, and why would she want to?

Mrs. Krugle had wrinkled her nose at the dining room and muttered under her breath about spoiled children as they maneuvered their way through the toy-filled living room. She had seemed to appreciate the kitchen, but she didn't look too impressed with the family room or the three well-groomed kids sitting side by side on the couch. Beyond a very polite "hello" the children hadn't said a word to the woman. Then again, Mrs. Krugle hadn't been too keen on starting any conversations with them. The kids had managed to throw a couple mutinous glares his way.

The tour of the upstairs rooms hadn't gone any better. Mrs. Krugle didn't seem to consider the master bedroom with its own private bath as a perk. She had even asked about getting a window air-conditioning unit for the room.

Quinn waved a hand toward the kitchen table. "Would you care for a cup of coffee, Mrs. Krugle, or something cold to drink?" So far the woman hadn't given him permission to use her first name, nor was it likely she ever would.

"Lemonade if you have it, please." Mrs. Krugle frowned at the old jelly jar sitting in the middle of the table filled with wildflowers the kids had picked yesterday for Jocelyn. A few dead petals littered the table, but they were still a bright and sunny spot in the room.

Quinn opened the refrigerator door and tried not to cringe at the half-bare shelves. "I'm afraid we are all out of lemonade, Mrs. Krugle. We have iced tea, orange juice, and what appears to be blue Kool-Aid." There was also half a bottle of white wine left, and three cold beers. He had a sinking suspicion that Mrs. Krugle wouldn't approve of alcoholic beverages before or even after the lunch hour.

"Ice water will do, thank you." Mrs. Krugle wrinkled her nose at Max, who had come over to investigate now that there were people in his favorite room of the house, the kitchen. Mrs. Krugle waved her hand at Max and said, "Shoo."

Quinn poured two glasses of ice water and carried them over to the table and sat. Max took one look at the stern expression on Mrs. Krugle's face and silently padded his way back into the family room to flop in front of the children. Quinn didn't blame him one bit. Out of everyone in the room, Max looked the happiest. Hell, Max looked ecstatic compared to the kids.

"I can see why you are in such a hurry to get a housekeeper in here, Mr. Larson. This place could really use a good scrubbing." Mrs. Krugle looked directly at Max. "If I decide to take the job, the dog has to go. I can't be spending my days cleaning up dog germs and hair. It would be too much to ask of one person."

He frowned at the glass of ice water in his hand. The dog wasn't too much for Jocelyn to handle. In fact,

Jocelyn had been the one insisting Max stay from the beginning. The kids loved Max, and there was no way he was getting rid of the mutt now. Somehow, during the last month, the mutt had managed to become a member of the family.

Hell, Tori managed to bring more germs and dirt into the house than Max. Would Mrs. Krugle want to get rid of Tori, too?

He glanced around his house and tried to see it from this stranger's eyes. He couldn't. There was absolutely nothing wrong with the place. In fact, it was probably the cleanest it had ever been. Jocelyn had gone through the place an hour ago like a madwoman, pushing the vacuum with one hand and dusting with the other. The children and he had been given no other choice but to get out of her way. All that work on what should have been her day off for what? For Mrs. Krugle to turn up her nose at his home and tell him it needed a good scrubbing?

Mrs. Krugle was never going to work out. He had known it the minute she had walked in the door. Feeling guilty, he had proceeded with the tour of the house and explained a little about what the job would entail anyway. They were now at the interview part, and he couldn't think of a single question to ask.

He smiled at the kids. "Come here, guys."

The kids slowly made their way into the kitchen. Ben looked worried. Issy looked ready to cry at any moment. Tori tilted up her chin and glared at the woman.

"Ben, do you have a question for Mrs. Krugle? Something that would be very important to you if she lived here and took care of you." He was curious as to what his children thought their nanny should be like, and what qualities they were looking for.

Ben thought for a minute and then asked, "Can you throw a curve ball?"

Mrs. Krugle seemed taken aback by the question. "Certainly not, young man. I'm a firm believer in academics over sports. You should be reading, not playing ball."

He didn't even bother explaining that Ben hadn't even started kindergarten yet, let alone mastered the art of reading. "What about you, Issy? Anything you'd like to ask?"

Issy studied the floor and softly asked, "Do you like ballerinas?"

"Oh, my, yes," said Mrs. Krugle with what he had to assume was a smile. "Ballet is a fine hobby for a young lady to pursue."

"What about horses? Do you like horses?" asked Tori excitedly.

"They're filthy beasts." Mrs. Krugle looked directly at Tori and snapped, "Young ladies don't ride horses. You should be spending your time doing something constructive, like taking piano lessons."

He had to put a stop to this right now before Tori did something outrageous, like pop Mrs. Krugle one in the nose or cry. Tori very seldom cried, but had been known to pitch fits worthy of a banshee. "I think you children should go upstairs and have a tea party or something while I finish up here with Mrs. Krugle." He nodded to the stairs and gave them all a reassuring smile. "Take Max with you, okay?"

His children looked ready to disobey, but they kept their mouths closed and marched out of the room. They didn't even have to call Max; the dog seemed more than glad to follow them without being told.

He pushed away his glass of water and softly said, "I'm sorry, but this isn't going to work out. I appreciate you taking the time and coming for the interview."

Mrs. Krugle stared back at him for a full minute before saying, "I see."

He got to his feet, and Mrs. Krugle followed him out to the front porch. Without saying another word, Mrs. Krugle got back in her big boat of a car and drove away. He stood there for a moment feeling nothing but relief. Jocelyn wouldn't be leaving. They would still have time to explore their feelings for each other. They hadn't talked about or named those feelings yet, but he knew where he was heading. He was falling in love with Jocelyn.

So what in the hell was he going to do about it?

When no insightful answers came to him, he turned and walked back into the house. His step faltered as he spotted his kids sitting on the stairs. Issy and Tori were on the bottom step, and they were holding hands. Ben sat on the step behind them. All three were looking at him as if he had just told them Santa wouldn't be coming this Christmas.

He glanced around the room. "Where's Max?" It was unusual to see the kids without their hairy companion.

Tori raised her chin and said, "We hid him."

"Why?" Hiding Max would be like hiding an elephant in a cardboard box. Senseless.

"Because we aren't going to let you get rid of him," answered Ben.

"I never said I was going to get rid of Max." He knelt down and looked each of his children in the eye. "I did say if his owners showed up we would have to do the right thing and give him back to them." He saw Issy's lower lip tremble and tried to head off the flood of tears and a broken heart. "But, since the 'found' posters have been up for weeks and no one has come to claim him, I have a feeling Max is part of the family now."

"What about that lady?" Tori pointed to the screen door and pouted. "The one who doesn't like horses or baseball?"

"Mrs. Krugle won't be back, hon." He reached out

and wiped away a tear that was slowly rolling down Issy's cheek. "I promise that when we find someone new to take care of you guys, you will like them." He didn't know how he was going to keep that promise, but he would somehow.

"We don't want anyone new," Tori said.

"We want Jocelyn to stay," added Ben.

"We like Jocelyn, and she likes us," whispered Issy as she rubbed at her tears. "She plays castle with us, and she always lets me be the princess."

"Jocelyn teached me to bake cookies. Special cookies, too," Tori added. "She lets me smash them with a fork to make the pretty designs."

"I know, honey, and they tasted delicious." He pulled the girls into his arms and hugged them tight.

"She's still teaching me to spit and scratch." Ben gave him an imploring look.

"Spit and scratch?" He couldn't keep the amusement out of his voice as he stared at his son. He had no idea where this would be going.

"Jocelyn said all great baseball players know how to spit and scratch."

He tried not to chuckle. "I see." He tried not to visualize Jocelyn giving his son scratching lessons. What he did see was how important Jocelyn had become not only to him, but to the children as well. "Since Jocelyn is so nice to you guys, I think she deserves a special night out." It would be a shame to waste his one night off just sitting home. "How about we treat her to a trip to Sullivan?"

"Happy Meals," shouted Tori as she bounced out of his arms.

"I was thinking more on the line of pizza, maybe a visit to the arcade, and we can top off the evening with double dip ice-cream cones."

All three kids shouted their agreement. Somewhere

above his head he could hear Max's muffled barks. With a deep sigh he said, "Ben, please go let Max out of the girls' closet. There's no telling what he has chewed up by now."

Chapter Sixteen

Jocelyn squeezed Quinn's hand. "Are you sure they're okay by themselves?" She watched as the merry-go-round did another complete turn and waved to the girls as they went by. Issy was riding a beautiful and fanciful white stallion, while Tori opted for a black beast that seemed to have smoke pouring from his flared nostrils. Both girls were holding on to their poles with two hands and grinning.

"They're fine." Quinn waved to Ben, who was on the horse directly behind Issy. Strong arms tugged her closer. "Relax, Joc, they aren't going to get hurt."

She snuggled up against him and glanced around at the other parents surrounding the amusement ride. No one else seemed to be worrying about their kids. A couple of parents were even on the ride, holding little ones that were too young to hold on for themselves. It seemed everyone had the same idea as Quinn. Tourists and the locals, who had been cooped up all day because of the rain, had all come out to play now that the storm had passed. It was turning into a real family night in Sullivan.

Jocelyn watched as the kids made another pass. Flying horses, tinny organ music, swirling lights, and three of the most beautiful smiles she had ever seen. One of Quinn's hands rested on her hip, and she was holding three little zip-up sweatshirts for when the night turned cooler. Damn if she didn't feel like they were a family.

When she had returned to Quinn's home after visiting with her sisters, the kids had announced they were taking her out for pizza, ice cream, and a trip to the arcade. Quinn had been awfully quiet, but the kids had filled her in on Mrs. Krugle. She was thankful that Quinn hadn't hired a woman like that for the kids. How could one person want to get rid of Max, hate horses, and not like America's greatest pastime, baseball?

She looked at Quinn and said, "I'm sorry Mrs. Krugle didn't work out." She knew how important it was for Quinn to find someone to permanently fill the position.

Quinn gave her a long, measured look before asking, "Are you really sorry?"

She saw the gleam of hurt in Quinn's eyes before he hid it. She didn't want to hurt Quinn or the children. Her emotions played a tug-of-war, and no one was the victor. She was falling in love with Quinn and the children, but she couldn't give up being a lawyer permanently. Her hand reached up and tenderly cupped his jaw. "I'm not as sorry as I should be." The pad of her thumb traced his lower lip, and a heated flush swept up her cheeks when she thought about what his mouth was capable of doing to her. "You still haven't tried my spaghetti and meatballs."

White teeth nipped at her thumb. "It's not your cooking I'm interested in." Quinn captured her hand and gave it a gentle squeeze. "You okay with staying?"

"After a comment like that? Try getting rid of me." She laughed at the frustrated look on Quinn's face. The children's bedtime was still hours away. The crowd of parents rushed forward as the merry-go-round slowed to a stop. Someone bumped into her, and Quinn's hands steadied her.

"Stay here, I'll go get the kids." Quinn headed for the ride.

She watched as Quinn reached for Ben first and then swung both girls up into his arms. Quinn laughed at something Issy was saying. Tori was trying to get his attention by patting him on the jaw. Ben, not wanting to be separated, had grasped the back pocket of his father's jeans as they worked their way through the crowd.

She saw the laughter dancing in Quinn's eyes and the smile that turned the handsome sheriff into a loving father. She felt the noise and confusion of the arcade fade into the background as her heart slammed against her rib cage. She wasn't falling in love with Quinn and the children. *She was in love with Quinn and the kids!* Hell, she even loved the hundred-pound hairball back at the house.

Her whole world was before her, yet her life was supposed to be back in Baltimore.

Quinn stopped in front of her and frowned. "Joc, are you all right?"

She could read the concern in Quinn's dark eyes. "No, I'm not all right." There was no way she was going to be blurting out the truth while arcade games were blaring all around them, or when they had such an audience. "I just realized something very important."

"What?"

She traded Quinn the sweatshirts for a sticky-faced Tori. She swung the laughing child around in a circle. "I just realized I haven't had cotton candy in about ten years." Which wasn't a lie. She'd been eyeing the dozen or so plastic bags one of the vendors was selling for about ten minutes now.

Quinn glanced over to a red-and-white-striped cart. The white-aproned vendor was selling cotton candy, candy apples, and bags of freshly popped popcorn. "Well, it looks like you get a choice of either pink or blue."

"Pink." She swung Tori around one more time, just

to hear her shriek of laughter. "I'm definitely in a pink mood tonight."

Quinn stared at the ceiling in what once had been his bedroom. Now it was Jocelyn's bedroom, but he had been enjoying the view of the ceiling night after night. More important, he had been enjoying the woman lying in his arms. A naked, warm, and tonight, totally aggressive woman.

He took another deep breath and tried to calm his pounding heart. It wasn't working. Jocelyn had rocked his world, and destroyed his body. He felt a wide grin spread across his face and was thankful that at least his facial muscles were still working. The rest of his body was a total wash.

Jocelyn had been acting funny since the arcade earlier. He couldn't really pinpoint exactly what had been different, but something had changed her mood. Whatever it was, he prayed it happened every evening. His fingers toyed with the ends of her long blond hair as it lay across his chest. Jocelyn's face was buried into the pillow next to him, and her long, luscious legs were tangled with his. The sheets and comforter had been kicked off sometime during their first ten minutes in bed.

"So"—he took another deep breath and tried to brush some of Jocelyn's hair away from her beautiful face—"this is your 'pink' mood?"

Jocelyn snorted into the pillow. "The sugar made me do it."

His fingers trailed down her spine and softly traced the sweet curve of her bottom. "Remind me to feed you cotton candy more often." Tonight's lovemaking had been wild, heated, and fantastic, which wasn't that unusual for them. But there had been an added element. Something different. Something more.

Jocelyn turned on her side and snuggled up against him. "Did I thank you for a wonderful evening yet?"

"If you thanked me any more, I'd be dead." He pulled her closer and placed a kiss on the top of her head. He liked the feel of her breasts against his chest and the way her one thigh nestled against his groin. "If all of this was from one evening spent fighting crowds, heartburn pizza, and sticky-faced children, I would hate to think what would happen if we actually went out on a real date."

"Define a 'real date.' "

"Just you, me, good food with a great wine." He skimmed his fingers over her hip and felt her shiver. "Maybe some slow jazz and a very dark dance floor." He used the palm of his hand to cup her bottom. "Definitely a dark dance floor."

Jocelyn smiled against his shoulder. "You like jazz?"

"What saxophone player doesn't?"

Jocelyn's head snapped up. "You play the sax?"

"All through high school and into college." He liked the astonished look on her face. "Surprised you with that one, didn't I?"

"How good are you?"

"Better than Bill Clinton, but not as good as Lisa Simpson." He gave her a quick kiss. "If you play your cards right, I might give you a private concert one night."

Jocelyn's fingers toyed with the hair on his chest. "I wasn't thinking about playing with cards." Her fingers danced lower.

He sucked in his gut. "No, you're playing with fire."

Sweet laughter tickled his chest. "Am I going to get burnt?"

"Give this old man a couple more minutes to recuperate, and you just might." He grabbed her wandering fingers and smiled up at the ceiling. His heart rate still wasn't down to normal, and already she was boosting it up again. The woman was insatiable, and he was the luckiest man in the world. He needed to pull his mind off her luscious body and made-for-sin mouth. "So, did you straighten out Abraham's and Millicent's legal problems?"

"I found a very nice and reputable lawyer for Abraham's mom, but they are going to have to drive about forty minutes to get there." Jocelyn's fingers entwined with his. "Millicent's problem is a little more difficult. Her lawyer made a complex problem a lot more complicated than it needed to be. It's nearly impossible for me to untangle it all and explain it to her in English."

"So what are you going to tell her?"

"My recommendation is either her lawyer rewrites the entire thing, or she gets a new lawyer. One that will take his time to explain everything to her." Jocelyn kissed a path across his chest and up the column of his throat. "What Misty Harbor really needs is a good lawyer."

Quinn felt his heart slam against his chest. There was something in Jocelyn's gaze he couldn't decipher. It was as if she was testing him. "True. You happen to know of anyone that might be interested in hanging out their shingle?"

With a seductive move that raised his blood pressure along with one obvious appendage, Jocelyn straddled his thighs. "Maybe." Jocelyn leaned forward and nibbled on his lower lip. The sway of her breasts teased his chest. "Taking another bar exam would be a bitch, though."

Was Jocelyn saying what he thought she was saying? He was almost afraid to ask, but he had to know. Was there a chance that she would be staying in Misty Harbor for good? "Are you considering taking it?"

Jocelyn's chuckle was low and sensual as she raised her hips up and slowly lowered herself onto him. "Yeah, I'm taking it."

Quinn felt her warm, wet flesh surround him as she lowered herself inch by inch onto his shaft. He had no idea if Jocelyn was referring to the bar exam or him, but he couldn't voice his question. Somehow he had managed to lose his ability to think, let alone talk. All he could do was feel as Jocelyn arched her back and started to ride him.

Quinn paced the family room. Every third step he looked out the patio doors and tried to see down to the cove, where Jocelyn and his sister had taken the kids and Max about fifteen minutes ago. Jocelyn had been upset with him as he ushered them out onto the patio. He hadn't kept the interview with a potential nanny/housekeeper from her to hurt her. He had done it so she wouldn't fret, worry, and run around the house cleaning it like some possessed madwoman.

There were crayons scattered around the family room, along with coloring books and papers. A handful of dirty dishes were in the sink, and the dining room table was piled high with clean, folded laundry. Max's chew toys were scattered throughout the house, and the living room held two blanket tents and a massive Lego tower he had helped Ben make last night. His house was just the way he liked it, and if the potential housekeeper didn't like it, she wouldn't be the right one for the job.

He also couldn't go through another tearful guilt trip from the kids. The best thing to do was to interview this Ms. Starr, and if she was indeed the ideal person for the job, he would take her down to the cove and introduce her to the kids, their aunt, Max, and Jocelyn. If Ms. Starr turned out to be another Mrs. Krugle, then he would hustle her on her way, and the kids would never even know he had interviewed another nanny.

Seemed like a perfectly reasonable plan to him. So why did he keep thinking about that hurt look in Jocelyn's eyes. Or the murderous glare Phoebe had thrown over her shoulder at him as she helped Jocelyn gather up the beach towels and sand toys to take with them.

It had been three days since Jocelyn had teased him about taking the Maine bar exam. He still wasn't sure if she had been serious or not. She hadn't mentioned it again, and he had been too chicken to bring up the subject. In regard to the upcoming interview, it really didn't matter if Jocelyn had been serious or not. If Jocelyn went back to Baltimore and picked up her life and career, he would need a new housekeeper. If Jocelyn opened her own law office in Misty Harbor, he would still need that housekeeper and nanny.

Jocelyn was way overqualified for the position. She had a career to get back to, one that didn't include finding a ballet studio for Issy, pony-riding lessons for Tori, or teaching his son how to scratch and spit. He knew that Jocelyn liked the kids, really liked them. But liking them was one thing. Giving up her career was another.

Their own mother had refused to give up her career. He had never blamed Diane, so how could he even consider asking Jocelyn to stay and become a full-time mother? Hell, he wasn't even sure he wanted a full-time mother for his kids. He had fallen in love with Jocelyn because of who she was, not because of how well she had gotten along with the kids. Jocelyn was smart, funny, and loving. She was also a lawyer, and he had no right to ask her to give that up. Nor did he want to.

The sound of a car pulling into the driveway destroyed his thoughts. By the noise it was making, the car obviously didn't have a muffler.

He headed for the front door and frowned at the rusty, dented car. He thought it must have at one time been blue, but now it was mostly a rust-colored primer. As a young woman stepped out from behind the wheel, he stepped out onto the porch.

A bubble of laughter threatened to overtake him as he got his first look at the prospective employee. Ms. Starr was wearing skin-tight jeans that boasted about six holes in them. Her blouse was one of those midriff things that showed a good inch or two of her belly. Short black hair was spiked in every direction, a row of sparkling earrings outlined her entire right ear, and her complexion was so pale she actually looked sick. Ms. Starr wasn't old enough to order herself a beer.

The woman spent a long while studying his sheriff's car before walking to the porch. She planted her feet on the bottom step and stared up at him.

"Ms. Starr?"

"Crystal. Everyone calls me Crystal."

Crystal Starr? Lord, it sounds like a country western singer or a porn star. "I'm Quinn Larson."

Crystal nodded toward his SUV. "You're a cop?"

"Sheriff, actually." He waved a hand toward two of the rockers lining the porch. "Why don't we sit for a moment." There wasn't any use going through an interview with her. There was no way he was hiring her.

"Gee, I don't know about living with a cop." Crystal plopped herself down in one of the rockers.

He lowered himself into a chair and tried to figure out what to say. "Crystal, can I ask you why you are applying for this job?"

"Well"—Crystal glanced at his uniform and sighed—"I was hoping to get out of my parents' house. They are always trying to run my life and tell me what to do."

"I see." He could see a lot of things, and the main one being Crystal Starr wasn't going to be living in his house.

"I like kids and all, but I don't think I want to live with a cop." A red tide swept up her pale face. "I don't mean any disrespect or anything. It's just that I think you might even be worse than my parents when it comes to rules and all."

He tried not to smile. The silver hoop pierced through her one eyebrow really wasn't so bad after all. Of course, his girls would never be allowed to do such a thing

when they became older. "I do have a whole list of rules.
Plus you won't be getting any weekends off."

"I'd have to work every weekend?" Crystal looked at
him in horror.

"Afraid so." Maybe he should consider conducting
these interviews over the phone. It would save everyone
time.

Crystal stood up and politely held out her hand. "I
would like to thank you for the opportunity, but I really
don't think this job is for me."

He stood and shook her hand. "Sorry to hear that."
Crystal seemed like a nice enough kid. Way too young,
but polite. Her parents obviously had been doing something right. He was just thankful he didn't have to tell
her she wasn't right for the job.

Crystal hurried to her car, gave him a final wave, and
with more noise than a Mac truck, drove away.

He stood on the front porch for a long while trying
to decide if Crystal's departure was a good thing or a
bad thing. He hadn't seriously considered hiring her,
but if she had been an acceptable candidate, what would
he have done then?

He was out of options. He would have to hire a new
housekeeper and nanny soon. Jocelyn wouldn't be filling that position much longer, no matter where their
relationship led.

With a weary sigh, he headed for the cove and his
family.

Phoebe stood at the counter and peeled the skin off
another warm potato. She was helping Jocelyn make the
potato salad for tomorrow's big barbeque. She glanced
at Jocelyn, who was peeling the shells off of about two
dozen hard-boiled eggs. "How many did you say are
coming to this thing?" Every inch of the countertop was

crammed with food in one stage or another of preparation. It was a hell of a way to spend a Friday night.

Jocelyn brushed at her cheek with the back of her hand and continued peeling. "I lost count. There's Quinn and the kids, me, you, and your parents." Jocelyn placed the egg on the tray and picked up another one. "Then there are Gwen and Daniel, Sydney and Erik. Erik's brother Gunnar, his wife Maggie, her daughter Katie, and Erik's grandfather Hans and his date."

"That's seventeen." She glanced around her brother's kitchen. "Seems like a lot of food for just seventeen people."

"Millicent is coming with Daniel's grandfather."

"You're up to nineteen." She shook her head at Jocelyn. "Are you sure all this is necessary just for Katie and Ben to get to know each other better before they start kindergarten?" She picked up another potato. "Seems like an awful lot of trouble for one play date."

"It had started out a lot smaller, but it just kind of mushroomed into this big production. I couldn't invite one sister without the other. Then I realized your parents haven't been over for dinner since I started here. Erik and Gunnar don't like to leave their grandfather alone, so I had to invite him and his date."

She chuckled at Jocelyn's blabbering. "Relax, Joc, it's going to be great. The weatherman is predicting perfect weather, and Quinn's got the grill raring to go. My brother hasn't done much entertaining, and he's really looking forward to this."

"You think?" Jocelyn frowned at a stubborn egg in her hand. The shell wasn't coming off nicely at all. "On Monday I told him it would only be about ten of us. Tuesday it was up to over a dozen, and now it's pushing twenty."

"Quinn's happy, Joc." She picked up the last potato in the pot. "In fact, I would have to say I have never seen my brother so happy. You're good for him."

"Really?"

"Really." Phoebe shook her head at the hopeful gleam in Jocelyn's eyes. "The kids love you, Joc, and so does my big brother." She eyed her friend with a knowing smile. "If I'm not mistaken, I would have to say you love them back."

"How can you tell?"

"You're glowing." She chuckled at the absurdity of the whole thing. "I couldn't think of a nicer person for my brother to fall in love with. Of course if you hurt him, I will have to kill you."

This time it was Jocelyn's turn to chuckle. "I have no intentions of hurting him, or the kids."

"Good." She didn't want to see her brother hurt again. For the past several weeks Quinn was like a new man. Whatever Jocelyn was doing was working like a charm. She just hoped that it would last.

"Hey, speaking of tomorrow," Jocelyn said. "Did you invite Gary? I told you you could."

"No, I didn't call him." So much for her good mood.

"No?" Jocelyn sounded surprised.

"No." She wondered if Jocelyn was going to leave it alone.

"Why not?" Jocelyn lowered the egg she was peeling back to the counter and stared at her.

"Because, it's been over a week since we went to the movies, and he hasn't called me once." She finished the last potato and frowned at the small mountain of peeled potatoes. "I made the first move four times. If I call him again, it would make me desperate. I'm not desperate." At least that was what she kept telling herself.

"Four times?"

"Move number one was when you and I went to The One Eyed Squid for chili and a brawl. Number two was when I showed up on the docks and went lobster fishing with him all day, and then I asked him out to dinner. Which was number three."

"Fourth was the movie date, right?"

"Right." Phoebe tried not to let it get her down, but she was about as low as she could go. Gary hadn't called her once. Now she was doubting the look she had seen in his eyes. She had been imagining things. If Gary was still interested in her, he would have called. Plain and simple. She needed to move on with her life.

"How did the movie date go? You never did fill me in on the details." Jocelyn started to slice the peeled hard-boiled eggs in half and dump the cooked yolks into a bowl.

Phoebe sat on a stool and frowned at the amount of food spread out before her. She now knew why she hated to cook. It was one hell of a lot of work. Jocelyn and she had been working for over an hour so far, and nothing was done. Not even something as simple as deviled eggs.

"The movie was good." What parts she had concentrated on had been real good. Problem was, most of her brain cells had been focusing on the man sitting next to her. "As a date it was a bust. No hand holding, no nothing." In a motion of pure disgust she waved her arm, and the sound of her clanging bracelets filled the room. "Hell, he didn't even try to kiss me good night."

"Good," snapped Quinn as he entered the room. The front of his shirt was wet from where he and the kids had been hosing down all the patio furniture in preparation of the big event tomorrow. "Franklin knows better than to mess with you."

"What do you mean by that?" she demanded.

"It means that eleven years ago me and Franklin had a little 'chat' about how he better not even look at you ever again." Quinn poured himself a glass of iced tea.

"You didn't!" A sick feeling twisted her gut.

"Of course I did. You're my sister, and he broke your heart." Quinn glanced between Jocelyn and her, and then shrugged. "It's what big brothers do."

"Did you beat him up?" asked Jocelyn.

"Of course not. He was three years younger than me, and it wouldn't have been fair." Quinn looked confused, as if he hadn't a clue as to why the two women in his kitchen were so upset. "Phoebe, do you remember what you were like when you went off to college?"

"Of course I do. I was a total wreck." She had been worse than a wreck, but she eventually pulled herself together and got on with living.

"Was I supposed to stand by and do nothing?" Quinn held her gaze and waited for an answer.

How in the world was she supposed to answer that? Older brothers were supposed to protect their sisters, but this had been Gary he threatened. The man that she loved. The man who had broken her heart. She could feel tears filling her eyes and lowered her head. She softly said, "I guess not."

Quinn rounded the counter and cupped her chin. "If Gary had any feelings for you, Phoebe, what I said eleven years ago wouldn't make any difference to him. He'd come after you, and it wouldn't matter who was standing in his way." Quinn's lips brushed her forehead. "You're a very special woman, and if he can't see that, then he's a bigger fool than I ever thought he was."

She managed a watery smile. "Thank you."

"For what?"

"For now." She reached up and kissed his cheek. "For eleven years ago." Big brothers could be a pain in the ass sometimes, but she never doubted Quinn's love.

"You're welcome." Quinn stepped back and picked up Max's brush. "You two get back to cooking while the kids and I brush Max."

She snorted. "How did you get the easier job?"

Quinn held out the brush. "Want to trade?"

She had tried brushing Max once. The dog was worse than the girls when it came to getting his hair brushed. "No way. Jocelyn's teaching me how to make potato salad that's actually edible."

Quinn gave Jocelyn a quick kiss, whispered something that sounded suspiciously like "good luck," and disappeared out the back door.

Jocelyn watched Quinn through the screened patio doors. "He's right, Phoebe."

"About?"

"Gary and you. You are a very special lady, and if Gary can't see that, it's his loss. I've seen the way Gary looks at you, Phoebe. He sees that special lady, too." Jocelyn handed her a stalk of celery. "I think he just needs more time."

Her smile didn't hurt so much this time. "Thanks, Joc." She felt a little better. Not much, but a little.

Chapter Seventeen

Jocelyn carried out the last bowl of food and set it on the already groaning table. There was enough food laid out to feed a small third world country, and then some. By the hungry gleam in all the men's eyes, she wasn't sure if it was going to be enough.

Most of the men were gathered around the grill offering advice and tips to Quinn, the designated cook. Somewhere in the "male" handbook it was written that since it was Quinn's house, he was the sole hamburger flipper. The other males in the species stood around him at the altar of flaming propane, drinking cold beers and talking about sports and fishing. Since she had put Quinn in charge of what meat to grill for the big day, they were having hamburgers, hotdogs, chicken, and sausages. Quinn couldn't make up his mind, but she forgave him because he looked adorable in his "Kiss the Cook" apron.

She maneuvered her way across the patio, turning down offers of help as she went. A quick glance over at the swing set showed little Katie fitting right in with Ben and the twins. Operation "play date" appeared to be a success. Ben and Katie were both hanging upside down from the crossbars on the swing set jabbering up a storm. Tori was trying to tug a chewed-up Frisbee out of Max's mouth, and Issy was showing Millicent and Quinn's mother her latest dance moves.

She came up behind Quinn and glanced over his shoulder at the burning, sizzling, and smoking meat. "Are you about done?"

"They're as ready as they will ever be." Quinn started to pile everything on plates and passed them off to the surrounding men.

If she wasn't mistaken, some of the men grunted in approval as they carried the platters to the table. Thankfully her brothers-in-law, Daniel and Erik, had stopped by this morning with extra tables and chairs to handle the crowd.

Quinn turned off the propane tank and lowered the lid of the grill. He glanced around the backyard and smiled. "So, what do you think?"

She reached up and surprised him by planting a quick kiss on his mouth. "I think you're adorable in that apron." She eyed the apron and quickly glanced around them to make sure she wouldn't be overheard. "Wear that to bed tonight, and I'll show you what's cooking."

Quinn frowned at the smear of barbeque sauce splattered across the front of the apron. "Can I wash it first?" he asked hopefully.

She ran her finger through the spot of wet sauce and then stuck it into her mouth. "Ummm . . . I don't know. I love honey smoked barbeque sauce." She closed her eyes and seductively licked the tip of her finger.

Quinn growled deep in his throat. "I'm going to make you pay later for that, Joc."

She laughed with delight. "One can only hope."

"Hope what?" asked her sister Sydney as she joined them.

An attractive flush swept up Quinn's cheeks, which

caused her to love him more. "I was just telling Quinn that I hope there will be enough food for everyone."

Sydney glanced over to the two tables loaded with food. "You've got to be kidding? Gwen didn't even have this much food at Thanksgiving dinner."

"Maybe you're right." She winked at Quinn and then ushered Sydney back into the crowd. "I just wasn't expecting everyone to bring something." There were nearly doubles of everything on the tables. Millicent brought a bowl of potato salad. Quinn's mother brought cupcakes for the kids and a triple-layered chocolate cake for the adults. Sadie Hopkins, Erik's grandfather Hans's date for the day, had brought two blueberry pies. Sydney had even managed a bowl of cole slaw and a vegetable tray, and Katie's mom, Maggie, had brought cookies and brownies.

The part that worried her was her sister Gwen, who she had figured to bring a dish in every major food group, had only brought a relish tray. A sloppy relish tray that looked as if she had dumped a jar of olives and pickles onto the fancy glass tray.

"Syd?"

"What?"

"Has Gwen been in to see you yet?" She nodded to where their sister was sitting under a tree and sipping from a bottle of spring water. Sadie Hopkins was talking to her, but Daniel was hovering nearby. Gwen's husband had been hanging by her side since they arrived an hour ago. Daniel wasn't the clingy type.

Sydney frowned. "No, but I think it's about time. She's been acting awfully funny lately."

"So has Daniel. He hasn't left her side for more than two minutes." She watched as Gwen laughed at something Sadie said. "Gwen looks perfectly normal and healthy, except . . ."

"Except what?" Sydney's expression turned to one of concern.

"The Gwen we know and love wouldn't be sitting under a tree passing the time of day with Sadie Hopkins during a barbeque. She would be manning the grill and trying out a recipe for grilled tuna or conducting a lobster bake in the middle of the yard. She might even be in the kitchen whipping up a quiche or something equally delicious. But sitting on the sidelines?"

"Never." Sydney worried her lower lip.

"Did you see the relish tray that she brought?"

"Was that what it was? Daniel had to have done it, because there is no way Gwen would have opened up some jars and dumped their contents on an antique serving platter."

"Agreed." She frowned at Daniel when he and Gwen looked their way. "So what are we going to do about it?"

"We'll wait until everyone has eaten; then we'll drag her and Daniel into the house and demand answers."

"Sounds like a plan." She watched as Daniel and Gwen put their heads together and whispered. "They know we are talking about them."

Sydney gave her the same smile she used to use when they had been growing up. The smile that said she was the older sister, and what she said goes. "Doesn't matter. We'll still get our answers."

An hour later the remnants of the main meal were put away, and everyone was getting ready for a trip down to the cove. The kids were all in their bathing suits and lathered with sunblock. Most of the adults had on their bathing suits, but some opted to sit on the shore and watch. Since everyone was stuffed, they had voted to hold off dessert until after swimming.

Jocelyn checked the kitchen one last time to make sure everything that had to be put away was. She came out the back patio door and was surprised that no one had started the short walk down to the cove. "You all didn't have to wait for me."

"Your sister made us," said Quinn as he came up to her and took the load of beach towels out of her hands.

"Sydney?" She glanced over at her sister, who was standing next to her husband and shaking her head.

"Not me, it was Gwen," explained Sydney.

"That's right," said Gwen. "We wanted everyone here." Gwen reached out and grabbed her husband's hand. "Daniel and I have an announcement."

Jocelyn looked at her sister and the radiant glow about her and knew what Gwen was going to say before the words left her mouth.

"Daniel and I are going to have a baby." Gwen laughed as everyone started talking at once.

She looked at Quinn and grinned. "I'm going to be an aunt!"

"Looks that way," whispered Quinn as he pulled her close and hugged her.

"Do Mom and Dad know yet?" she asked Gwen when the noise level lowered enough that she could shout over it.

"We called them this morning." Gwen was nestled up against her husband. One of Daniel's hands was spread across her still flat stomach. "They're flying up in September to check on us."

"We stopped at my parents' before coming here, so they know they are going to be grandparents again," added Daniel. "Between Gwen tossing her cookies all morning and being on the phone, I'm afraid our contribution to the barbeque was a bit sad. I pulled it together at the last minute."

"It's my fault," grumbled Gwen. "I have all the ingredients for key lime pie and those baked beans you love so much, Jocelyn. But, when I got home from work last night, I crashed and didn't get out of bed until nine this morning."

"You're forgiven"—she leaned forward and kissed her sister's cheek—"Mommy." She could breathe easier now knowing why her sister had looked so sick the other day.

Gwen beamed. "Has a nice ring to it, doesn't it?"

"Sure does."

"Who's your doctor?" asked Sydney. "When's the due date?"

"We don't have a doctor yet, and as close as I can tell, the due date will be around the middle of February."

Everyone started to walk toward the cove. Questions, children's laughter, and excitement filled the air. Sydney was grilling Gwen and Daniel.

Erik puffed out his chest and elbowed his identical twin brother in the ribs. "I'm going to be an uncle."

"Yeah." Gunnar shoved him back. "Well, I'm a step-dad, and that's better."

"Is not."

"Is too."

Jocelyn chuckled at the muscle-bound Vikings trying to outdo each other. The clash of the pacifist Titans. Phoebe was walking with the twins while Ben and Katie seemed to enjoy each other's company. All in all, it was a wonderful day.

"So, Jocelyn, what do you think about becoming an aunt," asked Millicent, who had fallen in step beside her.

"I can't wait." She allowed Millicent to go before her through the tight squeeze on the path. "I wonder if Gwen is going to find out if it's a boy or a girl." She joined Millicent again once the path widened. "I don't know if I would want to know if I was pregnant. It seems to take all the surprise out of the big event."

"Ah, so you want children of your own one day?"

"At least two, maybe three," answered Jocelyn.

Quinn, who had been following behind Jocelyn, stopped dead in his tracks. His father walked right into him.

"Quinn, what's wrong?" asked his mother with a frown.

"Nothing." *Everything! How could I be so stupid?* "Go on, I'll be right there." He waved to the path in front of him and watched as his parents joined the rest of the crowd. Erik and Gunnar were already halfway out in the cove. Max was with them. The kids were all running up and down the small sandy shoreline, and Hans and Daniel were setting up folding chairs for the ladies in the shade. Jocelyn was trying to smear more sunblock on Tori.

Jocelyn wants her own kids! Why in the hell hadn't he seen that one coming? He knew everything had been going too easily. Here he had thought Jocelyn's dream was to be a lawyer. She had even hinted at taking the Maine bar exam and opening up her own practice in or near Misty Harbor. Her dream had matched his. He had wanted Jocelyn to stay. He had allowed himself to dream and to hope.

He had been waiting until he had hired another housekeeper and nanny before asking Jocelyn to become his wife. It was the logical thing to do. If he asked her while she was still living with them, she might get the impression he was only interested in a mother for his children. He had been waiting to not only declare his love for her, but to propose. He wasn't about to let Jocelyn give up her career to become his wife and a stepmother to his kids. They could have worked out something.

Now, knowing that Jocelyn wanted children of her own, he couldn't marry her. All those times they had made love he had never once used a condom. He had never really thought about it, except he assumed Jocelyn was on the pill and that was why she hadn't mentioned birth control. In today's society it had been a stupid risk on both of their parts.

There was a reason he had never thought about

using a condom. He couldn't father Jocelyn's or anyone
else's babies. He had had a vasectomy three and a half
years ago, when Diane had been pregnant with the twins.

He was as sterile as a capon.

Phoebe stepped into her makeshift studio and sighed
in relief at the silence. Quinn and Jocelyn's barbeque
had been great, but she really hadn't been in the mood
for a crowd. The party was still in full swing, but she had
bailed early. Right after the desserts had been served.
Gwen and Daniel's announcement of impending parent-
hood was the main topic of everyone's conversation. She
was happy for them, but it also made her realize she was
twenty-nine and didn't even have a date tonight.

Another fun-filled Saturday night in Misty Harbor.

She turned on the lights above her worktable and
studied the window laid out below. It was breathtakingly
beautiful in its simplicity. There was no other word to
describe it. Rocky shoreline, Misty Harbor's lighthouse
in the distance, and a white-and-green lobster boat riding the waves gleamed under the lights. Gary's boat, the
Winter's Rest.

The tip of her finger tenderly traced the individual
pieces of colored glass that formed the boat. She had already surrounded each piece with copper foil, and they
were now ready to be soldered together.

A deep voice came from the direction of the garage
door opening. "Quinn told me I could find you in here."

Phoebe felt her heart start to pound, but she didn't
turn around. She needed a minute to pull herself together. She would know that voice anywhere at anytime.
It was Gary's voice. "This is where I usually am"—her
finger skimmed the ocean waves beneath the boat—
"seven days a week."

Gary stepped into the garage and glanced around
with interest. So this was where Phoebe spent all her

time. This was what took the woman he had loved away from him. Wooden bins held individual pieces of colored glass. A huge worktable was set up near the back windows, and a rainbow of colors danced around the area.

He had no idea if coming here was a good idea or not. All he knew was that he couldn't stay away from Phoebe one more day. He had tried. "I called your parents' house, but no one answered."

"They're out back. Quinn and Jocelyn are throwing a barbeque."

"You weren't invited?"

"I was there for a while." Phoebe turned halfway around and looked at him. "I thought I would catch up on some work while I was here."

"Am I holding you up?"

Phoebe shook her head, but he wasn't looking at her any longer. He stepped up to the table and stared down at the glass picture. "It's the *Winter's Rest.*" His voice held awe and surprise. "It's beautiful."

"Thank you, but it's not finished yet."

He studied her light brown eyes for a long while. He remembered once telling Phoebe she had whiskey eyes. She hadn't been impressed with the comparison. Being a part-time bartender for the past five years he had come to regret that comparison on numerous occasions. He had served a lot of whiskey over the years, and more times than not he had thought of Phoebe's eyes with each shot glass he poured.

He stepped around Phoebe to get a better view of a two-foot by three-foot stained-glass window already done. This one had green leaves, three purple and blue irises and a brilliant yellow butterfly fluttering on one of the delicate petals. Fine and loving craftsmanship was in every detail. Phoebe Larson was one very gifted artist. Hell, he had trouble staying in the lines when he colored with his niece. He couldn't imagine doing such delicate

and intricate details with his big clumsy fisherman's
hands.

Another piece caught his attention. This one was
modern with bold lines and angles. The only curved
piece of glass was a two-inch orange circle positioned
perfectly within a golden square in the upper right-
hand portion of the window. He had no idea how
Phoebe had gotten the pieces to fit so precisely, but he
was impressed.

"You made the right decision to go to school instead
of staying here in Misty Harbor." What else could he
possibly say? Her gift and dream was laid out before
him. If he had gotten his way eleven years ago, Phoebe
would have about three kids by now, a husband who
spent more hours on the water than on dry land, and
the closest she would ever get to stained glass was in
church every Sunday morning.

"Did I?" Phoebe stared at him. "What are you doing
here, Gary? The afternoon is still young. Shouldn't you
still be out on your boat hauling in lobsters?"

"I knocked off early." He tried to appear nonchalant,
but he had a horrible feeling he was failing miserably.
"Why be your own boss if you can't take advantage of
it?" He had absolutely no idea how to handle this Phoebe.
An eighteen-year-old Phoebe had been easier. He would
have backed her against the wall and kissed her senseless.

He still wanted to kiss her senseless. Hell, he wanted
to kiss her until he was senseless.

"You still haven't answered my question. What brings
you here?"

"I was worried."

"About?"

"You. I was worried about you." He ran his fingers
through his hair, and he felt as though his shirt collar
and tie were choking him. Funny thing was, he wasn't
wearing a dress shirt or tie; he was only wearing a T-shirt.

"I haven't heard from you in a while, and I started to think something might be wrong."

"The phone works both ways, Gary." Phoebe propped her hip against the table. The tremor that had been in her voice earlier was gone.

"I told you I tried about an hour ago, and no one answered."

"We haven't seen each other in over a week, and after one attempted phone call you conclude something must be wrong?" Phoebe crossed her arms and glared at him. "Did it ever cross your mind that after four times of being the one to make the first move, I just gave up and assumed you weren't interested?"

"No." Lord, he had hurt her again. He could see the pain in her whiskey-colored eyes. "The Phoebe I remember wouldn't have given up after four tries, or forty tries."

"People change." Phoebe lowered her head and seemed to be studying the cracked cement floor.

"Yeah, they do." Gary took a couple of steps and stopped in front of her. He cupped her chin and made her look at him. Tears swam in her eyes, but so did hope. "The real reason I came by was to apologize to you."

"For what?"

Phoebe's cheek felt like satin beneath his weatherroughened fingers. At one time he had thought she was the most beautiful girl in the world. Now he didn't have to think it; he knew it. His fingers itched to yank the rubber band off the end of the thick brown braid hanging down her back nearly to her waist. He wanted to bury his face once again into the silky softness of her incredibly long hair and breathe in her fragrance of lavender.

He lowered his hand. "You were right the other day when you said I was unfair to both of us when I made you choose between college and me." He had wanted to say that for years. "I was a world class fool who was scared to death that you would go away, see the world, and never come back to Misty Harbor or me."

"That's exactly what I did." Phoebe's gaze never left his. "I never even came home in the summer months."

"I know, and it was my fault, wasn't it?"

"Some." Phoebe shrugged as if the whole thing didn't matter any longer. "The other half of the blame was mine. Partly because I was chicken, somewhat because Misty Harbor didn't feel like home any longer, but mainly because I didn't want to run into you and have my heart broken all over again."

"What made you move home now after all this time?"

"I realized Misty Harbor was still my home and I missed it. I traveled a lot during the last eleven years, and no place ever felt like home. So when I decided to start my own business there was only one logical place to set up shop." Phoebe moved back a couple of steps, away from the stained glass laid out on the table, and then sat on the edge of the table. She nodded toward the lone chair in the garage. "Quinn was nice enough to offer up his garage as a temporary shop until I can find something better."

He ignored the chair. "And you were nice enough to help with his kids when Diane was killed down in Boston."

"That's what family is for, Gary."

"Why haven't you gotten married and started a family of your own by now?" He knew she had wanted children of her own one day. Two to be precise. One boy, one girl. Phoebe had even picked out the names, Dillon Franklin and Colleen Franklin. They were both going to have his red hair and green eyes, but her sense of humor.

"No one would have me, I guess." Phoebe swung her sneaker-clad feet. "Why haven't you tied the knot and started populating the town with little Franklins?"

He didn't for a minute believe that the men she had

met over the years had been that stupid or blind. "I almost got married once."

Phoebe's head snapped up, and she stared at him with surprise. "You did? Mom never told me that."

He forced himself not to smile. So Phoebe had been keeping tabs on him over the years. He had to wonder if Phoebe knew her mother was in the same quilting club as his mother. Mrs. Larson had kept his mother updated on Phoebe's every move. His mother had made it her mission in life to relay every word spoken at those quilting club sessions right back to him.

"Yeah, I was young and incredibly stupid back then." He hoped to hell he had grown some brain cells since then, or he was about to make the biggest ass out of himself. "I was still in high school and couldn't afford an engagement ring, so I bought her this little gold ring with three of the tiniest diamond chips you ever saw. I got engaged to be engaged. In other words, I was waiting until I had some serious money saved up to buy a real engagement ring."

Phoebe's legs stopped swinging, and tears filled her eyes. "Maybe she didn't want some big, fancy, expensive diamond ring; maybe she only wanted you."

"A man only gets engaged once; he should do it right." He felt hope bloom in his heart. "Doesn't matter anyway, I never bought that big diamond ring. I screwed up long before I could even afford it. I made her choose between her dream and me. Here I was living in Misty Harbor reaching for my own dream, and having her by my side. I had it all." He reached out and with the pad of his thumb tenderly wiped at the lone tear rolling down Phoebe's cheek. "I was scared to death that if she went away for four years searching and reaching for her dream, she wouldn't want or need me any longer."

"Stupid fear." Phoebe wiped at her other cheek.

"She tried to tell me; but I was too stubborn to listen, so I lost her anyway." His fingers trembled, and his heart was thumping like a demented rabbit's; but he needed to tell Phoebe how he felt. How he had always felt. "I would like to think I grew and changed over the last eleven years, but I'm not too sure I did."

"What do you mean?" Phoebe's eyes were awash with tears.

"I wouldn't be afraid of her reaching for that dream now, but in other ways I'm still the same." He eased himself closer and lightly brushed her mouth with his lips. "I'm still in love with her."

Phoebe's smile was radiant. "Really?"

"I love you, Phoebe Marie Larson. Always have. Always will." This time when his mouth captured hers there was nothing light or tentative about it. He kissed Phoebe with all the heat and promises of eleven long and lonely years. When she wrapped her arms around his neck, deepened the kiss, and melted against him, he knew it was going to be all right.

Phoebe might have finally returned to the town, but in her arms, he was finally home.

He slowly broke the kiss and smiled at the desire flaring in Phoebe's eyes. For what he had in mind they needed more privacy than a studio garage with a big party going on about a hundred yards away. His sister and niece were at the party, but more importantly, so was Phoebe's brother.

Sheriff Quinn Larson didn't worry him any longer. But back when he had been eighteen, Quinn had threatened to rearrange his face on more than one occasion. If Quinn walked in on them now, Gary was afraid Phoebe's older brother's very protective gene would kick in. Especially if Quinn figured out what Gary was planning to do to his baby sister. He wasn't about to let Phoebe get away from him this time, and he figured the best place for her would be his bed for the next month or so.

He brushed his lips across the tracks of her fallen tears. "Come home with me?"

Phoebe's arms were still around his neck as her gaze searched his. "I know I promised, but you won't be my first lover."

He tenderly smiled at her concern. He hadn't expected her to be a virgin. He wasn't. "That's okay, because I'm planning on being your last."

"I love you, Gary," whispered Phoebe. Then she returned his own words to him. "Always have. Always will."

He could finally breathe again. After eleven years he could finally draw a deep enough breath to feel alive. With a shout of joy he swung her up into his arms and headed for his truck.

Phoebe laughed with pure happiness as her feet left the ground. She wrapped her arms tighter around Gary's neck as they stepped out into the sunshine.

Chapter Eighteen

Jocelyn paced between the kitchen and the family room. She didn't know what else to do with herself. Television held no appeal to her, and the current book she had been reading couldn't hold her attention. It was all Quinn's fault. Something was wrong. Something had gone wrong in their relationship.

One night last week Quinn had been suggesting that she stay in Misty Harbor, and she had been hinting about taking the bar exam. Now he was not only avoiding her, but he was avoiding the kids and his own home. She could even pinpoint it to the exact minute everything had changed.

Saturday, early evening and as soon as his parents, the last to leave the barbeque, had pulled out of the driveway, Quinn had changed. He had kissed the kids good-bye and headed for the office to catch up on something or other. She hadn't thought much about it at the time. Quinn and she very rarely showed any signs of affection in front of the kids. But later on in the night, when he had gotten home, he hadn't joined her in her bed. Quinn had spent the night in his own bed. He also had been heading out of the front door when she had been stumbling down the stairs to start breakfast for the kids the following morning. Sunday he had pulled a double shift, claiming his deputy, Rick Roberts, needed to spend some time with his wife and newborn son.

She had no idea what time he had gotten home last night, because she never saw or heard him. His bed had been slept in at sometime, but that was about all she knew. This morning he had been gone before she even awoke. Something definitely was wrong, and whatever it was happened at the barbeque. She had been racking her brains, but she couldn't remember anything happening that would affect their relationship. They hadn't argued at all. In fact, the entire party had gone off without a hitch.

Gwen and Daniel had surprised and delighted everyone when they had announced they were pregnant. Ben and Katie had become best friends. Quinn's mother had even complimented her on her deviled eggs. Gary Franklin had showed up, found Phoebe in her studio, and then driven away with her in his pickup truck. Phoebe's Jeep had sat in front of the garage abandoned until sometime Monday morning. Jocelyn had considered that a good sign. As to what Quinn thought about his sister and Gary finally getting back together was anyone's guess. Hell, she wasn't even sure if he realized that one yet.

So what was the problem?

The sound of a car engine and crunching gravel out front pulled her from her thoughts. Quinn was home. Tonight she was getting some answers. She didn't care how tired and cranky he was. The man was going to start singing like a canary.

She was standing quietly at the far end of the family room staring out into the backyard when Quinn entered the kitchen.

"Oh, are you still up?" Quinn asked as he opened the refrigerator and pulled out a can of soda.

She didn't answer his question, because if she wasn't still up, she wouldn't have been standing there. She studied the bags beneath Quinn's eyes and the lines on his face that seemed to be etched deeper than they had been on Sunday morning, the last time she had seen him. "You look like hell."

Quinn cringed, then lifted the can in her direction before muttering, "Thanks." He then tipped the can to his mouth and drank.

In the refrigerator, front and center, where he had to have seen it, was his neatly wrapped dinner. Quinn didn't seem to be interested in eating it. So much for her meatloaf and mashed potatoes. She walked to the kitchen table and stared at him across the width of the room. "What's wrong, Quinn?"

"Nothing." Quinn tipped the can again and finished off whatever had been remaining. He wouldn't meet her gaze.

"Bullshit." She liked the surprised look on Quinn's face. If he thought she would stand meekly by and watch whatever they had together fall apart, he was sadly mistaken. "I want to know what in the hell went wrong." Direct and to the point. Her grandfather Michaels would be so proud of her. If this line of questioning didn't work, she'd get her baseball bat and start aiming for the kneecaps. Both of them with her Louisville Slugger. Then she'd start on his thick head.

"The kids are becoming too dependent on you." Quinn's fingers were slowly denting the empty can in his fist. "They are going to be hurt when you go back to Baltimore."

"I've been talking to the kids. They're fine, so leave them out of this discussion." During the barbeque the kids barely even knew she had been there, let alone talked to her. There had been too many other people there to hold their attention. Whatever happened to Quinn hinting to her to stay? Did he think she would joke about something as important as taking the bar exam and starting her career all over again in a different state? "I want to know what in the hell is happening between us? If you don't find me attractive any longer, then just spit it out, Quinn. I'm a big girl; I can take it."

Of course, after spending weeks in her bed if Quinn suddenly realized he didn't find her attractive any longer, she wasn't sure his knees would be able to take it.

Quinn felt his hand crunch the empty can into nothingness. *She thinks I'm not attracted to her any longer!* If it wasn't so depressing, he would have laughed hysterically. He was standing in the kitchen with the same hard-on he had rolled out of bed with this morning. The damn thing never went fully away, because all day long he kept thinking of Jocelyn and the life they would never have together.

"Not want you?" he shouted. How could Jocelyn have even doubted his desire? "You've got to be out of your freaking mind."

Jocelyn's hands gripped the back of one of the kitchen chairs. Her knuckles turned white with the pressure. "Okay, Quinn, you have to help me out here. I have absolutely no idea what's going on."

"Okay," he snapped, "I'll spell it out real slow for you." He tossed the smashed can into the recycle bin. "You don't belong here. You belong in Baltimore chasing your high-power career, not doing pirouettes out on the back lawn with Issy."

"I can be a great lawyer in Maine if I wanted to." Jocelyn's fingers trembled against the wooden chair.

"I don't want a lawyer. I want a wife." He tossed his hands out wide and practically shouted, "I want a real family, Jocelyn. I'm in love with you."

"You are?" whispered Jocelyn. Her eyes widened in shock, and the beginning of a broad smile pulled at her mouth.

"It doesn't matter if I love you or not, Jocelyn." The

crumbling of that smile broke his heart. "I can't give you your dream."

"What dream?" Jocelyn's expression showed nothing but confusion. "Being a lawyer?"

"You were already a lawyer when I met you, Joc. You reached that dream, and I have one hundred percent confidence in you that if you took the Maine bar exam, you would pass with flying colors." He leaned against the counter and gripped the edge with both hands. Anything to prevent himself from dashing across the room and pulling her into his arms. "I was referring to your other dream."

"What other dream?" Jocelyn asked in the same tone of voice she would have used to ask *What other head?*

"Your dream of having children one day." His fingers were trembling against the counter. "I heard you tell Millicent that you wanted at least two, maybe three children of your own one day. I can't give you that dream, Joc. I can't father any more children." There, the truth was finally out.

Jocelyn blinked. "What do you mean you can't father any children?"

"I said *any more* children." He hated this part, but if anyone had the right to know his private business, it was Jocelyn. "Remember when I told you Diane was a little upset when we discovered she was carrying twins?"

Jocelyn nodded.

"Diane was more than a *little* upset. Our marriage started to crumble right there and then. I was desperately trying to hold it all together. To make her happy and to try and save our marriage I had a *vasectomy.*" The word seemed to get stuck in his throat, gather unearthly power, and then come out sounding like a vile curse.

He stood there as a tense silence filled the room. Jocelyn was staring at him as if he had just sprouted another head. He didn't blame her. His vasectomy wasn't something that cropped up in everyday conversations. "Didn't you ever wonder why I never used a condom?"

She shook her head and said, "I'm on the pill to regulate my periods. I didn't think about birth control."

"In today's world, we still should have used condoms, Joc." It was one of the many stupid things he had done recently. The first being falling in love with a woman who wanted children. "The one thing I might have been able to give you, I can't. The one act that I thought might have saved my first marriage has doomed any chances of my second one." He sadly shook his head at the irony of it all. "I'm truly sorry, Joc."

There was nothing else left for him to say to her. What was done, was done. He walked out of the room and headed for his lonely bed.

Jocelyn listened to the sound of Quinn climbing the stairs and wondered if she had crossed over into an alternate universe. Quinn loved her! Quinn wanted to marry her! Quinn was walking away from her because he couldn't father any more children. It was all her dreams come true, except for that last small detail.

If she married Quinn, she would never carry his child under her heart. She would never know the joy of giving birth. No midnight feedings. No first words of "mom mom." No gaining weight and having swollen ankles the size of oil drums. No precious toothless drooling smiles. No pouring over baby name books to pick out the perfect name. No morning sickness. No sitting in rocking chairs holding a warm sleeping bundle that smelled like baby powder.

Was she willing to give all of that up?

Jocelyn felt her knees start to shake. She pulled out the chair she had been clinging to and sat down with a heavy thump. Major decisions in life were always tough to make, especially when you were alone. She couldn't very well call her sisters and discuss this with them. Quinn had seemed embarrassed by the whole procedure. Like the simple surgery had lessened him as a man. There wasn't anything to be embarrassed about. Vasectomies were a perfectly acceptable form of birth control if you happened to not want any more children.

Diane had obviously not wanted any more children. Then Diane should have been the one to do something about it. Not Quinn.

Mention the word "vasectomy" in front of a man, and he would actually cringe and develop a reflex motion of protecting that "sensitive" part of his anatomy. A woman could deliver a ten-pound two-ounce screaming bundle of joy naturally out of an opening designed for nothing larger than a well-endowed male, and no one thought anything of it. Let a man hear the words "Snip, snip," and he would shake in terror. Hell, males even displayed empathy for male dogs when they went to the vet's to be fixed.

Men were definitely from Mars.

Quinn must have loved Diane very much to go through that procedure. Or he had been desperate to hold his family together. The reasons behind his decision didn't matter now. It was done and in the past. The question was, did it matter to her?

The simple answer was yes it mattered. The choice of her bearing Quinn's children had been taken out of her hands. She didn't like it. But could she live with it?

Hell, how did she even know if she could have children of her own? Who even said she was definitely fertile? Thousands of perfectly healthy women could never carry a child, yet they hadn't known that fact until after they were trying to get pregnant and couldn't. Who was to say she wasn't one of them? Life was full of surprises. Some were great. Some were heartbreakers.

She already had problems with her monthly flow.

That was why her gynecologist had put her on birth control pills over three years ago. Just because she now had her period every month didn't mean she would be able to conceive.

The silence of the house mocked her as she tried to justify her reasoning. The simple truth was, she loved Quinn. End of statement. It didn't matter if he couldn't father one baby or a thousand babies. She still loved him.

The amazing part was, Quinn returned her love. What more could she possibly want? The only children that had entered into the equation of her love for him had been his own. She didn't want to replace Diane in Ben's, Issy's, and Tori's hearts. All three children had an amazing capacity for love. She knew there would be enough love in their hearts if she chose to join the family. Quinn hadn't officially asked her to become his wife, but he wanted to.

Phoebe's words from weeks ago came back to her. Quinn's sister had told her about his flaw. Quinn always put everybody else's happiness above his own. Phoebe had been right. Quinn was doing it again. Quinn was putting what he conceived her happiness to be above his own. Phoebe had warned her to use the knowledge of Quinn's flaw wisely.

She was very wisely going to point out the errors of his ways.

Quinn was a fool. It was an admirable trait, but not when it came to her happiness. Who was he to decide what made her happy and what she wanted in life? He had it all wrong. Quinn made her happy, not his sperm count. His children made her happy. The possibility of Quinn returning her love made her delirious.

When they became a family, they would already have three wonderful children. If she should suffer some uncontrollable urge to go change a dirty diaper, she would go visit one of her sisters.

Her decision was relatively easy to make. A life with Quinn or a life without him. There hadn't really been a choice after all.

Jocelyn slowly got up from the table and locked the back patio doors. After turning out all the lights, she slowly climbed the steps and listened to the shower in the kids' bathroom running. For a moment she debated just walking in on him in there, but with the kids' rooms on either side of the bathroom it might not be the best idea. Things might get a little vocal.

She slipped into the room Quinn was using as a bedroom. The twin bed looked far too short for his tall frame. The rest of the crowded room was a mess. The desk, which took up half the room, was piled high with papers and folders. How in the world did Quinn actually find anything?

The door squeaked lightly as Quinn stepped into the room. A damp towel was wrapped around his hips. She felt the desire that was never completely cooled start to simmer. Quinn was breathtakingly beautiful in his masculinity.

Quinn took one step into the room and froze. "I thought we were done talking."

"You thought wrong." She shoved a pile of papers out of her way and leaned against the front of the desk. Ben's bedroom door was directly across the landing from them. "Close the door so we won't disturb the kids." She didn't know what she was prouder of: the fact that she hadn't raised her voice, or that she hadn't tossed Quinn onto his bed and had her wicked way with him yet. That low-slung towel was too much temptation for one woman to deny.

Quinn's one eyebrow rose, but he softly shut the door. "If this is going to take some time, can I at least get some pants on?"

Her gaze dropped to the front of the dark green towel. The subtle movement behind the terry cloth made her smile. Quinn wasn't as immune to her as he was trying to make her believe. She considered it a good sign. Husbands should desire their wives.

Quinn cursed and started to mumble something about cold showers not working as he turned his back on her and stepped into a pair of faded and soft-looking jeans.

She grinned at his hairy legs and pale behind as the denim slipped over them. Quinn was adorable when modest.

Quinn snatched up a T-shirt and tugged it on over his head and growled, "Enjoying the show?"

"Immensely." She wasn't going to get all shy and modest on him now. "Are you ready for our talk?"

"I think we've been over everything."

"No, you had your say downstairs; now it's my turn." She wiggled her butt onto the edge of the desk and avoided looking at the rumpled bed.

Quinn leaned against the closed door and folded his arms across his chest. "I'm listening."

"No matter what happens between you and me, I'm staying in Misty Harbor. So get used to seeing me around town. I love it here, and I love being close to my sisters." She studied the hard line of Quinn's jaw. He hadn't taken the time to shave before or after his shower. "I'm going to be opening a private practice either in Misty Harbor or maybe Sullivan. I'll worry about location after I can practice law in Maine."

She tried to read his expression, but couldn't. She didn't know if her staying in the area made him happy or not. Lord, Quinn was stubborn. "I decided not to go into criminal law, so I don't think there will be too much of a conflict of interest between us."

"Your chosen career had never been an issue."

"That's good to know." It was one less hurdle to get over. "I'm not going to be making a fortune practicing here, but being rich was never the reason I went into law in the first place."

"I'm sure you will do very well in whatever you choose." Quinn's voice was polite and ambiguous. He might have been discussing the weather instead of their future.

She jumped off the desk and snapped, "Stuff it, Larson!" She took two threatening steps toward him. There was only so much a woman could take, and she had just reached her limit.

Quinn blinked in surprise and pressed his back against the closed door.

"I don't appreciate your 'Lord and Master' routine," she snapped.

"What are you talking about? What 'Lord and Master' routine?"

"The one where you decide what makes me happy." She took another step closer and batted his arms down. "The one where you decide what my dreams are."

Quinn looked flabbergasted. His mouth opened, but nothing came out.

She took another step closer, went toe to toe with him, and jammed a finger into his chest. "You can't announce you love me, and then practically ask me to marry you, and then just walk away." Her fingertip jabbed at Quinn's rock-solid chest. "Since you practically asked, I'm practically answering."

Her finger stopped jabbing, and her palm pressed against Quinn's chest. She could feel the rapid pounding of his heart beneath her hand. Her anger drained away with a sigh. She gazed into his eyes and softly smiled. "Yes, I'll marry you." Her hand trailed up to his stubble-covered jaw. "I love you, Quinn." Her fingertip slowly outlined his lower lip. "Besides, we have to get married. Living together would set a bad example for the children."

Quinn closed his eyes as his hands reached out, grasped her hips, and pulled her near. Quinn tucked her close to his heart and held her tight for a long while.

She pressed against his warmth and breathed in the

scent of the soap and shampoo he had just used. This was where she belonged. In Quinn's arms she was happy.

Quinn's chest expanded as he heaved a heavy sigh and gently pushed her away from his chest. His fingers were gentle as they cupped her chin and raised her face so she was looking directly at him. Sadness pooled in his dark eyes. "What about children, Joc? I can't give you a baby."

"No, you can't." She felt the hot burn of tears in the back of her own eyes. "I'm asking for something far more important than some baby that might or might not be in the future."

"What?"

"You can give me a little boy and two beautifully adorable girls who already own a piece of my heart."

The love burning in Quinn's eyes was blinding. "What about a baby of your own? I thought you wanted one."

"If you were able to father children, and if I had gotten pregnant in the distant future, nothing would have made me happier, Quinn." She reached up and brushed a light kiss over his lips. "It's not going to happen, and I still love you. I still want to spend the rest of my life with you."

"But—"

She pressed another quick kiss on his mouth. "Quinn, do you have any idea how much it is going to cost us to send three kids through college?"

Quinn groaned. "I don't even want to think about it."

She grinned. "They are each going to want their own car." She stood on her toes, and her mouth teased his ear. "Then there's the car insurance and gas money. I won't even mention the trips to the mall for clothes shopping." Her teeth nibbled on Quinn's earlobe as he groaned. She couldn't tell if his moan was from the insurance premiums flashing in his mind or her playfulness.

"What about the prom, Quinn? Got any idea what a prom dress is going for nowadays?" She laughed against the side of his throat. "Let's not forget about dating, boys, talking about the birds and the bees, PMS, and staying out late."

Quinn swept Jocelyn up into his arms and carried her to the bed he had been using these past nights. He couldn't fight her any longer. He knew he would never let her out of his life as soon as she had told him she loved him. Her fate had been sealed.

He captured her next words with his mouth and pressed himself against her warm and willing body. Jocelyn's arms pulled him closer, and he cursed the fact that both of them had on way too many clothes. Desire threatened to ignite as he broke the kiss. "Are you trying to talk yourself out of marrying me?"

"Never." Jocelyn wrapped her arms around his neck and laughed. "Do you have any idea what two weddings are going to cost?"

He stared down at the woman who made his life complete, Jocelyn. Joy, laughter, and happiness were all dancing in her gorgeous gray eyes. So was love. He tenderly brushed a golden lock of her hair away from her cheek. "I only care about one wedding right now, ours." He gently placed a string of kisses from her ear down over her jaw and chin. He arched his hips and let Jocelyn know how much he wanted her. "The sooner the better, I would think."

Jocelyn's smile couldn't have gotten any bigger. "My father had been afraid of this as soon as he heard I was heading for Maine."

"Is he going to be upset that he's losing another daughter to Misty Harbor?"

"A little." Jocelyn reached up and tugged on his lower lip, sending the heat between them spiraling. "What he's really afraid of is paying for another wedding."